A Yankee Musician in Europe

Studies in Music, No. 110

George J. Buelow, Series Editor

Professor of Music
Indiana University

Other Titles in This Series

A
Yankee
Musician
in Europe

The 1837 Journals of
Lowell Mason

Edited with an Introduction by
Michael Broyles

UNIVERSITY OF ROCHESTER PRESS

Originally produced and distributed 1990 by
UMI Research Press
an imprint of
University Microfilms Inc.
Ann Arbor, Michigan 48106

Reprinted in paperback and transferred to digital printing 2010
University of Rochester Press
668 Mt. Hope Avenue, Rochester, NY 14620, USA
www.urpress.com
and Boydell & Brewer Limited
PO Box 9, Woodbridge, Suffolk IP12 3DF, UK
www.boydellandbrewer.com

Paperback ISBN: 978-1-58046-355-3
Cloth ISBN: 978-0-83572-002-1

Library of Congress Cataloging-in-Publication Data

Mason, Lowell, 1792–1872.
    A Yankee musician in Europe : the 1837 journals of Lowell Mason / edited
with an introduction by Michael Broyles.
        p. cm. — (Studies in music ; 110)
    Includes bibliographical references and index.
    ISBN 0-8357-2002-0 (hardcover: alk. paper)
        1. Mason, Lowell, 1792–1872—Diaries. 2. Composers—United States—
Diaries. 3. Music—Europe—19th century—History and criticism. I.
Broyles, Michael, 1939–. II. Title. III. Series: Studies in music (Ann Arbor,
Mich.) ; no. 110.

    ML410.M4A3 1990
    780'.92—dc20
    [B]   89-20256
                                                                          CIP
                                                                           MN

A catalogue record for this title is available from the British Library.
This publication is printed on acid-free paper.

to Margaret and Tracy

Contents

viii   *Contents*

Preface

I first became aware of the 1837 journals of Lowell Mason when I was a graduate student in the 1960s. Bryce Jordan, then Professor of Musicology at the University of Texas at Austin and now President of Pennsylvania State University, obtained them for scholarly examination from Mrs. Helen Endicott, great-granddaughter of Lowell Mason. As Professor Jordan's research assistant, I spent a fascinating summer examining them. Jordan's rise up the administrative ladder, however, subsequently claimed much of the time that he would otherwise have spent on scholarly pursuits. In the early 1980s he and I agreed to work on the journals jointly. The duties of administering a large, state-wide university system severely restricted his activity in the project, until finally he concurred that I should complete it on my own. I wish to thank him first for piquing my interest in these journals and then for generously turning over to me his materials.

A second person to whom I owe a considerable debt of gratitude is Nicholas Temperley of the University of Illinois. We have had several stimulating conversations about European and American music in the early nineteenth century, and he has generously provided me with the resources of the Hymn Tune Index in locating sources for some of the tunes that Mason recorded.

The journals are now in the John Herrick Jackson Music Library at Yale University. I would like to thank Yale University for permission to reproduce them. I would especially like to thank Harold Samuel, Music Librarian at Yale University, and Victor Cardell, Assistant Librarian at Yale University in the early 1980s, more specifically in making material available and more generally in making a scholar's life less difficult. Work occurred at many other places but I would like to single out for thanks Gillian Anderson and Wayne Shirley at the Library of Congress, Diane Ota at the Boston Public Library, and Edwin Quist at the Peabody Conservatory Library. Some of the material in the Introduction appeared in the *Journal of the American Musicological Society.* I am grateful for permission to use that material.

I would like to acknowledge the debt of many other colleagues who have provided various types of assistance during the course of this project: R. K. Webb, James Mohr, Hubert Henderson, Katherine Preston, Daniel Preston, Carol Pemberton, Richard Crawford, Paul Machlin, and Pamela Fox. Robert Webb and James Mohr were especially helpful in directing me to historical sources. Finally I want to thank Nina Fedoroff, who, applying the sharp eyes of a scientist, suggested many improvements. I also wish to thank her for much other support.

Introduction

By the middle of the nineteenth century Lowell Mason was probably the most famous native-born musician in America. Concentrating almost exclusively upon vocal music, he had built a spectacular reputation in Boston as a choir director and teacher. He had revolutionized music education and was in constant demand as a lecturer. Most of all, he had published many collections of sacred music, some of which sold into the hundreds of thousands, a figure that surprised even Mason and far surpassed any normal expectations.[1] These collections included many original compositions, especially hymns, that attained a level of popularity almost unimaginable for a religious song today. They were in every way "hit" tunes, comparable to our popular secular songs, and they made Mason's name a household word throughout the country. Mason, himself, was the first American musician to accumulate a small fortune through his publications.

In December 1852, when he was nearly sixty years old and at the height of his fame, Lowell Mason embarked upon a fourteen-month sojourn in Europe. This trip came at a natural break in his activities, just as he had decided to retire from Boston and move to New York. It was a carefully planned grand tour, and Mason, accompanied by his wife and briefly by his sons William and Henry, played the role of elder statesman of music with great relish.

When Mason returned to Boston in 1853 he published a detailed description of his 1852–54 travels, entitled *Musical Letters from Abroad.*[2] In a series of chapters, or "letters" that were clearly intended for publication,[3] Mason described at length many musical activities and events in England and on the continent.

This was not, however, Mason's first trip to Europe. That occurred in 1837 and stands in marked contrast to the later one. It came when he was forty-five years old and in one of the busiest periods of his life. It was a solitary journey, with Mason traveling alone and in many cases picking up letters of introduction along the way. It seems to have originated on the spur of the moment, there being no reference to it in Mason's letters before 1837, and was undertaken at a time when European study by American musicians was practically unheard of, whereas such travel had become commonplace by 1852.[4]

Mason made no attempt to publicize the 1837 trip, but he did keep a detailed account of it in the form of three journal books in which he made daily entries. These journals were first described by Daniel Gregory Mason (Lowell Mason's grandson), who recognized their significance and published some brief excerpts from them in

The New Music Review.[5] They remained in the Mason family until 1970, when they were given to the Yale University Library along with other Mason material. Except for some brief discussion and occasional citations, scholars have generally ignored them, and they have never been examined as an entity.[6]

Mason's account merits consideration on several levels. It contains specific information about musical activity of its time. It reveals much about Mason himself. It elucidates antebellum American attitudes toward music and religion. It calls into question the nature of the relationship between European and American culture in the early nineteenth century. While it may be examined profitably on each of these points independently, its richness and complexity as a historical document become fully apparent only when it is regarded overall.

On the first level it is a primary source about musical practice in Europe in the early nineteenth century. In spite of certain biases—for example toward vocal music as opposed to instrumental, or toward the Protestant worship service as opposed to the Roman Catholic liturgy—Mason, in a straightforward, almost off-hand way, recorded a great deal of information about both the musical life and the society around him.

Mason concentrated upon church music, an area that is difficult to document in the early nineteenth century. In both England and on the continent he frequently visited four or five churches on a Sunday. The observations he made in England are particularly important as they vividly portray the state of church music at a critical period in its history.[7] In some respects, these observations directly contradict prevailing musicological opinion.[8]

Mason's observations are not, however, limited to church music. He attended many concerts and operas and had the opportunity to meet and speak with many musicians. He recorded much about both the musical activities and the social settings surrounding performances. Mason's criticisms of what he heard suggest a musician of some acuity, and his descriptions are precise enough to afford insight into performance practice of the time.

A collection of programs and hand bills that Mason retained supplement the diary entries. These not only provide further information regarding the performers and the pieces themselves, but in a number of instances contain notes and comments that Mason made about what he heard. Most of the concerts that Mason annotated extensively were in England, and almost all were choral or vocal. Many of the annotations are not duplicated in the journals.

Mason's most detailed comments appear on the programs of two performances of *Messiah.* He originally heard *Messiah* in London in May and then at the Birmingham Music Festival in October. He discussed several aspects of the performances: the tempos, the forces used, the instrumental accompaniment, the level of ability of the soloists, the style of singing, and the use of ornamentation. A transcription of the original programs with Mason's annotations to both *Messiah* performances is included in appendix 4.

Mason did not ignore instrumental music. He heard many of Europe's best virtuosi and not only described their performances but frequently compared them directly to each other. He also compared the relative quality of instrumental ensembles, such as the principal orchestras in London, Paris, and Berlin.

Since Mason's primary interest was church music, he made a special effort to observe and record musical practices in churches both in England and on the Continent. According to Mason, the state of church music in England was abysmally low.[9] This observation is not surprising, as Mason arrived in England precisely when the Oxford movement was gaining momentum, and when English musicians and members of the religious establishment themselves were calling for reform.[10]

Mason found church music on the Continent more acceptable, although the quality was not universally good. More than any other aspect of church music, the power and force with which the German congregations sang made a deep impression upon him. In the first church he visited in Germany he described the chorales as sung by "the whole congregation and sung loud—it was very solemn and devotional. The hymns were very long." He soon began to tire of this unrelenting large sound, although he still seemed to find it more to his taste than what he heard in London.

Mason perceived instrumental music in Europe to be superior to that in America. Since the heavy influx of German musicians and the establishment of the symphonic societies in the United States was still a decade or more away, this is not a surprising observation. Mason was particularly impressed with the level of organ performance found in Europe. Although many organists whose names Mason did not record elicited his disapprobation, Mason did hear a number of well-known organ virtuosi whose abilities far surpassed anything he had heretofore encountered.[11]

On a second level, the three journal books that Mason filled provide the first detailed account of an American musician's reaction to European musical culture. Many European musicians had come to America, of course, and later it would be commonplace for American musicians to go to Europe. Virtually all of our comparisons between European and American musical culture before the 1840s, however, are seen through European eyes. And by the 1850s, when European travel by American musicians became more common, the aura and the mystique of European musical culture had been imprinted upon America. The revolts of 1848 had brought to America large numbers of European, particularly German, musicians, and in the second half of the century, European virtuosi became familiar figures throughout America. Mason's account is unique in that it predates this significant change in the American musical landscape.

It is frequently difficult to distinguish the reportorial from the reactive level in the journals, particularly in regard to sacred music. Mason expressed his musical prejudices frequently. He preferred a solemn, dignified, restrained, precise, "chaste" style, but praised enough church music so that his criticism seems balanced. The lack of choirs in most churches, their small size when they did exist, the persistence of lining out, the reluctance of the congregation to sing, and the use of Rippon's collection—all events reported by Mason—is factual evidence, independent of Mason's biases. His willingness to compare church music on the Continent directly with that of England lends credibility to remarks about the music that are somewhat more subjective. His preference for German church music is well in keeping with his own aesthetic, and in this instance his description of its power and force is convincing.

Mason's trip probably did much to convince him of the artistic significance of secular music, not only because of the performance levels that he encountered, but also because of the settings in which it was found. For instance, he marveled at the theater in Europe. It was not the rough, immoral place that it was in America, in which the worst elements of society congregated. This forced Mason to acknowledge that his objections to opera in the United States were social rather than musical, although he did find certain operas objectionable because of the content of their libretti. He admitted, however, that some oratorios were no better.

Mason's longest description of a musical event was of a concert at Linchen Erben or "Lingershurbard," an outdoor garden on the Elbe River (July 10, see chap. 4). Mason was astounded that a large orchestra would play a fine symphonic program in an outdoor setting, in which the listeners could drink beer, wander about the gardens with their many bowers, groves, and gazebos, or picnic, read and write. He described the program, the orchestra, and the performance in great detail. He was particularly struck by the composition of the crowd. The people were almost all middle class, there being "evidently no rich or great ones there." The social significance of the occasion was not lost on him: "No wonder that the Germans should have a cultivated musical taste when for 12½ cents they may hear symphonies of Beethoven and music of the highest order."

This and a number of other instances demonstrated to Mason that art music could be very much a part of everyday life and that it could be treated with proper decorum while being enjoyed not only by the cultivated few but by the many. As Mason's general idealistic philosophy of music was already well established by 1837, this idea was not new in itself, but Mason's surprise in what he found indicates that its social confirmation was indeed an important discovery. It may well have been the most important insight that Mason brought home.

On a third level these diaries present us with the most intimate glimpse that we have of one of the most important and powerful men in the history of American music.[12] The sustained candor of the diaries is found nowhere else in all of Mason's preserved writings.[13] Through both example and advocacy Mason promulgated a set of values and attitudes about music that went far toward shaping an American musical aesthetic of the second half of the nineteenth century, and in these journals we come to understand not only more about those attitudes but also about the nature of the man behind them.

These journals in some ways depict an archetypical antebellum American. They reveal Mason as a strong-minded, energetic, morally upright and deeply religious man. There is no doubt that his religious convictions encompassed all aspects of his life, that they provided central psychological support, and that they were sincere. The latter is apparent not only in the many moral lessons Mason drew from events but also in the number of sermons that he heard and outlined in the diary. Whatever the merit or historical value of these sermons, their very presence in the diaries indicates that Mason listened to them closely. As his tour progressed he recorded more and more descriptions of sermons and fewer and fewer of music in churches. Perhaps by the latter stages of his journey Mason had concluded that he had absorbed all that was worth absorbing about church music.

Even Mason's aesthetics have a distinctly religious tone. One of his principal criteria was restraint; he was interested in performances that were exact, precise, and lacking in excesses, such as extended cadenzas. In Mason's vocabulary of criticism, "chaste," "devotional," and "cultivated" are positive terms; "vulgar," "bacchanalian," and "coarse" are negative ones. Mason's vocabulary translates New England Congregational orthodoxy of the early nineteenth century into aesthetic terms. Strong remnants of puritanism remain, and antebellum revivalism, with its strict moral code, is acceptable only if its methods eschew the frenzy that characterized the revival movement in the West.

These diaries reveal a theocentric point of view which is characteristic of antebellum America. Historians of the past two generations have demonstrated how important evangelicalism was to this age,[14] and Lowell Mason, with his firm beliefs and his dedication to the improvement of church music, reflected his time. In that respect it is difficult to distinguish between the diaries as revelatory of Mason and revelatory of Mason's society.

The difference between Lowell Mason's outlook and a more modern one is succinctly illustrated in a criticism that Frédéric Ritter leveled at Thomas Hastings. In 1890, Ritter castigated Thomas Hastings for placing religious considerations above aesthetic ones (Ritter, 171–72). Yet Hastings was not alone in his opinion: In a letter written to his son William, Lowell Mason summarized his music aesthetic by classifying music according to the reasons it is cultivated, according to its ends and purposes. He delineated four aesthetic categories: the sensuous, the intellectual, the artistic, and the moral. There is no doubt about a hierarchy here—Mason's own metaphor is "ascending a ladder." And while he valued the artistic highly, claiming that only a few composers have reached that plateau—he specifically cites Beethoven, Schumann, Liszt, and Wagner[!]—he nevertheless placed the moral a rung above that.[15]

Today most of us would side with Ritter, but in the early nineteenth century, evangelical Protestantism and its important corollary, individual choice, were relatively new and disturbing concepts. Because of the profound implications of individual choice to a society that rejected predestination but still found salvation very real and immediate, moral education and persuasion was a pressing issue of the most fundamental importance. Mason's hierarchy reflects an urgency about religion so characteristic of its age that its prevalence shaped virtually all aspects of American life, from social reform to national purpose.[16] Most historians also consider revivalism to have peaked in the 1830s, and given Mason's close association with Lyman Beecher, there is no question that Mason was very much involved with it.

Anyone reading the journals seeking to understand Mason the man immediately encounters one of the principal mysteries surrounding the trip: Why did Mason go? The origins, purpose, and timing of the trip, as well as the details surrounding its planning, are unclear—even the diaries are tantalizingly vague on these points—but what deepens the puzzle is its uncharacteristic nature: this trip was one of the most atypical acts of Mason's career, inconsistent with both his activities and his personality.

If the trip is examined in relation to Mason's professional activities in the late 1830s, his decision to go to Europe in 1837 seems ill-timed. Mason's work schedule was staggering by the mid 1830s. He not only continued his activities as choir director,[17] but also had assumed teaching and administrative duties in the Boston Academy of Music, which by 1835 had three thousand students (Census, 1841). He had pioneered the teaching of music in the New England School for the Blind, had accepted an offer to teach music in the Andover Theological Seminary, and had continued to publish large quantities of music, averaging more than two books a year.

Most important, Mason had lobbied strenuously throughout the 1830s for the acceptance of music into the public school curriculum. The Boston Academy was founded in 1833 for that very purpose, and in 1836 Mason had the Academy reopen the question with a petition to the School Board (called the School Committee). Two other groups also petitioned at the time, and the School Committee appointed a sub-committee to study the issue. This committee presented a report supporting the teaching of music in the schools, with a recommended plan of action, on August 24, 1837.[18] The School Committee accepted this plan on September 19 and submitted it to the Boston City Council for funding. The City Council failed to grant an appropriation, but Mason, not wishing to lose the chance to demonstrate the feasibility of adding music to the school curriculum, offered to teach a year without salary. The offer was accepted.

Mason was in Europe from April to November 1837, precisely when the issue was before the sub-committee, the School Committee, and the City Council. Why Mason chose to go through with his journey at that particular time is difficult to explain. He may have specifically wished to absent himself from Boston during the deliberations, he may have felt that he had already done all he possibly could to argue his case, or he may have simply miscalculated. Certain of a positive recommendation from the Committee, he may have assumed the necessary appropriations would follow. The latter hypothesis is the most plausible, because much of Mason's activity while abroad suggests a man who is looking beyond this immediate victory to the years ahead.

One other possibility can be dismissed. A journey that lasted seven months and had an itinerary of twenty-five cities (see appendix 2) was a major undertaking in 1837. It would be reasonable to assume that Mason had worked out the details well in advance and that the complexity of the arrangements were such that the cancellation or postponement of the trip would be difficult. Mason's penchant for organization and the cautious manner in which he approached most of his career decisions reinforce such an assumption. The evidence, however, suggests precisely the opposite. Mason's letters prior to 1837 do not even hint at a trip, and the journals themselves reveal the extent to which Mason improvised once he arrived in Europe.

Had Mason been planning a European trip prior to 1837, he would certainly have mentioned it in his considerable correspondence with Sigismund Ritter von Neukomm. Between 1835 and 1837 Mason carried on an extensive correspondence with Neukomm, and when Mason arrived in Europe, Neukomm provided him with crucial introductions that did much to insure the success of Mason's trip. Mason's letters to Neukomm are lost, but most of Neukomm's to Mason have survived.[19] While we are thus reduced to listening to one side of a conversation, thanks to Neukomm's garrulousness and his many references to the contents of Mason's letters much of the correspondence can be reconstructed. The letters provide critical evidence regarding the background to Mason's trip.

Mason initiated the exchange. Neukomm's long letter of December 20, 1835, the earliest to survive, replies to Mason's first of September 20. Mason's immediate purpose apparently was to secure a copy of Neukomm's *David* for performance. Neukomm promises to send the orchestral parts and then thanks Mason "for the honor you have wished to make me," presumably the performance.

Evidently Mason also sent Neukomm a copy of his *Sacred Melodies* and expounded at some length upon his philosophy regarding sacred music and music education, for Neukomm praises Mason for his position: "You have taken the true, the only way to make certain that the music of your continent will have a durable as well as glorious future. Sacred music is the only kind which will be imperishable." Mason apparently painted a rather glowing account of his efforts in the United States, for Neukomm compliments Mason several times for his success and compares activity in England unfavorably with that in America: "I see with great satisfaction that in the part of the new world in which you live, they occupy themselves with our divine art in a manner more serious than is the case in our old Europe, where they are surfeited on everything, and where they descended rather low in order to believe that it is necessary for music to tickle one's ears."

At the close of his letter, Neukomm boldly offers to come to the United States in order to see what Mason has done. He suggests that "if it could be arranged advantageously for all parties," he "would not be adverse to a little voyage," and could direct some of his works with Mason.

Mason apparently responded favorably to Neukomm's suggestion, for in the next surviving letter Neukomm details specific plans to visit Boston.[20] He indicates that he will embark from Liverpool in July 1836, arrive in New York and be in Boston by September. Neukomm was to be connected with the Boston Academy, probably directing some concerts during the fall; he intended to supplement his income with organ recitals. He then planned to travel south and west, spend the winter in New Orleans, and then return to Boston for several weeks in the spring of 1837 before leaving for Europe.

That these plans took definite shape is indicated in Neukomm's letter of July 7, 1836: "I am on the point of embarking for Boston, and I hope to arrive almost at the same time as the letter. I have guaranteed passage on board the 'New Jersey' a ship which goes directly from Liverpool to Boston and which has been recommended to me as very good—we shall see." He then asks Mason to arrange lodging for him while in Boston.

Neukomm did not make the voyage and there is no explanation for this. There is no direct reference to it in his next surviving letter to Mason, dated April 3, 1837, and Neukomm does not mention a possible American trip in his autobiography (Neukomm 1859). This is not particularly surprising, however, as Neukomm was a constant traveler and often changed his mind at the last minute. He very likely made many plans of this sort which never materialized.

Neukomm's letter of April 3, 1837, is in reply to one from Mason dated January 6, 1837. Complimenting Mason upon the continued success of the Academy, Neukomm recommends that Mason find someone from Europe with experience in choral festivals to direct concerts and organize the endeavor—in essence to do what Neukomm would have done. Neukomm makes one veiled reference to his American trip. Discussing a work that will be performed at the Birmingham Festival, he regrets that since it is still in manuscript he cannot show it to Mason but notes that "if I were on your continent, all of that could be arranged easily."

If we consider Neukomm's proposed American venture in relation to Mason's plans, it is clear from this correspondence that as late as mid-1836 the idea of a European trip had not yet entered Mason's mind, and that even in early 1837 he still had formulated nothing definite. If he had, he surely would have mentioned his plans to Neukomm, who intended to spend a few weeks with him in Boston during the spring of 1837.

That Mason had no plans for a European trip as late as January 1837, is supported by a letter from W. A. Woodbridge to Mason dated June 5, 1837 (Mason P, Box 4, Folder 80). Woodbridge had lived in Europe during the 1820s and had returned to Switzerland in 1836. His contacts in Germany and Switzerland were extensive. On June 5 he sent Mason a circular letter of introduction to a number of educational institutions in those areas. In his letter to Mason Woodbridge strongly intimates that he had no idea Mason was to be in Europe until he had already arrived. Again had Mason been planning the voyage ahead of time, he would almost certainly have contacted Woodbridge as well as Neukomm.

Why then did Mason go to Europe? He alludes to the purpose of his trip several times in the diaries, but these allusions tend to be more tantalizing than informative. Puritan to the core, Mason viewed the trip as a duty and was particularly cognizant of the cost of his lengthy stay abroad relative to his own Sabbath obligation. He felt justified, however, as his Sunday activities conformed to his larger aims. After having spent one Sunday sampling music in various cathedrals and wrangling invitations into their organ lofts, he expressed regret that the Sabbath was sacrificed in the spiritual sense but noted, "[I] still feel as if I had been in the path of duty—I make the sacrifice to accomplish the great object of my tour—musical information, etc." [May 28]. "Musical information, etc." is about as precise as Mason is in the diaries. The two circular letters of introduction that Mason secured from Woodbridge and Neukomm, however, refer more extensively to the purpose of the trip, and they almost certainly reflect Mason's own explanations. Neukomm's letter reads:

London 21 June 1837

Mr. Neukomm begs those of his friends whose names follow to please welcome with kindness the bearer of this letter

Mr. Lowell Mason, Professor Music

at Boston, in the United States of America, and to help him in every way which will contribute to his attaining in the shortest time the aim of his journey which is to know the different methods of musical teaching and all the institutions which are associated with them.[21]

Woodbridge's letter reads:

Montreux (près Vevay) Suisse
5 June 1837

I take the liberty of presenting to you the name of my compatriot Mr. Lowell Mason, Professor Music in the "Boston Academy of Music," a man known equally for his Christian character and for his devotion to his science, as for his musical works and his efforts for the instruction of our young people. He travels at present in order to prepare for his important tasks and I hope that his purpose will serve as justification when I dare to request you to aid his research in your neighborhood and to accord him the information which

he desires as far as your convenience will permit. I beg of you to excuse this only way of providing your address. I am
sir—

Your very devoted servant
W. G. Woodbridge
Editor "des Annales d'Education"[22]

Both letters suggest that Mason was in Europe to learn more about musical instruction. Even this, however, is misleading, as both were written in June, after Mason had been in England for some time, and both refer to activities on the Continent. The diaries show that the journey had no one single, overriding purpose, but rather that objectives varied with locale. Because his activities in the two principal areas that he visited—England on the one hand, Germany and Switzerland on the other— were so different, it is impossible to speak of a single overall purpose that encompasses both.

The focus of the German and Swiss phase of his tour was primarily educational, with the bulk of his time spent visiting various teaching institutions. This may have been at least partly dictated by circumstances. With a few notable exceptions,[23] Woodbridge's letter turned out to be more valuable than Neukomm's as an entree into musical society on the Continent, and Woodbridge had few contacts with musicians outside of educational institutions. Mason, hampered by his total inability to speak German (and complete lack of any regret about it), not surprisingly found it much more difficult to make contacts and gain access to other phases of musical activities on his own than he did in England.

One of the principal purposes of Mason's visit to Switzerland was to meet with George Nägeli. Nägeli, who lived in Zurich, had pioneered the application of the Pestalozzian system to musical instruction and had also written a considerable amount of music for youth, some of which Mason had used in his anthologies. Nägeli had died the previous winter, and it is not certain when Mason learned of this. Woodbridge apparently did not know it when he sent Mason the letter of June 5th. The first reference to Nägeli's death occurs in Mason's diary on July 31, in St. Gallen, when Mason noted without comment that "A gentleman to whom Mr. Tobler introduced me gave me some pieces of music composed on the death of Nägeli" (chap. 5). Mason stayed in Zurich only long enough to hear Nägeli's daughter sing and to complete the purchase of all of Nägeli's music that he did not already own.

When Mason was in England his interest in music education was minimal. He visited the Royal Academy of Music only briefly and only after he had been in London nearly a month. He recorded the visit tersely in the diary with none of the detail that characterizes his German and Swiss education-related entries. Mason seemed to have had two goals while in London: to purchase music and to hear performances. Days were spent in music stores or publishing houses—Mason's diary indicating just how many there were in London at the time—evenings at concerts, and Sundays visiting as many churches as possible.

Mason does record one other reason for the European trip: simply to get away from it all and to have the opportunity to renew himself mentally and spiritually. Aboard ship to England he refers to this several times. Apparently feeling the press of his many activities of the 1830s, on the second day out he noted:

> I desire to praise God whose kind providence has thus separated me from those worldly concerns which have so sorely occupied my time and attention for years past. I now find time for meditation, self examination and for reviewing my past life, especially the few years past . . . I feel as though this separation from my worldly business would be greatly to my spiritual good. (March 27)

After lamenting that in musical matters he has conformed too much to this world, he observed:

> I feel that the time on board this ship is very precious and I desire to bless God for his good Providence by which I am thus brought into circumstances so favorable for religious reflection, etc. (April 1)

On the eighth day out he reiterated this point: "If I get no other advantage from this voyage than that ('reflection and self examination') I am already richly repaid" (April 3).

The remainder of Mason's trip gave him not rest and recuperation but a hectic schedule of business and professional activities: collecting music, arranging for his own works to be published, observing educational practices, interviewing musicians, and attending concerts. His desire to get away and the indications in the diary entries, that he was beginning to feel the wear and tear of his frantic pace in Boston, do support the apparently precipitous nature of the decision to travel as well as the puzzling timing of the trip itself. Mason may well have reached the point that he felt an overwhelming need for a temporary respite, although his own energetic, duty-bound character would never have allowed him the luxury of a trip that did not have a larger and more tangible purpose.

The manner in which Mason proceeded once he reached various cities not only confirms the relative looseness of his planning but also reveals much about Mason, himself. Mason secured most of his contacts only after he had arrived in Europe, and these by and large determined his itinerary. Even the two principal letters of introduction—by Neukomm and Woodbridge—were solicited only after Mason was in Europe.

Neukomm's friendship proved particularly valuable while Mason was in England, as he personally escorted Mason to a number of private gatherings and personally introduced him to a number of prominent musicians. Through Neukomm Mason met Moscheles, Thalberg, and Mendelssohn, among others. Yet not all of Mason's success can be attributed to these introductions. At times Mason was just lucky, being at the right place at the right time. Mason's luck, however, has a distinctly cultivated quality, and there is no question that when by chance Mason did meet someone of importance, he was a master at taking full advantage of his good fortune. His relationship with the Novello family illustrates this well. Upon first arriving in London, Mason visited Robert Gray, an organ builder, who must have known Mason, because Gray immediately abandoned his business for the day to show Mason around and then to have dinner with him. The next night Mason dined again with Mr. Gray along with J. A. Novello and another unnamed gentleman. The following day (May 20th) Mason visited Novello's business and, after remaining there for two hours, was invited to dine at the Novellos' home. From that point on Mason had a close rapport with the Novello family. He visited them frequently, accompanied various members of the family to concerts, and through them secured special concert passes that he would otherwise not have been able to obtain. The Novellos' cordiality was of course good business, for Mason not only purchased very large quantities of music from them but also worked out an agreement for Novello to publish his *Juvenile Songster.* Nevertheless, the relationship that Mason developed with the Novello family seems to have been one of genuine friendship.

The diaries also reveal Mason as a man of independent mind and strong opinion in musical matters, whether dealing with secular or church music. With no reticence whatsoever, he recorded his likes and dislikes irrespective of the fame or prestige of the performer or event. The Birmingham Festival in September was surely a highlight of his trip, possibly one of the motivating factors for the trip itself, since Neukomm's oratorio *The Ascension* was to be performed. The festival also featured a performance of Mendelssohn's oratorio *St. Paul,* which Mason had heard earlier in rehearsal in London with Mendelssohn present. Because he found it not to his liking, Mason walked out of the performance. He recorded his reasons for his opinion in the diary and gave only the briefest mention to his meeting with Mendelssohn (Sept. 5, chap. 6).

Many friends and professional acquaintances of Mason have spoken of his commanding appearance and charismatic personality. These traits are evident throughout the journals. More than once Mason received preferential treatment because he was taken to be a person of rank or station, and he was always perceived as a gentleman, in the antebellum sense of the term.[24] Much of his success can be attributed to this aspect of his person.

Yet in spite of what these journals reveal about Mason or about European musical life, their greatest value may lie in the questions they raise about transatlantic cultural identification in the early nineteenth century. Mason was willing to compare directly and in total candor many aspects of culture (including music) in America, England, and on the Continent. His comparisons reveal an underlying attitude at odds with recent musicological thought regarding the nature of the cross-cultural relationship between Europe and America at that time.[25]

Mason viewed American music as part of a single Anglo-American culture. In his eyes, the essential cultural line was drawn between English-speaking and other Continental cultures, not between Europe and America. Upon his arrival in Hamburg he commented: "Every thing here indicates that I am in a Foreign Land—In London it seemed only as though I was in another American City" (June 30, chap. 4). While he marveled at the extent and the quality of musical activity in London, which to him far surpassed that of any city in America, he viewed the difference between London and Boston, for instance, as analogous to that between London and Manchester. London was the capital of an Anglo-American culture, and Birmingham, Liverpool, Boston, and New York were smaller outposts.[26] Mason also found many members of the English musical establishment well versed in musical developments in America, which further helped him feel at home in England.

Germany, however, was an alien land. Mason's lack of knowledge of the German language hindered him greatly, but beyond that he found much to his dislike. He commented at length about minor matters, such as beds and bedcovering, dress, and the coaches. He found the circumstances of the peasantry abhorrent, seeing them as physically ugly and finding their living conditions evidence of an inferior society. His own attitude toward language is revealing. He considered it an imposition that so few Germans could speak English, and he made little effort to accommodate them halfway in their attempts to communicate with him. When a German did try to speak English, Mason made his grammatical errors and accent an object of ridicule. When he did meet a German who could speak English relatively well, he viewed that person as a true gentleman, his status validated by having learned the English language.

Mason was not, however, blind to the positive aspects of German society, particularly education. He was impressed with the enthusiasm that both German and Swiss children displayed toward music and found the discipline and the highly organized approaches to education laudable. He saw in the strictness of the German educational system an antidote to the corruption and temptations of the world, something that concerned him in many ways throughout the journal. He was sufficiently impressed with this aspect of German and German-speaking Swiss culture to consider sending his own sons to Europe for study.

The most fundamental question raised by Mason's Anglo-American stance is whether scholars have exaggerated the quasi-nationalistic aspects of American musical culture in the late eighteenth and early nineteenth centuries. If Mason's attitudes are not aberrant, and the shadow he cast over American musical thought suggests they were not, the issue of national identification in American music in the first part of the nineteenth century needs to be reconsidered.

The issue cannot be settled by Mason's diaries alone, but the diaries do suggest that to depict Mason as anti-nationalistic because of his European orientation may be an inaccurate judgment. Nationalism was indeed an important political concept by 1837, but in 1837 a conscious American musical nationalism seems, at least from this evidence, unformed. Mason was interested in taste, quality, and decorum in music, irrespective of its national orientation. While he encountered a level of musical activity in London far above what he had known, that was only because it was London, a city that in Mason's eyes culturally eclipsed any other in the English-speaking world. To Mason, English music, especially English church music, was not superior overall to American, and whatever the differences, they had little to do with national identification.

In 1842, some five years after Mason's journey, Louis Moreau Gottschalk left for Europe as a youth of fourteen, intent on becoming a virtuoso who could rival the best that Europe had to offer. As such, Gottschalk was a pioneer. During the nineteenth century this course would become more and more common until it became almost *de rigueur* for an aspiring performer. Lowell Mason's own son William followed precisely in those steps.

In 1837 Lowell Mason was not an aspiring musical talent but a man of maturity who already viewed his mission with considerable clarity. The purpose of his trip differed from Gottschalk's, to observe rather than to participate. Yet it was a bold move for 1837, and its impact on Mason was without doubt considerable. The trip may have changed Mason's viewpoints or direction little, but, judging from these diaries, it did confirm and solidify what he already sensed: that it was possible to base a musical culture upon the European masters, that such music was not beyond the grasp of the majority of the population, that demonstrable results could be obtained from the proper musical education, that performance levels above those commonly found in America were attainable, and that American music, while weak in some areas, did not lag behind its European counterparts in others. Mason recognized the value of the study of European music and was undoubtedly encouraged and stimulated by what he saw. Intending less to conquer than to learn, Mason, in the candor and detail of the diaries, recorded a series of comparisons that sheds light on musical activities and attitudes on both sides of the Atlantic.

Notes on the Transcription

In order to reproduce Lowell Mason's journals faithfully and precisely, corrections have been made only where necessary for intelligibility and where they transgress neither the content nor the flavor of Mason's original. For example:
1. Emended words have been left out when the emendation is clearly by Lowell Mason and when it involves only minor grammatical or spelling corrections. More significant emendations have been indicated in the text. Emendations made by Lowell Mason's grandson, Henry Lowell Mason (HLM), who began editing the journals in the early twentieth century, have been corrected without comment if it is certain that they were by HLM. Those few passages where doubt exists have been indicated.
2. Lowell Mason's unusual or archaic spelling has been retained, unless it is clear that the misspelling was only a slip of the pen. This is usually evident by comparing the spelling with other occurrences of the word. Where proper names are misspelled the correct spelling is indicated in brackets immediately following the first occurrence only. Mason abbreviated some common words—such as "thro" for "through," or "accompd" for "accompanied." He seems to have done it for purposes of speed and efficiency in writing, and it is not a stylistic characteristic of his prose. In such instances the word has been spelled out.
3. One of the most individual characteristics of Mason's writing is his unusual and often inconsistent capitalization of words. This has been reproduced as it stands in the journals.
4. Mason frequently used dashes in place of other punctuation marks. These have been retained, with one exception: when a period is clearly intended. This is almost always obvious from the context and the physical properties of the entry, as the dash is separated from the subsequent word, which, itself, is capitalized, indicating that Mason had in mind the beginning of a new sentence. In such cases a period has been substituted for a dash.
5. Doodle-like marks appear frequently throughout the journals. These were apparently used to indicate breaks in writing and thus convey information in themselves. They have been reproduced in this transcription by the symbol ~~~~~~~
6. The original pagination has not been indicated, but the point at which each of the three journals begins and ends has.
7. Material enclosed within parentheses ( ) is part of the text. Editorial material that is not part of the original is enclosed within brackets [ ]. Emended text is enclosed within braces { }.

Annotations

Mason refers to many people in these diaries, some of whom are historically or musically important and some of whom receive mention simply because they happened to be in close proximity to Mason—in the same hotel or coach, or on the same ship. Through heroic archival efforts, that latter group of people could be identified in many instances. Even with such diligence however, some must remain unknown. At times Mason simply does not provide us sufficient information, as he often, for example, records only the surname. At other times archival searching can yield at best several possibilities. Even when a positive identification is possible, whether such would actually contribute to the understanding of the narrative is questionable.

Every attempt has been made to identify all professional musicians, important historical figures, and persons who play a substantial part in Mason biography. Even in such cases the search has not been entirely successful. Some individuals have proved frustratingly elusive, and it is hoped that biographical information that allows these persons to be more fully identified will eventually come to light. As it stands, however, the roster of musical personalities, especially in England, is remarkably complete. Mason's diary is a virtual compendium of musical activity in what was probably the richest musical center in Europe at that time.

1

The Voyage to Europe

A new era in transatlantic travel opened in 1816 with the inauguration of the New York–Liverpool route, the first regular packet service between America and Europe.[1] At that time Atlantic crossings were still reminiscent of the days of the *Pinta, Niña,* and *Santa Maria.* They continued to be made in wooden, square stern, high-rigged sailing vessels very much at the mercy of the elements and completely out of touch with the rest of world save an occasional sighting of another ship. Storms, fog, icebergs, and even piracy were constant dangers. Travel time, totally dependent upon the wind, was unpredictable.

In spite of the presence of steam vessels by the 1830s, most voyages were still made in sailing packets, although in size and contour they had changed dramatically. They were longer and sleeker and had attained a degree of luxury hitherto unimaginable.[2] Most packets carried approximately fifteen passengers in first class and catered to their needs with comfortable berths, elegantly appointed cabins (or lounges) and lavish meals. These packets also carried about fifty passengers who were crammed amidship in steerage, and their accommodations were anything but comfortable.

For even the first-class passengers, however, the voyage presented difficulties. Seasickness was a constant discomfort, and only the most seasoned traveler escaped it entirely. And even though these packets attained sizes of 500 to 750 tons, an Atlantic storm was still a terrifying and a realistically dangerous experience. Fog was even more threatening, particularly where icebergs were present or when the vessel began to approach land.

Most of all the first-class passenger had to cope with boredom. Voyages usually took between three-and-one-half and six weeks, and first-class passengers had no duties. Consequently many accounts of ocean travel exist, and here Mason's journal is far from unique.[3] Reading, writing, and reflection were common on board ship, and Mason, himself, indicates that the latter at least, was an unusual activity for him.

———————

MASON'S DIARY

On board Ship Virginian—bound from New York for Liverpool—Wednesday April 26th. 1837. Lowell Mason.

We sailed from N.Y. yesterday 25th. Ins. at 12 o'clock—the Packet having been detained one day beyond our regular time by bad weather. We sailed in company with Packet Ship Albany for Havre which vessel is still near us. I find myself most comfortably situated on board the vessel—having an entire state room in the Ladies Cabin to myself. There are on board 15 passengers and also 49 in the Steerage. Everything on board seems to be in fine order. Thus far we have had a moderate breeze, and have only made about 4 or 4½ miles an hour[4]—but little motion and no one (so far as I have seen) sick. I rose at about 7 this morning—had breakfast ½ past 8—after which I spent an hour delightfully in my room. Read in Daniel and also Matthew. It is very pleasant to think of home—of each individual in my family, and to commend them individually and collectively to Him who can keep them all in safety. ~~~~~~~

¼ past 11. Spoke [to] a Schooner bound to Boston. Captain Watson requested him to report us—so that I hope my friends will be cheered by hearing of our good passage thus far. ~~~~~~~

Thursday 27th

Second day out. The wind has continued fair thus far though but a moderate breeze. We have averaged from 5 to 6 miles an hour—some part of the night Seven. It was very cold yesterday, and especially towards night—I could not get warm untill ½ an hour after going to bed. In the night I rose and took Magnesia—and feel much better for it this morning. I desire to praise God whose kind providence has thus separated me from those worldly concerns which have so wholly occupied my time and attention for years past. I now find time for meditation, self-examination, and for reviewing my past life—especially the few years past. It is a mercy that I know not how to estimate that I am thus taken away from my worldly pursuits, and I feel as though I could leave all in the hands of God. He knows what is best for me and my family—may we always put our trust in him. I feel as though this separation from my worldly business would be greatly for my spiritual good. I know it will be so, if I improve it aright which God grant me grace to do.

The Ship Albany is still near us. Among the Steerage passengers are two fine little Irish girls about 10 or 11 years of age, and two or three boys 12 to 14. Some of the Steerage passengers look quite respectable—especially the Parents of the girls above mentioned.

Friday 28th. April

Third day Out. The wind still fair. The weather is somewhat warmer this morning. The wind is from the Southward and is mild, soft and pleasant. The ship sails faster than when the wind is directly aft. We now go at the rate of 7 m. an hour. All is pleasant as possible thus far. How glad I should be to have my wife and children look in and see how comfortably I am situated here. Some of the passengers amused themselves yesterday by catching Mother Cary's chickens.[5] They threw out a string with a little piece of cabbage tied to it, and the birds would fly down to catch the bait, and become entangled with the string. Several were caught that way. I became acquainted yesterday with a farmer from N.Y. state. He came from England 6 or 8 years ago—from Yorkshire and settled in this country—he likes it much—he is now returning to secure a legacy that has been left to his wife, and expects to come back again in 4 months. There is a great difference on board the ship between Cabin and Steerage passengers. The latter 49 in number are all crowded together, men women and children into a little dark hole forward—without fresh air, and with hardly room to turn round—while we in the Cabin have everything we could desire. I feel much for two females in the Steerage. They appear to be well educated and respectable, and to have seen better days. I have tried to do something for them—but have not succeeded at it. This morning the Albany is not to be seen. She was 6 or 8 miles behind us at dark last evening. ~~~~~~~

A day on board. Rise at 7

Saturday 29th. Ap.

Fourth day out. This day the weather continues pleasant and rather warm—though we need an outside coat when on deck. The wind is quite light, and we only sail about 4 m. an hour this morning. I have found on Board the history of the Bible and I find it very interesting to read a passage and then compare it with the original history of the sacred writers. Today I think of Mr. [Gideon French] Thayer's school [Chauncy-Hall] and Mr. [William Bentley] Fowle's [Female Monitorial School]—of my class in afternoon, and of the Choir in evening.

When at breakfast this morning one of the passengers handed around "The New York Mirror" of this date—having got it before he sailed in N.Y. and 4 days before the publication. He assured the passengers that he had just received it from N.Y. and that it was brought by one of Mother Cary's chickens—in jest of course. A day on board. Rise from 6 to 7—wash—dress, etc. take a walk upon deck—read—breakfast at 8. ½ past 8—retire to room—read etc.—walk on deck and read—12 lunch—

then we all eat. Afterwards hot water—shave etc.—3½ Dinner which takes just about an hour—from 4½ till 7½ walk about deck—read—talk etc.—at 7½ tea—at a little past 8 to bed.

~~~~~~~~~~~~~~~~~~~~~~~~~~~

Sabbath 30th April 1837

Fifth Day out. It is quite a warm and pleasant day—so warm as to be comfortable without an outside coat. But little wind, so that our progress is but slow.

This morning I love to think of home. I imagine I see all the family collected and Mr. Lawrence in my place reading the family worship. Billy [William Mason] playing Arlington, etc.[6]

It is nearly time for Church to begin. How I should like to step in unobserved, and hear the exercises—especially the singing. Mr. [Jonathan Call] Woodman will have Hannah [Hannah Call Woodman] to help him to day, so that the singing must go unless he hinders it. I hope to be enabled to spend this day aright, and although I cannot mingle with God's people in the exercises of worship, I have my Bible, Hymn Book and other religious books by me, and a room that is entirely private, where I am not liable to interruption. May the Lord bless me and my absent family and friends this day. ~~~~~~~

Monday 1st May 1837

Sixth day out. First morning in the month. A delightful day—with a strong and favorable breeze—warm and pleasant. Ship moving 9 miles an hour. Several of the passengers are a little seasick. I do not feel it in the least. I ate a very hearty breakfast and feel perfectly well this morning. Felt disposed to chant a psalm of praise—read and sung over "Praise the Lord O my Soul" and also "O Sing unto the Lord a new Song." I have read yesterday and to day "Biddolph on conformity to the world"[7]—it condemns me. In musical matters especially I have been to much conformed to the world. The Boston Academy of Music is the cause of my associating much with merely worldly people—and I need more Christian influence—I need the strength and encouragement that I should certainly derive from a more constant intercourse with Christians—such as I used to have in Savannah.[8] I feel that the time on board this ship is very precious, and I desire to bless God for his good Providence by which I am thus brought into circumstances so favorable for religious reflection, examination, meditation, review etc. ~~~~~~~

This is May-day—very likely Billy has enjoyed the morning. ~~~~~~~

5 o'clock P.M. At ½ past 11 this forenoon came on quite a squall. The scene was new and full of interest to me. It blew strong. The sea

was quite in a rage and the ship danced up and down so that it was difficult to walk or even to stand upright. All hands were on duty—taking in sail etc. The Captain stood at the windward side of the ship steadily watching the weather—occasionally giving an order to one of the mates, or going to the compass to see how the ship headed. But the mates were loud enough—giving their orders from the very top of their voices. The men had many of them on caps similar to firemen's caps—they ran up the shroud—out onto the yard, and all over the vessel as spiders run over their web. It was truly sublime. Just before 12 I took a glass [of] soda water with lemon syrup, and immediately after went down to Lunch and took a bowl of soup. They did not agree and together with the extra motion of the ship produced sickness—I threw them up—and took my berth for an hour or two.

The wind has abated—but it still blows finely. We are making good progress today. During the squall as I was standing on deck there came a sea which washed across the ship and gave me a thorough wetting. ~~~~~~~

Tuesday 2nd May
Seventh day out. A week at sea. We have had a heavy motion—rolling of the ship all night, and it still continues. The wind is fair and we go at the rate of 9 or 9½ knots per hour. I took some cold yesterday and do not feel very bright to day. Took a cup of tea, and some dry toast for breakfast. It is wonderful to stand upon deck and watch the rolling waves of the troubled Sea—the rising and sinking and pitching and rolling of the ship. I braced myself up on a deck and read the 29th Psalm

> "The voice of the Lord is upon the waters:
> The God of glory thundereth;
> The Lord is upon many waters, etc."

The Captain says we are now "up to the banks" (Grand banks of Newfoundland) having been about 1000 miles. A ship is seen at 5 or 6 miles ahead—we are fast overtaking her. I stood on deck this morning as the vessel was rolling along through the mighty waters—I thought of each member of the family and how it would please them could they now look out and see "Father"—in these circumstances. There is one who always looks out and watches and guards and protects us. May he ever be with us all. ~~~~~~~

Wednesday 3rd May
Eighth day out. We have had rather rough weather, and I have been mostly in my berth yesterday and to day. I have not dined with the com-

pany at all since Sunday. I find it difficult to keep warm, and especially my feet. I need thick stockings and India rubber over shoes very much—having only very thin boots. The decks are most of the time damp and my feet get cold. The weather is pleasant to day—the wind has decreased but the rolling of the ship remains—we go at the rate of 5 or 6 miles. The steward has prepared some stewed prunes which are very good.

Evening, ½ past 8. I found myself so much better as to be able to dine with the company to day, and have felt quite well since. We are now sailing pleasantly 6 or 7 miles per hour with fair wind. I have been sitting alone on deck in the dark thinking of home, and all my relations there to individuals, societies etc.

Alas! In how many things have I come short of duty—what an unfaithful Steward have I been. I desire to bless God for this opportunity of reviewing the past. If I get no other advantage from this voyage I feel that I am already richly repaid. Perhaps I never should have found so much time for reflection and Self examination as I now find. The Lord help me to improve it aright, and enable me to carry into effect when I get home again these resolutions that I now make.

I suppose it probable that the Oratorio of 'The Feast of Tabernacle' [by Charles Zeuner] will be performed this evening. If so it will begin there when it is about 10 o'clock here—for there is now about two hours difference in the time.

I will put down some little account of our passengers as I become more acquainted with them—thinking I shall like to look this memorandum over hereafter. I begin with Capt. [Robert Field] Stockton. He is from Princeton, N.J. He is a Captain in the Navy. He is very much of a gentleman—and although I cannot approve of some remarks bearing on religion which I have heard him make, yet I very much respect the man, and think it is an honor to our country to have such men to fill offices. He has a family, and I suppose a man of fortune.

Mrs. Anderson and her four sons. She is a Scotch woman—quite a Lady. We see but little of her as she is most of the time in her room. Her oldest Son appears to be a very unpromising young man—perhaps 20 or 22 years of age. He is forward in his conversation—drinks several kinds of wine at dinner—besides ale or port, and at evening whisky punch, etc. His countenance already betrays him. It would make me miserable indeed to see Daniel pursuing such a course.

Mr. [Joseph] Sturge of Birmingham England. He is a sworn anti-slavery man—has devoted much of his time for years past to this subject, and is now on his way home from a visit to W. I. [West Indies] Islands made on purpose to examine personally the condition of the colored population. He seems a very fine man. He is much of a gentleman and is always ready to give information of England etc. etc.

Thursday 4th. May 1837
Ninth day out. 11 o'clock. It has been blowing very hard for 12 hours or more—so that with but very little sail we are going at the rate of 10 m. per hour. The wind exactly fair. Weather cloudy, squally, rainy, but not cold—S.W. wind.

There is now a higher, and more troubled sea than I have seen before. My sickness is pretty much over. The Captain supposes our passage to be about ½ made. But we depend upon the wind and waves, and he who holds them in his hands only knows when and where our voyage will end.

Friday 5th May
Tenth day out. We have had a fine days run—Wind enough and fair. A heavy sea, and although I can hardly be said to be sea sick, yet I do not feel right. A Head ache and cold feet almost constantly. I desire to make record of the goodness of God to us thus far, to be grateful for past mercies and thank him for future good. My thoughts are daily with my family, and my prayer is for their temporal and spiritual good. The ship rolls so much that it is very difficult to write. ~~~~~~~

Saturday 6th May 1837
Eleventh day out. A very pleasant day—wind from N.W. and a good breeze from 8 to 10 knots. Had considerable conversation with Mr. Sturge to day—on War—He is a thorough peace man—on slavery—He is a thorough abolitionist—on music—being a Quaker he is perhaps rather opposed—but from my conversation I should judge that it is principally if not altogether the abuse of music to which he would object. He is however, very decided against uniting religious and musical exhibitions, and says religious people generally in England are opposed to the great musical festivals. Two ships in sight—both bound the same way as ourselves—but at a great distance from us. Mr. Sturge offered to introduce me to Rev. Mr. [John Angell] James of Birmingham, the author of the Sunday school teachers guide. ~~~~~~~

5 o'clock. We have just dined. It is the first dinner I have relished since last Sunday. Boiled ham—Boiled Mutton—Boiled Cod Fish—Roast duck—Roast Chickens—Curried Chicken—Lobster—Vegetables—Puddings, etc. ~~~~~~~

9 o'clock. It is now not far from 7 o'clock in Boston. Soon the choir will meet. How I should love to be with them. May they have the presence of him whose blessing will make them united, happy and useful.

Sunday 7th May. 1837
Twelfth day out. This is a fine day—wind from the South, and a good breeze by which we run about 8 knots. Three sail are in sight—all four

of us bound the same way. To day I think much of Bowdoin Street.[9] It is a great privilege to be so retired as I can on board the ship. I can read, and sing, and pray undisturbed and without disturbing any one. How precious appear the ordinances of the Sabbath when deprived of them. May all my dear friends be abundantly blessed this day. The passengers are generally quite still to day—and make quite a difference between this and the other days of the week.

I had this morning a very pleasant conversation with Mr. Sturge— who appears to have much feeling similar to my own on religious subjects, etc. ~~~~~~~

Monday 8th May 1837
Thirteenth day out. Light wind from N.W.—some rain—we make little progress today.

This day I remember is the birthday of my oldest son now in college Daniel G. Mason—17 years old. My prayer this day for him is that he may be more a child of God—a partaker of true religion. ~~~~~~~

Tuesday 9th May
Fourteenth day out. Not much wind since yesterday—but what there has been has been fair—This morning exchanged signals with a Packet from Havre for N. York, so that on the arrival of that vessel we shall be reported, and our friends will hear of our safety and progress thus far. I have not been well for some time—am much troubled with cold clammy feet, headache etc. Also sore mouth—to day I feel better, however, having taken early this morning a Seidletz powder—which operated kindly.

The Rochelle powder that I brought only made me sick. We now suppose ourselves to be about 900 m. from Liverpool.

Wednesday 10th May
Fifteenth day out. The wind still fair and we make constant progress. The hope now is that we may get in, in three or four days. Since yesterday I have felt quite well. This evening perhaps, The Oratorio will be again performed. I took much pleasure this morning in reading a chapter in the Bible thinking of each of the family, and supposing each to read in turn, thus: Father, Billy, Lowell, Daniel, Mr. Lawrence, Elizabeth, Julia, Grandmother, Mother—and then Henry to say "Lord how delightful."[10]

Since I have been on board I have read several Quaker tracts which are excellent—several of the New Jerusalem Books also in which there is much that is good since there is so much scripture—I have also looked over some books of travels and also the biography of Bonaparte and of Newton.

Thursday 11th May

Sixteenth day out. We commence this day with a storm of rain—wind S.W.—It is fair for us—but blows too hard—we are under close reefed sails. Were we nearer to the land it would be dangerous. Nine or ten knots an hour, and much pitching and rolling about. 10 o'clock. The wind and the weather have changed and both favorably. The Captain expects to make the land tomorrow, if our present breeze continues.

Friday May 12th. 1837

Seventeenth day out. The day is pleasant—wind fair, and we are sailing at about 8 knots per hour. The present appearance is that we may see the land and enter the channel this afternoon.

¼ before 2. Land seen from the mast head. 6 o'clock. We are now sailing up St. George's channel, being about 280 miles from Liverpool. We have just spoken to the Packet Ship St. Andrew bound to N. York—so that I hope my dear family may hear of my safe arrival thus far much sooner than they will expect to.

Saturday May 13th 1837

Eighteenth day out. Sailing up St. George's channel. A pleasant morning, but not much wind. Last evening we passed by the place where the Packet Ship Albion was lost about 20 years ago. After having made her passage across the Atlantic, and when congratulating themselves upon their safe arrival, a strong S.W. wind drove them upon the Irish coast, and all but one of the passengers, and most of the crew perished. We pass along now in view of Ireland. The land is very uneven—we frequently pass high hills or mountains. We are about 10 or 12 miles from the shore.

Last night I had a pleasant conversation with Mrs. Anderson. She seems to be a pious woman—quite decided—she is also a Lady. Her husband was formerly a planter in Jamaica—she has been lately residing in Brunswick N.J. Her eldest son having received a college education is now attending to the study of medicine—but alas! for the Mother—her trials with him are great. He has formed a habit for wine etc. which will probably be his ruin. The mother feels it and laments over it; she spoke to me about it. It commenced when in college by taking occasionally a glass of wine. It grew up into a confirmed habit—to wine he has now added brandy etc.—he drinks so much as to disguise himself every day, and once or twice since we have been on board has been quite beside himself. The next Son appears to be a very fine, sober and intelligent young man. The mother seems to think that had she kept the eldest at home he would have done well, and says that she does not intend to send the next away.

Mr. Sturge, Dr. [Pliny] Earl (who is also a Quaker) and myself had some pleasant conversation—religious—but principally relating to slavery, etc. both warm abolitionists—but candid and rational.

I also conversed yesterday with Capt. Stockton. He is not a religious man—although in theory he highly approves of it. His wife is a devotedly pious woman by his account of her, and constantly devotes herself to her children. They have four children—oldest are boys 11 and 9. They have never been to school, but are taught at home. He says he will never send his children to school where they are sure to learn more evil than good. From the account he gave me of his boys I should suppose they have been well managed thus far. Physical and moral education are the grand points with him.

Mr. Schaffer (a german) appears to be a man of general information and a gentleman. Always ready on any subject. Speaks the language well.

Mr. [John Gadsby] Chapman of N.Y. (a painter) far enough from anything serious or good in a religious sense. Is a man of education and has once before visited Europe—(France and Italy.)

Mr. King, an englishman, forward, always talking—though often ignorant—although genteel in his appearance and address he is light, trifling and an unpleasant companion.

Mr. Vignaud is a Frenchman very modest, sensible and pleasant.

Mr. Fincke says but little but appears quite a pleasant man.

3 o'clock. We have just past Tuska Rock on which there is a light house. ~~~~~~~

We are now about 160 m. from Liverpool.

Conversed today with Mr. Anderson on dangerous tendency of his present course, and advised him by all means to leave off all drink that intoxicates, as his only hope. He received it kindly. May the Lord bless it to his good. ~~~~~~~

Sunday May 14th 1837

Nineteenth day out. We have had very light winds and make but slow progress. This morning the wind continues light, and hardly can be said to be fair. We are now passing near the coast of Wales on the right— Ireland being on the left. We are perhaps 100 miles from Liverpool—so that another Sabbath must be spent on board. It is now between 9 and 10 o'clock. In Boston the people are not up yet.

Evening. 8 o'clock. We have been beating all day against a head wind and have made but little progress. We are now nearly up to Holy Head. I have been greatly interested to day in reading the Memoirs of Mrs. Judson.[11] It was more interesting from the fact of my acquaintance with her parents and sisters. It has occupied me much of the day, and I desire to be grateful that I have thus been led to read a book so full of interest and instruction.

2

England: May 1837

When Mason landed in England, his natural destination was London. Remaining in Liverpool and Manchester only long enough to make brief contacts, Mason arrived in London on May 18. He remained there for five weeks, far longer than in any other city. After returning from the continent Mason spent another ten days there. Mason's concentration upon London may seem odd, for Germany, Italy, and France all contributed more to nineteenth-century European musical culture than England, and in the 1830s even Londoners were aware of the extent that their musical life was dominated by foreign elements.[1]

Yet London offered a variety of musical experiences unmatched by any other city. Its population of over one million was at least twice that of any other European city in the early nineteenth century and far exceeded that of New York, Boston, or Philadelphia. And London was a prosperous city, containing many well-off, upwardly mobile families. As a consequence London attracted the best artists in Europe. They knew that they could command larger audiences and fatter fees there than anywhere else. Mason's five weeks in London permitted a sampling of the best that Europe had to offer, and these pages of his journal vividly reflect the dazzling concentration and variety of musical life that characterized the capital city.

MASON'S DIARY

Monday May 15, 1837

Twentieth day out. This morning we find ourselves at about 50 or 60 m. from Liverpool—but as the wind has changed we now hope to get in this day. I have written letters to on board for Mrs. Mason and for Elizabeth C. Belcher—to send by the Packet of the 16th which sails from Liverpool tomorrow—also to Daniel [Mason] at N. Haven.

At ½ past 11 a Pilot came on board. We see on the Welsh coast mountains covered with snow.

At a little past 11 (having left the Ship in a Steam Boat) I landed in Liverpool, and went to the "King's Arms Hotel." Here I had an excellent room—good bed—and every thing in fine order—all was clean and neat.

[Tuesday May 16, 1837]

After a good night's sleep, I rose at 7. Going out into the street the first thing that attracted my attention was a school of boys (orphan boys I suppose) 300 in number and all just about the age of 9 to 12—nearly all of a size and all dressed alike in plain blue. After a short walk I went back, and took breakfast in Company with several of the Virginian Passengers. Excellent bread and sweet new butter, also muffins uncommonly good. The Tea is put onto the table in a caddy, with a pot of hot water, and it is mixed, or made at the table by the persons who drink it. After breakfast I went down to the ship and to the Custom House to get trunk, etc. Every thing was carefully examined and I had to pay duties on every book with a fee for entry etc.—amounting to about 2.50—a little more than ½ of which was for Dr. Wainwright.[2] This took untill nearly one—we then returned to Hotel and at 2 took an early dinner—after which I called on Mr. Molineaux but did not find him in—and on Mr. Smith composer and Teacher of music whom I saw—called at [Humphrey] Hime & Son Publishers but found that Liverpool is not the place to learn anything on this subject. Called on Dr. [Thomas] Raffles but found that he had gone to the continent. So I concluded to leave Liverpool at once.

The chamber maids look singularly—all quite neat—with short gown coming down below the waist—generally quite light color, and an apron covered as a petticoat. They are very attentive and modest in appearance. The men servants are quite genteel in appearance, and look neat—entirely different from that class in American Hotels generally. The whole arrangement of an English Hotel is vastly superior to an American—everything is far better. The Pavements are of square stones—and uppermost—so that the streets look as if they were paved with bricks i.e.—the size is just about the same as a brick. In Liverpool the buildings are good—large and commodious—stores of stories high we see. I wrote another letter to my wife, and sent newspapers containing a list of passengers in Virginian to several persons—by packet Orpheus—which vessel was detained one day. At 5 o'clock took the Rail way for Manchester.[3]

#The Tunnel under a part of the town through which the cars pass is 1⅓ miles in length. The country is beautiful—every field cultivated—but no fine seats on this route.

Arrived in Manchester at a little past 6, and put up at the "Star" Hotel. Mr. King who came with me said that they took me for some important foreigner, and therefore gave me a good room, etc. He ascertained this from some of the attendants.

Manchester is just about what I expected from the accounts I have had of it. My first business was to see if Neukomm was here. I ascertained that he was not—so I am disappointed. I then looked for Mr. Hutchinson—took a carriage and rode to Mr. Thornton's house to inquire. There being some misunderstanding between the coachman and the boy at the door of the home—a Lady came to the door, and as soon as she saw me in the carriage, said "Mr. Mason I believe"—"Please to walk in, Sir."—I found thus she used to be in Boston, and had seen me at church. She informed me that Mr. Hutchinson had been gone to America about a fortnight—here I was disappointed again—delivered a letter of introduction to Mr. Homer—from Mr. [Melvin] Lord and also from Mr. Ch. Homer of Boston.[4] He was not in—Returned to "The Star" overhauled and repacked my trunks, and wrote this. It is now ½ past 9—but it is hardly dark yet. So much for Tuesday 16th May. 1837.

 Wednesday 17th. May
This morning I called on Mr. P. F. <u>Willert</u> the friend of <u>Neukomm</u> and ascertained from him that The Chevalier is now in Paris.[5] Mr. Willert was very polite, said that he should be happy to have me remain but as there was no music now in Manchester, and as it is exactly the season for London he would advise me to go directly to London. He said that The Chev. Neukomm will be very glad to meet me, and that if I will address a line to him from London he will come from Paris to see me, etc. He also gave me a letter of introduction to Mr. Beale (Cramer, Addison & Beale, London). I returned to the Hotel and took my passage immediately for London to start at ½ past 12. Just before I started Mr. P. T. Homer (to whom I was introduced by a letter from Mr. Lord and another from Ch. Homer) called to see me—urged me to remain and dine at his home with some musical gentlemen—but as I had taken my passage I could not accept. Mr. King (one of the Virginian passengers) was very attentive to me, being himself well acquainted in Manchester—with him I went round the town here—and especially to the Collegiate Church.[6] It was here that the grand musical Festival of 1836 took place—and here [Maria-Felicia] <u>Malibran</u> sang for the last time.[7] She died in this town soon after. While I was in the Church Service was performed in Chapel, previous to which about a dozen couples were married all at once—all sorts of looking people. There were two or three ministers to officiate and they went through the ceremony like a race horse. I remained untill after the weddings and untill Divine Service commenced. There were some 10 or 12 priests—and the Choir consisting of 6 or 8 Men and Boys, all dressed in white. The audience consisted of 6 or 8 old women and one or two men—but they seemed to go on just as if the Church had been full. I left Manchester at ½ past 12 in the coach called "Peveral of the Peake." It carries 4 inside and 8 outside. I took an inside seat (Cost £ = 5. which together with fees to Driver and guard and meals came to about $30.) and found for company two young Ladies, very pretty, modest, well educated together with the Brother of one of them. They were all free to converse and we had a pleasant ride. The country

through which we passed was very beautiful—highly cultivated, etc. The Hawthorn Hedges look beautifully. The Coach drives at the rate of 9 miles an hour, over a road as smooth and level the whole way (180) miles as possible—we rode all night and arrived in London a few minutes past 10 on Thursday morning. The coaches are far superior to the American, and the Hotels are altogether better. We had at 4 o'clock a most luxurious dinner which only cost 2/—less than a very poor one would have cost in America.

Thursday 18th May

11 o'clock. Write this at London Coffee House Lindgate Hill. ~~~~~~~
Called at 12 oclock on Mr. R. [Robert] Gray organ Builder who immediately left his business and walked to see various things and places with me.

We walked untill 4—then dined together at London Coffee House.

Evening at ½ past 7. Went to the Italian Opera. "Malek-Adel" by [Michael] Costa. Heard

Sig. [Giovanni-Battista] Rubini—Tenor No. 1
  " [Nicolai] Ivanoff   "
  " [Luigi] Lablache Base No. 1
  " [Antonio] Tamburini Baritone
Siga. [Giulia] Grisi Soprano No. 1
  " [Emma] Albertassi Mezzo Soprano
  " Castelli
Sig. [Filippo] Galli
  " Salabert[8]

The orchestra consisted of about 60—of the best performers in London. Costa himself was conductor, and [Nicholas] Mori Leader. Draginnetti [Domenico Dragonetti], [Robert] Linley and others of like standing in orchestra. ~~~~~~~

Friday 19th May

Finding it necessary to remove towards the west part of town, I went down to call on Mr. [John?] Slade[9] thinking he might assist me. I found there, not Mr. Slade but Mr. [Daniel?] Colby from Boston who instantly recognized me, and kindly offered to go with me. I concluded to "take lodgings"— by which is meant hiring such room or rooms as may be wanted and then providing meals some other way.

After going to many places I selected two rooms—Parlour and Bed Room at Mr. R. Webb's No. 24 Haymarket. From Mr. Colby I heard bad news from Boston. Proctor and Palmer's failure and others.[10] Closed a letter for Mrs. M. to go by Packet tomorrow. Dined with Mr. Gray at No. 9 Fitzroy Square new Road in company with Mr. Alfred Novello and two other gentlemen. Evening heard Beethoven's beautiful Opera of Fidelio. It is admirable indeed. I was vastly more pleased with this than with Costa's opera.

Saturday May 20. 1837

Found my new room very comfortable—a good clean bed, and things in good order. This morning after breakfast I went down in town about 1½ miles slowly and looking at the shop windows, etc.

What a wonderful place this is—what New York is to a country village London is to N York. Presented my letters to Messrs. Barings [Baring Brothers & Co.], and found all right there. Afterwards called on Messrs. Lee Coats & Co. and presented letter and saw Mr. Coats (letter from Mr. [George William] Gordon). Dined in a club house—a piece of boiled beef, and greens—bread and beer—a hearty dinner for /8. ～～～～～～

I then got into an omnibus, and rode up to Haymarket—from whence I went to Mr. J. A. Novello's. I got there at about 2—and after remaining untill 4 he invited me to go and take a plain family dinner which I did. Here I met <u>Vincent Novello</u>, the father of J. A. N., and also his sister an accomplished singer Miss <u>Clara Novello</u>.

Mr. V. N. is out of health, and is much depressed in spirits in consequence of the death of a Son [Edward Petre Novello], about 2 years ago. He said but little—after the Ladies had retired and the conversation became a little more scientific, he cheered up a little, and spoke of Haydn's Masses etc. Mr. V. Novello presented me with a ticket to the Philharmonic Society (of which he is a member) for 12 o'clock on Monday May 27th. These tickets cannot be bought—and there are only about 150 issued so that I was highly favored in obtaining one. He also gave me a ticket to a concert of the Royal Society of Musicians New Rooms Hanover Square on Monday 5th June. When Handel's Messiah is to be performed. This also was a very great favor, as tickets cannot be bought. Mrs. Novello invited me to go to a concert this evening, but as I was fatigued, and had no outside garment I was forced to decline—accepting one however for Monday next. Mr. J. A. Novello invited me to go to church with him tomorrow, saying that they should sing Haydn's Mass No. 16.

Sunday 21 May 1837 ～～～～～～

This morning Mr. Novello called for me, and we went to his church. On our way we passed several public buildings—Horse-guards—Admiralty office—and Whitehall. We called a few moments at Westminster Abbey and walked about in some of the apartments of this beautiful and magnificent building. Looked a little at the poets corner and saw the monuments to Milton and many others. Also Handel's monument. They were chanting the service in the Chapel. Crossed Westminster Bridge and went to

Mr. Novello's chapel.[11] Here we had the Roman Catholic Service. There were four priests and four boys to assist. It commenced by some Gregorian chanting, and afterwards was performed the entire Mass of Haydn No. 16. But I cannot say much in favor of the performance. The organ was well played. After Service the Choir stopped to rehearse some music for next Sunday evening when there is to be some extra occasion—they were joined by a sister of Mr. Novello Mrs. [Cecilia Novello] Searle who sang beautifully. At the same time one of the ministers was baptizing 6 or 8 children below. Remember the ill-natured and peevish manner in which the minister performed this observance—catching hold of the child—putting it on the other arm, etc. Service was out at ½ past 1. At 2 I stopped at an eating house and took dinner of cold roast beef, and then went to Westminster Abbey and heard the whole service. Organ by Mr. [John Bernard] Sale. They sang an anthem by Dr. [William] Croft. But it was poorly done—the choir was inefficient. The harsh tone of the Boy's Soprano was disagreeable. It was so cold that I did not stay to the sermon, but came home and after having rested and warmed, I got into an omnibus and rode down to Bury St., St. Mary Axe—Visited the chapel and attended service where Dr. [Isaac] Watts used to preach.[12] The preacher's name was <u>Yorkley</u>—a good sermon upon the <u>source</u>, <u>superiority</u> and <u>security</u> of the joys of the Christian. The singing was wretched—the Clerk standing up under the pulpit and giving out the psalm—2 or 4 lines at a time. They sang miserable tunes from Rippon's collection.[13]

I observed they had a female for sexton. The following is from a tablet behind the pulpit—

Proverbs: 10-7 (Hebrew)
The following humble inscription was composed by
Dr. Watts a short time before his death
and according to his desire is written upon his tomb stone
in Bunhill-field
Isaac Watts DD
Pastor of a church in Bury Street, London
successor of the Rev. Jos. Caryl,
Dr. John Owen, Mr. Clarkson and Dr. Isaac Chauncey,
after fifty years of feeble labor in the gospel
interrupted by four years of tiresome sickness
was at last dismissed to rest
November 25 A.D. 1748. Age 75
2 Cor. 5.8 Absent from the body and present with the Lord
Col. 3.4 When Christ who is our life shall appear I shall also
appear with him in glory.
In Uno Jesu Omnis.

This tablet was erected when the chapel was enlarged in September, 1820, by the church and congregation under the pastoral care of the Rev. Henry Heap, as a tribute of their high veneration and sincere regard for the inestimable character of this eminent man of God and our incomparable sweet singer of Israel, whose praise is in all the churches.

      The righteous shall be had in everlasting remembrance.

                        Ps. 112.6.

The chapel is a mean place.

Monday, 22 May 1837

Spent a part of this forenoon at Green's Soho Square, and made some selections of music—afterwards went to Mr. Novello's, and made selections from his music. I was occupied there from 1 to 5. At 5 I dined in company with Mr. V. Novello and Lady—Miss Clara Novello. Mr. A. J. N. [Novello] and two other ladies. After dinner Miss Clara sang two or three songs accompanied by her Father. At 8 o'clock I went with Mrs. Novello and Miss Clara Novello to Mr. [Charles Kensington] Salaman's concert where Miss Clara N. [Novello] was to sing. Mrs. N. took me into the room where the singers assembled—here I saw several of the [illegible][14] singers and amongst others Madam [Giuditta] Pasta. While I was in there, she was walking about exercising her voice—running over very difficult passages, and carrying the voice very high—B or C.

      The concert commenced and I hastened to take my seat. It was altogether a different thing from any concert I ever before heard. The orchestra consisted of about 50 performers. Conductor Sir George Smart. Mad. Pasta sang twice—Madam [Wilhelmine] Schroeder-Devrient twice— and Miss Clara Novello once. Mr. [Michael William] Balfe sang and also Sig. Ivanoff of the Italian opera. I was greatly pleased with the Harp of [Theodore] Labarre—a Sinfonie by Beethoven in A. The overtures to Der Freyschütz and to Zauberflote [*sic*]. The singing was all excellent. Devrient had the most feeling and Miss Novello the sweetest voice. Mad. Pasta did not do as well as either of the others and had it been any one else perhaps I should have thought her nothing wonderful. Devrient is in her prime— about 30 years of age. Miss Novello will continue to improve for many years—but even now stands quite at the head of English singers.

Tuesday, 23rd May

This morning wrote to Mr. [H. Theodore] Hach at Lubeck—via Hamburg.[15] Afterwards I went with Mr. Webb to the daily parade of the footguard where I heard an excellent Military Band in the yard of St. James' Palace— afterward passed out by the Buckingham Palace, and walked through St. James' Park—a large lot of ground containing many acres with gravel walks—trees and flowers in abundance. There is quite a large pond running through it in which are a great variety of ducks, geese and swans. These birds are very tame. I saw a man feeding a large swan from his hand. The little birds also that fly about among the trees and shrubs are very tame, and will hardly get out of your way as you walk along—and this right in the midst of London. Afterwards went to the Museum of the United Military and Naval Service—containing curiosities in the war line from every part of the world. Guns, swords, etc., of every descriptions—many rooms full—also models of ships of war, boats, etc. etc. all free. Then went to Mr. [John] Green's Soho Square and completed a purchase of music— also to D'Almaine's [D'Almaine & Co] 20 Soho Square and purchased. Evening, went in company with Mr. Novello to a concert at the London Tavern where was performed "The Mount of Olives," "The Bell," and several other pieces. The band consisted of about 50 or 60, and the chorus about the same number. Miss [Charlotte] <u>Birch</u> was the principal solo singer and an excellent singer she is. Mr. [name omitted] sang Tenor and Mr. Novello Base. The chorus was not so good as ours in Boston—but the solos, and the band were far better. Got home a little past 12. Twelve o'clock here is about as late as 10 with us in Boston.

Wednesday, 24th May, 1837
Spent the greater part of this day in looking over Cramer, Addison and Beale's Music—went also to Boosey and Co. This is the birthday of the <u>Princess Victoria</u>—the heir apparent.[16] It is a holiday. Streets are full. It is wonderful to pass along the streets, and see them crowded with thousands and thousands of persons. I could not have conceived of the one half of what I see had it all been told me. ~~~~~~~ Evening—The city is illuminated—crowds of carriages, and foot passengers throng the streets. I went out and mingled with the multitude. I soon got lost and knew not where to turn, but at length found my way back. The Princess Victoria is 18 today.

Thursday, 25th May
This morning went down town to [Thomas Edward] Purday's opposite St. Paul's and looked over and purchased music—afterwards went up to Mr. Novello's—sorted music and prepared a package to send to Mr. Webb. On returning to my lodgings, I found cards from Mr. Alfred Slade and Mr. Jarris Slade.[17] Mr. Novello presented me with tickets to four concerts. ~~~~~~~ Evening heard Cinderella—principal performers Albertazzi— Ivanoff—and Lablache. I was not much interested in it. ~~~~~~~

Friday, 26 May, 1837
This morning met Mr. William Gardiner of Leicester at Mr. Novello's. I

was sorry to hear profane expressions from the compiler of Sacred Melodies and Judah. I had about an hour's conversation on musical subjects, but we should never agree on many things relating to Church Music. At two o'clock went to Madam Dunkin's [Louise Dulken's] concert—here I heard nearly the same performers as is usual at these concerts. Madam Schroeder-Devrient who is rather my favorite, sang the earl king by Schubert, and another song by the same author with admirable effect—both encored. She is truly a singer of great pathos and feeling. The Concert continued from 2 till ½ past 5. Dined and went to the grand performance of the "Sacred Harmonic Society" at Exerter [Exeter] Hall.

Handel's Messiah was performed by about 400 persons. The solos were sung by Miss Clara Novello, Miss Birch, Mrs. A. [Mary, Mrs. Alfred] Shaw a fair mezzo, Mr. [John William] Hobbs, Tenor, and others. I did not like the ad libitum passages—cadenzas—so common. [Thomas] Harper's trumpet was fine in the Base song. He tripped a little in Hallelujah chorus. The choruses were well done—though not better than our choruses in Boston often go. They were generally slower than I have been accustomed to hear. The Solo Singers almost all changed the vowel sounds more or less—shall was almost always pronounced shawl, etc.

The effect of this performance was far enough from anything devotional. ~~~~~~~

Saturday, 27th May, 1837
At 12 o'clock this day went to the rehearsal of Philharmonic Society.

Here was decidedly the best music that I have ever heard. A band of 60 to 70 instruments. 6 Bases and other instruments in proportion.

A sinfonia The Heroica—Beethoven
A sinfonia by Haydn
An Overture by B. [Bernard] Romberg
An Overture by [William Sterndale] Bennett a young Englishman
were played and some songs, etc. sung—by Madam Pasta and Mrs. Shaw.

Afterwards I called on Mr. [Henry Joshua?] Banister, but did not find him in.

Evening saw a new opera by Balf [Balfe]—Catherine Grey.[18] I am quite sick of opera music, however, or rather, of the other circumstances attending the opera, and I think I shall confine myself mostly to concerts hereafter. ~~~~~~~

Sunday Evening. 28th May, 1837
This morning I went to St. Paul's Cathedral. Mr. Novello had kindly given me a note of introduction to Mr. Atwood [Thomas Attwood] the organist, and who is also one of the first English composers and musicians. The Service had commenced when I arrived. I enquired for Mr. Atwood, and was

immediately directed up into the organ loft. {He looked around as I came in, and} as soon as he stopped playing I stepped up to him and told him that I had an introduction from Mr. Novello which I would hand to him as soon as the Service was through. {The Service went on, and I had an opportunity of assisting him to a book that he wanted once or twice, [which] possibly perhaps prepared him to give me a kind reception.} After the Service he read the note, and expressed himself very glad to meet me, etc. His deputy Mr. Cooper [George Cooper, Sr.] came in, and he introduced me. He is organist both to St. Paul's and Chapel Royal, and usually goes from one direct to the other, as St. Paul's is at 10 and Chapel Royal at 12—though his deputy often supplies. He was now going direct to Chapel Royal, and invited me to go—but added we have so little room that I cannot ask you to stay—but will show you the Chapel etc. So went with him—{we got into an omnibus, and talked about his music, etc. on the way} and when we got there he said if I would like to hear one of his anthems he would have it done. This was a matter of great importance to me and I was delighted to remain. He took me up into the organ loft. It is very small—indeed the whole chapel is very small—being intended only for the Royal family and a few others. The Kings pew is in the gallery and in full view of the organ loft—but he was not there being quite sick— but one of the family was there viz. Princess Augusta who is I suppose about 50 years of age. The choir who were in a gallery directly opposite to the organ loft consisted of 9 boys (usually 10) and 8 men. Among the men Mr. Vaughn was pointed out to me and Mr. [William] Hawes. The boys are dressed with red coats much trimmed with yellow lace—Black breeches and Stockings and a military hat. But in Service time they are all covered with the white Surplice, as are all the Choristers.

Before the Service commenced Mr. [William] Ayrton (a Composer, etc.) came in to whom Mr. Atwood introduced me and afterwards Sir George Smart to whom I was introduced. Both gentlemen were very polite and attentive. Mr. Ayrton upon being informed that I would probably be in town a fortnight longer took my card and said he would get permission for me to attend the next and last concert of the Philharmonic of which he is a director, and Sir George said he was so fortunate as to have left a ticket for their concert tomorrow evening which he presented me. This was a very great favor—for tickets to the Philharmonic cannot be purchased for love or money. The Service commenced. Mr. Ayrton played a Service by Boyce, and at the close played his own anthem "My Soul truly waiteth upon God."

Before leaving Mr. A. invited me to go to St. Paul's in the afternoon telling me that there was to be a grand procession etc. I went immediately on towards St. Pauls—called on my way and got some dinner, and was just in time. The crowd was great—when I got up to the Iron door that leads to [the] organ loft, it was locked, and the keeper said no one could go up. Upon my saying that Mr. A. had invited me, he said he would take up my card. He did so and came down, and requested me to follow him. I went in under the organ in a dark passage, and soon came out in the organ loft. Mr. Cooper was there and also Sir George but Mr. A. had not arrived.

At the door of the Church I was much amazed at the Carriages and splendid liveries of coachmen and footmen. Some were literally covered with gold or silver lace, with red, green or yellow coats, breeches and white stockings. The Carriage of the Lord mayor was truly a curiosity—drawn by 8 beautiful bay horses, richly trimmed—with coachmen—footmen and attendants walking by the side with long poles in their hands. By and bye the procession came into the Chapel—first came judges—all the judges of the land about 20 dressed with white wigs, and covered with long scarlet robes. Then came the Lord Mayor—Aldermen etc. These had generally blue robes, and each had in his hand a large bunch of flowers. When they had all got seated—the organ was stopped (Mr. Cooper had played voluntary) and the Service commenced. When it was about half through Mr. Atwood came up. Sir George was next to me and said a good deal about music etc. in America. I did not stay to the Sermon but went out and crossed Blackfriars Bridge to go to St. George's Chapel, where Mr. Novello directs the music, and where I had promised to meet him. After walking about 1½ miles I found it. Here I heard the Gregorian, and some fine Motetts etc. by Miss Clara Novello her Sister Mrs. Searl and others. Got home at 9 o'clock—not quite dark—very much fatigued. The day has in one sense been sacrificed that is in a religious, spiritual sense—but still I feel as if I had been in the path of duty—I make the sacrifice to accomplish the great object of my tour—musical information etc. The Sermon at Chapel Royal I heard, not very evangelical, but many good things.

There are many customs here strange to one accustomed like myself to the plain and simple manner of doing things in America—the pomp splendor and parade—even servants and those who perform the office of sexton—door keepers etc. are dressed in such a style that a simple American might take them for the Lords and great ones!

~~~~~~~

This day I met near St. Paul's Cathedral Dr. Parkman and wife from Boston.

~~~~~~~

Monday 29th May, 1837
Spent most of this forenoon in writing—wrote letters to
   Mr. [George J.] Webb
   The Choir—M. E. Crockett

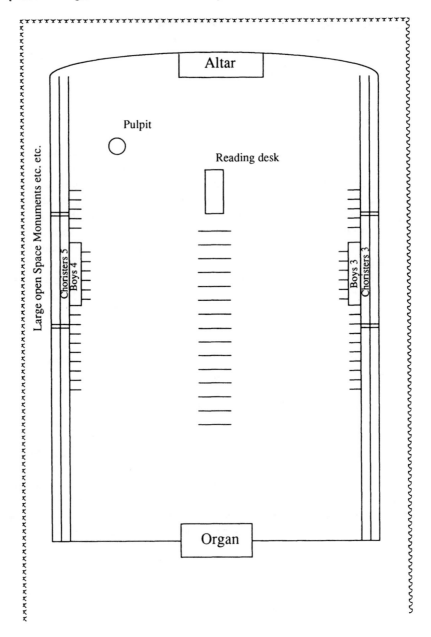

H. C. [Hannah Call] Woodman
Daniel New Haven
Lowell Medfield
Dr. [Edward] Hodges Bristol

Received a case from Mr. H. J. [Henry Joshua] Banister (son of C. W. Banister) and also from Mr. A. Slade with whom I walked out an hour—at ½ past 9 went down to Lee Coates & Co. to carry letters for America. Mr. Coates impressed me that the news from America as late as 5th May is of the most gloomy kind. ~~~~~~~

This evening attended the best concert that ever I heard viz: The Philharmonic Society. It commenced at 8 and continued till nearly 12. The Sinfonia Eroica of Beethoven was perhaps the most splendid piece.

Tuesday 30th May 1837

This morning at 10 o'clock went to St. Paul's to hear the Charity Children.[19] Here were about 6000 of them together and about 4000 spectators. I heard them sing from the organ loft awhile and then went up into the whispering gallery—but I could not look down from this eminence with comfort. I went as high as the golden gallery and coming down I counted 376 steps. The Singing of so many children with the powerful organ was quite sublime. This was what so much affected Haydn. They sang the same chant to day, that he heard. Afterwards I went to Mr. [Ignaz] Moscheles concert at Concert Room of Kings Theatre—It commenced at ½ past 1 and at 5 I left in company with Mr. Banister with whom I dined, and from whose house I have just returned at 11 o'clock.

Note. Temporary seats were erected in St. Paul both for the Children and for the Audience. Each school was seated by itself—and each had its own appropriate dress—boys usually in Breeches—and with bands like clergymen. The girls with white caps etc. ~~~~~~~

Wednesday May 31. 1837

This morning called by appointment on Mr. Ayrton—conversed on music in America etc. Ascertained that he was the editor to the Harmonicon and also Sacred Minstrelsy. He is quite a literary and musical man. I spent an hour and a half with him, and gave him a copy of my 'Manual' [*Manual of the Boston Academy of Music,* Mason 1834]—and accepted an invitation to breakfast on Saturday Morning at ½ past 9 to continue our conversation. Just as I was coming away Mr. Nivore from Birmingham the principal manager of the festival in September next came in, and I was introduced to him. Afterwards visited two music stores, and made some purchases—called on Mr. Novello, and was presented by him with a ticket to St. Paul's tomorrow—went home and to my great joy found a letter from my wife. I had not expected it quite so soon—it afforded me great happiness indeed. In the evening I went to the Concert of Ancient [Antient] Music at the King's Concert Rooms—Hannover [Hanover] Square.

This is a concert which is attended mostly by the Nobility—the present one was under the direction of the Archbishop of York. The music was very splendid—though not so good as the Philharmonic on some accounts. Here is a Chorus, and several Choruses with which I am acquainted were done.

The Creation to the end of the Chorus "The praise of God." The Recitative at commencement was much slower than I have heard it. "The Horse and his rider" by Handel was slower than I have heard it, and in very exact time—[John] Braham sang the recitatives. The Treble Solo by Mrs. [Anna] Bishop—in time and without any instruments. After the Concert 'The Duke of Wellington'—'Archbishop of York'—Bishop of Hereford and other Lords and great ones were pointed out to me. I had a fine view of Lord Wellington and heard him converse for some time.

This was a very superior concert—but too long—commencing at 8 and closing at 12 or a little past. At this concert I saw Lord Burgersh who has composed some music.

Thursday 1 June 1837

At 11 o'clock after doing some errands, I went to St. Paul's where the Charity Children were assembled—this is the great day—the other one (Sunday last) was the rehearsal. The audience was larger to day—but not very much—perhaps 1000 persons more.

Afterwards went to Baring & Co. and to Lee Coates & Co.—found that the London Packet had been detained a day and that I could yet send letters—so I went home to Haymarket 1½ or 2 miles—finished some letters which I had begun and returned to Lee Coates & Co.—sent two letters to Mrs. Mason One to Clarissa A Woodman (Choir) one to George Cushing Colonial Bank. Made some little purchases of Music on my way home, and in evening heard Beethoven's Fidelio. This evening there was a famous Full dress Ball at the King's Theatre which was fitted up for the occasion. As I came home (about 12 o'clock), I stopped and saw multitudes of people going—Carriages coming and leaving Ladies and gentlemen in splendid dress.

3

England: June 1837

After Mason had been in England slightly more than a month, unsettling financial news from America reached him. Caught in a credit squeeze, a number of financial institutions had failed, touching off the panic of 1837. The financial worlds of England and America were closely interlinked in 1837, and the monetary crisis that occurred in the United States was precipitated by decisions made by the Bank of England. Fearing an outflow of gold and a preponderance of loans secured with American properties, the Bank of England raised interest rates and severely curtailed the use of American collateral for loans. As a consequence Anglo-American trade practically came to a halt. Failures in financial houses that depended upon that trade were common, and the crisis reached a peak in April 1837 when the American branches of three large London houses—Wilson & Co., Wild & Co., and Wiggins & Co.—were forced to turn to their competitors for assistance. In this crisis they were tagged the "three W's."

Mason had real cause for personal concern, since he depended upon one company that was directly involved, Baring Brothers, for the transfer of funds to finance his trip. Mason could not have known, however, that he was relatively safe with Baring Brothers. Their directors had anticipated the impending crisis for several months and had done all they could to improve their capital position. When the panic hit, they were not only in a position to survive it, but, realizing that it must be contained, they were able to offer such assistance to the "three W's" as to help avert a broader and more disastrous financial collapse.

MASON'S DIARY

Friday June 2. 1837

This morning {after Breakfast, the Taylor brought here some clothes, which I tried and which took some time.}[1] At 1. went with Mr. and Mrs. Banister to Mr. [Philip Cipriani Hambly] Potter's Concert, Hanover Square. Out at 5—dined and called at Hart's—Hutton Garden and [Zenas Trivett] Purday's 45 High Holburn—music publishers—called also at Mr. Novello's—he is to publish a small collection of Juvenile Songs by me [*The Juvenile*

Songster].[2] Mr. Purday seemed to be well acquainted with me by reputation, and we had quite a chat about America—he is acquainted with Mr. Webb.

Saturday June 3
Breakfasted with Mr. Ayrton—the Editor of Harmonicon—Sacred Minstrelsy, Musical Library etc.

Explained to him the Pestalozzian system of teaching with which he seemed to be much pleased, and expressed a wish to have it introduced here. Am to see him again shortly—He has a large Musical Library which he is to show me. A man of general information, etc. ~~~~~~~

At 2 o'clock attended 'Concert of the Royal Academy of Music' at Hanover Square rooms. Dined and at 7 took tea with Mr. Banister and went with him and Mrs. B. to Mr. [Charles] Neate's Soirée at Hanover Square. Home a little before 12.

Heard this day of the failure of the great American Houses Wilson & Co., Wild & Co. and Wiggins & Co. of London, and which must produce great distress in America. {Probably I will suffer among the rest.}[3]
~~~~~~~

Sunday 4 June 1837
This morning went to the Foundling Hospital—having a letter from Mr. Jones of N.Y. to Mr. [Edward] Sturges the organist.

Mr. Sturges was quite polite to me and after the Service walked with me through the apartments. I saw the girls in one room and the boys in another at dinner—about 100 of each—saw also some celebrated paintings belonging to the Hospital. The building is an admirable one—surrounded by Gardens, gravel walks, etc. The Choir consisted of 2 Sopranos, 1 Alto 2 Tenors and one Base. The organ was powerful and played very loud.

The organ was presented by Handel—but has since been enlarged.

Afternoon I went by agreement with Mr. Atwood to St. Paul's—Service much as before. Evening went to St. Sepulcher's Church near Newgate and heard a very good Sermon "Let the words of my mouth and the meditations of my heart etc." applied to public worship. Mr. Cooper is the organist to whom I had been introduced—there is no Choir but the Singing and the responses as mostly by the Charity Children there being about 100 girls on one side of the organ and 100 boys on the other. Mr. Cooper has a Son 17 years of age [George Cooper, Jr.] who after the Service played a Fuge by J. S. Bach with pedal obligato very well. When I came home I heard that Mr. Colby had called to say that he was going to Liverpool tomorrow to sail for America immediately.

Monday 5th June 1837

This morning went down to the office of Lee Coates & Co. to see Mr. Colby and send a letter by him.

{Enquired of Mr. Coates as to the Security of Baring & Co.—he said that he considered them as safe as the Bank, and that I am as secure as I can be while I depend upon them for funds.}⁴ Mr. Colby consented to take a small package of music for Mr. Webb. Afterwards at 12 went to Hanover rooms and heard the Messiah—performed for the Royal Society of Musicians—a very excellent performance—3½ hours. Dined from 4 to 5—and went to Mr. Novello's where I found that my package for Mr. Colby had not been sent—or rather it had been sent and brought back for Mr. C. could not be found, so I took it and went to Lee Coates & Co., and they sent it for me. The Messiah to day was very much better than at Exeter Hall. Solo's were better, and Choruses more exact and in better time. I observed, however, that the vowel sounds were often changed by solo singers. I also observed in the Hallelujah Chorus, in the passage where the Soprano leads off King of Kings and Lord of Lords—first D then E. F♯ and G—that there was the same want of firmness, precision, and unity as I have often witnessed in choirs. It is a very difficult passage—there was however, no flattening from the pitch in this passage. The Messiah is to be performed again on Wednesday next—but as tickets cost a Guinea each I think I shall not attend. ~~~~~~~

Wrote to William and Henry—to Daniel—to Mr. Webb and to Miss Forbes (Choir letter) to go by the Packet of 8th June. ~~~~~~~ Also to Mr. Lord. ~~~~~~~

Tuesday 6 June 1837

This morning wrote letters—afterwards went to Barings & Co. and drew £50 on account Edwards & Stoddard for Bos. Ac. Mus. [Boston Academy of Music]. Called at Mr. Novello's and did up some bundles of music etc. Afterwards went to Purdays 45 Hoburn and to Harts 109 Hutton Garden where I made some purchases. To day is quite a warm summer day— walking through Regent Street it was filled with Carriages and people of all kinds. As I walked along I imagined Mrs. Mason to be with me, and her surprise at the various shops, carriages, liveries etc. we passed. ~~~~~~~ How much pleasure it would give me if I could take the members of my family round with me and show them this great city. ~~~~~~~

Evening went with Mr. Novello to hear some band and instrumental music.

Wednesday 7th June 1837 ~~~~~~
Spent the whole day untill 4. at Lindsdale's [Lonsdale's] Bond Street and
Chapell's Bond St. looking over and selecting Music—at 4 dined, and at
5 called on Mr. Banister and went with him to a Concert of "Classical in-
strumental Music at Horn Tavern, Doctor's Commons."[5] ~~~~~~
Home ¼ past 11. ~~~~~~

Thursday 8th June
Spent most of this day in visiting the wine vaults—London Docks—and
the Tunnel under the Thames.[6] The distance to the Tunnel from my
lodgings is about 4 miles. I went to the end of the Tunnel and recorded
my name in a book kept for the purpose. Evening—with Mr. Novello at
Italian Opera. Don Juan by Mozart—the most beautiful music. ~~~~~~

Friday 9th June 1837
At about 11 this morning Mr. Gear called on me—at ¼ before 1 I went
to Mr. Benedict's concert thinking I would be in season for a good seat
as it did not commence till ½ past 1. When I got there every corner was
full and it was only by pressing through a crowd that I just got inside of
the door. Ladies elegantly dressed and gentlemen were all crowded close
together—I could hardly raise my arms from my side. So great was the
crowd—here I stood—the air so bad that I could hardly breathe from 1
till ½ past 5. The concert was very fine—and much talent was brought
together—The singers were Grisi, Pasta, Schroeder-Devrient, Albertazzi,
Clara Novello, Rubini, Ivanoff, Tamburini, Lablache, Balf,—and besides
there was a new singer from Berlin, her first appearance in London Signor
Eckerlin a very fine Singer, but not equal to several of the others. [Sig-
ismund] Thalberg, Moscheles and [Julius] Benedict Pianists—Labarre Harp,
[Giovanni] Puzzi Horn, [Auguste-Joseph] Franchomme Violoncello. Among
the most interesting pieces was a Triple Concerto on Three Piano Fortes
by the above named performers, accompanied by full orchestra—
Composed by J. S. Bach—and a Duet by Grisi and Pasta. A Boy 10 years
of age (M. [August] Moeser) played with wonderful execution a solo on
the Violin. From 6 to 7 I dined, and at 8 went to the Concert of "Societa
Armonica"—where was a full orchestra, and Grisi, Rubini and others.
Beethovens Symphony in C minor was played—and Mori played a solo
on Violin. ~~~~~~ Home past 11.

Saturday 10th June
At ½ past 11 Mr. Banister called for me to go to the rehearsal of Philharmonic. It is very difficult to get in to hear this Society but I received tickets
by a special vote of the directors both for the rehearsal and for the Concert on Monday next.

The Pastoral Symphony of Beethoven—A Symphony by Spohr—an Overture by Weber and one by Cherubini were played. Just before the music began Miss Clara Novello introduced me to The Chevalier P. Neukomm who had just arrived in London {and he was so kind as to come and sit by me}[7] during a great part of the performance.

By appointment I am to meet him on Tuesday morning next. Went home with Mr. Novello and dined—after tea Miss Clara went and seated herself at the Piano, and at my request sang over many of her Solfeggios—in beautiful style—and afterwards several songs. Mrs. Searle (Miss Novello's Sister) also sang very beautifully. I was very near to Miss Novello so that I could hear the manner of bringing out the voice etc. I also attended to consonants and vowels. ~~~~~~

The Band at the Philharmonic is splendid indeed—six double Bases and other instruments in proportion—I should suppose about 30 violins—besides tenors. ~~~~~~

Sunday June 11th 1837
This is my eighth Sunday away from Boston—and my fourth in London—(one was spent in N.Y. and Three on the Sea). ~~~~~~

This morning Mr. Banister called for me to go to Surrey St. Chapel to hear a favorite preacher (Mr. [James] Sherman) to whom I have a letter of introduction but have not yet delivered it. It is a long walk say ½ mile—when we got there we found quite a crowd, but our appearance (I suppose) procured for us a very good seat, though many were standing.

When the preacher took his place in the pulpit Mr. B. whispered to me that it was not Mr. S.—and soon after he began to speak I recognized Mr. [Edwin] Kirk of Albany. He preached a faithful and excellent sermon from the text "I am the vine, ye are the branches." I felt that it was good to be within the sound of the gospel again. The singing was by the whole congregation, but miserable enough. The men mostly singing the soprano—The organ only tolerably well played. After the service I spoke to Mr. K.—who had before seen me in the Congregation. We exchanged cards and agreed to meet on Wednesday. I walked home with Mr. Banister to dinner 2 or 2½ miles and at ½ past 6 went with him to his church (Baptist) where I heard a very good sermon from the text "For the Soul to be without knowledge (no-ledge) is not good"—Headings.

1. All knowledge is useful
   1. Mechanical knowledge
   2. Musical knowledge
   3. Intellectual knowledge
2. Spiritual knowledge is preeminently important—on account of its
   1. Excellence

appearance in London. Signora Eckerlin a very fine singer but not equal to several of the others. Thalberg, Mochelles & Benedict Pianists — Labarre Harp, Puzzi Horn, Franchomme Violoncello — Among the most interesting pieces was a Triple Concerto on three Piano Fortes by the above named performers, accomp.ᵈ by full Orchestra — (composed by S. S. Bach — and a Duet by Grisi & Pasta — a Boy, 10 years of age (M Moeser) played with wonderful execution a solo on the Violin. From 6 to 7 dined, & at 8 went to the Concert of "Societa Armonica" — there was a full orchestra & Grisi, Rubini & others. Beethovens Symphony in C minor was played — & Mori played a solo on Violin. came Home at ½ past 11.

Saturday 10th June.

At ½ past 11 Mr. Banister called for me to go to the rehearsal of Philharmonic. It is very difficult to get in to hear this Soc.ᵗ. but I rec.ᵈ tickets by a special vote of the directors both for the rehearsal & for the Concert on Monday next —

Book 1, pp. 64 and 65 of Lowell Mason's Diary
The emendation at the top of p.65, "we were together," is not by Mason.
All of the others are.
(Photo courtesy the John Herrick Music Library, Yale University)

The Pastoral Symphony of Beethoven — a Symphony by Spohr — an Overture by Weber & one by Cherubini were Played. But before the music began Miss Clara Novello introduced me to the Chevalier Neukomm who has just arrived in London, ~~he was so kind as~~ we were ~~to sit by me during~~ a great part of the performance.

By appointment I am to meet him on Tuesday morning next.

Went home with Mr Novello & dined — After tea Miss Clara ~~seated~~ seated herself at the Piano, & at my request sang over many of her Solfeggios in beautiful style & afterward several Songs — Mrs Leal (Miss Novello's Sister) also sang very beautifully. I was very near to Miss Novello so that I could trace the manner of bringing out the voice &c. I also attended to consonants, & vowels. ~~Max~~

The Band at the Philharmonic is splendid indeed — Six double Basses ~~& all~~ & other instruments in proportion — I should suppose ~~nearly~~ about 30 violins — besides tenors.

2. Accompaniments
3. Permanency
4. Prospects

The singing here made it abundantly evident to me that a little musical knowledge would not be amiss—awful indeed.

Returned and remained with Mr. B. till ½ past 10—then walked home—about a mile.
~~~~~~~

Monday 12th June 1837
At 11 called at Mr. Novello's, by appointment and heard Miss Clara sing about an hour—her Father accompanying her—here I met Sir John Tryllian—who had made a morning call on Miss Clara. At 1 went to Mr. Labarre's concert but it was so full I could not find a place to stand—so I left, and walked to Regents Park, and visited the Zoological Gardens (a walk of 7 or 8 miles). Here my wonder and admiration were as much excited as at any thing I have seen. A vast field with hills and valleys and lakes and ponds—partly natural but mostly artificial—with every kind of tree, shrub, plant and flower that can grow in the climate, and all kinds of birds and animals* that are to be found in the world. (*Elephants—Giraffe's or Camelopards. ~~~~~~~ [LM's footnote]) But it would be in vain for me to describe it so I omit any attempt—this will be enough to bring the circumstances to my mind. I returned—very much fatigued—dined at 6 and at ½ past 7 went to the last Philharmonic concert that I ever expect to hear—a splendid one it was indeed. Beethovens Pastoral Symphony was the great piece. Thalberg's playing on the Piano far surpassed anything that I have before heard—and a concerto on the Double Base by Sig. [Luigi] Anglois was an astonishing performance. From ½ past 1 untill ½ past 5 to day I was walking, and must have walked in all as much as [   ] miles.

Tuesday 13th June 1837 ~~~~~~~
Spent this forenoon with Neukomm in his room 15 Duke Street Portland Place. Afterwards went to Mr. Novello's, and to <u>Lonsdale's</u> Music Store where I purchased music to the amount of 5 £. ~~~~~~~ Dined and went to Mr. Banister's to tea, after which I heard the two Banisters and Mr. Westrop play Trio's—Piano Forte, Violin and Violoncello—mostly by Beethoven. Received a letter by Mr. Hach—Hamburg ~~~~~~~

Wednesday 14th June 1837
This morning went to Lee Coates & Co. and ascertained that Mr. A. Slade had left for Boston. After calling at Baring & Co. I went over to Southwick

Bridge to Mr. Blackman Music Publishers and spent several hours in selecting music—returned and after dinner walked for several hours through the streets seeing what ever was to be seen.

Sent letters this day to Miss Penniman, Daniel, Miss Field for Choir and T. [Timothy] B. Mason Cincinnati.

Thursday 15th June

At ½ past 10 started in the Stage Coach for Southampton, on my way to the Isle of Wight to see Mr. Webb. I rode outside. A fine day—warm sun shine—but a cool breeze and I found my wrapper quite comfortable. We past through a delightful Country—and in the most pleasant season. The air was filled with the fragrance of the flowers.

I saw many flowers which were new to me. A yellow flower on a tree similar to a locust—but without smell, and a tree covered with a rich crimson blossom. The hawthorn hedges were some of them in full white blossom. From 3 to 6 miles out of London the road was filled with carriages, and it was wonderful to me to see how the coachman would steer his four horses through the crowd.

We had four greys—each handsomely trimmed with flowers. The rich field in the country looked beautifully. In many cases I saw women working in the fields. Every thing is neat around the dwellings—very different in this respect to New England. After about 3 hours ride we came to a barren country and passed over much poor land.

The names of Inns is amusing—

The Red Lion
White Hare
Crooked Billet
Rose and Crown
King George
King William
The Angel
The Bugle

Fighting Cocks and a multitude of others. Arrived at Southampton (about 80 miles) at 7 o'clock, and as there was no Boat going over was obliged to stay over night.

Friday 16th June

Left Southamptom at 9 in a Steam Boat and arrived at West Cowes, Isle of Wight, at a little before 11.

Mr. Webb's residence is close to the landing place, and I went directly to his house and delivered my letter from his son G.[George] J. Webb.

I met with a very cordial reception from the family, who all seemed to devote themselves at once to me. They would hardly hear to my leaving them so soon as I proposed, but when I assured them that I must return the next morning—they immediately began to think how they might spend the day so as most to amuse me.

In a few moments we had a carriage at the door and Mr. Webb, two daughters and Miss Withers who was there on a visit together with myself got in and went to <u>Shanklin</u>—about 20 miles. After a walk of about one hour through the wild scenes of the place we returned and dined at Williams Hotel—and soon after started for home. We had a delightful ride, through a most pleasant and highly cultivated country.

Miss Fanny Webb and
Harriet Webb went with us
Mary Ann remained at home
After tea, I went up into the young ladies room and they played for me
Mary Ann—the Harp
Harriet—the Piano
They played several duets—"Overture to the Barber of Seville" amongst others.

They both play very well. The Harp was rather better played than the Piano. A young Lady from Hamburg (a german) is on a visit to Mr. Webb. She sang and played Guitar.

Mr. W. and all of them asked many questions about George—all of which I was able to answer.

At about 12 oclock I took my leave of them and went to bed.

Saturday 17 June
Rose at ½ past 5 refreshed—took an early and excellent breakfast which I found all ready for me and started in a 4 wheel Chaise from Cowes and went as far as Newport—7 miles—here took the Stage Coach to Ryde—then Steam Boat to Portsmouth, and at Portsmouth the Coach (Rocket) for London—where I arrived at 6½ oclock—well tired.

Evening at 8 attended Mr. Neate's concert at Hanover Square. At this Concert I was introduced to Mr. Potter, Pianist, etc.

Something to tell Mr. Webb. Captain Miller had just left Cowes—he is in a Cutter.
Sally is there still. ~~~~~~~

Mr. W. has also the same Coachman that he had when George J. W. was born.

In writing home to children—remember the Prisoners, chains—carts—soldiers at Portsmouth. ~~~~~~~

Rev. Richard Krill of St. Petersburg was lecturing on missions etc. at Isle of Wight. address

J. Webb Esq.
Fountain Hotel
West Cowes
Isle of Wight

Sunday 18th June. 1837
Morning attended St. Bride's Fleet Street—Mr. [George] Mather the organist.
I went expecting to hear a popular preacher but did not. Text "Sin is the
transgression of the law." The Congregation pretty generally sang, and
responded. Commenced singing 117 Psalm (Watts) to an adaptation of
"The Heavens are Telling."

Dined, and went to deliver a letter to Mr. Sharp No. 7 Church Yd.
Row—Irvington—beyond Elephant and Castle. I found him at home—
was introduced to Mrs. S and four sons all of whom were very polite and
agreeable. Next to Church with them and heard Rev. George Clayton—
Walworth Surrey—to whom I had a letter from Dr. [John] Codman.

Text. Proverbs 29.18 "Where there is no vision the people perish."
By vision is meant revelation etc.
1. God has given a revelation of his mind and will to his creatures.
2. Where this is not enjoyed the most disastrous consequences ensue.
3. The happiness of those who prosper, believe and obey the lively
    oracle of God. A very good sermon.
Sung 119 Psalm 8 pt. to Missionary (Tune)[8]
Sung 19 Psalm 2nd pt. to a poor tune.
Sung St. Michaels for the last tune.
The singing was Congregational but poor enough. The Clerk gives out the
1st and 2nd hymns and the minister gave out the last, and read it two lines
at a time.

In prayer the minister prayed for a family that had removed from one
dwelling to another. Mr. Sharp told me that this is customary.

The people at close of Service do not hurry out but remain quietly
for a few moments, and then retire slowly and in order! After tea at Mr.
Sharps his two oldest sons went with me to St. George's Camberwell to
hear the celebrated Mr. [Thomas] Adams play the organ. We went into
the organ loft, and after telling him who I was he received me very kindly. He is a wonderful player—I never before had heard any thing to compare with it—wonderful powers of execution. After supper at Mr. Sharps,
and singing 5 or 6 tunes (the family singing and myself playing) I came
home in an Omnibus—having made a circle to day in attending Church
of 9 or 10 miles.

Mr. Sharp's family are very pleasant, intelligent and pious. She thinks very highly of Mrs. Codman with whom she was intimate when Mrs. C. was in London.

Monday 19th June 1837
Morning wrote to Mr. [Horace] Mann—
      Lowell, William and Henry
      Choir—Julia A. Belcher
      G. J. Webb etc.
      J. [Julius] A. Palmer—by Mr. Slade
Spent most of the forenoon or untill 3 oclock in getting ready a little package to send to Mrs. M. by Mr. Slade who leaves London this day for Boston. Sent Mrs. M. a bible I bought a few days since—sent the boys a book—some gloves and a map—also some nut cakes. ~~~~~~~ Afterwards dined and went to Mr. Novello's—thence to Mr. Banisters from whence we went to a Concert at the Horn Tavern Doctors Commons—where I heard some fine instrumental music. ~~~~~~~

Tuesday 20th June 1837
This morning I breakfasted with Mr. W. Ayrton James St. 4 Buckingham Gate at ½ past 9—I remained untill ½ past 11. Mr. A. gave me much information on the subject of Royal Academy of Music and a note of introduction to "The Rev. Frederick Hamilton Royal Ac. Mus. Tenderden St. Hanover Square," who is the principal agent of the institution for further particulars.

The King [William IV] died last night, or this morning and as I came home by St. James I found a large collection of people expecting the formal proclamation of the New Queen Victoria—I waited some time and happened to meet Sir George Smart—he informed me that it would not take place today but tomorrow at 12. Sir George invited me to Chapel Royal next Sunday to hear the Funeral Anthem for the King. ~~~~~~~

Afterwards went down the City to get my passport for the Continent—I spent several hours in book stores. Dined with Mr. Webb—(Richard Webb in whose house I have a room.)
~~~~~~~
Evening—went by invitation from Mr. Neukomm and called on Mr. Mochelles [Moscheles]—it was ½ past 9 when I arrived, and the family were taking tea. At about 10 or ¼ past Mr. M. took his Seat at the Piano, and played a very difficult Concerto of his own. Mr. Neukomm took me by the arm and placed me down by the side of Mochelles where I could do no less than turn over, and I had enough to do to keep my place, and turn over for him. It was a splendid performance.

Afterwards Miss [Elizabeth] Masson sang a song from Romeo and Juliet by [Nicola Antonio] Zingarelli accompanied by Mochelles. She then sang several Scotch songs and afterwards she sang to Neukomm's accompaniment two of his songs "Consolation" and "Farewell." She is an excellent Singer—one of the best English singers I have heard—sang with great feeling. She is a Professor. A gentleman from Germany but whose name I have forgotten then played for about ½ an hour at the Piano with great execution—but I suppose with less than Mochelles. Neukomm prefers Mochelles to any of them. This has been one of my richest musical treats. Mrs. Mochelles offered me a letter to her Father in Hamburg. ~~~~~~~

Mr. Mochelles teaches from 8 oclock in the morning to 7 in the evening. He takes no time for rest and takes no lunch except what he takes in his carriage in going from one pupil to another—at 7 he dines—a Guinea per lesson. ~~~~~~~

Wednesday 21st June 1837

This morning at ½ past 10 went to Charing Cross to see the procession and proclamation of the new Queen—afterwards went to St. Sepulcher's where Neukomm was to play the Organ. He played upwards of an hour without stopping and in a most beautiful and finished style. Dined and on my return home found a letter from Mrs. Mason and Elizabeth and also another from Mr. Palmer which gave me great pleasure. Date May 26.

Thursday 22nd June

This morning sent off a large packet of letters and papers for America—afterwards spent all the morning in looking over and fixing my papers etc.

Called on Mr. [Charles] Lucas to whom I was introduced by Mr. Webb of Isle of Wight—who gave me some information on the subject of Royal Academy of Music, and letter to "The Right Honorable Lord Burghurst [Burghersh] etc."—Evening went to Italian Opera and heard Pasta. ~~~~~~~

Friday 23rd June 1837

This morning went to Mr. Novello's—paid my bill there, and ordered my music to be packed. All the music that I have bought elsewhere has been sent there. Called on Lord Burghurst to whom I had a note of introduction from Mr. Lucas, to make enquiries about Royal Academy. His Lordship received me very kindly—gave me such important information as he could and referred me to the institution, giving me liberty to see it etc.

Went to Royal Academy and was Mr. Hamilton the Superintendent—found him very busy and agreed to call again on Tuesday next.

Called on Mr. T. Philips Lecturer etc. in Music, and who was formerly in Boston. He received me very warmly—here I heard two young ladies sing Psalmody, Mr. Phillips singing base and another young Lady playing. It was very beautiful—and interested me much.

Went down in town to Lee Coates & Co. and also to Baring Brothers & Co. to make my arrangements previous to departing—obtained a passport. ~~~~~~~

Evening at Mr. Gear's concert Hanover Rooms—heard Madame Giannoni a very excellent Soprano—and Miss F. Windham with whom I was much pleased. Then Schroeder Devrient sang beautifully. ~~~~~~~

Saturday, 24th June 1837

This morning at ½ past 10 called, by appointment on Chevalier Neukomm—spent an hour or more with him, and received from him a circular letter of Introduction to various parts of Germany.

Afterwards at Mr. Novello's—At ½ past 1 went to Kensington 6 Bedford Place and called on Mr. [William] Crotch to whom I was introduced by a note from Mr. Ayrton. Spent nearly an hour with him—he played to me an overture by Handel on the Organ. Dined at 4—and at ½ past 5 went to Mr. Banister's and heard some music.

Duets by Romberg for Violin and Violoncello J. Banister and H. J. Banister.

Duets for Violoncello and Piano Forte or rather Violoncello Solo with Piano Accompaniment.

—Violin Solo by [Charles] de Beriot with Piano Accompaniment. Also a Violin Solo by J. Banister with Piano Accompaniment.

The Banisters also played a Chorus by Handel on the Piano Forte as a duet—

Home at 12 oclock, and examined proofs till 1. Proofs of a Juvenile work, prepared by myself for Mr. Novello—"The Juvenile Songster." ~~~~~~~

Coming home from Mr. Banister's the streets were filled with people (11 to 12) Men, women and children—buying or selling —talking and laughing, running, riding, etc. etc.

Sunday 25th June 1837

Tenth Sunday away from Boston

Sixth Sunday in London. ~~~~~~~

This morning at 11 went to Craven Chapel not far from the corner of Regent and Oxford Street. Dr. [John] Leifchild is pastor—I should suppose it a popular Chapel—quite full. Singing by Congregation, and I think better than I have before heard. There is solemnity and devotion about it that is delightful. Text "He setteth up Kings and pulleth down Princes" (Daniel.) I did not stay the sermon out but went at 12 to Chapel Royal—Sir George Smart had invited me here to hear the funeral Anthem—on the occasion of the death of the King. Earl Wilton [Sir Thomas Egerton, 2nd Earl of Wilton] was in the organ loft and played a Sanctus and Response composed by him, also a voluntary. Sir George played the Anthem. Better of the kind than any thing I have heard. Text Job. 30.23.

I dined and went to the Temple Church—one of the oldest Churches in London. I did not hear the text—and could not feel much interest in Sermon. I then went to St. Paul's and heard a part of Mr. Atwood's concluding voluntary.

Took tea with Mr. Cooper deputy-organist of St. Paul's—and then went to St. Dunstan's and heard Mr. Adams play. I did not wait for the Sermon but went to Christ's Church—near St. Pauls—and heard a very fine organ built by Hill [Hill & Son]. The organist to whom I was introduced (Mr. [Henry John] Gauntlet, or something like it) played very well. The Sermon was ½ through when I got there.

Returning passed a poor woman with two children by her side. She held her face down with a paper before it on which it was stated that she had been deserted by her husband, and that she had been driven into the street etc. I gave her all the penny's I had. ~~~~~~~

Monday 26th June 1837

This morning before breakfast I received three calls—Two Mr. Greatorex [Henry John and Thomas Westrop], brothers and Chev: Neukomm. All the morning was spent in making preparations for my tour. I have now no wife to look after my things and am obliged to do a thousand little things that I should find already done were I at home. Went to Barings—Lee Coates & Co.—and Novello's—wrote letters home—received a call from Mr. Sharp (son). At 8 o'clock I went by appointment to see some drums made after a new fashion by C. Ward (see his advertisement.)[9]

At 9 o'clock went to a music party at Mr. Mocheles in Company with Mr. Neukomm—soon after we arrived music commenced—the following pieces were played—

1st. Quartetto by Beethoven
The first violin being played by Mr. Moëser [Karl Moeser]—a very excellent Violinist from Germany and also has often played with Beethoven himself. Mr. Mocheles told me that he considered it the very best style of Quartett playing.

2. Concerto on the Piano Forte by Mr. Mocheles, with accompaniment for Quartetto—composed by J. S. Bach.

3. Solo on the Violin (Concerto) by <u>Master Moeser</u> 10 years of age. This was indeed a most wonderful performance. Few good players could do the piece as well. Mr. Mocheles accompanied on Piano Forte.

3. Quartetto by Beethoven

4. Piano Forte Solo—or Trio for Piano Forte, Violin, and Violoncello the Piano by [   ] a new player just arrived in England.

5. Solo—Fantasia—Piano Forte by Mr. Benedict

6. Solo—Piano Forte—by Mr. [Jacob] Rosenhain from Frankfurt a/m Germany.

7. Solo—Fantasia—Piano Forte by Mr. Thalberg. All the piano Forte playing was first rate—all wonderful—but Thalberg's was certainly the most astonishing—but nothing that I can write can convey an idea of it.

It was nearly one o'clock when I started for home having to go from Charter place Regent's Park to Haymarket.

I was this evening introduced to Mr. [William?] Horsley—who gave me his Card and invited me to call when I returned from England. ~~~~~~~

Tuesday 27th June 1837
This day has been spent in getting ready to go to Hamburg.

Visited the National Galery of Fine Arts—or Royal Academy of Fine Arts [Royal Academy of Arts in London]. ~~~~~~~

Finding my trunk too large—I purchased a new one, and leave my Boston Trunk also my Carpet Bag containing my Cloak in care of Mr. R. Webb wine merchant No. 24 Haymarket.

Wednesday 28th June 1837
Last night I went to bed rather late—and a good deal fatigued. The preparations for my departure from London, packing up my things etc. had so much excited me that I could not sleep well—besides I was afraid of sleeping so late as to lose my passage.

I got up at ½ past 3—there was a disturbance in the street, and some women were carried away—at ½ past 4—the door bell rang. Mr. Webb had engaged a watchman to call us in this way—he had determined to go from London to Gravesend with me (60 m.). We started in a Cab at a little past 5—it being 1½ miles to the ship.

We were obliged to go on board in a small boat—as foreign vessels are not allowed to come to the wharf. The moment I got on board I began to perceive indications of a foreign country—The appearance of the passengers—but especially the language, as many were speaking German— Men, women, and Children—Masters and Servants on board. The Ship (steam) is far less convenient than an American Steam Boat—built in a very different manner necessarily as they go to Sea. We commenced our voyage down the Thames at ½ past 6—breakfasted at 8½ and directly after Mr. Webb left with the Pilot. The Parents of two fine looking boys came on board with their sons to send them away—probably to School—when they parted with them—it brought home—and my own family so strongly to mind, that I could not avoid joining them in their tears. It would be very pleasant to me were I now commencing my voyage home. We start with a pleasant day—but Head wind. ~~~~~~~
—Steam Ship "Countess of Lonsdale"—London to Hamburg. ~~~~~~~

Thursday 29th June

I was quite sick after getting out to Sea—so much as to take to my berth—not, however, untill I had written several letters. To day I feel better and have written letters to the following persons Viz:

Mr. G. F. Thayer—for the boys of his school—

Mr. W. B. Fowle—for the girls of his school

Daniel G. M. [Mason] New Haven

Lowell M. [Mason] Jr. Medfield

S. A. [Samuel Atkins] Eliot Esq. Boston

Mrs. Lucy Slade Boston

Ea. W. Pray Boston

Mr. W. [William] Cummings Savannah

[In margin to left: "Eight full sheets."]

10 o'clock—evening—we have just taken a pilot at the mouth the River Elbe—and are about 18 Danish miles from Hamburg—or 72 English miles. At this hour twilight still lingers in the west. ~~~~~~~

Had a pleasant conversation with one of the boys mentioned on last page—they are going to school in Germany—to be absent 3 years—were never away from home before. Their Father whose name is Hodgkin is editor of the London Courier.

4

Germany

When Mason traveled from England to Germany he went from a progressive, unified, prosperous country with a burgeoning middle-class population to a group of independent, autocratic, agricultural and relatively poor principalities. Germany was divided into thirty-nine states in 1837. A few, such as Prussia and Bavaria, were large; most were small. Mason's travels took him first through Prussia and then parts of Saxony, Baden, the Thuringian States, Hessedarmstadt, Frankfort (one of four free cities), and Wurttemberg.

Shortly after the Congress of Vienna in 1815 several attempts at political reform occurred in Prussia. These had failed utterly by 1822 and the Prussian state reverted to its conservative orthodoxism, in which the Junkers, as nobility were called east of the Elbe River, maintained authoritarian control over county governance as well as their estates. Serfdom had been officially abolished, but peasant life had not markedly improved. Germany as a whole suffered under economic hardships during this time, and life for the peasants, as Mason observed with horror, was harsh.

The Germans, however, did not ignore education. Goethe, Schiller, Herder and Jean Paul had called for educational reform. In Prussia Fichte specifically championed Pestalozzi's approach, even though the educational philosophy of Pestalozzi (1746–1827), which was premised upon the capacity of the individual to rise above his lot both morally and socially, was not entirely compatible with the political conservatism of the time. The responsibility of the state to educate the population was taken seriously in Prussia, and under Prussia's leadership education had become almost universal throughout Germany in the early nineteenth century. By the Revolution of 1848 as many as 93 per cent of the children attended school in some of the German states. And in most states it was a Pestalozzi-inspired education.

MASON'S DIARY

Friday morning 30th June
This morning we are sailing up the river—it is very pleasant, ½ past 6 o'clock,—we see villages and farms on the shore close by—and smell the new hay—see men mowing, and men and women engaged in making hay.

See many wind mills —and often pass churches. I have found the passengers
very pleasant—German and English are about equally spoken on board.
~~~~~~~ At 12 o'clock found myself at <u>Hotel Belvidere</u>—Hamburg.

Every thing here indicates that I am in a Foreign land—In London it
always seemed only as though I was in another American City—the
language being the same. But now it is all another language—and everything
is different—houses are very old—

and often project over the street—look as if they would fall over. Streets
narrow and lowest in the middle. At 2 o'clock saw Mr. Hach and was
disappointed to find that he cannot start so soon as he expected, so that
I suppose I must go alone on my German tours. ~~~~~~~

I will attempt to describe my first dinner in Germany—At 4 o'clock
we commenced with soup—this being served and cleared away, next came
boiled beef—with potatoes, cabbage and new turnips in melted butter—
this being through—next came stewed pigeons and green peas—i.e. both
stewed together—after these came some kind of fish I do not know what
with sauce of oil, catsup, and steamed over with parsley.—next came a
fore quarter of roast Lamb—with a piece of paper wrapped round the bones
so as to enable the carver to take hold of it—he took it and cut the shoulder
nearly from the rib so as to lay it open, and then put in first say about
¼ lb. of new fresh butter—then salt—then pepper—then sprinkled over
it herbs, which were before prepared—then squeezed the juice of a lemon
over it, and shut it up. He then cut it up in small pieces and the servants
handed it round together with stewed strawberries—the strawberries
appeared to be stewed in something a little acid and were made very sweet
with sugar—and also cucumbers cut up and dressed in oil and vinegar.
The lamb was eaten with the strawberries—as venison is with jelly. Next
came pudding—I do not know what kind but very nice—after this bread
and cheese and butter and oranges. ~~~~~~~

It took a little more than 1½ hours. ~~~~~~~ While at dinner the
Landlord who was next to me took snuff fragrents—he asked me but I
declined—he asked "do you not take snuff"? No—Smoke? No—"Why surely," said he "you will go to heaven then if you commit no Sin." I asked
do you think it Sin to snuff and smoke—"Yes—tis folly and folly is Sin"—
Here the conversation dropped. ~~~~~~~

After dinner I took a walk about the City—the people in the streets
seem to be mostly the laboring class—much of the work is done by

women—we see them engaged in almost every kind of labor. They walk mostly in the middle of the street. A beautiful little girl dressed like a Swiss came up to me with a red rose to sell—she talked to me as fast, and smiled—I could not help laughing right out—but she kept talking faster than ever, and put the rose up to my nose to let me see that it was good. I saw many more—having branches of roses to sell. The dress is common to count as proper on market women. Passing by a "Pavillion" or Resterateur I heard very good music and went in and took my seat. The waiter came, and as I was obliged to say something I said "Coffee" as I saw others round me taking coffee. He brought me a cup and I took it at my leisure and listened to the music. There was two Violins one Tenor, Two Clarinets and Double Base and they played truly well. As soon as they got through with the piece which appeared to be an overture they came round for a contribution—{So I was obliged to pay for my curiosity which I did willingly enough.} [Emendation probably by HLM] I passed a very good band in the street—playing at the Doors of gentlemen's houses—there were four Clarinets—two Horns—Trombone and Drums.

Heard also very superior hand organs or Barrel organs. Many of the women (they look like Swiss) walk with a kind of flat basket turned bottoms inwards on their heads—it Serves for a Bonnet—but more go without any thing but a cap on the head. Wooden shoes are very common and make a great noise on the pavements. The streets smell bad from the dirty water that runs down the middle of them.

Saturday July 1, 1837
It is quite cold to day—I feel chilled through without an outside coat. Called on Mr. Schröder to whom I was introduced by Captain Gregerson—also on Mr. Gossler, (brother to the one to whom I was introduced by Mr. Eliot).

Mr. G. promised me letters to Berlin, Leipzig, etc. Called on Mr. [Johann Friedrich] Schwenke—Organist—introduced by Neukomm. He was very pleasant—invited me to his church tomorrow—showed me a new piano with 2 sets of Keys and pedal—2 Grand Pianos in one—as I was coming away said he hoped I would write in his album before I left. A small man—looks very delicate, fingers and hands small and very soft—dressed in a morning gown.

Called on the music store of Mr. Cranz and selected some pieces.
Met this day with Mr. Fincke one of the passengers in the Virginian.
~~~~~~~

Sunday 2nd. July 1837
This morning at 9 I went not knowing where I would go. I fell into the train of some women who had books and appeared to be going to Church and followed them to St. Jacob's a very old, and large building. When I

went in they were singing a <u>Chorale</u>—the whole congregation and sung loud—it was very solemn and devotional. The hymns were very long. Of the sermon or prayers I could not judge not being able to understand German.

In coming from the Church I passed through a square where was a military review and a Band of music. At ¼ past 11 went with Mr. Hach and called at Mr. Romberg's[1]—where I was introduced to Mrs. R.—two Miss R's—to one of whom Mr. Hach is engaged—also to a son of Mr. R.—took tea and bread and butter and at ¼ past 12 went with Mr. H. to St Nicolai Church where Mr. F. Schwenke plays the organ. J. F. Schwenke organist Hamburg.

The congregation did not consist of more than about 20 persons, in a church large enough to hold nearly as many thousands. The singing was wholly <u>Chorals</u>. The organ is large and very well played.

At the close of the Service ½ past 1—went out with Mr. H—but returned directly to another Service commencing at 2 o'clock.

Mr. <u>Schwenke's</u> little son was with him and he could speak a few words of english—so I could just make myself understood. Service as before.

There are five sets of keys on this organ—and five more of registers on each side of eight each—so that there are in all 80 registers. There are 16 bellows—and it is hard work for two men to blow. I went into the bellows room—it is much larger than the whole space for the Bowdoin Street organ. The bellows are worked by the feet—each man having to work 8 bellows. The dress of the ministers is strange to me—a black gown—a Cap on the head, and a <u>ruff</u> round the neck extending out say 3 or 4 inches all round alike. ~~~~~~~ This day has been so cold that I could hardly be comfortable in my room without a fire.

There are two English Churches here—to one of which I intended to go after dinner—but mistaking the hour (½ past 6 for 6) I was too late. So I took a little walk out as far as one of the gates of the City—and found just beyond the City a most beautiful place—gardens and walks etc.

Came home and at 8 went to bed—not having been very well to day—or for a day or two past.

Monday 3rd July 1837

Spent the morning at Mr. Crantz music store and made selections, etc.

Dined at 3 with Mr. Hach at Belvidere—Room.—

Called on Mr. Schwenke who showed me the organ at St. Nicolai.—

When I went to take my passage for <u>Berlin</u>—I could not obtain a seat because I had left my passport. So I returned and got it. I found all the seats taken except Nos. 7 and 8, and I was told by my interpreter that these were so situated that I could get no Sleep, and as I was to be out two nights in succession, I was at a loss what to do—but being told that I might take No. 9 which would entitle me to the first seat in an extra as soon as 7 and 8 were taken I did so.

Mr. Hach was engaged and could not go with me to the coach office so I went by myself—at the hour for starting. I found three coaches were going and that I had the best seat in No. 2. As soon as our passengers collected—six in number—I looked around to see if I could find any one who could speak English. I fixed upon one that I imagined by his looks might speak, and addressed him and asked him if he was going in that coach. He answered "yes." I found that he could speak a little so that I was quite relieved. The coaches were rather comfortable—but their Horses were miserable, and tied to the carriage by ropes. There was a Coachman or Postillion and Conductor or guard. Both had on Prussian uniform. The Postillion had Blue coat faced with red—Buck skin pantaloons and military boots and spurs. The coach was marked "Koenigl: Prueuss Schnell-Post"—meaning I believe "The King of Prussia Post coach, or mail coach. We started at 8 o'clock, and had on the whole quite a good journey and arrived at Berlin at 7½ o'clock—Wednesday morning—having rode 36 hours—2 nights and one day. I slept considerably and felt much better on my arrival at Berlin than expected. After the first night I was removed to the first coach, as a part of the passengers stopped—but I had a good seat, and found a man who could speak a few words of English. He was so kind as to wish to converse—so he began a conversation with me by saying (having found out that I was an American) "There is a very great calumny in America now." I was puzzled for a moment but soon thought that he referred to the mercantile distress and had mistaken calumny for calamity—and this proved to be the case.

From Hamburg to Berlin is 38 German miles—or 152 English miles.

Berlin July 5th
Arrived at the Hotel "King of Portugal" at 8 o'clock. Found that there was no one in the house could speak English—but the keeper of the hotel informed me through Captain Otto (the man with whom I started from Hamburg) that he could secure me a person for $1. per day who would remain with me the whole time—interpret—give me information, etc, etc. So I told him to employ one and he has brought me a very good looking young man whose name is John who is now at my Service. ~~~~~~~

Called on Mrs. Simpson 33 Charlotte Strasse and delivered a package sent by Mr. Novello for her daughter. The bundle was untied but I delivered a Music Book Blotting Paper Package of Letters and 2 dozen rasors in boxes. ~~~~~~~ Mr. and Mrs. Simpson were away from home—left letter of introduction from Mrs. N. and Card. Called on Mr. Rungenhagen Professor Music and director of a Choral Society [Singakademie]—was sorry to learn that the Society did not meet untill next week Monday—Mr. R. introduced me to Mr. Lichtenstein Professor Natural History in University a great lover of music who conversed in English, giving me much information relative to music in Berlin. Called on [Gasparo] Spontini (le director General) but was informed he could not be seen untill 5 tomorrow. He is a sick man and his carriage with servants in livery stood at his door.

Called on Mr. [August Wilhelm] Bach—organist, etc.—he was very polite and attentive—showed me some manuscripts of Jno. Sebastian Bach—of Jos. Haydn, of [Johann Gottlieb] Naumann and others. Haydn's and Naumann's were original letters of theirs. Invited me to attend his school Friday morning and to go to his organ with him Friday afternoon. Dined and at 4 o'clock went to the performance of Haydn's Creation in a large church. Although we went nearly ¾ of an hour before the time we could not get good seats, and were obliged to stand a part of the time—the church was crowded and must have contained 4 or 5000 persons.

The Orchestra was just about as large as Philharmonic London. 6 Base etc. The Choir as near as I could judge were say 120—½ ladies, ½ gentlemen.

The orchestra was to me almost perfect—and the solo singing was admirable. The Solo's, Recitative's, etc. were sung in a chaste, simple style with a strict adherence to the text—and only in a few instances were cadenza's introduced—and when introduced they were exceedingly simple and chaste. The choruses were better (I believe) than I ever heard before anywhere. The soprano predominated largely. There was a precision and energy about the choruses that I have seldom heard. C 2¼ hours in performance exactly. ~~~~~~~

I find my interpreter "John" quite pleasant and indispensably necessary to me. Having had no sleep except in the coach for two nights past, I go to bed early to night. I have a pleasant room—the river runs directly under my window, and opposite on the other bank is a large palace.

Thursday 6th July 1837

This morning called on Bernard Romberg now here on a visit to his daughter. He received me with great kindness—and after a little conversation he offered to play to me—which offer was most gratefully accepted on my part.

He played three pieces—which took with preluding etc. nearly an hour. I shall never hear the Violoncello so played again.

He gave me an introduction to a friend in Wursburg—advising me to go there.

Visited the museum—of King of Prussia.[2]

The lower rooms are filled with antique statues, etc. from various places.

The upper rooms with paintings—I passed through about thirty rooms—each containing about 25 pictures. ~~~~~~~

Visited the palace in which the Crown Prince resides. Here I passed through perhaps thirty rooms, all furnished in a superb manner—with pictures and various curious things. ~~~~~~~

Called upon Spontini but he was engaged in hearing a candidate for the opera sing, and could not attend to me for ½ an hour—and as I was engaged at that time I left my card and went to hear Rossini's Barber of Seville—a good thing—poorly done. ~~~~~~~

Purchased a few musical works from Bechtold and Hartje.[3]

Friday 7th July 1837

At 9 o'clock this morning I visited the "Institute for Church Music," Berlin—by invitation from Mr. Bach, one of the professors.

This is an institution supported by government where young men may receive a musical education free of expense—having only to board and clothe themselves. They are taught music practical and theoretical—vocal and instrumental.

Each day of the week is appropriated to some particular music study. There are three professors, each of which attend two days in the week. This was Mr. Bach's day. When I went in they were attending to thorough base—Mr. B. wrote a lesson on the board—base figured, which the pupils all copied in full in their books—and some of them also wrote it out on the board.

Two lessons which Mr. B. wrote upon the board—one in harmony the other in counterpoint he afterward wrote down for me at my request.

At 10 o'clock the pupils played the organ. The whole class were present (about 20)—four or five played, one after another—the others listening. Some of them played difficult Fugues. ~~~~~~~

At 11 o'clock—singing—when Mr. B. was at the Piano Forte. They sang a choral piece and a psalm in very excellent style as I thought—though Mr. B. considers them all as pupils.

They were young men from 18 to 22 years of age—and some of them would do well in America and stand high as they now are. ~~~~~~~

This was a forenoon well spent. Afternoon at 3½ went to Marion Church where Mr. Bach is organist. He played untill 5 in a most masterly manner—confining himself principally to the music of John S. Bach—but playing a few pieces of his own—particularly a Quartetto extempore—fugue—which was excellent. He played three or four fugues of J. S. Bach and closed by one of the most extraordinary difficulty. Mr. Lichtenstein

and his daughter—and several other persons were present. (pronounced
Lish-ten-stine)

Afterwards called on Spontini—found him home. He received me very
politely—expressed regret that he had not met me before—and urged me
to remain longer. He lives in very splendid style. ~~~~~~~

At 6 went to the grand opera where Alceste by Gluck was performed
to a crowded house.

The music of Gluck is very popular and this is the first time for five
years that this opera has been performed. The principal singer—Miss
Faszman—did her part admirably—as well as anything that I have heard.
The orchestra consisting of about 80 was very effective. The largest orchestra that I have heard. ~~~~~~~

The opera was over at 9—or an hour before dark.

August William Bach.

Left Berlin Saturday morning 8th July in the "Schnell-Post" for
Dresden—Capital of Saxony. In the coach I found two Englishmen with
whom I could converse. We passed through a number of old towns some
of them fortified—among the best was Jüterbryk—pronounced Guterbrok.
Potsdam soon after leaving Berlin is a beautiful place. The country is much
of it barren through which we passed—and when we came to a town the
buildings are almost all very old—mostly built of frame work filled with
clay, etc.

Arrived at Dresden (capital of Saxony) having rode all night—suffering
much from the cold air.

Sunday morning, at 8 o'clock.
July 9, 1837

12th Sunday absent from Boston. Went to "Hotel de Saxe." The master
of the house speaks English—but he informed me it would be impossible
for him to procure a "Valet de place" who can speak it. I went to the
church called "Sophine Church" where Mr. [Johann Gottlob] Schneider
plays the organ. The congregation were singing a choral as I went in—the
effect was sublime and highly devotional. But it is power that produces
the whole musical effect, as there is no variety. The organ is always very
loud and all sing loud. Here was a choir of about 8 or 10 boys and as many
men—the boys sang treble the men base and all very loud. I thought there
was less screaming than by the boys in cathedrals in London. The base
was admirable. Of course I could not understand a word the preacher said.
I observed that as he preached the people or some of them would often
exclaim after the manner of Methodists in New York—Ah—a—o—e—or
Amen—and sometimes a short sentence of three or four words.

After I came out I passed a military parade and the band, a superb
one, were playing magnificently—dropped into a very large Church. It is

circular, and I should suppose must contain at least 8 or 10 thousand persons—seated—yet the whole congregation did not amount to 60 persons although service was going on as if it were full.

At the "Sophine Church" at the close of the service the minister went to the altar at one end of the Church and kneeling before a Crucifix chanted—the organ first giving the tune—like this

The choir and organ would respond—occasionally a short sentence or Amen. Hanging around the pulpit were about 20 or 30 portraits—appeared to be those of former ministers.

The large church in which was so few called <u>Frauenkirche</u> (Church of Our Lady) is built in a circular form—much like a theatre—and is partly divided into private apartments or boxes. In all the churches there are rooms separated from the main body of the church and which merely look in by a window—and which appear to be occupied by persons of high rank—who can thus go to church and be quite retired from the public—altogether so if they choose. ~~~~~~~

At 6 walked out—but found no churches open. I saw by advertisement that the Theatre was to be opened this evening and an opera performed—but of course did not feel inclined to go. The bells on churches strike the ½ and quarter hour—as ¼ past one, ½ past one, etc. . . .

It has been very cold all this day—more like 20th of October than 9th of July. Went to bed at an early hour and made up for riding the night before. ~~~~~~~

Monday, 10th July, 1837
It is impossible to procure a "guide" or "Valet de place" who can speak English. The keeper of the hotel sent a servant with me to a Professor who teaches English, and French—to him I explained my situation, object, etc.—he was so kind as to go with me to Mr. V. Schneider to whom I have introduction and interpret. Mr. S. was very obliging. Invited me to attend a Society this evening at 6—and an organ performance tomorrow at twelve o'clock. ~~~~~~~

Spent the remainder of forenoon in walking about the streets mostly about the market. Where they were selling everything. The whole market—a large square is filled with little tents in which the people mostly women sell various articles—everything indeed that can be thought of—and in various places in the streets are little Stands where things are sold.

Cherries and strawberries are very excellent—I never saw so many large before—Cherries are cheap and strawberries not dear. ~~~~~~~ Afternoon at six Mr. Scott (Professor of Languages) went with me to Mr. Schneider's Singing Academy. The choir was small owing to the summer months, etc.—about 60 present—Mr. S. at the piano. They sang a Mass by Jos. Haydn in B♭ and a Mass by Naumann in A♭—both excellent. I was most interested in the latter as it was entirely new to me. Naumann formerly lived in Dresden. The performance interested me much. Mr. S. introduced me to one Lady and one Gentleman who spoke english. Mr. Schneider is brother to the celebrated composer of that name. ~~~~~~~

Tuesday, 11th July, 1837
Spent the morning in looking over the map, etc., and in considering where I shall go. There is so much to do, and so little time that I know not which way to turn. ~~~~~~~ Wrote letters to Mrs. Mason and to Daniel [Gregory Mason]. Went by appointment to a school of boys and heard the singing class.

The class consisted of about 50 or 60—one half of the voices had changed and there was a good proportion of <u>Soprano</u>, <u>Alto</u>, <u>Tenor</u>, and <u>Base</u>.

They sang several hymns—in good style—including quite difficult fugues. They threw out the voice with great power and sang with such energy and force—promptness and decision as I scarcely ever before witnessed. Afterwards went to the Sophine Church where Mr. Schneider played the organ for an hour in a most masterly manner. I hardly know which played with the greatest skill, he or Mr. Bach of Berlin—both were excellent, and by far surpassed any organ playing I ever heard in this style. [Thomas] Adams of London is a style so different that there is no comparison between them. I think on the whole that Mr. Schneider used the pedals with greater execution than Mr. Bach. ~~~~~~~

After dinner, Mr. <u>Rivimus</u> [Edwin Florens Rivinus] United States Consul called on me and said he was very sorry he did not know I was here before, as it would have given him pleasure to have served me. He leaves Dresden this evening for Leipsig. ~~~~~~~

At 4 o'clock I went about a mile and a half out of the city to a place of resort called "Linchen Erben"—or more commonly, I believe, "<u>Linger</u>-shur<u>bard</u>."

Here was to be a concert.

It is a place on the banks of the Elbe consisting of a house with several acres of ground around it—laid out in walks, shade, groves, with trees, flowers, shrubs, etc. There are tables and chairs, benches and seats enough scattered around in different places to accommodate many hundreds—tents, booths, small houses, etc.

I suppose there were there this afternoon, say 4 to 600 persons—and they were seated around tables, in groves, shade, etc., in various parts of the grounds—1, 2, 3, 4, 5, or 6 at a Table, or in a party. There were men, women and children of all sizes and many dogs. Some were eating, some drinking, some smoking, many smoking pipes and cigars, some snuffing, walking, talking, sitting, reclining, standing; sewing, knitting (most of the females were knitting), reading, writing, etc. etc. Old men and little children were playing—young Ladies and little girls were walking about through the shade and playing, running, jumping, swinging, etc.

There was a railroad with horses and carriages on which children were riding.

As I walked about I would come suddenly upon party after party sitting by the fresh blooming roses or in secluded dark and shady bowers drinking Tea, Coffee, chocolate, Beer, water, Lemonaid, etc. etc. Eating cakes, Tarts, or confectionary. There were some regular eating parties where 8 or 10 were seated round a table. Beer seemed to be the favorite drink, there were glasses of beer, bottles of beer and jugs of beer, and many different kinds Some sweetened their beer, some watered their beer—but almost all had more or less to do with beer. There were some little houses about 10 feet high and 10 feet square, furnished with sofas, chairs, tables, etc.—with a little plot of green and flowers before it. These seemed to be occupied by families, or parties of 6 or 8 or 10 persons.

In a dark, green bower would be seen perhaps a solitary individual Lady reading or knitting just as quietly as if she was in her own house,—or a gentleman smoking or sipping his Beer—or two persons—or families as parents and children might be seen in such places. When I went in I met a man with a plate in his hand—he held it out to me and spoke German—of course I knew not what he said, but while I was pondering what it meant, a lady came past and dropped two or three groshiens into the plate—at the same time saying "de music." I imitated her example and all was well—I observed as the people came in they immediately selected a seat, and had some of the good things brought forward—generally beer.

~~~~~~~

I soon saw that everyone was expected to take a seat and order something—as soon as I was seated a servant came up and began to talk dutch as fast as a mill clacker. "Beer, Beer," said I, and away he went and brought me a quantity of the precious beverage and a large piece of cherry pie. I paid him two groshiens, and this entitled me to my seat at the table all afternoon—for if a seat is once taken you need not fear of losing it though you get up and walk all over the grounds—the beer glass being left on the table is your security. It was not yet time for the concert to begin, so I walked about making my observations. When I was seated again a little dwarf boy came to me with a large basket of flowers—I suppose he wanted to sell, but knew not what he said. I handed him all my cherry pie—he stared me in my face as if he could not believe me sincere—when he saw that I was—he received it with great joy—put it on top of his flowers and ran away. But it was 5 o'clock, and time for the music to commence. In a central place was built the orchestra—a kind of shed—open at the sides. The performers were as follows—

Three double bases
Two violoncellos
Four Tenors
Sixteen violins
Two Flutes
Two octave flutes
Two oboe
Two clarinetti
Two fagotti
Two Trumpets
Four corni
Two Tromboni
Kettle Drums
Common Drum
Base Drum
Triangle
Cymbals
Tamborine—but the last two instruments I did not see used. They played the following music:

1. Overture (Tebaldo e Isolina) Monacht
2. Introduction Euryanthe, Weber excellent
3. Overture—Onslow
4. Duetto. Meyerbeer
5. Sinfonia in D♯[E♭]—Beethoven
6. Overture—Cherubini (Ali Baba)
7. Duetto. Norma. Bellini
8. Ballet and Air. Bartrelli
9. Overture. Marschner
10. Finale. Meyerbeer

A better concert of this kind I have not often heard—perhaps never. They played admirably—great attention was paid to p's and f's and I never heard fz.'s so well done before. I was highly delighted—the more so as I would walk about them and hear them at different points—be close to them, look over the music to some of the instruments, etc., and between the pieces could go and sit at my table and sip my beer.

I found one old man at a table near mine when I first took my seat—I believe he did not rise once the whole time, and I left him there when

I came away, say ¼ past 8—but I observed his beer was almost gone and I presume that when this was gone he went away also.

By the side of us were boats with parties of Ladies and sailing up and down the river. I came home—took my tea and just as I had finished writing the clock struck 10 but it is yet twilight. ~~~~~~~

N.B. There were fireworks at <u>Lingershur-bard</u>, but I did not remain there to see them. What I saw and heard there this day takes place frequently I believe almost always daily. ~~~~~~~

{Wednesday 12th July 1837
It is strange to see the women coming to market with their great baskets on their backs filled with <u>peas</u>, <u>cabbages</u>, or some vegetables—enough one would think for a horse load.} [emendation probably by LM]

I observed at Lingershur-bard that the people were almost all of the middling class—there were evidently no rich or great ones there. No wonder that the Germans should have a cultivated musical taste when for 12½ cents they may hear the symphonies of Beethoven and music of the highest order.

Wednesday, 12 July, 1837
Morning—visited the Picture gallery—which is said to be one of the best collections of painting anywhere to be found in Europe and the best north of the Alps.[4] ~~~~~~~

At 3 o'clock went to hear a class or choir of Mr. Schneider's. I was in hopes of seeing them taught but in this was disappointed, as they only sang. There were 6 Soprano boys—4 alto boys 3 Tenors and 3 Bases.

They sang a <u>Coral</u>—interspersed with figurative music composed by Mr. Schneider which was very excellent, and also the Kyrie and Gloria to Beethoven's Mass in C. They sang admirably with such precision, force, energy and accuracy as would put all the English chorus singers to the blush. There is no comparison in this respect.

In answer to questions Mr. S. said these boys are taught 1 hour every day. Some have been taught 6 or 7 years—others 3 months. It does not injure the voice to sing the high soprano. Female voices are much better for Soprano and Alto than boys—more Rich, melodious, etc. Men's voices are not fit for Alto—it makes the part harsh, thin or squeaking. ~~~~~~~

The arrangement of the parts I find is always the same as that I have adopted—soprano on the right in front of Tenor; Alto on left in front [of] Base. In speaking of Mr. S's organ playing I should have said that he took for his subject a common <u>Coral</u> and worked it up in all manner of ways in Fuge with Obligato Pedals, etc. for about ¾ of an hour—without the least hesitation or want of thought or imagination. The first playing of this kind that I have heard was by Neukomm in St. Sepulcher's London—but there was greater strength and execution about Schneider. Bach's fugues are considered the highest style of organ music by everyone here, and also in England. Mr. S said he would play Bach's fugues to me, but on my observing that Mr. Bach of Berlin had done so, he omitted them and took another course.

Mr. Schneider has been uncommonly kind and attentive to me—as I was coming away he gave me a copy of a drawing of an organ.

Mr. Schott my interpreter and who is not a Valet de place but a professor of modern languages, has been of great service to me.

At seven o'clock left Dresden and after riding all night arrived in Leipzig at seven o'clock in the morning—a distance of 12¾ German or 61¼ English miles.

There being no one in the coach to speak English, I was quite solus the whole distance. Just as we got out of the coach I found a gentleman who could speak a few words and who aided me when the police officer came for passport, and also in getting a porter to take my trunk to Hotel de Saxe where I am on

Thursday morning, July 13, 1837

Called on Mr. [Johann Friedrich] Rochlitz—to whom I was introduced by Neukomm. Found him an old man, and also a public man, and although very polite I cannot expect assistance from him. Called on Mr. Fink Editor of Musical Gazette[5]—and found him also quite an old man and one from whom I cannot expect aid. His daughter Miss Charlotte Fink played nearly an hour to me on the piano—better than I ever heard a female perform. She is 18 years of age. She played first a very difficult study by some author I do not recollect—then a Fuge by J. S. Bach in the key of C$\sharp$—with seven sharps—Then the beautiful fugue by Handel in E minor, and finally a very difficult Fantasia No. 69 as by Thalberg. She executed not only with perfect accuracy but also with great expression, force and character. Wonderful that such a young lady can execute in such a manner.

My disappointment was great to day in not receiving letters from home. They were to be sent here from London. It is now more than two and ½ months that I have have been away from home, and have had but two letters. ~~~~~~~ My last letter from Mrs. M was received 21st June and was dated 26 May—she would not probably write again untill about 6th June—and as passages are often long at this season of the year it is not surprising that I have not heard. ~~~~~~~ Having ascertained that it will not probably be of advantage to remain here—and as if in case I remain I must remain until Monday or travel all the Sabbath, I have resolved to go on this evening for Frankfurt.[6] ~~~~~~~

While resting a little after dinner I had pleasing dreams of Mrs. Mason teaching Daniel to read. ~~~~~~~

Left Leipsig at 7 o'clock on Thursday, 13th July, having remained there only twelve hours—had a comfortable seat with the Conductor and one passenger, on the front seat which afforded a fine view of the country. The passenger with me (Mr. Rothchild from Frankfurt) spoke a little english. Had a pleasant ride and slept quite well a great part of the night. In the morning the Conductor left us and a new one took his place who took his seat in the coach, and another German passenger came on to the front seat who also spoke little english. He was on his was to England and I believe he desired to practice speaking.

During the night it had rained, so that there was no dust—nor was it too hot or cold. The second night I also slept quite well. We arrived at Frankfort on the Mein on

Saturday July 15. 1837 (11 o'clock)
Took a room at "White Swan" hotel which was recommended by Mr. Rothchild.

The whole distance from Leipsig to Frankfurt is 44¾ German or 215½ English miles—we were 40 hours on the road. We passed through many villages and several important towns as Weimar, Erfurth, Gotha, Hanau and others. Soon after leaving Leipsig we passed over the ground where the celebrated Battle of Leipsig was fought which continued three days in Oct. 1813.

Weimar is the place where Schiller, Göthe, Herder and other distinguished literary men resided.

At Erfurth is Luther's cell in the Augustine Convent—and at a short distance is the Castle in which he was confined after the diet of Worms. We passed near to the Castle.

Several things observed on the road that were novel or interesting.

Women mowing, and doing all kinds of farming work. Carrying heavy burdens—as peas, potatoes etc. etc. to market on large baskets tied to their backs—they are often without shoes or stockings. Towards the latter part of the journey I observed the women carried their baskets on their heads.

The Shepherds keeping their flocks. They always had dogs and a pole with a small crooked shovel or knife at the end. It is surprising to see what command they have over the sheep. I saw them feeding often in the little passages between fields of grain or of grass, and although there were 40 or 50 sheep in a flock, and no fences they were all kept within their bounds, and were sent into the cultivated fields or fields of clover and grass to which they were always very near. If the dog saw one approaching to the field he would run and drive it away immediately. There are no fences or walls—all the land lies common. Thought of David as a Shepherd, and of the beautiful allusions to pastoral life in the Bible—particularly John 10th Ch. and 23rd Psalm.

—As a sample of the German's English who was riding with me—I mention the following.

As we were riding along—he said to me "I very dusty" "very dusty"—as it had been raining and there was not the least dust—I could not think what he meant—he saw that I did not understand and repeated "very dusty" "I want some water"—"Oh! thirsty" said I—"ah thirsty that's what I mean" he replied.

When we were at supper a dish was handed round that looked to me like roast veal, but I was not sure what it was, so I said "Is this veal"? No, he replied "It is cough" (or corf)—meaning that it was "calf" ~~~~~~~

At ½ past 12—having shaved, washed and dressed—I have written this, and hardly feel any the worse for my three nights successive riding in the "Schnell post." ~~~~~~~

Called on Mr. Andre [Carl André] to whom I had a letter from his brother in London[7]—

He speaks english a little, was very polite, and went with me to call on Mendelssohn—but I was greatly disappointed to find that he is out of Town.

After dinner made several calls but found all out of Town, viz: Ferdinand Ries—Mr. [Ferdinand] Hiller, Mr. Schnyder de Wartensee and Mad: Wendelstadt. Spent the afternoon in selecting music from Mr. André. In the evening he took me about a mile out of Town to a meeting for singing for Men's voices. The Society consists of about 80 but not more than half that number were present. The singing was very excellent—a few pieces were accompanied by three Horns and Trombone. It was in a huge hall—and all around the hall eating and drinking were going on. The Singers many of them had bottles of wine before them. It is expected of every one that goes that they will take something to eat or drink.

I do not like this in musical performances. ~~~~~~~

Home at 11 o'clock—well tired. ~~~~~~~

Sunday 16th July 1837

Frankfort on Mien—13th Sunday absent from Boston.

This morning called into a church (without a Steeple or Bells) which appeared to be something different from Lutheran. There were no images, crucifixes, etc., of which Lutheran Churches are filled—everything was plain and simple which gave me a favorable impression, and led me to suppose that it might be a Calvinistic Church. The Organ occupied the whole end of the house, opposite to the pulpit. The house was of regular construction and similar to our American Churches. The Organ was playing a voluntary until the minister got into the pulpit when it stopped and the whole Congregation commenced a <u>Choral</u>. It was grand indeed—far surpassing anything of the kind I have before heard. All seemed to sing— all seemed to be interested—I wish such singing could be introduced with us in Boston. There was no choir. ~~~~~~~

(To New Book)

[END OF JOURNAL ONE]

[JOURNAL TWO]

Sunday 16th July 1837

Frankfort on the Main. Mr. A[ndré] called and proposed to me to go first and hear a celebrated organist and large organ. Afterwards to visit the picture gallery—then to call on Mad. Wendelstadt and hear her play the piano—at 3 o'clock to go in company with himself to Offenbach to his Father's, and then to conclude the day by going to the Opera where Masaniello was to be performed. I was fortunately a little unwell, and could therefore excuse myself on that account.

The Sabbath seems only to be a holiday. The Chev. Neukomm when I was in London proposed to me to go and see an improvement in Kettle Drums on a Sabbath morning.

At 3 o'clock Mr. Schnyder de Wartensee called to see me. A man of 55 perhaps very gentlemanly in appearance—a man much respected. He remained a hour conversing on Music very pleasantly—offered to introduce me to Switzerland of which Country he is a native. ~~~~~~~

From my window I see females at the windows on the opposite side of the street sewing and knitting.

Between 5 and 6 walked out hoping to find a Church open—but could not. In my wanderings I fell in with a train of people who led me to a Garden, somewhat similar to the one at Dresden where was Military Music—but I did not stop. As I passed along the streets females were seen sewing, knitting etc.

I write this at ½ past 6. It is now about 3 oclock in Boston—perhaps afternoon Service is about commencing and Jonathan [probably Jonathan Call Woodman] may be playing his voluntary, or the choir may be singing an hymn—May the presence of the Lord be with them to help them, and also ever with my dear family at Medfield and D.[aniel] at New Haven.

Monday July 17th 1837

Frankfort on the Main

Spent the forenoon at Mr. André's music store, and made many selections.

After dinner Mr. André called for me in a carriage and himself with Mr. Schnyder de Wartensee, Mr. John Barnett (the english composer of songs) and myself rode to <u>Offenbach</u> (2 english miles) to see Mr. J. [Johann Anton] André the father of Mr. André and a distinguished composer of Music. The old gentleman was very cheerful and entertaining—but not being able to speak english we could not converse. He showed us several old Books etc. and also a large quantity of Mozart's original manuscripts. Mr. André purchased these manuscripts of the widow of Mozart some time since and has 15 boxes full of them. He keeps them very carefully and seems to prize them very much. There were two oratorios among the Music. Mr. A. is now printing a Mass of Mozart's which has never before been printed.

Mr. Barnett is studying with Mr. Schnyder de Wartensee whom he says is the first Theorist in Germany. Mr. Neukomm told me he was one of the most learned. He is certainly much of a gentleman.

Mr. Barnett married Mr. Linley's daughter (violoncello Linley) and his wife is with him here.

Stricker[8] the celebrated piano maker of Vienna married a daughter of Mr. André who is now on a visit at Offenbach.

Home at 8 o'clock. ~~~~~~~ The widow of Mozart still lives at Saltsburg—were the distance not so great I would be disposed to go and see her.

Tuesday July 18. 1837
This morning before breakfast closed letters which were partly written before to Mrs. Mason, Daniel and the Choir.

Called on Messrs. Frères Bethmann Banker and drew from him £30.

Paid bill to Mr. André £14.2.0. Mr. Bethmann extended my letter of Credit to Berne Switzerland inserting the name of <u>Marchand & Co</u>.

Had a package of music done up and left with Mr. A. to be sent by him to N.Y. by way of Bremen—marked
Lowell Mason
Boston
Care of Holbrook & Nelson
N.Y.
Wrote letters to Holbrook and Nelson One to be sent by the vessel from Bremen and one care of Lee Coates & Co. London.

After dinner fearing I might not have money enough—I drew £20 more from Messrs. Bethmann.

Mr. André's agent in Bremen to whom my music is to be sent is
J. H. & G. von Zengerke
Bremen.
At six o'clock went to the opera and heard <u>Medea</u> by Cherubini. The principal objections to the Opera in America do not exist to it as it is here. It ends before dark—there is nothing but the Opera itself—and it does not

seem to be a place where the worst characters are brought together, as the Theatre is with us. Indeed the only objection to it is the impurity, or immoral tendency of the text. This is certainly objectionable—often profane etc. but perhaps not much more objectionable on this account than most oratorio music is—where the most solemn addresses are made to the Deity in a manner not much better than in a mock prayer at the opera. ~~~~~~~

      Dinner today was
1. Soup
2. Beef boiled
   Cucumbers—oil and vinegar
   Boiled potatoes
   Butter and Radishes
3. Cold salted Fish
   Cold sausages
   Boiled String beans seasoned with herbs
   Mashed potatoes also seasoned
4. Boiled Fish with Lemon juice
   Hashed Chickens—mixed with sundry other things
   Puddings with sauce of Cherry Juice
5. Lobsters
   Roast Duck with small potatoes done with them
   Stewed Cherries
   Salad
6. Cherries
   Currant
   Cheese
   Confectionary

===

Wednesday 19th July 1837
Left Frankfort this morning at 6 o'clock. Mr. Schnyder de Wartensee was in the coach, and went about half the way with me, and Mr. André was also in another coach. It rained a little—a little before coming to <u>Mainz</u> we passed through fields of vines for wine. Arrived at <u>Mainz</u> and took a room at the Hotel—die drei Kronen (the three crowns) at ½ past 9 o'clock—distance 21¾ English miles.

    Called on Mr. [Johann Andreas] Schott introduced by Neukomm and found one in the store who could speak english—made selections of music. He informed me that this afternoon I can have an opportunity of hearing a new <u>Te Deum</u> composed by <u>Neukomm</u>, and tomorrow an oratorio by C. [Carl] Loewe—so I shall remain longer than I intended. ~~~~~~~
    Today at dinner there were two things that I have not seen before—1. a

woman came round the table with a plate or basket of beautiful flowers for sale—2. When dinner was half through two musicians a player on the harp and one on the Violin came in and played beautiful music during the remainder of the time. A contribution was made for them.

At 4 o'clock Mr. Schott called on me and took me to hear about 50 boys learning a Te Deum by Neukomm and which is to be sung here on the [   ]th of August (next month.)

On that and the two succeeding days there is to be a grand musical Festival in commemoration of <u>Genofleisch</u> (called Gutemberg [Gutenberg]) the inventor of movable types. Mainz it seems is the place where printing was first carried to any degree of perfection. A monument to the memory of Gutemberg is now erecting in a public Square. At the musical Festival are to be 1200 vocal performers. An oratorio by C. Loewe has also been composed which is to be sung on that occasion.

Neukomm's Te Deum is all in unison and accompanied by Brass or Military Instruments. It is to be sung in the open air—a large scaffolding is now building. Mr. Schott told me there would be 700 boys, and they sing astonishingly loud. He introduced me to Mr. [Franz] Messer conductor of vocal music etc. ~~~~~~~

| No. of Inhabitants | 35000 |
| No. of Soldiers here | 15000 |

50000 in all ~~~~~~~

Learning from Mr. Schott that it is much quicker to send to America by way of Havre than by Bremen, I have written to Mr. C. A. André Teil, D. 208 Frankfürt a/M requesting him to send my bundle of music here to Mr. Schott's care, and as I shall have another small bundle here—they may both be sent together.

Evening at 8. went with Mr. Schott to the first meeting for learning the New Oratorio of "Gutemberg."[9] The men's voices only present—Tenor and Base.

A drilling something after our fashion—though with a much more able Conductor than ever I saw before, and a Choir most of whom could sing at sight well. Almost 60 or 70 present. Staid till 10 o'clock.

In coming from Frankfort to Mainz we frequently passed Crosses on which was hung the image of the Savior—hewn in Stone. I suppose we passed 10 or 12 such crosses by the side of the Road. This is a Catholic country—there being but very few Protestants in <u>Mainz</u> or round about.

Thursday 20th July 1837
This morning at 8 o'clock Mr. Wihlein who has a large School of Charity
Children sent one of them to conduct me to it. I saw him last evening—he
speaks a little english. There were about 80 boys and 60 girls. They are
altogether under the care of Mr. W. who resides with them in the building
appropriated to their use. They are all taught music—I heard them sing
several songs by Nägeli—"How Sweet 'tis to play" and "Through the Love-
ly fields to run" were among the songs sung.[10] Mr. W. used a Violin. Music
is taught in all the Common Schools under this government. At ½ past
9 went to Mr. Schott's and completed my selections from his music—and
paid him my bill £4.4.8.

Afternoon spent some time in walking about the City—Went into the
Cathedral.

This ancient building was commenced in the 10th and finished in the
11th Century. Met Mr. Wihlein who walked about with me and showed
the town. ~~~~~~~

Evening at ½ past 7 went to a meeting for the practicing of the new
Oratorio "Gutenberg"—Given in the Theatre—about 40 Ladies and 60
gentlemen present—Piano Forte accompaniment. Some parts of it are very
beautiful—but as a whole I did not think very highly of it.

Having determined to go to Carlsruhe in the morning, I have left word
with Mr. Schott to forward any letters to Care of Mr. Woodbridge—and
also to forward my music—both that which I have brought here, and also
from Mr. André in Frankfurt—care of Holbrook & Nelson N.Y.

Friday 21st July 1837
At 5 o'clock went on board Steam Boat Frederick Wilhelm—to go up
the Rhine to Carlsruhe—distance about 60 miles.

The steward could speak a few words of english. There was an english
family on board who went about half the distance viz: to Mannheim—
Two Gentlemen and Lady and female servant—one gentleman appeared
very ill. They left and also most of the other passengers at about one
o'clock. Immediately afterwards the Steward came and said "dinner"—at
the same time holding out a bill of fare in German, for which I was none
the wiser. I asked him what he had got, and among other things he said
"Beef Steak"—"well Beef Steak" said I "with potatoes and beans"—and
took my place at table. There were but three others dining—a Gentleman
and Lady at the next table, and a young gentleman at the same table with
me. Their dishes came quick but I had to wait ½ an hour or more. At length
it came—a small piece—which was soon gone. They had their regular
courses but I had no more. I saw that something was wrong—by and bye

the Steward came down (the Servant who tended table could not speak) and I asked if I had anything more coming. He said what will you have. I asked him again what he had, and he replied among other things "Duck"—"Very well bring me some roast duck and sallad" and he went away. The others finished their dinner and I continued to wait a full hour—at last I got up and went on deck and found the Steward sitting down reading—I asked him if my dinner was coming. "Oh" said he "the duck was no roast"—"it will be done"—and away he went to look—in ¼ of an hour more it was done—but turned out to be Chicken—so badly cooked I could not eat it.

We arrived at the landing at 9 o'clock—and there I found that we had to ride about 10 or 12 miles in an "Eilwagon." I had some difficulty in being understood, but on the whole got along very well, and arrived at Carlsruhe Hotel d'Angleterre—at 11½ o'clock where I found the Servants could speak to me in a known tongue.

I have been very much favored again this day and preserved by him who has thus far led me in safety on my journey, and find myself at 12 o'clock in a comfortable room, having everything I need—except gratitude for such constant goodness and humility under a sense of my own unworthiness. ~~~~~~

Saturday 22. July 1837
Carlsruhe ~~~~~~
This morning called on Prof. [Anton] Gersbach—and found with him a gentleman who could speak a little english. He invited me to his school on Monday at 11 o'clock—was very polite, and gave me the sheets unbound to a book he had lately published. Afterwards employed a teacher to go with me and introduce me to Prof. Stern to whom I was introduced by Mr. Woodbridge and also by Mr. Schnyder de Wartensee. Prof. Gersbach was with him—had some further conversation and an appointment to see a school on Monday at 8 o'clock. Called on a teacher of Female school to see a School Organ,—a small organ of an octave and a half with two stops—Diap. and Prin. He invited me to see his school on Monday at 10 o'clock. In all the schools in Baden (dukedom) Music is taught. There has just been a vacation in all the schools—while I was at Prof. Stern's six of eight students came in having just arrived from the country on a visit to parents, etc. They always walk and carry a little wallet or pack etc. on their back containing whatever is necessary for their journey. They walk often 100 or 150 english miles. I told the teacher who was with me that I had a son in College—and that he was home on vacation—he said it was much better to walk—all the students here would walk that distance—or 130 miles. They walk 8 hours a day—about 3 miles an hour. ~~~~~~

After dinner Mr. [   ] the teacher who speaks English went with me and called on Mr. de St. Julien—but he was out of town (introduced by Neukomm). We then called on F. S. [Ferdinand Simon] Gassner (see his Tabellen) who is a Teacher—he was just beginning with a class and allowed me to stop and hear them.

There were about 20 or 24—boys and girls—they have been to S. School 6 months twice a week—average age perhaps 8 or 9 or 10. They have been well taught. I wrote a lesson for them which they examined Rhythmically, and Melodically and then sang it. Afterwards they sang several Songs—some of Nägeli's. We then called on a Teacher Mr. Rider—who showed something of his manner—and recommended Solfeg: in Paris (see memo: at end of this book) [appendix 1]—his daughter—13 years old sang a song well—very well indeed. Purchased a few works by Mr. Gersbach and some others.

Sunday, July 23, 1837
Carlsruhe—14th Sunday from Boston This morning went to a Lutheran church—very few present. I only remained to hear one Coral, and went to Catholic Cathedral, afterwards to the Chapel in Palace where was the Grand Duke. Heard a coral there which was very good—first part as follows[11]

Afterward to the Cathedral again and heard part of Mass, and home at ¼ past 11. It is a warm delightful day—and sitting in my chamber fronting the market place—I think of home and of a Boston Sabbath with delight. Fourteen Sabbaths away from the home of God and religious privileges—they now appear pleasant and desirable indeed. May the Lord this day be with his people and bless them with peace and salvation.

Saw many men today with three cornered, or cocked hats—also having large square shoe buckles. I was told they are from the country living a short distance from this place.

At ½ past 12 a military company passed my window—the Band played admirably—15 Clarinets and Oboes—2 Bassoons—8 Horns—4 Trumpets—3 Trombones—3 Base horns—Drums, etc. There was a gentleman near me today (and also yesterday) who very much resembled the late D. H. Kollock of Savannah. His size—general appearance and address—double chin, mouth—especially when speaking—nose—eyes (though I think his eyes were a little darker), forehead and hair—all. I could not keep my eyes away from him and often exclaimed to myself "is it possible." Indeed I would not have thought it at all probable that another man would be found the world over so much to resemble a man whose appearance was so different from every other person I ever before saw.

In the afternoon I remained in the house. At six o'clock the Opera of Oberon was performed—had it been another day I should have heard it. ~~~~~~~

Some things out of place

In coming from Mainz to Carlsruhe we passed Worms. It was here that Luther was summoned to answer for his heresy—and when advised not to go by his friends who supposed his life might be in danger he replied "I will go to Worms though there be as many devils there as there are tiles on the houses." This speech of his appears much more natural and much more sensible after having seen these German cities where the houses are covered with red tile.

We also passed Speyer or Spire. It was here that the famous decrees were passed against which the reformed Princes and cities protesting gave rise to the name Protestant.

In the Museum at Dresden may be seen relics of Luther. His beer jug, his sword and his ring are preserved. In the library are original letters by Luther and [Philipp] Melancthon, and at the library in Berlin may be seen the very copy of the Hebrew Bible from which he made his translation with marginal notes in his handwriting.

In Wittemberg Luther's apartment in the Augustine Convent remains almost as he left it. The chair and table at which he wrote are there, and on the wall is written "Peter the Great" in Luther's hand. ~~~~~~~ (Journal to Choir brought to this place.)

I should suppose from what I see in riding through the country that almost all the work on the farms is done by women. I see them hoeing, mowing, reaping and doing all kinds of field work. I have seen them also loading or unloading carts of gravel, and indeed doing all kinds of outdoor work of men in New England. They are accustomed to carry heavy burdens upon their backs. For this purpose they have a basket filled to the shoulders and tied on. In these baskets we see them carrying potatoes, peas, beans, grass, etc. to market. The women are used for the same purposes that market men near Boston use horses.

Cows are not generally turned out to pasture as in New England but are kept up in the stable or barn, and to feed them the women go out with their baskets and cut and bring up the green grass. It is very laborious work.

The peasantry, or laboring country people, do not live on their farms as they do in New England but live together with their cows, pigs, etc. in villages. These villages are the dirtiest, slovenly looking places imaginable.

There seems not the least attention paid to appearance or cleanliness about the houses. The houses for the people and the houses for the cows are just about alike so far as I can see and are close together. Men, women, children and cows are all together—often under the same roof. In passing through one of these villages one would think as well from the testimony of his eyes and his nose that he was in a great cow yard. The houses are close together and streets very narrow, crooked and dirty—and are often filled with carts, ploughs, wheelbarrows and implements of husbandry. The houses are usually built of wooden frame, filled up with clay and straw. The clay is left natural color so that you would suppose they are what they really are, houses built of mud. The roof is commonly thatched—sometimes tiled.

North of Leipsig I do not remember to have seen oxen; but south of this place I saw occasionally oxen and often I saw cows yoked, or tied together performing the labor of these useful animals. Sometimes a cow would be thus yoked or tied to a horse, and side by side these good natured animals would be doing the work of their master—not knowing but what they were made to go together in that way—although the poor cow had hard work to keep up with {so swift an animal as the horse} her companion.

The laboring women, country women, wear nothing upon their heads or arms and are often without shoes or stockings. They are much tanned or blackened with the sun and look beyond description ugly. Even young girls of 16 or 18 are as rough in appearance as an up country New England farmer. By neglecting to attend to their persons, I doubt not that they grow ugly—and more and more so from generation to generation—thus proving that beauty may be lost by neglecting to attend to it, and vice-versa that it may be cultivated by a constant and proper attention to personal appearance, just so it is with our physical and moral powers. ~~~~~~~

In cities we see some pretty faces—but not many.

There are no fences or walls in the country to separate one field from another, as in New England, and we pass along by field after field of wheat, rye, oats, potatoes, peas, etc. etc. There is a beautiful wild red flower common in the fields that gives them a lively appearance—as I often see whole acres of poppies cultivated for oil.

Beds

The beds are all single—or made for a single person. The bed stead is nothing more or less than an open box raised about a foot from the floor—just wide enough for one to turn over in, but often not long enough for a person of moderate stature. The bed itself is good—but the pillows reach from the headboard down nearly half way, and form such an angle that the body is supported in a half sitting posture—much as we would sit on a sofa. There are no blankets—but instead of these there is a very light feather, or down bed to go on top—so that you have a feather below and above—but the upper one is so small that unless a person lies as still as a statue, he will surely kick it off—so that in cold weather one will freeze unless he keeps awake to take care of his covering, and in warm weather he must be suffocated with a feather bed on the top of him, or else be without any covering but the sheet which is not enough.

Milk is brought into the city by women in tin vessels in baskets on the head—a girl of 16 or 18 just passed by my window having five cans on her head which would hold I suppose a gallon each. Here everything is carried on the head—further north on the back. ~~~~~~~

Monday, 24th July 1837
This morning at eight I visited the school under Professor Stern and Professor Gersbach. This is a school for boys—a public school. the pupils pay 8 florins a year only—about $3.00. There [are] 250 pupils—5 classes 1st class 6 to 8—2nd class 8 to 10—3rd class 10 to 14 4th 13 to 15 or 16 5th 14-upward.

Music is taught to each class. The 1st class only learn by rote—the other classes all learn the Theory. I heard from 8 to ½ past 9—the 1st, 2nd and 3rd classes.

At ten o'clock went to a girl's school, also public—the pupils paying only about 12 florins per annum. 350 pupils—4 classes, arranged much after the manner or Professor Stern's school. The 1st and 2nd classes only learn by rote. Visited all the classes. Heard another class sing—but did not see any teaching.

At 11 o'clock returned to Messrs. Stern and Gersbach's school, and saw the 4th and 5th classes exercised together—rhythm and melody mostly the former according to Gersbach's method. Afterwards they sang <u>Corals</u>.

Rhythmic exercises of this kind were new:

taking the short notes as 1, the next as 2 and reading them in this way without singing.

There are not many songs used in this school—lessons mostly and Corals—Corals they think highly of—for forming and giving strength and firmness to the voice. This [illegible] I also heard from Bach of Berlin and Schneider of Dresden.

Messrs. Stern and Gersbach advise me to go to Stuttgart and have offered to give me letters of introduction. Many of the pupils in Professor Stern's school are educated for Teachers. He has many teachers under him as Mr. Thayer has. I observed that Professor Stern, also Professor Gersbach, and all the teachers seemed to be familiar with music—and the different teachers taught in their respective rooms. The smallest class is taught by one of the more advanced pupils. I understood that the 5th class take turns in teaching the smallest class in music and I believe also in other things.

Music is more of a study and less of a play or amusement in this school than it has been where I have taught. ~~~~~~~

Sent letters this morning by way of Havre—to
> Mrs. Mason
> To the Choir
> Holbrook and Nelson

I also wrote to Messrs. Baring Brothers & Co. London requesting any letters to be sent to Paris care up to 20th August. ~~~~~~~

Afternoon at ½ past 2—called on Professor F. L. Gassner and was present when he taught a class of about 15 or 20. Three of the girls and one of the boys copied a song and gave me with their name etc. Professor Gassner also gave me a song composed by himself.

The name of the Teacher who has been with me, and who has enabled me to converse etc. is <u>William Haas</u>—Carlesruhe.

Afternoon—got my hair Cut—went to Bath—returned and wrote a letter to Mr. Woodbridge—Vevay—and to Miss Woodman—Ipswich—and made preparations for departing from Carlesruhe—where my visit has been very successful as it relates to Children's music etc. ~~~~~~~

Tuesday July 25, 1837

Left Carlsruhe this morning at 7—and arrived at Stuttgart at a little past 4. I went to the Hotel "King of England" having been told that I should find some one who would speak English there—but when I arrived I found there was no one. I left my luggage and went to another hotel "King of Wurtemberg" where I found one the keeper of the hotel Mr. Macklet who could speak—sent for my luggage, and now have a good room in the "King of Wurtemberg" Stuttgart. There was no one in the Coach (5 of m[en]) who could speak english so I had quite a solus ride—about 50 miles.

Made enquiries but could not find a Valet de Place who can speak English—but am told there is a young man a merchant from N. York in the house.

Called on Professor Klumpp—introduced by Mr. Woodbridge—but did not find him in.

Having dined early and feeling hungry I requested some supper to be brought—without giving any more particular order—in a few minutes came up into my chamber as follows: ~~~~~~~

1st course—Soup

2nd—Boiled Fish with melted Butter

3rd.—Roasted Chicken and String Beans

4th—Fried Veal, Sallad and Stewed Cherries

5th—Cherries, Frosted Sponge Cake and Confectionary ~~~~~~~

So that I concluded I was likely to get food and drink here, if I did not succeed in finding an interpreter to speak English. ~~~~~~~

Sent a messenger to ask Professor [G. F.] Kübler to whom I was introduced by Prof. Stern of Carlsruhe when it would be convenient to have me call—and in a short time after he called on me—the gentleman here who speaks english Mr. Macklet the keeper of the hotel was so kind as to come up and interpret for us. Mr. Kübler was very open and free and received me cordially—and invited me to attend his class tomorrow.[12] Mr. Macklet after Mr. K was gone invited me to attend a rehearsal of vocal music at a Society of which he is a member this evening.

So Providence leads me. I was directed to the other Hotel—went and found no one spoke english and felt quite disappointed—but on my way there I had observed that one of the passengers of to day stopped at this hotel—otherwise I should not have known where to find another—I came and found not only a man who can speak—but who seems perfectly willing to do so—and who is himself a member of a musical society, and invites me to attend with him. Surely there is an invisible hand in this. ~~~~~~~

Went out at 9—to hear a Men's Society of singers. There are about 15 such societies in Stuttgart. They sing Glees, etc.—arranged for men's voices. It is similar to the Society I heard in Frankfort.

I also heard one in <u>Mainz</u>—but did not record it. ~~~~~~~

Wednesday, July 26, 1837
Stuttgart

This morning a little after eight, while I was at breakfast Mr. Klumpp called—offered any assistance and was very kind indeed. We conversed (through an interpreter) untill 9 when he accompanied me to the orphan home where Mr. Kübler is teacher. Mr. K is teacher not merely of music but of the other branches, as Geography, Arithmetic, etc. etc.

They were singing when we got there—there were children and young men—say altogether about 100 in the room—singing in 4 parts music composed by [Conrad?] <u>Kocher</u> who was also present and to whom I was introduced, and who speaks a little English. There was also another gentleman there connected with the institution who speaks English. All were very attentive to me and seemed to conduct the singing with reference to my gratification.

The young men who sang Tenor and Base are preparing to be Teachers. The teacher of music in a seminary at [   ] was also there to whom I was introduced but who spoke no English. After the singing I went with Mr. Kübler and Mr. Kocher to the dwelling of the former (in the building) and remained ¾ of an hour, and then Mr. Kocher came home with me to the "King of Wurtemberg" and remained untill ½ past 11.

Opposite to my room is a young lady at her singing lessons—singing passages—vocalizing passages—scales, etc. as

 etc.   etc.

just as Hannah—Miss Belcher and others ought to function for hours every day.

After Mr. Kocher was gone I walked out and went past a girls school where a class was practicing singing. The singing I heard satisfied me that there is no native capacity in the children which we have not already in America. It is by constant practice—and by learning from childhood upwards that they acquire such proficiency in Music. Passed by homes and heard individuals practicing with piano forte. A military band passed. Called at a Book Store and purchased a few Music Books. ~~~~~~~

When Professor Klumpp called this morning after finding that we could neither converse in English or German—he proposed Latin—which did not help the matter at all. ~~~~~~~

At two o'clock Mr. Kocher with Mr. [   ] called on me and we went to the Lyceum, a school where young men are prepared for the university. Here Mr. Kübler teaches music, and I saw him give a lesson to 40 boys—"the transposition of the scale." There are about 250 students—all the young ones learn music untill they become of a certain age or enter a certain class and then it is left to them whether to continue or not, but in case they intend to study Theology then they are required to pursue the study of music.

Afterwards went into the first church where Mr. K. is organist. The organ contains 6000 pipes and has 4 rows of keys, 64 stops—sub base 32 feet, but not so large in size I would think as our largest pipe in Bowdoin St.

In this church they have an orchestra in addition to the organ, on Sundays, of about a dozen instruments—on feast days they have a larger orchestra. ~~~~~~~

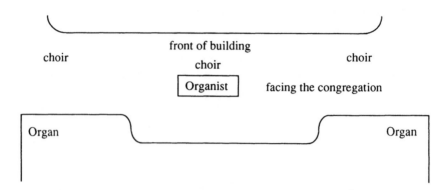

At six o'clock Mr. <u>Kocher</u> called to have me go with him to a meeting of his choir. I found assembled

20 sopranos

8 boys (and) nine young ladies alto

8 or 10 tenor

20 basso—a great part of which were full, grown-up voices. It was a very powerful choir. They sang music from Mr. K's books—which I have. They have a good room—but want some conveniences that we have at Bowdoin St. The Ladies have seats without backs—the gentlemen have no seats—but stand the whole time—they all stand when they are singing.

They sing quite loud—there are no <u>Pianos</u>, although there was some difference in the passages, it was all loud. Nothing sung was softer than mezzo—a mezzo forte.

The treble was very powerful.

I observed that although they spoke together there was less noise than at Bowdoin St. between the pieces.

The books were changed during the hour (for it continued just an hour), and I observed when they were changed—they did not throw them carelessly down, but collected them all carefully and put them on the piano. This seemed to be a habit. It looked well—not so slovenly as it does to throw down the books just as they happen to be when we have done singing. A good lesson for our Choir.

Here was a choir meeting right in the middle of the afternoon—from 6 to 7 for the purpose of singing church music. Mr. Kocher told me that he had continued this for 15 years past—during which time he had been the organist and intended to continue it. I asked him what would become of it when he was gone. He said that if the work was the Lord's he would raise up some one to carry it on. If not let it perish, but added it will not perish. Some one will be prepared to take my place. This is more like Bowdoin St. than anything I have seen. There is much more power in this choir—more good voices in all the parts—but less delicacy—less accuracy of execution. There was more strict decorum—order and propriety of conduct—indeed in this respect everything was perfectly right. ~~~~~~~

So it seems also in the Boys school—taught at Lyceum today—they were all silent and attentive and at the close of the lesson walked out like young gentlemen—without riot or noise.

I think I have used the piano too much in teaching. I have also allowed them to sing too many songs—especially in Mr. T(Thayer)'s school and Mr. F(Fowle)'s.

Thursday 27th July 1837
Stuttgart
This morning early—finished a letter to Daniel to be sent by way of Havre. At ½ past 6 a military band passed—playing admirably. ~~~~~~~

Having been advised by Prof. Klumpp to visit a school in <u>Stratten</u> about 12 or 14 miles from here—I took a carriage and Mr. <u>Kocher</u> and Mr. <u>Kübler</u> went with me, by invitation.

I was greatly pleased with the school. It is kept in a large building in originally a Castle—containing about 70 Rooms—with a beautiful garden and trees etc. including some 20 or 50 acres around it. It is at a little distance from a village. Mr. <u>Kocher</u> is a particular friend of the Principal or Director. There are now about 100 boys—all preparing for the University which is the design of the school. There are 14 Teachers. Rooms are large and airy and in all respects commodious. The boys were mostly dressed very plain—all appear healthy and happy. The Director is a preacher—they have public worship in the Chapel once on Sabbath and once go to the Parish Church.

Music is taught to all—there are 5 classes in music—each of which is taught 2 hours in the week. There are also some of the Boys who learn the Piano Forte, or Violin. There is a music teacher attached to the Institution—who is engaged most of the time in group lessons. I heard a class sing—well—also saw a class taught, and wrote myself on the board lessons for them. We dined at the Hotel. After Dinner Mrs. [   ] (wife of the Director) invited me to take coffee, and we went out into the Garden, and took it in under the green trees—and after coffee <u>Wine</u>. They find fault with me that I will not drink wine.

We passed through several villages of the peasantry and I had an opportunity to see more of the filthy manner in which they live. Cows, men, women and children all together—the front door often opens into the cow yard.

The men (peasantry) are dressed often in Buckskin yellow breeches, and cocked up hat. Little boys are also dressed in the same way, and look strangly indeed to me.

Mrs. [   ] sang from the Messiah "He Shall feed his flock" and "I know that my Redeemer liveth" in very good Style—an excellent voice and chaste and tasteful singer.

The grounds around Stuttgart the way we went out of the City are most beautifully laid out. There are rows of large trees for miles and red and white roses growing all along each side of the road. In some places two carriage paths and one or two foot paths separated by trees or roses. There being no fences or walks, but all being common gives the country a delightful appearance.

We got home at ½ past 8 in the Evening.

The Hotel "King of Wurtemberg" at Stuttgart I have found better than any other at which I have been in Germany. The Master of the house has been uniformly kind and attentive—and the Servants quick to answer calls ~~~~~~~ My apartment has been kept clean and in good order, and the Table excellent.

5

Switzerland and France

When Mason left Germany and entered Switzerland he also left the orbit of Neukomm and entered that of Woodbridge. As a consequence the focus of his trip changed dramatically. In Germany Neukomm's letter of introduction had provided Mason with most of his contacts. Neukomm had few connections in Switzerland, and Woodbridge's letter served as Mason's principal entree into Swiss society. In contrast to Neukomm's associations, which were principally with musicians, Woodbridge's were almost exclusively educational. Since the language barrier made it as difficult for Mason to fend on his own in Switzerland as it had in Germany, cultivating contacts outside of those provided by Woodbridge was difficult. Other circumstances contributed to Mason's almost exclusive focus upon educational issues. Switzerland had no great concert tradition as London and many cities in Germany did, and Switzerland was the home of Pestalozzi and Nägeli. Visiting the latter was one of the original objectives of Mason's tour.

Paris offered Mason more variety, but the fatigue of his lengthy trip plus his anxiety to move on had already begun to show in Switzerland. Consequently he only sampled briefly the rich musical scene of Paris. He did contact a number of important musicians, but in Paris Mason began to unwind. We see as much of Mason the tourist as Mason the ever-efficient professional.

MASON'S DIARY

Saturday 29th July 1837
St. Galen—Switzerland.

Yesterday morning at 5 o'clock I left Stuttgart. There was but one passenger besides myself when we started and he could not speak English. The Morning was fine, and the ride was delightful as we ascended the highest hills that surround Stuttgart. This place is thus surrounded on all sides—the hill is so steep that a carriage cannot go directly up, and the road is made zig-zag—or like this

Stuttgart

We have in leaving the town by this road many beautiful views as we wind up the hill—and look down upon Stuttgart in the valley below. Weather was delightful. After say 30 m. we took in another passenger—he could not speak english.

As we passed through the German villages I saw more and more of the filthy manner in which the working class live. The front yard is almost a Cow yard and filled with manure,—and the steamy smell of it fills the whole village.

Shepherds tending their flocks.

Women tending geese.

How rough the out-door working appears—I should hardly have supposed a female could have been found so rough, coarse and horridly ugly in appearance. Soon after dinner the gentleman who got in last left us and two ladies got in the coach—neither could speak.

At 12 o'clock at night—another Lady and Gentleman got in but none could speak in my language.

At ½ past 4 this morning we arrived at Friedrichshale—on the Weberlinger See or Lake Constance—at 6 we went on board a Steam Boat and in two hours crossed the lake 10 miles to Rorschach. Here we took coach and arrived at St. Gallen at ½ past 10.

When we got to Friedrichshale I was not aware of it, and supposed that we had yet 5 or 6 miles to ride in the coach—untill the Captain of the Steam Boat came up to me and spoke in English. I then learned where we were etc. etc. (Footnote by LM: I had not time to go to Constance. It is the place where John Huss was burned.)

When we went down to the Boat, as soon as we came to the Border of the Lake Constance Switzerland with its lofty mountains opened to our view—beautiful, sublime. We saw the lofty range of mountains of which Mount Santis is the highest. Alp-Tyrol—They were all covered with snow, and presented a strange contrast to the green fertile valleys below.
~~~~~~~

There is also a range of smaller mountains between the lake and the mountains—called the Rorschach Mountains—

At the hotel "zur Hecht" or in French "de Brochet" or in english "the pike."

After washing and dressing I walked through the market where every thing was selling as at Dresden and other places. Bought needles and thread, and returned home and sewed two buttons on my pantaloons.

Dined at ½ past 12—while at Dinner we had music—a man and woman came in and played a Guitar and sang.

After dinner took a little sleep and feeling refreshed—although very warm weather—I determined to go up one of the neighboring mountains—took a guide—but he could speak no english.

It was ¾ of an hour up a steep hill all the way—very fatiguing—but I was amply repaid when I got up to have such a fine view of the surrounding scenery. Twenty miles distance was Mount <u>Santis</u> in the range of the alps. Through the telescope I could distinctly see the snow in the crevices of the rocks—Sublime indeed. Below on the other side lay the beautiful little City of St. Galen, and half way between us were some lakes in which boys were swimming. The boys looked so small that I should not have seen them—but my guide pointed them out. ~~~~~~~

Home a little before 8—and almost immediately to bed after writing this. I have a pleasant room, and it appears to be a fine Hotel.

While on the mountain I plucked some flowers for my friends at home—one beautiful blue flower for my wife—it seemed to bring her to me as I carried it along, looking at it, and thinking how I should like to give it to her. It gives me pain to think that neither Mrs. M. nor the children can enjoy the beautiful scenery with me.

Sunday 30th July 1837
St. Gallen—Switzerland
15th Sunday from Boston

I awoke this morning at 8—after a long night's sound sleep—feeling refreshed and quite well—I hope grateful for the constant goodness that follows me. A rainy morning. When I had finished my breakfast it was nearly 10. I went out and came first to the Cathedral (Catholic). Here they were performing Mass. In addition to the organ, which is large and powerful they had orchestral accompaniment—I believe only Stringed Instruments. The Cathedral is very large, and was filled with people—men on one side and women on the other. I found myself on the side with the women—but as I observed several english gentlemen and Ladies near me, having made the same mistake, I remained near them untill the service was over, and then walked about to look a little at the building. It is the most showy building of the kind I have seen. The walls and all over head being painted with various scripture subjects. There is also much carved work. Besides the great organ at the end of the Church opposite the altar—I observed two smaller organs near the altar—one on the right and the other on the left hand. The music was not very good. At the close of the Mass I walked out and went to two other Churches but found them shut. I then came home and spent the remainder of the morning in my room.

I observed that all of the people in the Cathedral seemed to be of the laboring class—and looked poor. The women either had nothing on their heads, or else a peculiar kind of dress that looks [like] a peacock spread tail form though not in color. I have sometimes seen Swiss in U.S. with this head dress on.

Afternoon I went out and called into a Luthern (I suppose) church. The Congregation was small and more than ⅔rd females. They began by singing a Choral (Luther's Hymn, or Monmouth, though not exactly as in our books) but I did not stay to hear it through—the organ was not well played, and the voices were coarse and rough. Went to another Church where the minister was preaching—out of a congregation of about 200 I could only see three or four men. The people all seemed to be poor—the churches furnished in a very rough manner. In these protestant churches I did not see a single instance of the peculiar head-dress.

Went again to Cathedral—an old man with a black cap was preaching—staid but a few moments and come home to my room and spent the remainder of the day. ~~~~~~~

Monday 31st July 1837
St. Gallen

It continues to rain gently. ~~~~~~~

This morning at 7 o'clock I left St. Gallen to go to <u>Trogen</u>—a distance of not more than 6 or 8 miles but the road is so bad, and the hills so steep that it takes two hours or more to go. There is no coach, so I provided myself with a four wheel chaise and one horse with a driver.

It rained, though not fast, and we went slowly up the long hills, not being able to speak a word on account of the language. I had an introduction to M. M. Tellweger Merchant and to Rev. Mr. Le Pasteur Fry and Mr. Le Director Knisi from Mr. Woodbridge—and also to the latter from Mr. Schnyder de Wartensee of Frankfurt a/m. We arrived at about 10 o'clock and at the first good looking house to which we came a gentleman was standing in the door which, as it afterwards appeared, the driver knew. He stopped and speaking to the gentleman asked him if he would speak to me and ascertain where I would like to stop—telling him at the same time that I did not speak German. The Gentleman stepped out and spoke to me in French—I told him I could only speak English—upon which he spoke to me in my own language. I told him I wished to go to the principal Hotel. Just as the driver was about to start, I thought I would ask him if I can find any one who could speak english. He replied "no—there is no one here but myself," and then offered his assistance. I took my letter from my pocket book and showed him. Upon reading it he informed me that Mr. <u>Knisi</u> did not now live in Trogen and that Mr. Tellweger was out of town—that Mr. Fry was in town but could not speak English—and added that he was the son of Mr. Tellweger and should be happy to render me any assistance in his power. He then invited me into his house, introduced me to his wife, etc.

After explaining my object he proposed to go to the schools which would be interesting. We went to two—in the first they could not conveniently have the Children sing to day. In the 2nd school there was a class of about 30 who sang for half an hour, and the Teacher gave me a list of several books.

I then returned with Mr. T. to his house—took <u>Wine</u> and <u>Bread</u>—he afterwards went with me to call on a Gentleman to procure books—not being able to do so, he said he would send them to St. Gallen for me this evening.

After trying to express my gratitude for such attention—I bid him good bye—having taken up his time from 10 to about 1 o'clock. He said repeatedly to me that <u>it was a duty to attend to strangers</u>.

His name J. C. Tellweger Jr.

    Trogen,

      Appenzell

        Switzerland.

he gave me his card. He was very much of a gentleman, and I doubt not from appearance a wealthy man.

The Providence of God has thus wonderfully led me and provided for me this day.   Returned—dined—and purchased some books—and prepared to go in the morning to Zurich. ～～～～～～～

Mr. T. also gave me a note to Mr. Weishaupt of Gais—author of some music—and to Mr. Titus Tobler [Titus added in pencil by HLM]. Mr. W. was not at home, but from Mr. T. I purchased two little books. A gentleman to whom Mr. T. introduced me gave me some pieces of music composed on the death of Nägeli. ～～～～～～～

Sent letters to Father in Medfield and to Choir. ～～～～～～～ Note: It seems quite remarkable that Mr. T. should have been standing at the door as he was the moment we passed—had it been otherwise I should have gone to the Hotel and finding no one who could speak—and ascertaining that Mr. Knisi was out of town—should probably have returned to St. Gallen—disappointed and having lost my journey. In several instances, has Providence thus favored me.

Bread and wine—this is what we get here—not cake and wine but plain bread.

At 8 o'clock I received a package of books from Mr. T. with a note requesting me to accept them as a remembrance of the Canton of Appenzell Switzerland.

Tuesday Aug. 1 1837
Zurich

Left St. Gallen this morning at 7. My seat was on the outside of the coach back of the wheel. The coach was more like an English or American one than any I have seen before. There was one man with me who could speak a very little english so that by the help of a book that I had in my hand we could occasionally exchange a word or two. The morning was pleasant and cold. As we left St. Gallen the cemetery presented much the appearance of N. E. except that the scenery is more bold. We soon came in sight of the lofty Santis—an eternal rock covered with snow. It brought to my mind the figure used in the Scripture "God is a rock"—unchangeable, eternal, fixed and immoveable—but not like the Santis covered with Snow—he is a God of love, full of compassion and tender mercy. On the first church we passed, in a small village I saw on the outside a large cross on which was an image of the Saviour nearly as large as life hewn out of stone. Having ascertained that my companion was from Zurich, I mentioned to him the name Nägeli—where he lifted up his hands and exclaimed "Nägeli is my friend"—and shaking his head with a sad look added "he is now dead." After some difficulty I made him understand that the songs of Nägeli were sung by children of America—where he exclaimed "glorious glorious."
~~~~~~~~

The country appears to be settled much after the manner of N. E. and not at all as Germany—I see none of the disgusting german villages. There are frequently hedges as in England. All the houses are supplied with a constant, running faucet of pure spring water from the mountains—we see it every morning as we pass. At 8 o'clock we passed through a village and stopped a few moments just before a church. The door was open—I saw candles burning and heard the peal of the organ, and the loud sound of the choral song. How quickly it started the tears. Is there any thing more delightful than to hear a large congregation singing the praise of the Lord. The catholics appear to be very attentive to the external of worship— here on a Tuesday morning at 8 o'clock there was (as it appeared) a large congregation assembled. They are also externally more devout in relating exercises than Protestants. Why should our principles lead to irreverence, or carelessness about externals? I was anxious to get a little nearer the organ but was afraid the coach would leave me. We drove away and the sound of the music was lost amidst the noise, the Postillion and the rattling of

the carriage. We frequently passed little villages—say at 1 or 2 miles apart—
often two or three churches would be in sight at once. We often passed
flower gardens—a pretty sure indication of civilization, cultivation and
taste within. At 10 o'clock the interweaving hills shut out <u>Santis</u> from our
view. Just as we were losing sight of it my Companion said "Now we lose
Santis forever" meaning that we should see it no more on our journey.
In this, however, he was mistaken, for it seemed to follow us—nor did
we leave it for at least 40 or 50 miles. To me the remark of my fellow
passenger was undoubtedly true "it is gone forever." There is something
peculiarly solemn as I leave different places, and persons with whom I
have formed a slight acquaintance, in the thought that I will never see them
again in this world. At 11 we passed the beautiful town of Wye—and soon
after we passed many crosses. On some was a carved image of the
Saviour—on some were pictures coarsely painted on wood and having a
little roof or box to shelter them—the subject always had relation to the
Saviour, and generally to his crucifixion. On some were only the letters
I. H. S. I do not like to see this Emblem of our Religion made so common.

About 12 we dined—and arrived at Zurich a little before 6. Switzerland
is indeed a beautiful country. The valleys are rich with wheat, rye, barley,
oats, potatoes, grass, hemp, peas, etc. etc. and on the sides of the hills
in a lighter soil are vineyards.

Men travel much on foot—we often see respectable men having their
packs on their backs, and a staff in their hand evidently on long journeys.
Boys too, of 12 or 14 years of age travel in a similar way alone.

The large places through which we passed were <u>Wye</u>, Frauenfield,
and <u>Winterthur</u>—at the latter place I heard a choir of men singing near
where the coach stopped. It was quite warm in the afternoon, and the
hot sun in the valley through which we were passing, presented a strange
contrast to the range of mountains on our left covered with snow. A hot
sun over our head, and the snow in full view—at only 15 or 20 miles
distant.

When we arrived at <u>Zurich</u>, my principal business here being to call
on the family of Nägeli, and procure music, I thought I would try and do
it at once and be ready to go in the morning. I took a guide and went
to them—but no one could speak a word. They read my letter from
<u>Mr. Schnyder de Wartense</u> but we could not say a single word to be
understood. At last I pointed to the music books and said "gute gute" and
hummed over to them "Charming little valley" which is one of Nägeli's
songs—they seemed surprised and greatly pleased that I should know it.

The best Hotel in the place was entirely full the queen of Naples oc-
cupying many apartments and I could not get in—but found a place at
"Zum Storchen"—where I have written this. The Lake of Zurich is right
under my window, and the bells of Zurich are on the opposite side say

as far as from Bowdoin St. Church to Cambridge St. and the chimes of
Zurich have already sounded in my ears. ~~~~~~~
To bed at 8—much fatigued.

Wednesday Aug. 2. 1837
Zurich ~~~~~~~
Awoke this morning after a night's sound sleep much refreshed.
~~~~~~~

Mrs. Nägeli sent to the house "Zum Storchen" to say that if I would
call at 9 o'clock, a friend would be there who could speak english.

I went and staid untill 12 o'clock—selecting music—purchased all the
pieces by Nägeli they had except what I had before. Nägeli himself died
last Spring—Mr. Woodbridge did not know of his death, and gave me an
introduction. The wife of Nägeli is quite an ordinary looking woman—
but his daughter who is about 30 years of age is a very interesting young
Lady—she plays the Piano but not much—plays also the Harp and sings.
She sang two songs of her Fathers to me and accompanied on the Piano,
but said she had not sung since her Father's death, and could not do well.

She gave me an introduction to Mr. Muller of Burgdorf—saying that
I should be pleased she thought to call on him—and recommended also
that I should call Doctor <u>Niederer</u> of <u>Iverdon</u> whom she said could speak
English and would be of great use to me.

Nägeli left a Son who is a musician and composer—but for some cause
or other, he retires from the world almost altogether. Hearing that I was
there he sent his respects to me with a manuscript song by himself, making an apology for not coming down, as his eyes were weak. Mrs. N. gave
me a small piece in her husband's hand writing and the daughter (Ottilia)
did likewise.

I have hesitated this afternoon whether to spend a week in going into
the mountains or go direct to Bern—and have determined on the latter,
principally because I have so little time. Went to see the house where
<u>Zwingle</u> [Zwingli] the reformer lived—Lavater afterwards occupied the
same house—the Church is near by where both preached. ~~~~~~~

This afternoon at 4 o'clock 'tis truly hot weather—yet from my window I see mountains covered with snow, and they do not appear to be
further from me than Dr. Porter's meeting house in Roxbury Rd. from the
head of Boston common. They <u>are</u> about 15 to 20 miles distant.

Zurich is said to have been founded nearly 2000 years before the Christian Era and is one of the most interesting cities of Switzerland. At 5 o'clock
I walked out with the Gentleman who interpreted for me at Mrs. Nägeli's—
we went to a beautiful, shady spot ½ or ¾ of a mile where a monument
is erected to the memory of the poet <u>Gessner</u>—also another to <u>Lavater</u>
and returned at ½ past 7—tired. ~~~~~~~

My music became so bulky that I was obliged to buy another Trunk here, in which to pack it. ~~~~~~~

Thursday morning 5½ o'clock
August 3. 1837
Zurich
This morning while I write I hear "the Chimes of Zurich" for the last time. The sound comes from the bells of the <u>Minster</u>—the same that <u>Zwingle</u> or <u>Zwinglias</u> left on account of his reformation principles and established a new church on the opposite side of the River—more than 300 years ago. ~~~~~~~

Left Zurich at 6 o'clock—and after a hot days journey arrived in <u>Berne</u> at 9 o'clock—a distance I suppose of 75 miles.

My seat was in the inside—so I had not much prospect. The coach was full most of the way—but no one could speak english whom I saw this day. I did not make minutes of this ride, as I did the last. Switzerland is much like N. E.—we saw much reaping going on to day—men or women not young all in the field reaping and gathering the wheat, rye, etc.

I often saw women with baskets tied before them going carefully over the fields from which the grain had been gathered picking up all the scattering ears—like Ruth the daughter in law of Naomi who went into the fields of Boaz and "gleaned in the field after the reapers." Ruth 2nd.

I should like to remember the great frenchman and lady (apparently his daughter) who rode most of this day—and also the young Lady from whom I bought a knife after dinner—all of whom were very social and tried to converse and by the help of my book—travellers guide—succeeded.

Went to the Hotel "<u>Zum Distelzwang</u>" "Hotel Des Gentilshommes" where I found no one who could speak—but I easily made them understand that I wanted a room, and something to eat—(for we had dined at 12 and I had not taken much at dinner and nothing since). I soon had an excellent cup of tea—sweet good bread and butter just from the churn with new delicious honey.

There are two beds in the room—the children would like to hear me tell them how I told the servant that the other bed must not be occupied. ~~~~~~~

This is the worst hotel I have found. The principal building is on the opposite side of the street, and ringing does not call a servant under a quarter of an hour. The food is good—but attendance bad, and a dark and dreary passage to my room.

Friday morning 4th Aug. 1837
Berne ~~~~~~~
Rose at ½ past 6—quite refreshed by sleep. Took breakfast of fresh honey,

butter and bread. Wrote on a paper "can you find some one to speak english" and gave it to the Servant who returned directly with the Servant of an English family staying here. I made known my wishes to go to Hofyl, and am likely to be gratified at once. ~~~~~~~

So I find the good Providence of God ever provides. ~~~~~~~
(Wrote to Daniel—4 months from date of paper.)

Afternoon at 5 o'clock. Left Berne at a little past 9 this morning and went to Hofyl—a pleasant ride of perhaps 5 miles. I found Mr. Fellenberg at home but there was a vacation in the schools which commenced on Monday last and continues until 25th Instant. He conversed with me (speaking english a little) and sent for his daughter who speaks very well to interpret or help him along. He thinks that Switzerland is behind those parts of Germany that I have seen, and thinks that I shall not find much to interest me here, after having visited Carlsruhe, Stuttgart, etc.

He gave me manuscript copy of a piece of music composed by Rink at his request, and for his institution. He sent for one of the Teachers who speaks English well—and he went round and showed me the different rooms etc. and explained whatever I wanted to know about the institution. He also gave me a little tract written by himself and translated and printed in English relative to his institution. There are several American Boys here—Two Eagers from Charleston, S.C. and one or two from N.Y. or Connecticut. He has a teacher also (Mr. Dole) from Boston—but he and all the pupils were absent on a mountain tour during vacation. Left my card for Mr. Dole.

Returned to dinner—and afterward walked out (having a valet de place) who spoke mostly in french, partly in german and partly in english to guide me.

Berne is built upon very high land and is almost surrounded by the river Aar—so that it is a peninsula somewhat like Boston only much less in extent. The homes are almost all alike and have low arches in front— Stores, workshops etc. below and houses above. The arches protect from rain.

The bear is the emblem of Berne. In a low spot of ground or trench just out of one of the gates are constantly kept a number of bears—I saw four. The trench is walled up high so that we look down say 15 or 20 feet upon the animals. At the entrance to the city from the South—there are two large white bears hewn from stone, one on each side of the way. They look like a powerful guard.

We see work of all kind going on as we pass along the streets. Women washing, mending, knitting, carding wool, etc.—in streets as public for Berne as School St. or Washington St. for Boston. Carpenters, Blacksmiths, groceries and dry goods all mixed together. There is a class of laboring women who have a curious dress around the waist with iron chains attached to it. Through the principal street in Berne there is a running stream of water—some parts of the way covered—some parts open—the lowest part of the street being in the center.

In visiting the institution at Hofyl, I could not help regretting that Lowell, and William and Henry could not enjoy such a school—in a quiet, retired, place—where it would seem if anything they can be removed from temptation. It is worth serious thought whether we had not better send them—I will converse with Mr. Woodbridge on this subject. ~~~~~~~

While I have been writing we have had a beautiful shower. It rained very fast—and thundered some. Drew this afternoon from the Bankers, Messrs. Marcu and Co. £ = 25.00—<u>for which I received 616 franks</u>. The hotel at Berne was the poorest that I have seen on my journey. ~~~~~~~

Saturday 5th. Aug. 1837
Berne. ~~~~~~~
Spent the morning in my room—wrote a letter to Choir—<u>14th</u>—at 12 o'clock left Berne and after a pleasant ride of 4 hours arrived at <u>Freiburg Hotel des Marchands</u>. I rode in front in the <u>Coupa</u> as it is called—there was a frenchman with me who spoke english well, and as soon as it was ascertained that we could converse he was very sociable, and pleasant. He had been to call on <u>Fellenberg</u> but did not find him at home. He could not speak German. I have a pleasant room here, and the servant who showed me up speaks a little. It seems as if I could spend the Sabbath pleasantly here so far as it relates to temporal things at least.

The suspension Bridge as we enter Freiburg from the North is one of the most wonderful works of art I have seen. It is really frightful to come over it. It is made of Iron—905 feet long and 175 feet high—or above the water—within about 20 or 30 feet of the Park St. Steeple. The chains that support it are made of wires—and one would suppose that it would fall by its own weight—but the heavy coach went over, and I could hardly see that it trembled.

At 7 o'clock we sit down to dinner—I was very hungry having eaten nothing since 8 in the morning. The gentleman who was next to me spoke to me in English, and asked "Pray Sir is this a dinner or supper"—I told him I believed it was dinner—at all events it was very acceptable to me—in a little further conversation that I had with him, he informed me that himself and wife who was next to him are on a pedestrian tour in Switzerland—walking 10 or 12 miles a day.

There is a very celebrated organ here in the Cathedral which I hope to hear tomorrow. ~~~~~~~
To bed at ½ past 8.

Sunday, 6th August, 1837

Sixteenth Sunday from Boston. I was quite unwell last night in the night—having gone without food through the day and then at 7 eating hearty was more than I could bear. I got up and took some magnesia—and an hour after took a Rochelle powder. Did not get up untill the sound of an organ in a church close by told me it was time for public worship—this was 8 o'clock.

Felt better after I got up and went out at ½ past 9 to the Cathedral. Grand Mass was performed—an orchestra, and an organ, and a very good choir—but I could not determine the number of instruments or voices.

A most beautiful effect was produced by the organ accompaniment to the priest as he chanted some part of the Service. The chant being plain and the accompaniment florid with flute and tremlant. Service was out at 11—immediately after which the organist Jacques Vogt—played several pieces on the organ. The servant at the hotel sent for Mr. Vogt previously and introduced me to him—through my circular letter from Neukomm, and took me into the organ loft. This organ is the greatest curiosity I have seen since leaving home—it surpassed all belief—nothing but hearing it can convey an idea of its wonderful power—and nothing but playing on it can satisfy you that you are not deceived after all.[1] The organist played first a fugue by Jno Sebastian Bach in a very perfect manner. He then played a number of pieces by different authors—an adagio and allegro by Beethoven in which the complete orchestra was wonderfully imitated—some pieces by Haydn, and a storm which was very much superior to anything of the kind I have heard before. But what surprised me most of all—and what is almost incredible—he played a motetto by Haydn in which the voices Soprano, Alto, Tenor, and Base were distinctly heard, and so exactly imitated that I defy any one not fully accustomed to this organ to tell the difference. I could not believe for some time but that the whole was a deception, and that there were voices concealed within the organ. I walked about in different positions—went to the side doors and put my ears to the key hole, etc. not being satisfied that I was not deceived. The voice parts came in distinctly, with that little tremulous effect always perceived—then, and especially in Catholic singing—and they would leave off or close and the organ would continue the Symphony. Sometimes a Soprano Duet and a response by Tenor and Base—sometimes a Solo and then a chorus, though never very loud, showing that there was but one or two stops by which it was done.

He played an hour, after which some ladies and gentlemen came up into the organ loft, and at their solicitation he played another vocal piece—a motetto by Beethoven—in which the same effect was obvious. It was indeed so exact a representation of the human voice that I could not tell the difference—listening with all the attention that I could bestow. To put an end to all doubts on the subject after he had done playing—a Lady put her fingers on the keys and ran over a few notes and the same tones were produced and also a gentleman played a few chords.

Mr. Fellenberg at Hofyl had told me of this organ and told me to be sure and see it. A passenger in the coach yesterday spoke of it as being very celebrated.

I copied a list of the stops—and enquired if any description of it had been published and was told there had [been] none—nor could they let any one see its internal structure. The King of France sent sometime since for the maker to build him one—but he would not undertake it—saying he was too old to build another, and he wished Switzerland to have the only organ of the kind.

Left hand side

Bandon	8 pieds		Quintade	16 pieds
Solicional	8 "		2nd Principale	8 "
Calcan	4 "		Cornet	8 "
Flute a quinte	4 "		Octave	8 "
Cornet			Nazard	3 "
Krumhorn			Fourniture	
Trombone	8 "		Trompette	8 "
Bombarde	16 "		Montre	16 "
Prestand	4 "		Octave	8 "
Octave	4 "		Bourdon	16 "
Soubasse	16 "		Gambe	8 "
Bourdon	32 "		Dulciana	4 "
Montre Echo	8 "		Doublet	2 "
Bourdon	8 "		Cimbal	
Flajolet Echo			Trombone	
Flute e quinte			Copula	

Right Hand Side

Principal	8 pieds		Tremblant	8 pieds
Flute dome	8 "		Viole	8 "
Gambe	8 "		Prestand	4 "
Flute	4 "		Dulciana	4 "
Flute a chemince			Flute B	4 "
Doublet			Flagolet	2 "
Flajolet			Ped Trompette	
Principal	8 "		Prestand	4 "
Cornet	16 "		Principal	4 "
Bourdon	8 "		Montre	16 "
Prestand	4 "		Flute	8 "
Cornet	3 "		Flute Echo	
Fourniture				Solicional Echo
Scharf			Cornet Echo	
Clarion			Bassoon-Hautbois*	
Tremblant Echo				Voce humana [in pencil]

*The organist told me this was the stop that imitated the voice and with his pencil wrote <u>voce humana</u> under it.

The builder's name is Moser (Mooser).[2]

After dinner I went into a French church near the hotel—here was a large congregation. After the Service a procession marched around the aisles of the church consisting of priests, boys, females, etc. carrying images, Crosses and banners.

On one side of the church were about twenty or thirty females all in white, with red or blue ribbons round the waist, and white veils—these I took to be nuns. They were not afraid to show their faces, and some of them were very pretty to be seen.

I walked into another church for a few moments and also into the Cathedral, but saw nothing worth recording.

This is a Catholic place—there is only a small protestant society who meet in a hall—but they are thinking of building a church. ~~~~~~~~

One would think after seeing the forms and ceremonies of the Catholic Church that their religion and that of New England congregationalists cannot be the same. It seems incredible that both can be derived from the same source and impossible that both can be according to the will of Christ.

I observed that almost all the people seemed to be of the lower class—they must be very ignorant. Almost all had strings of beads. I saw many saying their prayers and counting their beads.

Some would kneel down 6 8 or 10 feet or more from the church, on the outside and begin to say their prayers.

While at dinner today a military band played in the entry of the hotel for our gratification—marches, waltzes, etc. ~~~~~~~~

At 5 o'clock Mr. Vogt played the organ again at the Cathedral. It was much the same as in the morning. He commenced with a full organ piece—in the old organ style. Afterwards played something like an overture—full orchestra—totally different from the first. I do not think, however, that as an organist he is to be compared with Schneider of Dresden in the old school or Adams of London in the orchestra manner of playing. He also played a vocal piece—I believe by Beethoven—the same wonderful effect as in the morning—past belief. I do not expect to be believed when I tell of this organ—I would not have believed it myself. My own sense of hearing is the only evidence that could have convinced me. He closed with a storm—and amidst the thunder and lightning were sometimes heard the solemn chanting of the choir (vox humana) and at others the tremulous and distant warblings of the flute.[3]

It is quite evident that the vox humana is far in the rear of the organ. The whole end of the Cathedral is filled with the organ—its front extends across the building—so that no one can go round—or back of it.

Walked round a little afterward—returned. I took a cup of tea and felt much better than I had through the day.

Having ascertained that the Diligence (as it is now called) does not go 'till 4 tomorrow, I have decided to go to Vevey in a private carriage, and to leave here at 5 o'clock in the morning.

Monday 7th Aug. 1837
Friburg ~~~~~~~
This morning at ½ past 5 left Freiburg in a private carriage—two horses and a driver to go to Vevay. The morning was very foggy and thick—as we left the gates we passed four priests—and soon after four more with books in their hands going to take a morning walk, I suppose. Here I was alone in a carriage riding a day through the beautiful scenery of Switzerland. How much I did want my dear Wife to enjoy it with me—or the Children—or all. But having no one, and being all alone in the carriage I found it an excellent time for looking back upon my past life—reviewing the mercies of God which have followed me in my crooked path. God grant that the meditations of this day may not be forgotten.

The fog cleared away and I rode through the splendid mountain views—at 10½ o'clock we arrived at Bulle which is half way to Vevay. As it was necessary for the driver to rest his horses and feed them here, I took another one horse vehicle to go about 3 or 4 miles to visit a Castle upon the mountains—Castle and town of Gruyeres—we could only ride part of the way. I had a guide who could speak a little. All in a perspiration I arrived at the Castle. Several of the different apartments were shown by an old woman who was there—among others the torture room, and the room where cattle were slaughtered—with a fire place at which whole oxen were roasted. ~~~~~~~

The country is famous for the Cheese that is here made—said to be the best in Switzerland—not far from us in the valley was a small house where they were making cheese and I had the curiosity to go and see them. As we approached the house we found the front door surrounded by some 8 or 10 boys, who made it their place of rendezvous—and through their mud and filth we must pass to get in. In the home were two apartments— divided, however, not by a close partition but by a kind of railing only. In one apartment were forty one fine looking cows—and in the other were two men and a boy—one of the men was making a cheese. It was very large—as large as 6 or 8 common New England Cheeses. A large Kettle full of milk was boiling over the fire in the center of the room. No floor except the earth itself—this was not very clean because of the cows which were so close along side—before going in I thought I should like to taste of the cheese—but after I was there I had no desire for any thing but to get away as soon as possible. The vallies are very rich with green wild clover on which the cows feed. We were close to the foot of a lofty mountain.

Returned to <u>Bulle</u>—dined and at 1 o'clock pursued our way to Vevay where we arrived at 2 o'clock. Here I took a horse and carriage—(chaise on low wheels—hung sideways—so that we ride as we do in an omnibus) and went up the mountains 3 miles to "Chateau de Blonay" the residence of Dr. Woodbridge—the road passed through vineyards about the whole distance. Arrived at a little past 5 and was greatly pleased to meet Mr. and Mrs. W. who also seemed as much pleased to receive a visit from me. On Tuesday Mrs. Bruen (wife of the late Dr. Bruen of N.Y.) came to spend the day with Mr. W. so that we had quite an American Party. Wednesday I also remained with Mr. W.—and left him on <u>Thursday</u> at ½ past 5 for Vevay where I expected to take the Steam Boat at ½ past 8—but having to walk to Vevay, and then having much to do to get ready, I found myself too late for this hour.

While I have been with Mr. W. he has urged me very much to go back again through Switzerland that I might visit the oberlands (highlands) and see more of the Swiss country and hear more of the Swiss singing. I had partly considered to do so, but upon arriving at Vevay I find that I cannot possibly be in Paris untill nearly 10 days after the time I had fixed upon for being there if I do so—and besides I cannot bear the idea of spending so much time in travelling back through a country I have already passed, and where it is with difficulty I can make myself understood. I have therefore determined to go on to Paris by Geneva.

My disappointment has been great here in not receiving any letters from home, as I had ordered them to be sent here—So I have been disappointed at <u>Leipsig</u>, at <u>Mainz</u> and at <u>Vevay</u>—hope I may not be also disappointed in Paris.

Vevay Thursday 10th Aug. 1837
"Hôtel Les Trios Couronnes"—
Pronounced La Trau Cooron [This line circled]
Nine o'clock. Have breakfasted—written the foregoing minutes from 7th Instant and have now to wait for Steam Boat this afternoon. ~~~~~~~
From this place to day sent letters to
    Mrs. Mason at Medfield
    Choir—Susan Copeland—Boston—15th letter.
Left Vevay at ½ past 1—and after a pleasant Sail along the Lake Geneva—stopping at <u>Lausanne</u>, <u>Morges</u>, <u>Rolle</u>, <u>Nyon</u>, and <u>Coppet</u> arrived at Geneva at ½ past 6 o'clock. I have a room at the most splendid hotel (externally) that I have seen.
    "Hotel des Bergues"—No. 13. ~~~~~~~
<u>Hotel de Berg</u>
When I went to Mr. Woodbridge's I was not very well—while there I took pills and also Castor oil and injections—and lived light. In conse-

quence of this I feel the fatigue of this days journey—though in a boat—and also feel very hungry. ~~~~~~~

Exactly in front of my window is the lake—between this and the other side is a small island—with trees, etc. and a promenade.

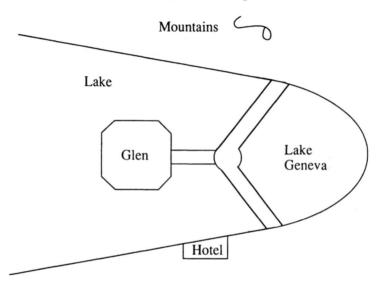

Geneva Friday Aug. 11. 1837
Hotel des Bergues

Rose at 7—feeling languid—owing no doubt to the very hot weather—this is truly hot summer weather. I have taken off my netting shirts, and felt the need of their pantaloons. ~~~~~~~ At 10 o'clock I went out and called on Rev. Dr. [César] Malan to whom I had an introduction from Mrs. Bruen. He invited me to be seated, read the letter and said "ah! dear Mrs. Bruen." After making some inquiries about her, and a few about my object, etc. He asked me though not in the exact words "How I enjoyed religion in my journey"—upon my giving him an answer saying that sometimes more and sometimes less, etc. He said that journeying is unfavorable etc. He asked me when I was converted—and whether I knew it to be so or only hoped it to be so. Not being satisfied with my answer he went on to prove that every Christian should at all times know and be assured of his acceptance and good standing with God. Hoping is not enough—we ought all to have assurance.

He asked me on what my hope was founded—I began to reply "On my acceptance"—"ah" said he stopping me—"acceptance not on your acceptance" that is Arminianism. He then got the Bible and spent perhaps ¾ of an hour in showing what true faith is—simply receiving God's testimony—then those who believe shall be saved—wherefore doubt?

He brought up various illustrations which I do not remember—but one was

"My son comes to me and says my Father forgive me for such an offense—the son does not doubt that he is speaking to his Father,"—etc.

"Once when the Emperor of the French was reviewing troops he accidentally let the reins fall and the horse spring but a soldier seeing it ran quickly and caught the horse and stopped him—"well done Captain" said the Emperor. "Captain of what" replied the soldier. "Of my guards" said the Emperor. He put away his gun and took his station as an officer, when he was told by some one to go away to his place—he replied "this is my place for I am a captain—the Emperor says so." Here was faith in the Emperor's word. Finally—he promised me some books on the subject, and then turned to music. He called in his wife and three daughters, and they sang to me some of Dr. Malan's compositions—one of his daughters playing on the Piano. ~~~~~~~ He then gave me a note to Rev. A. Bost who has composed some music—on him I called, and procured his publications, and returned to the Hotel at 12½ o'clock. On looking over the Book of the Hotel I found the names of Mr. Gray and Mr. Cogswell from Boston—and left my card for them. ~~~~~~~

Afternoon bought a number of Tyrolese Songs (30) just published.

Received a small package from Rev. D. Malan containing a copy of "The New Bartimaens"—"Chants de Sion" [Malan 1824]—and letters of introduction to Mon. J. J. Risler and Monsieur Lutteroth Paris.

Ascertained that I cannot get a good seat in the Diligence for Paris untill Tuesday Morning next. ~~~~~~~

Saturday 12th. Aug. 1837
Geneva
This morning called upon Mrs. Wolf to whom I had a letter from Mrs. Bruen. Saw Miss W. who speaks english—saw also Rev. W. Salsbury from Boston there. Mrs. W.'s daughter married a Dr. Buck of N. York and the family are quite attentive to Americans.

Received cards from Mr. F. C. Gray and
J. G. Cogswell who have left Geneva this morning.
Came home and wrote business letters
to Aug. Crantz Hamburg
Jos. Sturge Birmingham England
and letters of friendship to
Ch. McIntire
Lizzy C. Belcher
Johnson Mason Jr. Cincinnati
Business letters also to Mr. Schott—Mainz
Mr. André—Frankfort a/m.

Sunday 13. Aug. 1837
(17th Sunday from Boston)
This morning at 8 breakfasted at Mr. Wolf's—with Mr. and Mrs. W.—two daughters—Mr. Salsbury and others—they almost all spoke english—except Mr. and Mrs. W. On the Piano I found "The Boston Academy Collection of Church Music" [Mason 1834] and "Spiritual Songs" [Mason and Hastings 1843]—also "Musica Sacra." [Hastings 1815] It is quite a musical family. There were two Pianos in the room.

At 9 went to church at the Oratorie—the sermon was in French—and of course I could not understand—but Miss Wolf handed me an English testament by which I learnt the subject was in Luke 7—36 to 50. At 10 o'clock there was a lesson in singing—about 50 or 60 persons assembled and sang three or four pieces. The teacher singing the principal melody with the females. It was coarse and uncultivated. ~~~~~~~ At the Hotel met Mr. Henry Cabot from Boston. He is on an European Tour with his family. Mr. H. G. Otis Jr. is in Geneva, and lives in the Hotel at which I stayed.

From one to two o'clock I walked about the city—passed the home where J. J. Rousseau is said to have been born—at 2 called into a church where service was just about to commence—a Baptism similar in form to our own—then singing—a plain coral by Congregation—with the man in front of the pulpit to lead singing the prime melody. Some of the female voices sang tenor an 8ve. too high. ~~~~~~~

At 6 o'clock I went to Dr. Malan's Chapel—he preached in French. There is a small organ which his daughter plays. The music was plain and devotional. After the Service I went by invitation to Dr. Malan's house. His whole family were together viz: Father and Mother and Eleven Children—five sons and seven daughters. Miss Wolf was also there—two young English gentlemen and two or three others—after walking sometime in the Garden we went in to Tea—there were 16 or 18 at table and more in another room. All the Children (now grown up) speak english. So that the conversation was mostly in english. As tea was over a plate with folded papers was handed round—when it came to me Dr. M. said "take one, it is our dessert"—I took it and found a text of Scripture in french. After all were supplied Dr. M. called on me to read mine—which I did in english—a bible having been handed me. They were read in order round the table—the Doctor making remarks as they went along. I told them I would like one for my wife, and the plate was handed for "Madame Mason"—

My text was Nahum 1.7. Mrs. Masons was John 3.27—Miss Wolf also selected for her sister in N. Y. and gave it in charge to me.

We afterwards spent an hour in singing "Cantiques" or french hymns—and I sang one English or American hymn.

Home at ½ past 10.

Dr. Malan was ejected from his place as minister of the national church in 1817 on account of his orthodoxy—that church is now socinian—he gave me an interesting account of it. At the time of his ejectment he had 4 children and all his worldly property consisted of 100 franks.

Miss Wolf told me what a great trial it was for her sister in N. York to be called on to sing and play the foolish songs etc. of the day—at first she declined saying that she only sang hymns. She is sorry that Christians in America should not cultivate christian music more.

Monday 14th. Aug 1837
Geneva ~~~~~~~

This morning I wrote to Mr. Winslow—to Dr. Cotton of Marietta, and also an account of the organ at Freiburg which I sent to Mr. Palmer—requesting him to read it to the choir, and afterwards hand it to some of the papers for publication. ~~~~~~~

Received calls from two of Dr. Malan's sons and also from Rev. M. Salsbury. ~~~~~~~

This took me untill 2 o'clock, after which I walked out—went to see the monument to Rousseau—and sang Greenville.[4]

I am much obliged to him for this tune—and for his musical dictionary—although I cannot respect his religious character.

Went to Bathe—and at 5 dined. ~~~~~~~

Paris Aug. 18 1837

On Tuesday 15th. left Geneva—7 o'clock morning. I had No. 1 in the Coupé and with me were two english Ladies—Mrs. and Miss Patten—Mr. Patten being in the inside or <u>interieure</u> of the Diligence. There are 4 apartments and 4 prices—

  Viz: Coupé
       Interieure
       Retonde and
       Banquet—on the top.

I found the ladies very pleasant company—we passed the Jura mountains the first day and had some beautiful scenery from the high situations we occupied. It was quite cool—almost cold when we were high up. We were surrounded by and enveloped in the clouds. We saw the clouds above us for miles and continued to ascend untill we were in the midst of them—they were like a thick fog—we could see the sun shining at a distance from us in the vallies below. In the afternoon passed the first Custom house—our passports were examined—trunks etc.—detained almost 1½ or 2 hours. There were with us a man and his wife who we supposed introduced contraband goods. Perhaps watches or jewelry. They did it in this way. The wife feigned lameness, had her foot bundled up and could apparently but just walk. When in the coach her husband held her foot in his lap and when out he supported her as she hobbled about. But as soon as we had passed the custom house her lameness disappeared all at once, and she walked as sprightly as any one. The goods were probably concealed in her shoe, or stocking.

At almost 8 o'clock we came to another Custom house—here we had difficulty in being passed—several of us in consequence of not having the Vezay of the french Minister on our passports—but at last we all succeeded—detained two hours. The officer first told three of us—Mr. Patten, Dr. Parker and myself that we could not pass but afterwards we were permitted to do so. ~~~~~~~

On Wednesday morning at about 8 we arrived at [Dijon—crossed out] and breakfast and tea. I went out to find a Barber and was shaved by a woman. Here a change was made, and a french gentleman and Mrs. Patten got in the Coupé with me. At about 7 in the evening Friday, August 18 arrived at Dijon and here, the English family stopped and Dr. Willard Parker a young Physician from America—got into the Coupé. We were Wednesday Night 16th Aug.—Thursday 17th, Thursday Night, and Friday 18th untill 11 o'clock A.M. when we arrived at Paris. ~~~~~~~

Mr. George Patten
Mrs. George Patten
Miss Clara Patten

Dr. Parker is originally from Chelmsford—has studied and lived evidently in Boston—married in the Western part of Mass. and has been some at Cincinnati. He has been in Europe since last March, and was now returning from Italy. It made my journey very pleasant having him with me. We have had pleasant weather all the way, and usually a cool breese—without dust. The distance is about 375 miles. ~~~~~~~

After waking, shaving and dressing I went to the Banker Hottingues & Co. rue Bergere, No 11—and to my great joy found a letter from Mrs. Mason of June 20th—written just after having heard of my arrival in London, and also a letter from Miss Grant. Called on Mr. Cutter a Merchant Taylor from Boston who married a sister to Mrs. Andrews and Miss Woodward—and also on Messrs. Richards and Cromwell (3 Rue St. Barbe[)]. Dined at the Hotel, and attended Musard's concert. An orchestra of 90 musicians—who played well—but their selections were generally nothing more than Waltzes, Quadrilles etc. Price of admittance 1 fr.

Saturday Aug. 19. 1837
Paris Hotel de Meurice—
42, rue de Rivoli
Last night I went to bed at about 11—excessively fatigued—having rode

three days and three nights in succession and also a part of the fourth day. The weather we found very hot in Paris—and the novelty of the great French City and the running about all the afternoon had not served at all to rest me. Slept sound—and in the morning was much refreshed. Spent the day mostly in walking about the City with Dr. Parker. Bought Chockolate toys etc.

Called into the Church "Eglise des Petits Pères"—and saw the Catholic Ceremony of a Wedding. There seemed to be much mummery about it, and it all seemed a light and trifling affair to the parties. In the Church is a Monument to "Lully" the french composer of Music—who died about 150 years ago.

Called also and saw the Church "St. Germain L'Auxerrois."
~~~~~~~
Dined at 6 o'clock at Mr. Cutter's in company with Dr. Parker. Found Mr. and Mrs. Cutter very pleasant. They are Episcopal—but quite orthodox in sentiment. Both are also quite musical.

Sunday 20th Aug. 1837
Paris. ~~~~~~~ 18th Sunday from Boston
This morning I attended church with Mr. Cutter at the Marboeuf Chapel— Episcopal service. a congregation of two or three hundred—all good look- ing Ladies and Gentlemen. What a contrast to the Catholic congregations I have seen! The Sermon by Rev. Mr. Lovett the pastor was very good— Acts 15.11 "But we believe, that through the grace of our Lord Jesus Christ, we shall be Saved." In the introduction to his Sermon he gave an account of the disagreement spoken of in this Chapter.

Although the controversy has literally ceased, its Spirit still exists. It now assumes the form of Justification by faith or by works. Object—to prove the former—

1st. consideration. The origin of salvation is to be traced to the eter- nal purpose of God.

2nd. We find that it is the work of God to begin and carry on this work in the soul.
   Impossibility of it being the work of man
    Law to be kept
    Sin to be atoned for
    Son of God to fill the heart.

Concluded with punctual remarks—one of which was Salvation is a present gift—which was quite forcibly illustrated. ~~~~~~~

As I was going to church to day there was a woman playing a hand organ at the door of a Catholic Church—her object being to collect a few Sous, from the people as they assembled.

Went home with Mr. Cutter and in Afternoon at 3 attended the Chapel at which Mr. Wilkes (english) and Mr. Baird (American) officiate. We were rather early, and as I entered the Chapel the first person I saw was Mr. Henry Cummings.[5] He had just arrived in Paris this morning—had ascertained from the papers that there was english preaching at this chapel, and had come directly there. He knew that I was in Europe but did not expect to meet me. When we consider the great improbability of our meeting—it seems very providential that he should have found me this early. He is to remain here and study medicine.

Rev. Mr. Kirk[6] of Albany preached to a Congregation of about 50. "The carnal mind is enmity against God." A very powerful and searching Sermon.

After the Sermon I introduced Mr. Henry to Mr. Kirk. Mr. K. is to remain some time in Paris, and will introduce Mr. H. at once into Christian Society, and aid him in various respects.

The garden of the Tuileries is exactly opposite my Hotel, and here I found thousands were walking when I got home.

Monday Aug. 21 1837
Paris. ~~~~~~~
This morning finished a letter to the Choir (Sarah Anne Copeland)—being my 16th Letter.

At ½ past 8. I started to go to Mr. Cutter's—put on a new coat and took my old one under my arm to get repaired. I walked about an hour round and round and could not find the place—called at a Cafe and took my breakfast, and came home—went up into my chamber—consulted my map and was just going out when a Man from Mr. Cutter called on me to see how a waistcoat fitted that had been sent to my order on Saturday. So I walked with him to the store of Mr. C.

Afterwards called on Mr. Lovering—introduced by Edwards and Stoddard—there I saw Boston Papers up to 14th July—

J. G. Lovering   Cutter & Co.
9 rue de Chéry   Tailors
                  Rue Richelieu, No. 102

I afterwards walked about the City—calling on some Music Stores—but without finding anything useful. ~~~~~~~
Wrote a hasty letter to Mrs. Mason to go by packet of 24th—also finished a letter before almost done—for Mrs. Coffee.

Made out a list of the letters I have sent by way of Havre so far as I could to send to Havre through Mr. Lovering—fearing that some of them may have been stopped at the post office on account of postage.

Evening at the "Académie Royal de Musique" ~~~~~~~

Guillaume Tell

In the orchestra were 8 double Bass
        10 Violoncellos and violins in proportion—Orchestra 80 or upwards. A very Superior Orchestra—as good as I have heard.

M. Duprez—Tenor—is certainly one of the best Singers I have heard—without voce di testa he sings high with ease—he sang in medium with a few slight exceptions all the evening. Goes to A easy when singing full in Medium Register.

Sang with great feeling—a rich fullness and beauty of tone!
~~~~~~~

A duet in 2nd act near the beginning by Tenor and Treble was very fine.

The Horns echoing among the mountains (Scene Switz) was very fine.

The manner of taking breath struck me with force—they breathed with care—inspired full and quick. Remember the beauty with which they pass from 2 to 1—portamento in final cadence   sliding con expression.

Tuesday Aug. 22. 1837
Paris

Mr. Henry Cummings called on me at ½ past 9. We went out at 12— called on Mr. Cutter and on Mr. Lovering. Called at Mr. Draper's and left letter of introduction and Card. Spent the remainder of the day in looking over music—etc.

Walked with Mr. Henry—breakfasted with him in a Cafe at 1—and dined at 6 o'clock.

Evening Mr. Draper called on me at the Hotel.

Visited also to day the royal Library—containing
        900,000 Printed vols.
        80,000 Manuscripts

Wednesday 23rd. Aug. 1837

This morning at 8 I went to call on Mr. Mainzer having an introduction from Neukomm—out of Town—to call tomorrow morning.

Visited the Spot where the Bastile formerly stood. Visited the Cemetery Père la chaise—Tomb of Abelard and Heloise—covered with wreathes by the young lovers.

Saw the tombs of many distinguished men—some musical—Herold—Gretry—Boildieu [Boieldieu] and Bellini.

Many of the monuments are very beautiful. In several I saw a little room—with table and chairs—and door of open work Iron—furnishing a place for the friends of the deceased. Wreathes of flowers were every

where scattered over their tombs. Many women in the vicinity of the place
sell wreathes of flowers, so that (as) you approach it you see on the stalls
and up at the windows—hundreds and thousands of them at various prices.

One monument was pointed out by our guide which cost £12000.

There is a chapel for saying Mass for the dead—Mass is said every
morning. And for 2 franks any person can have Mass said for a deceased
friend—if he has music or if he has many tapers it will cost more.

Afterward spent three hours in search of the music establishment of
Mr. Choron's successor.

After finding the place I made some selections of Sacred Music from
a very extensive catalogue.

Mr. Henry was with me all day. We breakfasted and dined together
at 10½ and 6 o'clock. He speaks french very well, and is therefore very
useful to me.

Evening at "Academy Royal de Musique"—first part of "Moses in
Egypt" by Rossini.

Thursday 24. Aug. 1837

This morning Mr. Henry called and we went at 8 o'clock to call on Mr.
Mainzer (Jos.) to whom I had an introduction. Found him, and after sitting
½ an hour conversing on music very pleasantly left him.

Mr. M. teaches vocal music in large classes—he has two classes of 800
each—both of which he has invited me to see on Wednesday and Friday
of next week.

Breakfasted, and afterwards spent two or three hours in selecting
porcelain—to send home.

After this delivered a letter to Messrs. Wainwright & Co.—introduced
by Gordon & Goddard. ~~~~~~~

Called and completed my purchase of Music from Choron's and also
purchased from one other music Store. Called on Cherubini—but found
him engaged, and was requested to call again tomorrow morning.
Cherubini is director of the "Conservatoire de Musique"—and has his room
at the building. There are upwards of 300 pupils—but it is now vacation.
Fifteen years, I was told, is allowed for learning to sing. ~~~~~~~

Afterward went to Diorama[7] of Solomon's Temple and also of a scene
in Switzerland.

Met Mr. Patten with whom I started from Geneva and called to see
his wife and daughter.

Mr. Henry was with me all day—or untill 6—when we dined together
and he went home—he expects to commence his arrangements for study
tomorrow. ~~~~~~~

Friday 25. Aug. 1837
This morning having procured an interpreter or "Valet de place" I went
and finished the purchase of porcelain.

Called on <u>Cherubini</u> but he was engaged and could not see me.

Called on Mr. Muller's and saw his <u>Expressive Organs</u>. Called at Mr.
Cutter's and paid him for Coat, Vest and Pantaloons.

Took my passage for London on Thursday next by way of Boulogne.

Called at a Bazar—and purchased some yellow glass articles.

Visited the "Chapelle Expiatoire"—being on the spot where Louis 16
and his queen Marie Antoinette were buried in 1793—also the new and
beautiful Church of the Madeleine. Visited the Military Hospital (Hospital
of Invalides)—Chapel—Dome—Reading room—Sleeping rooms—Kitchen
etc. There are here upwards of 4000 disabled Soldiers—many have lost
a leg—many an arm and others otherwise wounded. It is a very extensive
and commodious establishment.

Visited the home of Chamber of deputies.

Came home and packed a box music etc. to send to Boston.
~~~~~~~

Dined from 6 to 7 at <u>Cafe de Paris</u>, an excellent house in <u>Boulevards</u>.
~~~~~~~

Saturday 26th. Aug. 1837
Spent the whole morning in writing letters, and in attending to the packing and delivery of Porcelain. Left with Messrs. Richards and Cromwell
3 Rue St. Barbe—three Boxes marked D and P to be forwarded by them
to Davis and Palmer, Boston.

Called and saw the church "St. Eustache" and one other—made purchases of toys etc. for Children—procured a box and packed the music
that I have been purchasing from place to place since leaving <u>Mainz</u>.

Dined at Meurice and afterward walked up the Boulevard—through
Rue Vivienne and Palis Royal home. To bed at 10. ~~~~~~~

Sunday 27th. Aug. 1837
19th from Boston
Slept late this morning—having taken some cold in night—felt unwell.

Mr. Cutter called for me to go to Church but I had not taken breakfast.

After breakfast went to the Chapel the service being in French, I only
remained through the 1st prayer and one Cantique. The Music was

 etc.

Afterwards called at a Catholic Church where I heard alternate chanting by Sopranos and Bases—the latter being accompanied by Serpents or Base-horns.

As we walk through the streets on the Sabbath we see almost all of the Stores open as usual. Now and then one will be closed. Mechanics—as Carpenters, Masons, Painters, etc. are at their work as usual—I saw Pavers—paving the streets to day. ~~~~~~~

At 3 o'clock returned to the same Chapel and heard an excellent sermon from Mr. Kirk.

II Cor. 4.2 "commending ourselves to every man's conscience in the Sight of God." The great duty of a ministers preaching to the conscience, was explained and enforced. Mr. Kirk's preaching is clear, pointed, searching, and highly practical—I have felt it good to listen to him this afternoon, and he kept my attention so as I was not much accustomed to have it kept throughout the Sermon. ~~~~~~~

Went to bed soon after dinner. ~~~~~~~

Monday 28th. Aug. 1837
This morning sent letters to
Mrs. Mason
Choir
Sister Lucretia
H. C. Woodman
Mr. Palmer

Left with Messrs. Richards & Cromwell 3 Rue St. Barbe four cases to be shipped to Davis & P. via N.Y.

The three large cases (D. & P. 1.2.3.) contain Porcelain as Ins. invoice (500 franks). The fourth case (smaller) contains music, collected at different places—and also a few toys etc. for children. The Value of this case happens to be $120. Wrote to Mr. Palmer requesting him to instruct his agents to receive and forward the above. If there should be any difficulty in passing the 4th Case (Music) through the custom house to let it remain there untill my return—requested him to write to me at N.Y. care of Holbrook & Nelson informing me also one of his agents in N.Y. so that I can apply to them on my arrival there for information etc.

Called on Mr. Wilhem but he was not in. Purchased three volumes of music edited by him.

Went to the Cathedral Notre Dame. Go in to these Catholic churches when you will, and you always find more or less persons at their prayers.

Went to "La Morgue." The Seine is raked often for dead bodies—and when found they are brought and deposited in this place for inspection.

Persons found dead in the Streets are also carried here. There were three bodies there when I visited it.

Called on Mr. Lovering and on Richards & Cromwell—Carried and delivered to R & C. a box of music to be forwarded with Porcelain to Boston.

It has rained a little to day since about 11 o'clock.

Bought Slippers for Daniel and myself in Palis Royal.

Tuesday 29th Aug 1837

This day has been spent in visiting the Palace at Versailles—12 m. from Paris—Mr. Henry Cummings went with me—we breakfasted together at Meurice—and dined after we returned at a Cafe.

Home at 8½ o'clock.

Wednesday 30th. Aug. 1837

Visited this day the following places:

Palace of the Louvre
    Picture Gallery
    Musée Egyptian
    Musée de Marine
    Statuary
Marché des St. Germain
(market)
Church St. Sulpice
Palace of Luxembourg
    Picture Gallery
    Garden
Pantheon—
    Vaults—
Church St. Etienne du Mont
Jardin des Plantes
Manufacture Royale des Gobelins.

In doing all this we (myself and guide) walked about 10 miles. Came home at 6½ (having dined at a Cafe) much fatigued. For particulars of the above mentioned places see Galignani's Guide [Galignani 1837].

In the museum at the Louvre I was shown a small bone said to be one of the bones of St. Andrew. The Organ at St. Etienne (St. Stephen)[8] is very splendid in appearance. Case carved from Black Oak. An artist was employed 50 years in carving it. While in this church being much fatigued I took a seat. I was but just seated when a porter came up to me and told me I must not sit with my back to Christ.—(oui) In this church is the tomb of St. Geneviève—Candles were burning round it, and I asked my guide if there were always lights kept. He said no—but when people were sick their friends would cause candles to be placed here and thus intercede with the Saint for the restoration of the sick person—and that much efficacy was attributed to this mode of praying for the sick.

Passed by the building called the Grainary where the Bakers deposit flower. Every Baker is obliged by law to keep 20 bags of flower in the house, in good order and of good quality. They usually take it out 4 bags at a time—that is—deposit 4 and take away 4—always keeping 20. The object of this is to provide for care of needy.

At ½ past visited Mr. Mainzer's school—250 men—Mr. Kirk went with me.

Thursday 31. Aug. 1837
Paris ~~~~~~~
Morning—went out before breakfast to see military parade. The Military Band was very excellent—consisting of about 35 to 40 persons. ~~~~~~~

Went to visit one of the Abattor de Sossincourt—(Slaughter Houses) 900 oxen—900 calves and 4000 sheep are slaughtered every week. Killing sheep while I was there.

Church Notre Dame de Sovette

Here I saw 4 women at confession—a priest administering communion to a woman

Called on Cromwell & Richards—paid 77 franks for shipping boxes etc. Left orders and paid for 20 boxes—designed for music—at 2½ fr. each.

Called on Mr. Cutter.

Went to Cabinet of Anatomy—at Ecole of Medicine—also another Cabinet of Anatomy.

School for Blind—but could not be admitted.

Palais du Quai d'Orsay Built by Napoleon for foreign ministers. Purchased prints—Portraits of views—Home at 3 to pack up clothes etc. preparatory to departure from Paris.

Dined with Mr. Cutter and at 6 o'clock Aug. 31 left Paris—Mr. Cutter and Mr. Henry went with me to the Coach office to see me start.

Rode all night and the next day at 6 o'clock reached
Boulogne-sur-Mer—(near the Sea)

Saturday Sep. 2. 1837
Last evening went to bed feeling much fatigued—from imprudence in eating dinner just before I went to bed (having had nothing since breakfast). I was unwell with sour stomach in night—Soda corrected it—and this morning I feel much refreshed which is to be attributed to the presence of Him who follows me and preserves me from day to day.

Hotel De Nord

6

England: September 1837

Mason returned to England after being on the continent for nine weeks and immediately expressed relief at being "home" once again. This time Mason stayed only briefly in London and then went on to Birmingham, where an important music festival was taking place. The star of the 1837 Birmingham festival was Felix Mendelssohn, who was there to oversee a performance of his oratorio, *St. Paul.* For Mason, who had already heard this piece in London and was notably unimpressed, the festival's chief attraction was probably a performance of a new oratorio by Neukomm, *The Ascension.* A performance of *Messiah,* however, provided Mason the most moving experience of the festival (see appendix 4).

Other than the Birmingham Festival, Mason's activities involved little music. Mason continued to visit many churches on Sundays and spoke with decided opinion about what he heard. At this stage of his journey, however, we find him recording more about the sermons than the music.

Mason spent the remainder of his time visiting the many tourist attractions of England and preparing for his voyage home, preparations which were complicated by an incident of lost luggage which has a thoroughly modern sound.

MASON'S DIARY

[Saturday, September 2]
A Rainy day. Left Boulongne at 11 o'clock—in a Steam Boat to cross the Channel to Dover.

It rained so that most of the passengers were obliged to be in the Cabin—which was very small and close. There were not seats enough for half to sit down—being early I was one of the two or three gentlemen who obtained a seat. I with another gentleman was seated upon a seat which was rather large for two but not large enough for three. A lady came and squeezed in between us. In less than 5 minutes after the boat left the wharf sickup commenced—about all in Cabin were very sick, and throwing up the whole distance. I was much sicker than when I crossed the Atlantic, and do not remember of ever being so sea sick before. We arrived in Dover in 3½ hours.

I went to "Payn's Royal York Hotel" and went to bed. After two hours sleep felt somewhat better but no appetite. Walked out—took a Carriage and rode to "Shakespeare's Cliff"—300 feet above the water—returned and tried a cup of tea—but without appetite. At 8 went to bed, and between 12 and 1 got to sleep.

How beautiful England appears after the tour I have had—the moment I stepped on shore I felt the difference—In the appearance of the people—houses—and every thing that strikes the eye. England is centuries before all other countries in the arts of life. I felt almost as if I had got home at Dover—and feel, now as if I should never want to go into France, Germany or any Foreign land where habits, customs and language are so different again. ~~~~~~~

Sunday Sep: 3. 1837
Dover England
20th Sunday from Boston
Rose at 7—feeling much better—but without appetite.

At ½ past 10 I went to St. Mary's church—Episcopal—went into the organ loft and introduced myself to the organist whose name is <u>Mr. W.</u> [William Walter] <u>Sutton</u>—who was very polite—after Service invited me to come again etc. The Sermon by an old man was very good indeed— text John 16.32 "And yet I am not alone because the Father is with me." This he applied to every true Christian, and employed it as matter of Consolation and comfort to all such. Communion Sermon. After the service I walked up to the Dover Castle— ½ a mile from the Church where I was. The Scenery from the heights is beautiful—<u>See Dover guide</u>. Returned to Hotel and eat some dinner although without much appetite. At ½ past 2 I went to "<u>Zion Chapel</u>"—Independent—but was met by a man at the door who told me there was no Sermon this afternoon but Communion. I told him that I would like to stay—He said they required an introduction—"Ah! then" I replied "I cannot stay—I am an American—a member of a similar Church there but am not known here." "Well" said he "I hope you are known some where else"—and then directed me to <u>The Baptist Chapel</u>—where I went and heard—a somewhat singular—but discriminating gospel Sermon from 1st Peter 2.9—"a peculiar people." "In this short text" said the minister "two things are to be observed and on which we will dwell—

1st. a people peculiar and
2nd. a peculiar people ["]
1. A people peculiar

1 a chosen generation
2 a royal priesthood
3 a holy nation
2. A peculiar people
    1. peculiar as they are loved with a peculiar love.
    2.   "   "   purchased with a peculiar price.
    3.   "   "   have a peculiar guest within the Holy Spirit.
    4.   "   with respect to their views, feelings and actions
    5.   "   with respect to their destined end.

In speaking the minister generally omitted the h's when they began a word—and said them before an open vowel where they were not placed—
Thus instead of "an hearing ear" he said
"an earing hear."
—In praying for the Queen—he talked thus "during her reign the hart of war might be unknown—that the people might all live in peace and that God would give them an art to praise him."

For inheritance	—ineritance
" his	—is
" high priest	—igh priest
" forever	—for hever
" Israel of old	—Israel of hold
" see with one eye	—see with one high
" look at them	—look hat them
" their actions	—their hactions
" I have sinned	—Hi have sinned etc. etc.

In the evening at 6 I went to "Zion Chapel" and heard an admirable Sermon from Rev. Mr. Leifchild[1] of Craven Chapel, London—from the Text Matt. 12.35 "A good man, out of the good treasure of the heart, bringeth forth good things: and an evil man, out of the evil treasure, bringeth forth evil things." It was an intellectual, experimental and searching Sermon—doubtless carried many to enquire into the nature of the fruit they were bringing forth.

A Lady was next to me, in the next pew who had a fine voice and sang well. She appeared to sing from the heart, and no doubt was a pious woman. I wanted to speak to her after the service—but propriety seemed to forbid.

The Singing at St. Mary's this morning was nothing—two or three psalms—with full organ—without choir and congregation not heard.

At Zion Chapel and at the Baptist it was of a similar character, very different from St. Mary's—but at Zion Chapel much better than at Baptist.

Rippon's tune Book appears to be about the Standard—there is not the least merit in the music—and the performance is barbarous. The hymns were in both places given out by the Clerk and not by the Minister—and the verses were each read separately—or rather whined out in a sing song kind of voice before singing. ~~~~~~~

Home and to bed at 9. ~~~~~~~ No appetite all day—in other respects feel well.

Monday Sep. 4. 1837

In the morning early went out—got my coat mended—purchased some prints—and went up the "Shaft." At 10 o'clock left Dover in the Coach for London where after a pleasant days ride I arrived at 7½ o'clock evening. Mr. and Mrs. Webb had kept their room for me, and I was received very cordially by them which at once provided me with a home. I rejoiced to be back to London again. My face is now turned toward home. God has mercifully guided me thus far—may he still preserve me and direct my steps. After tea I gave Mr. and Mrs. Webb some account of my tour and went to bed at 11.

Tuesday Sep: 5. 1837

London

Immediately after breakfast, I went to Messrs. Barings where I found (to my great joy) a letter from Mrs. Mason dated July 21st. Went to Messrs. Lee Coates & Co. and wrote to Mrs. M and also to Daniel (now at Medfield) to go by packet of 8th.

Called at Mr. Novello's.

Dined at 5.

At 6 called in at a Church where there was Service.

At 8 went to rehearsal of St. Paul at Exeter Hall—the Author Mendelssohn was present. I did not much enjoy it, and left before it was over—home and in bed at 10.

Wednesday Sep: 6. 1837

London

This morning wrote to the Choir—18th letter directed to Harriet A. Loving.

Sealed letters to Mrs. M and D. and carried them all to Messrs. Lee Coates & Co. to go by packet of 8th.

Afterwards went to Surrey Zoological Gardens with Mrs. Webb. The collection of animals and birds not so good I should think as at Regent Park. (Dined at Mr. Webb's.[)] ~~~~~~~

On coming home I found letters brought by packet of 8th Aug: from Mrs. Mason, Daniel and Lowell and from Mr. Webb.

Called on Mr. Banister but he was not at home.

Thursday Sep: 7. 1837 ~~~~~~~
Called to see Mr. Neukomm but ascertained that he is out of town.

Purchased Drawers, Stockings, Handkerchiefs, and some few other things.

Went to the <u>Colosseum</u>
  Panorama of London
  Optical Gallery
  Marine Grotto or Cavern
  Swiss Cottage
  Interior of a Silver Mine
The ascending and descending room is a curiosity—by which the visitor is raised or lowered 55 feet in one minute by Steam power.

Visited Diorama
  —The Basilica of St. Paul[2]
  The Village of Alagra
          Piedmont
Same principal as the Diorama in Paris.

Dined at common dining rooms 1/6 [probably cost of dinner]. Afterwards went with Mr. and Mrs. Webb to see the eruption of Vesuvius at Surry [Surrey] Gardens.[3]

Friday 8th. Sep. 1837
Spent the Morning in writing a letter to Daniel to go by Packet of 10th from London—and also in writing an account of Freiburg organ for "the Musical World" [7, no. 80 (September 22, 1837): 19–21].

Afterwards dined at Mr. Novello's at 8 o'clock and was there introduced to <u>Dragonetti</u>.

Evening attended a rehearsal of St. Paul at Exeter Hall—and was introduced to the author Felix Mendelssohn Bartholdy.

On my return home found a letter from Mr. M. Lord—Boston.
    Bed 10.

Saturday 9th Sep. 1837
In the morning called at Mr. Novello's—business of the Juvenile Book etc.

Afterwards went to Bonner St. and purchased some of Dr. Malan's books, and other little religious works.

Called at Mr. Purday's music Publisher Holborn—introduced by Dr. Carnaby—and also to Mr. Eager from Edinburg—who is much interested in educational Music. Spoke of Pestalozzian Methods and manual and explained it to him—spent 2 hours with him. He was much pleased and wishes to introduce it. He gave me report of a female school etc.

Went with Mr. Eager and Mr. [   ] to hear the Apollinicon.[4]

Called on Lee Coates & Co.—also on Mr. Slade (just returned from America)—Dined—made some other calls and purchases, and returned home—in bed at 9.

Sunday 10th Sep. 1837
21st Sunday from Boston. ~~~~~~~

This morning went to the Moravian Chapel, Fetterlane Nevils Court, Fleet St. The Singing was by the congregation and very devotional. In some parts of the Liturgy the Minister sang the prayers and the congregation responded. It had a good effect—I like a liturgy to some extent, and should be glad to attend church where one is used.

Sermon Ps. 28.9

The Sermon was a plain exposition of the text.

Afterwards went over to Mr. C. Sharp's—No. 7 Ch. yd. row—Newington Bath—dined with them and attended Church.

A young minister—from Acts. 16. 30 and 31
"What shall I do to be saved?
Believe on the Lord J.C. and thou shalt be saved."

1. The question—Its importance—related to the eternal happiness or misery of the soul.

2.—It evidences a conviction of Sin—earnestness—no one can be half engaged in religion—it requires the whole heart.

3.—Betrays great ignorance

2 Answer. Faith—what is it? The work of the Spirit upon the heart—
It is not a general belief that Christ came to Save Sinners, but that he came to Save one—offers Salvation unto me and the answer is the same to every one—believe and thou shalt be saved.

Faith includes full belief in the word of God, and in the plan of Salvation—a belief in the gospel or acceptance of its doctrines into the heart.

One Doctrine seems to be more important than any other viz: divinity of Christ. His deity gave dignity to his sufferings. Had not C. offered up an infinite sacrifice our Sins are so great that we might have despaired—but the divinity of Ch. renders the atonement sufficient—the greatest sinner can rely etc.

Conclusion.

Sometime or other this question will be asked by every person—and in deep earnest too.

Took tea at Mr. Sharps—gave them some account of my tour etc.—home at 8. ~~~~~~~

Monday 11th Sep. 1837
Mr. Sharp called on me in the morning, and I went with him to the National Gallery—pictures—see catalogue. ~~~~~~~

Went also to Mr. [Robert] Mott's (manufacturer of Piano Forte's) Saw Piano's and also an instrument called—[   ]—power of retaining sound—[5]

To Baring Brothers—afterwards called and bought a Filtera[6]—suitors[?] coat and sundry small things for family.

Guild hall—

Dined with Mr. Sharp at 2 (at Dining rooms) and at 3 went to Steam Boat where we met Mrs. Sharp, and from thence by boat to Greenwich (down the river)—observatory—Park—Hospital for seamen.

Went over the buildings—galery of pictures—saw and conversed with a man named Wilhain Pettigrew who was a drummer at the Battle of Bunker's Hill June 17, 1775 and also at the previous battle of Lexington in April.

Saw and conversed with Joseph Kenter who was on board the Frigate Shannon when she captured Chesapeake off Boston—he was one who boarded the Chesapeake (time of Lawrence's death.) ~~~~~~~

Tuesday 12th. Sep. 1837
In the morning went and purchased cloak for Mrs. M—corner of Oxford and Regent St.

Went to Strand and attended to packing filter. To Baring & Brothers—Lee Coates & Co.

Met Mrs. King of Georgia.

Attend to various things preparatory to leaving London.

Dined with Mr. Banister. Evening from 7 to 11 heard the Oratorio of St. Paul—at Exeter Hall about 500 performers.

I was not much interested. There is too much narrative—and recitative—Choruses are good—some magnificent.

Wednesday 13. Sep. 1837
Spent the morning untill 2—in packing trunks—at 2 went to Lee Coates & Co. and left with them to be forwarded to Liverpool five packages as follows:

1 Leather Portmenteau—Trunk—Boston made
1 Hair trunk—Swiss made in Zurich
1 Paper Covered—Ladies packing case—square
1 Box—a packing case containing Filter £ = 2.2.0
1 Band Box—with Hat. To be forwarded to Baring Brothers & Co. Liverpool and by them to be retained for me.

Called at Messrs. Barings and took letter of Credit on Liverpool for £150.00.

Finished letters for Choir and for Lowell and William to go by packet of 16th—and left them at Lee C & Co.

On my way home purchased gloves, poplins for dresses etc.—also a bible for Mr. Webb.

Called at Mr. Novello's and bid them good bye.

Home at 7—Bed 9. ~~~~~~~

Thursday Sep. 14 1837

This morning at 10 o'clock I left London for Oxford. Having a desire to see Windsor Castle I left London in the Windsor Coach—having previously taken my passage and paid my fare in the Oxford Coach 12/ and agreed with them to take me up, at Slough—through which they pass, and which is two miles from Windsor. I left my luggage—trunk and Carpet Bag for Mr. Webb to send by the Oxford Coach (The Defiance). ~~~~~~~

On our way to Windsor We met the Queen—She was in a carriage drawn by four horses and an attendant carriage or two behind. The carriage was open—our coach turned out a little and stopped for her to pass—they were not driving very fast, and as they passed us the Queen looked directly towards us, so that I had a fine view of her. She is very pretty—was dressed very plain—white bonnet—hair separated in front and wound each side—not curled—looked very modest and dignified.

Arriving in Windsor I went over such parts of the Castle as are open to the public—say State rooms—Tower—Terrace and Chapel.

Called at a Book store and purchased prints of Windsor Castle.

Took a "fly" (one horse carriage) for Slough (2 miles) having agreed to pay what I considered a very high charge viz 4/. In addition to this however, I was obliged to pay tolls 1/ on the way—and when I got to Slough the Coachman insisted on my giving him something for his labor—this I refused—as I had already paid as much for these 2 miles as I did from London (20 miles). He staid by me a long time—untill I refused to converse or speak any more to him. When after waiting some time he left me saying "well sir I wish you no harm only I hope you will break your neck when you start from here."

I took dinner at Slough and at 4 the Coach (Defiance) came along. I enquired for my luggage but the coachman said he could not look for it then but when he came to the next port 5 or 6 miles ahead he would look. I got up and at the end of 5 or 6 miles ascertained that my things were not there. As there happened to be a coach there at the time for London—I got upon that and returned to London (25 miles) to look for them. Arrived at 8—Mr. Webb had left them according to promise—we went directly to coach office and found that my things had been sent by another coach. The mail was just about to start—so I got in and started immediately again for Oxford—where I arrived at ½ past 2 o'clock. Went to the Mitre Hotel where I found a good bed, and my luggage was brought to me in the morning.

On my way back from Slough to London I again met the Queen, returning from London, and had another view of her.

Oxford Sep: 15. 1837   ~~~~~~~
Rose at 10 o'clock and breakfasted. Took a guide and spent the forenoon in walking about to see this city of Colleges—for places seen etc. etc. see pencil marks in the Oxford Guide.

I expected to go this afternoon to Birmingham but the coaches were all full and I am obliged to wait till tomorrow morning.

Spent an hour or two in the afternoon writing to Mrs. M. and to Choir. ~~~~~~~
Walked about the City—Tea—bed ½ past 8. ~~~~~~~

Birmingham Sep. 16. 1837
Left Oxford at 8 o'clock. I had taken my passage on the outside—but just before starting it began to sprinkle a little and there being one inside seat left I exchanged. I had no sooner taken the inside seat than there was another application for it, so that had I been a minute or two later I would have lost it. It rained steadily much of the way, and was a cold and disagreeable day.

In the coach were three Ladies—two of whom were very sociable and intelligent.

Arrived at Birmingham at ½ past 3. I went immediately in pursuit of Mr. Sturge to whom I had written from Geneva to procure a room for me. I found that Mr. Sturge from a principle of conscience had declined acting but had handed over my letter to another person to whom he gave me a letter—on him I called and found that he had taken lodgings for me for a week for which I was to give three guineas or £ = 3.3.0—an enormous price indeed—but such high charges I found are made here on the festival week. The hotels charge from 15/ to 21/ for a bed. I went and took possession of my room at the house of Mr. Shearman,
Surgeon
Corner of Lionel Street
Newhall Street.
On my way here I passed through Stratford upon Avon and saw the house in which Shakespeare was born.

When in Slough day before yesterday I saw the home where the

astronomer <u>Herschel</u> lived—his observatory is still standing in the yard.
~~~~~~~

    Sunday Sep: 17. 1837—Birmingham
    22nd. Sunday from Boston
Last evening I found that I had taken Cold—bathed my feet in hot water
and went early to bed—did not sleep very well—but felt better this morn-
ing. Mr. Sturge called on me. At ½ past 10 went with Dr. Shearman to
Mr. James' church. I have long known Mr. J. as the author of Sunday School
Teachers guide and was anxious to meet him. Service commenced by his
reading 100th ps.—next Prayer—next Singing—then Sermon—Singing—
Lords prayer—Benediction.

    The singing was Congregational—they have an Organ and there was
something of a Choir of Boys who led in the Soprano. The singing was
devotional. Sermon from 1. Cor. 15.25. For he must reign etc.

    It was on the subject of the millennium. The Sermon was good and
practiced—though from the nature of the subject it did not relate so much
to personal religion as no doubt his preaching commonly does.

    Previous to his sermon he related the circumstance of a Lady having
lost her purse with £22. in it at the chapel last Lord's day evening—and
cautioned his congregation to beware of the pick pockets etc. who come
amongst them.

    In the afternoon, not feeling very well, I did not go out, but in the
evening at ½ past 6 I went again to Mr. James' and heard one of the best
Sermons that ever I heard—

    Matt. 5.7—Blessed are the merciful etc.
        1. Nature of mercy generally
        2.——of Christian mercy
        3. The vast importance to the Christian
(1)—a disposition to <u>pity</u> and a disposition to <u>pardon</u>. It is a very common
mistake to suppose that mercy is a mere disposition to pity. Mercy includes
forgiveness of injuries—a man is not merciful who is not also forgiving.
It consists not in mere feeling or sympathy but in efforts—doing something
for others—etc.
(2) Christian mercy supposes true Christian experience. It is exercised
according to the rules laid down in word of God and the examples found
there.
It is not mere instinct—but principle—The Christian does good to his fellow
men, not only on their account, but because in doing so he <u>serves God</u>.
It includes efforts for the soul as well as body. Many are ready to relieve
the wants of body who are not willing to contribute to send the gospel
to the ignorant etc. Such are not merciful.

(3) Man is the only being so far as we know who receives and dispenses mercy—and that only while <u>here</u>—when we leave this world we cease to receive or to exercise mercy.

Mercy should be our business—calling—vocation—Be merciful now—if we die—mercy leaves us forever.

   Very eloquent and affecting.

One of the loveliest attributes of God.

Good works are excluded from the justification of a Sinner by St. Paul— but include in the justification of a believer by Jesus.

Key of C. Soprano $\frac{3}{2}$ 5|5 - 8|8 7 8|11 10 9| - 10|| 5|5 - 5|5 10 8|8 7|| 9|8 - 7|
8 - 9|10 11 10|10 9|| 10|6 - 9|7 - 7|8||⁷

The above tune was sung at Mr. James' this evening. ~~~~~~~

  Monday Sep: 18. 1837 ====

In the morning called on Mr. Vaughan and presented a letter from Mr. Greatorex of London. Went with Mr. V. and his daughter to the rehearsal, preparatory to Music Festival.

  For Band, Singers etc. see books of performance.

  The Ascension by Neukomm and

  St. Paul by Mendelssohn were rehearsed

Commenced at 11 and closed at ½ past 5 o'clock.

  I do not know that I was ever fully satisfied with the power of a chorus before—but here was enough. There was another rehearsal in the evening but I did not attend.

  Saw today Mr. Neukomm
     Mr. Mendelssohn
     Mr. Ayrton
     Mr. Vaughan
     Miss Novello (Clara)
     Mrs. Vaughan
     Mr. Hogart [George Hogarth] Author of a history of Music introduced by Mr. Ashton.

  Tuesday 19th. Sep. 1837

Attended morning performance

  11 to 3 o'clock—see Bill. ~~~~~~~ Dined at 4—afterwards took a walk—bought some medals—Evening performance from 8 to 11½—See Bill—

  In bed at 12 very much fatigued. ~~~~~~~ Introduced to Rev: Mr. [John] Webb author to the words of Oratorio of David.

Wednesday 20 Sep. 1837.
This morning at 11—St. Paul, and a selection afterwards—out at 3.
~~~~~~~
In the evening there was no concert but an opera which I did not
attend. ~~~~~~~

Thursday 21st. Sep. 1837
This morning at 11 o'clock (from 11 to 3) was The Messiah. I thought I
knew the Messiah before but it surpassed all I ever imagined. I desire to
be thankful for its moral power which I felt, and which I wish might ever
continue—I hope sometime or other to try and express by writing the feelings of the morning—but at present I cannot do it.[8] ~~~~~~~
Evening—from 8 to 12 Concert.
Mrs. Shearman came in at the end of first part. ~~~~~~~
============ Family Prayers.
~~~~~~~

Friday 22 Sep: 1837 ~~~~~~~
This morning heard "The triumph of Faith"—Oratorio by Hauer—(not
good.)
Mr. Banister and his Brother dined with me at Mr. Shearman's—
John Shearman
Surgeon.
Left Birmingham at ½ past 4—Rail Road—arrived at Liverpool at 11
o'clock.

Saturday 23rd. Sep. 1837
Liverpool
This morning I find myself at the same Hotel at which I stopped when
I first arrived in Liverpool—The Queen's [emended from "King's"] (name
changed) Castle Street. What cause of gratitude to him who has conducted
me safe through my journey for upwards of four months past and has
brought me safe to this place again.
[END OF JOURNAL TWO]

[JOURNAL THREE]

Liverpool 23rd. Sep. 1837
This morning called at Baring Brothers & Co. and found that my packages
from London have not arrived—they were to have been here last week.
Wrote to Messrs L. C. & Co. and also to Mr. Richard Webb on the
subject. Requested L. C. & Co. to write to Baring Brothers & Co., Liverpool and Mr. Webb to write to me directed to their care.

Called on Mr. Humberston (Letter from Lambert & Slade) but I did not find him in. His partner sent a young man with me to find the Virginian—I went on board and went into my room—and thought how goodness of God had followed me from the time I left the Ship. The 2nd Mate (now promoted to 1st) remembered me, also the Stewards—I feel now a strong inclination to go home direct, and omit Scotland and Ireland. Captain Harris is now in the Virginian.

Took my passage for Dublin—but several hours after I went to the office and altered it to Monday so as to avoid embarking on the Sabbath. The boat does not arrive in Dublin untill 6 or 7 o'clock in the morning. I once before tried this and arrived at Dresden on Sunday morning but my conscience scolded so hard, I cannot do it again—though I have several times lost 24 or 48 hours in consequence of it. But if we make any sacrifice to conscience we are sure to be doubly repaid in some other way.

Dined at the Hotel "Queen's Arms"—and afterwards walked about an hour or two—and bought some small things for children.

Sunday 24th Sep: 1837
Liverpool.
23rd Sunday from Boston.
This morning I went to Great George Street Chapel to hear Dr. Raffles.[9]

He preached from Job 28:12 "But where shall wisdom be found? and where is the place of understanding?"

After a very admirable introduction in which he clearly showed that it was not in human Knowledge, Science, or philosophy, he preceded to enquire:

1. What is true wisdom and where does it consist?

Answer. In the fear of the Lord, and in departure from Sin.
The fear of the Lord—this is wisdom indeed—the alpha and omega—the beginning and end of wisdom. Without this every thing else is insufficient, he who has this is wise, and whatever other wisdom a man may have, if he be destitute of this he shall at last be confessed a fool. This fear is compatible with love—is the offspring of it—it is not the fear of a culprit, a criminal, a slave, but of a child. Its origin is in the knowledge of God—of God in all his excellence, kindness, beauty, as revealed in his word—as his truth, rectitude, justice as well as his mercy, love, compassion. To fear God thus we must be reconciled to him—it implies a new heart—submission—regeneration.

2. Where is this wisdom to be found? This has been already in part anticipated—not in human science, or philosophy, though if this be taught aright it will aid us in our researches. It is to be found in the knowledge of its great Author—in Jesus Christ, God manifest in the flesh—who is the Source of all excellency and knowledge.

This true wisdom is incompatible with Sin—they cannot dwell together etc.

Self examination—Have we this wisdom.

Singing by whole Congregation but mostly inferior to that of Mr. James' Chapel in Birmingham. Here there is no organ—the tunes are not appropriate to congregational singing—they are of the Rippon kind. One was nearly thus:—Key of G.

Between 2 and 3 I went out and happened to stop at a <u>welch</u> chapel— but as the Service was in an unknown tongue I did not remain. ~~~~~~~ From my window I hear a chime of Bells thus

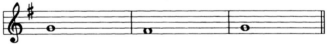

etc. always the same.

At 3 went to [   ] church—remained only through the Service and not to the Sermon.

A Choir of one Female and four male voices.—Chanting poor.

Evening at ½ past 6 went to the chapel of the school for the blind. Here the church service is beautifully performed—the responses are all done in the most exact and efficient manner by the blind, after the manner of Cathedral Service—i.e. in a musical

tone = thus

Minister: Glory be to the Father, etc.

Response: As it was   A   -   men
                    etc.

The Psalms for the day were finely chanted—and the common chants were done promptly, and all as one, in the most exact time.

I never heard chanting so exact before.

Kent's anthem "Blessed be thou Lord God of Israel"[11] was also sung. The Solo's were not so well as Choruses, and manifested a want of taste and cultivation—indeed I was surprised that they should be so coarse—a shake was two of three times attempted.

Sermon Rom. 10.10

"For with the heart man believeth etc."

The Faith which he described seemed to me to be only one aspect of the understanding—the heart seemed to be mostly omitted.

Home ½ past 8. Bed 9.

Monday 25 Sep. 1837

I have cold in my head, and what I suppose to be rheumatic pain in my left Jaw—and a little headache constantly—but good appetite.

This morning packed up a box of Gingerbread and some little toy things for Children which I sent to the care of Mr. Palmer by ship Caravan to sail for Boston on 27th.

Nothing yet from my luggage. There is danger that it may be lost—it would be a heavy loss indeed—more so than the mere amount of cost, because many things are there for Mrs. M. and the Children—indeed all that I have bought for them—also most all my own clothes etc. I hope to hear by mail tomorrow from Mr. Coates. My present expectation is that I shall not go to Dublin, and Edinburg as I had expected—but if I recover my trunks I may, perhaps, go.

Spent some time in Tract Depository—purchased several little books—some of the Epistles separate etc.

Feeling so unwell I came home and had a fire in my room. Took out of my trunk all my things—repacked etc.

Wrote a letter to Choir to go by 1st Oct. packet etc. etc.

Memorandum: Since I have always found it so good to be alone—to be separated from worldly business, since I have been on my journey shall I not have decision enough to take some time when I get home for religious purposes—I mean occasionally a day—when if necessary I can go out of Town—take a room and be entirely to myself? ~~~~~~~

In the evening I went to a Concert by Ole Bull.

Nothing good but his playing and a Quartetto by Mozart.[12]
~~~~~~~

Tuesday 26th Sep 1837

Liverpool

This morning I feel much better than yesterday—my cold appears to be leaving me. Thus the goodness of God follows me from day to day.

Received at letter from Mr. Webb, London, saying that there had been a mistake about my luggage but that it is now on the way to Liverpool. I wrote to Mr. W. on Saturday and requested him to attend to it.

Went down to the Ships Virginian and Oxford—hesitating in which to take my passage.

Purchased Spoons, Forks etc. also Merino cloth for Mothers and wife—also Silk dress for the latter—also cloth for Henry and William clothes and for Lowell and Daniel pantaloons.

Dined at ½ past 4—two American Gentlemen were at the next table— one from Baltimore and one from N. Orleans.

Evening went down again to vessels—and pretty much decided to give up Scotland and go in Oxford.

Purchased glass ornaments. Saw to day Mr. Humberston who was very polite and attentive.

Bed at 9. ~~~~~~~

Wednesday 27. Sep. 1837
This morning untill 1 o'clock was spent in walking about the City and in making a few purchases—Pictures of Birds and Beasts etc. for Children— a pair of Ship Boats for myself.

In the afternoon now—went to Arne's music Store and got a parcel of music to look over.

Fire in my room. Went several times in the course of the day to Baring Brothers & Co. but can learn nothing of my things.

Wrote by Caravan for Boston to Choir and also to Henry—with pro-files—informing of my intention to sail in Oxford or Virginian 1st. or 8th. of October.

Bed at ½ past 8.

Thursday 28 Sep. 1837
Last night, not feeling very well, I took a pill "Lathburg's Antibilious." It makes me sick today.

Carried out forks and spoons to have them marked. Bought a few Books.

Called at Messrs. Barings but can get no intelligence from my luggage— So that now I shall not have an opportunity of going to York.

Afternoon was in my chamber most of the time reading.

Evening went to Dr. Raffles Lecture. He preached to a small congrega-tion from Psalm 71:16

"I will go in the strength of the Lord God; I will make mention of thy righteousness, even of thine only."

Friday, 29th September 1837
Another day has past in waiting for my luggage in vain.

Walked about, stopped in at book stores, read some and passed away the day.

It is hard work to be idle . . . were I in London I could find enough to do, but here there is but little to see and anxiety of this constant and protracted waiting unfits me for seeing that little.

Evening went to Mad: Pasta's Concert—but notwithstanding the excellence of the music I only remained untill it was half over. ~~~~~~~
~~~~~~~

Saturday 30 Sep. 1837
This has been a day of anxiety to me.

On enquiring I found that I cannot expect my luggage here untill Tuesday next—and the Oxford Sails tomorrow—the question was shall I wait—or shall I go without my things? I decided after reflection and looking for wisdom to guide me aright to go—many things were then to be bought—Shirts—drawers—Stockings—etc. etc. All of which things I had provided myself within London. I made all my purchases—took my passage—wrote some letters—bought trunks and packed my things, and am now at ½ past 8 ready—to leave England.

I cannot omit to notice the unspeakable goodness of God to me in a multitude of ways since I left home—May his goodness make its suitable impression on my heart and future life—I now commit myself to the protection and guidance of Him who is the God of all his Children—the confidence of all the ends of the earth and of them that are afar off upon the Sea. May he preserve me during my voyage and bring me to my home in safety. ~~~~~~~

Finished packing etc. at ½ past 10. ~~~~~~~

Sunday morning Oct: 1. 1837
Liverpool
Queen's Arms No. 77.
The morning has arrived when I expect to embark for home. ~~~~~~~

It rains a little, and it may be doubtful whether we get away.

Last evening I received a letter from Mr. Hutchinson in behalf of the Choir.

The Lord be my refuge and my trust—my expectation is from him—may he cause me to go and meet my family and friends in peace and safety.

7

The Voyage to America

After being in Europe for four months, two weeks and two days, Mason departed for America. He was obviously tired and anxious to get home. Mason's voyage from New York to Liverpool had taken nineteen days, a good time for 1837. His return voyage took twenty-seven days, but must have seemed far longer, less because of the elements than because of the passengers. Other writers who have left accounts of ocean voyages speak of the camaraderie that the restricted confines and the forced idleness of these packets foster. This clearly worked against Mason on his return voyage, as he found himself thrown into close proximity with a group of passengers of whose conduct he thoroughly disapproved. During the voyage Mason's seasickness and general physical misery seem to be in direct relation to the amount of gambling, drinking and carousing that occurred on board.

Mason's Diary

Ship Oxford Sunday
Oct. 1. 1837

Came on board at ½ past 10. ~~~~~~~ Left the wharf at a few minutes past 12. Just before we left the wharf two of the men were thrown overboard. Ropes were handed, and they were soon on board again. One of the men, not one of those who fell over, soon after did something displeasing to the mate who immediately sprung upon him, threw him down, beat him, and kicked him with great severity. Hard and wicked is a Sailor's life. Hard because wicked.

At ¼ before one we passed the light and entered the channel.

The Sun shines and it is quite warm for the season.

I find that I have for my roommate Mr. Balfour, (Scott and Balfour) of Savannah. He knew me immediately, but I did not remember him untill he told me his name.

At about time that I commenced my voyage (allowing for difference of time) the Sunday School begins in Bowdoin Street.

When during my journey I have arrived at any place, or taken any new step, one of my first thoughts has been "How glad I should be if my wife knew now where I am" but now when I commence my voyage I hardly know whether I should prefer to have her know or not—thinking that if She did not know some anxiety might be saved.

What a relief to the mind to get away—there is now nothing to press upon it—and it is at liberty to go to this subject or to that, and to dwell comparatively without interruptions wherever the will may lead.

The Oxford is a larger Ship and more convenient cabins than the Virginian—but I shall not have the pleasure of a room entirely to myself as I had on my outward passage. ~~~~~~~

Dined at 7 o'clock—soon after I went to bed, but spent a restless night—feverish—pain in bowels, flatulent—costive—dreaming—waking—sleeping but little. Ship Oxford, Capt. Rathbone.

Monday 2nd. Oct. 1837
Rose at 6 and took a Seidlet Powder—which operated at 9 and relieved me considerably.

Took some homony and tea for breakfast. At Breakfast the Captain told us of his having run into a Ship on his outward voyage—In the night—very dark—both Ships were injured but principally the other which was full of German emigrants. In a moment they all came on board the Oxford—one woman in passing let her infant child drop into the Sea between the ships. The Oxford remained with the other vessel untill morning, when finding it safe to depart they did so.

We are now sailing down the St. George's channel with fair wind—we go out the northern passage—not by Cape Cleary [ill.] ½ past 12. Were it not that my appetite continues I should think myself sick. But at lunch I have just relished two baked potatoes and a piece of boiled mutton cold—felt quite hungry, but eat only a little.

Ireland is now south and Scotland north of us. Wind fair but light.

Friday morning 6th Oct. 1837
5th day out.
Tuesday, Wednesday and Thursday were spent in my berth—being quite sea-sick—more so, I think, than when I came out.

We got out of the channel on Monday night, and have had most of the time since a head wind, sometimes blowing hard, and a heavy sea. While on my berth these three days I have thought much of home—of wife, children, parents and friends, and of the great pleasure I hope to experience in meeting them again. This morning I feel much better—have taken some breakfast—but can hardly expect entire relief from sea-sickness so soon.

Passengers

Mr. David Sears, Boston.

Mr. Welsh, of Boston though not much there for 5 or 6 years past.

Maj. [David Emanuel] Twiggs of Georgia near Augusta

Col (James) [James Henry] Hammond, member of Congress from South Carolina.

Saturday 7th. Oct.

6th day out.

Stormy wind all night and tolerably fair—quite rough—rainy and squally this morning.

I was most of the time in my berth yesterday—but little inclination for food, and the little I took distressed me—even arrow root lay heavy upon my stomach.

This morning feel better, and have been composing simple chants while in my berth.[1]

Sunday 8th Oct. 1837

Second Sunday on board.

25th Sunday from Boston. We have all the time a rough sea and much motion.

I was in my berth almost all the day yesterday.

I am not sick at my stomach—but have no appetite, and what little I take, even arrow root, hurts me.

The Sabbath—this day may I be enabled to fix my mind upon the great things of religion, and although far removed from the common privileges of the day, may it be a day blessed to my soul.

Monday 9th Oct.

Eight days out.

Yesterday at dinner (5 o'clock) I relished my food for the first time for a week, and it did not hurt me, so I hope I am getting over sea-sickness.

To day we have light winds with rain—Southerly and tolerably fair.

Last evening some of the passengers played cards in the cabin, opposite to my state room, and much to my annoyance. We seem to have a set of passengers who have not the fear of God before them. It is misery to be confined in a Ship with such companions.

Soon after writing the above the wind came ahead—it has rained too, most of the day, and although I am better, I still feel sea-sick effects. Cold clammy feet trouble me much, and with them comes unpleasant feeling—sickness etc.

When I get into my berth and get my feet quite warm I feel much better and am relieved of sickness at stomach. I enjoy myself much while lying in my berth thinking of home etc.

Had some pleasant conversation with Mr. Sears on the subject of music as a common branch of education. He is much in favor of it.

Tuesday 10th. Oct. 1837
9 days out, at 12 o'clock.

Last evening at about 6 or 7 o'clock, the wind commenced blowing violently from the westward. Its force increased untill 12, and it continued through most of the night. The motion was great, the ship labored and creaked and rolled from one side to the other, as if in distress. The Captain was very briefly on deck. Amidst the terrific noise of the raging wind, as it passed through the rigging of the ship, his voice was heard giving orders; the response of the sailors with their "yo heave ho" mingled with the fearful howlings of the tempestuous elements. The Sea was all in a fury—its waves rolled mountains high, and dashed with such tremendous violence against the sides of the vessel, as seemed to threaten sudden destruction to all. But notwithstanding the awful grandeur and sublimity of the scene,[2] there was a party of thoughtless, foolish and wicked young men in the cabin drinking, swearing, playing cards, and talking louder and louder with the increasing winds and rising waves seemingly alike indifferent to the scene around, and to Him who "layeth the beams of his chambers in the waters = who maketh the clouds his chariot = who walketh upon the wings of the wind:—who commandeth and the stormy winds arise, and left up the troubled waves; or at who word—The waves sink down in gentle peace,

And tempests cease to roar."

"They that go down to the sea in ships, do behold the wonderful works of God."

~~~~~~~ Half sick to day—without appetite. Wind moderate at nearly ahead. About one third of our passage we suppose we have made.

Wednesday 11th Oct. 1837

Yesterday at about 5 came on a severe gale—more so than that of the day before—but I was not well and did not go up to see it. Drinking and gambling untill 12 in the cabin last evening—one young man (a Mr. Wainwright) was so much intoxicated as to be obliged to be carried to bed. This morning took Seidlitz powder.

Pleasant morning and not very cold—walked the deck ½ an hour—wind nearly ahead. ~~~~~~~

Thursday 12th oct. 1837
Eleven days out.

5 o'clock P. M. Took medicine this morning (Rhubarb) and have been quite sick with it ever since.

The wind has been fair through the day (S.E.). It begins to rain a little. I saw the mate putting on thick boots, and asked him if he was preparing for a Storm—"Yes" said he "we are sure to have it, when the wind comes from this quarter, at this season of the year."

Last evening they had a dance on deck—to day as I lie in my birth I heard them getting up a lottery.

Friday 13th. Oct. 1837
Twelve days out.

I was quite sick all day yesterday—this morning feel much better. The storm prophesied by the mate did not come with much severity—we had rather a smooth night—with fair wind S.E. This morning there was a sudden change of wind to N.N.W. The Captain likes this—says it is more likely to continue and indicates good weather. Ten days good wind would now carry us in.

Mr. Balfour composed a tune which I wrote down for him and put the parts to it.

There was much gambling going on in the ship yesterday. They made up purses and then raffled or cast dice for it.

Saturday 14th Oct. 1837
Thirteen days at sea.

I felt much better yesterday all day—had an appetite and perhaps indulged it rather too freely—as I do not feel very bright to day.

Wind again from Southward—but we are able nearly to lay our course. In the morning a Sail was seen at a distance.

When the wind is so near ahead, or when the ship sails so close to the wind, we have more motion, and it is also colder.

Last evening there was a total eclipse of the moon which we all had a fine view of from deck.

Sunday 15th. Oct. 1837
Fourteenth day out.
Third Sunday on Board
Twenty sixth Sunday from Boston.

Rough and head wind yesterday—I was so sick as to keep my berth most of the day. This morning we have a fair wind (N.W.)—but quite light so that we make only 2 or 3 Knots an hour—it is a wet and rainy day.

It is pleasant to have the Sabbath return, even though confined in a Ship at sea, and with a company that seem to have no fear of God before their eyes. My soul, make thou the Lord thy portion—rest upon him as thy refuge, thy strength, thy hope, thy salvation—find thy joy—thy happiness in him, and seek his face evermore.

Monday 16th Oct. 1837
15 days out.
The wind was favorable most of the day yesterday—but I did not feel very bright—spent the day mostly in my berth.

This morning we have but little wind—though fair.

Through the day a light Southerly wind.

Picture of the Cabin in the Evening after Tea—say 9 o'clock. In the Ladies cabin, 4 or 5 Ladies talking, laughing etc. At the end of the table in Gentlemen's Cabin, a party playing cards—next three or four persons reading—next Chess playing—afterwards two more parties playing cards, with two or three persons walking about, looking on etc.

Tuesday 17. Oct. 1837
16 days on board.
Weather mild—light winds most of the time tolerably fair for us—making but little progress—but much more comfortable than gale, squall etc.

Slept quite well last night, and feel better to day than at any time on board.

The Captain plays a little very coarsely on the Violin—a Mr. Baker plays a little better, but still in a low and vulgar style. A Mr. Wainwright plays flute a little, and we have considerable of what is called Music on board—but such Music as is calculated to disgust any man of taste with the whole subject.

Wednesday 18. Oct. 1837
17 days at sea.
Wind came on to blow last night, and it made me quite sick—got up to day at 11 o'clock, but feel quite unwell. The motion is very uncomfortable. Have taken two roasted potatoes and two baked apples.

The Steward told me this morning that there was a death on board last night—a child 9 years of age from disentary—in the Steerage.

Some of the passengers did not go to bed untill after light this morning.

Drinking and gambling are constantly going on at night.

Thursday 19. Oct. 1837
18 days out.
Yesterday towards night it was very cold and there was rain and hail. I kept my berth almost all the day—not only on account of sickness but

by doing so I get rid of the disagreeable, noisy company. Last evening the Captain was playing on a Violin and singing low and vulgar songs.

Friday 20 Oct. 1837
19 days out.

Yesterday we had a strong head wind all the latter part of the day with much motion of the ship. I was so sick as to keep the berth—though I got up for Breakfast at 9 and for dinner at 4½ o'clock. Passengers playing cards, drinking etc. untill about 2 o'clock. This morning it is pleasant with a northerly wind fair enough for the ship to lay on her course.

Saturday 21st. Oct. 1837
20 days out.

Sick all day again yesterday—cold feet—heavy head-ache—want of appetite etc. Much motion all day.

After dinner I walked on deck ½ an hour, and then went to bed. Wind became fair, and continued so through the night. This morning we have fair, but light wind. We are in hope of reaching the Banks to day.

At 12 o'clock the Captain's observation showed us to be on the Banks—Sailing with a fair wind—9 knots per hour. Six days thus would carry us to N. Y.

Sunday 22nd. Oct. 1837
21 days out
4th Sunday on Board
27th Sunday from Boston

We have had a fine southerly wind ever since 12 o'clock yesterday, and have been sailing at an average of 10 knots per hour. The scene was beautiful last night on deck, as the ship passed through the waves so rapidly.

We passed several fishermen on the Banks.

After dinner yesterday was a terrible scene of drinking, loud talking, singing etc. after dinner. It is painful to be shut up with such people who offend by their low, sensual, beastly conduct, and who seem to have cast off entirely all fear of God. I have never been where I have seen such men act out themselves before. After tea cards and gambling were introduced. To day is the Sabbath—I do not feel quite as well as yesterday—there is more motion. My wife and friends will know that I am now on my voyage, but will not suppose me to be so near home. I hope we may be at N. Y. before another Sabbath. The Lord bless all who this day call upon him, and be the God not only of those who meet to pray and praise in Zion, but also of all them that are afar off on the sea.

Rainy weather—but not very cold. At ½ past 11 the wind came suddenly ahead, and continued so about an hour, when it changed back again.

I do not feel well to day.

Monday 23rd. Oct. 1837
22nd. day out.
We made but little progress yesterday after 12—it was mostly calm.

This morning we have a fair wind but not much of it. It is thick foggy and damp weather—I feel better than yesterday.

There is on board a Mr. Neill a young Clergyman, going out to Canada for a short time to preach to a vacant Congregation. He is very pleasant, but says but little. He is the only man on board so far as I know who has any feelings on religion similar to my own.

A Mr. Baker from Providence seems to be one of the worst men that ever I saw—forward to speak—forward to drink and to do whatever is wrong. From some remarks he has made I suppose him an open infidel. In conduct he is certainly one.

There is a Mr. Van Dam, a german, who appears to me to be about as bad as any man can be—profane—drinking—gambling etc.

Several other young men are not much better and these are led on by Mr. Baker and Mr. Van Dam in all iniquity. It is but little short of hell to a man who fears God, loves the Bible, and respects the Sabbath to be in such Company.

Tuesday 24th Oct. 1837
23rd day out.
12 o'clock. For the last 24 hours we have had a fine run—2 to 250 miles. Wind N.E. We are now hoping to get in this week. Not very well to day. 630 miles from N.Y.

Wednesday 25th. Oct. 1837
This morning finished reading Irddridge's Rise and progress[3]—I have not read it before for many years. The latter part is well worthy of a daily perusal—I desire to partake deeply its spirit.

This day it is 6 months since I parted with my wife and Daniel in N. Y. Blessed be the Lord who has followed me with his merciful protection and provision since that day, and has now brought the prospect of meeting the members of my family and friends again, so near.

12 o'clock. We have had an excellent run again for the last 24 hours, with a very smooth sea—the wind is still fair, and we are now about 470 miles from N. Y. We are exactly East of Boston say 300 miles.

"Elijah the Tishbite"[4] which I have been reading since I have been on board is an excellent work indeed.

I walked on deck at a quick pace from a little before 3 to ¼ past 4—so that I could not have gone less than about 4 miles.

Thursday 26th Oct 1837
25 days out.
Last night I was sick all night—food hurt me—sour stomach and flatulency.
12 o'clock. The wind has continued fair—we have had an excellent run for the last 24 hours and are now not more than about 280 miles from N. Y. and perhaps 200 from Boston. Should we continue to be thus favored we may be in Saturday morning.

Friday 27th Oct. 1837
26 days out
12 o'clock. We are now not far from Block Island, and about 120 miles from N.Y. The wind is still fair for us, but there is not much of it, and there is a very thick fog. Hope to get in tomorrow.

A subscription was got up to day to present the captain with a diamond ring—I declined contributing for reasons arising out of a consideration of the nature of the case and of my own resources.

Finished reading "Elijah the Tishbite" from the German of F. W. Krummacher—a most excellent work which cannot be properly read but with great advantage to the Christian. I would recommend it to every one as calculated to deepen humility, strengthen faith, and brighten and animate the hope of future happiness. ~~~~~~~

At ½ past 3 wind came up from nearly ahead—so that the Ship could not quite lay her course—the change produced many long faces.

Saturday 28. Oct. 1837
27 days out.
Soon after the change of wind yesterday it became again more favorable, and at 9 o'clock a Light was seen on Fire island. At ½ past 11 the light at Sandy Hook was seen. Our Ship hoisted signals and fired guns for a Pilot—at ½ past 12 a Pilot came on board—the Ship then "lay too" untill 5 or 6 this morning—when she commenced beating in—the wind being ahead. Signal was also made for a Steam Boat and at ½ past 9 a Steamer came along side from N.Y. to tow us in.

New York Sunday 29th. Oct. 1837
28th. Sunday from Boston.
Arrived at the Clinton Hotel at ½ past 5 last evening. Mr. Neill came with me and took lodgings at the Hotel—also Mr. Saunders (a passenger).

After tea at 6—I went to Broome St. Church hoping to find the Choir together—thinking that if I could find Mr. Bartlett I might perhaps hear from home, not having any intelligence from there since August 1st.—but the church was shut. Called at the house where Mr. [Thomas] Hastings lived but another family were there who knew nothing of him. Called at Mr. Nevin's—he was out—but I ascertained that the Choir were at Mr. Doane's in Fourth Street. After a walk of upwards of an hour I found the place and Mr. B—who was recently in Boston—so that my object was accomplished and I heard that my family were well a few weeks since.

Returned to bed at 11 o'clock—Mr. Neill went with me.

Rose this morning at 7 much refreshed. Thus the goodness of God has brought me safe to my native land again, after a six months absence in safety, and health.

Morning—Mr. Neill went with me to Dr. [Thomas Harvey] Skinner's church [Mercer Street Presbyterian Church].

Heard a superior Sermon on the nature and evidences of regeneration. Went to Mr. Holbrook's and dined, and in afternoon to Mr. [William] Adams Church [Central Presbyterian Church]—Sermon from "I have a Message from God for you."

At tea at Mr. Holbrook's and afterwards to Dr. Skinner's and heard a lecture on the prophecies from Mr. Burk—played the organ. After lecture Dr. S. invited me to his house where we spent an hour, and I gave Mrs. S. an account of my interview with Mrs. Bauer at Chateau de Bloney.[5] Home at 11.

Monday 30th Oct. 1837
Called at Mr. Collyer's book store—on Mr. Eastman and delivered a letter from Mr. Woodbridge—on Holbrook & Nelson and found that my music had arrived—at the agent of Havre Packets and found that my things from Paris had also arrived—on Mr. Bartlett—on Mr. Nevins—on Mr. Schenk but could not find him—on Mr. [   ] who married Miss Colburn (Saxon?)

Dined at 3 at Hotel—½ past 4 called at Dr. Skinner's by appointment—afterwards on Mr. Hastings—delivered letter to Mr. Chubb from Mr. Banister of London.

Home at 10 o'clock.

Tuesday 31st. Oct. 1837
Called on Mr. Hastings—Dr. and Mrs. Buck—Col. Hammond—and Mr. [James Lang?] Hewitt.

Gave Holbrook & Nelson an order on Goodhue & Co. for my trunks expected by Virginian—to be forwarded to me at Boston.

At 4 left N.Y. in Steam Boat Massachusetts and arrived in Boston on

Wednesday 1 Nov. 1837 at 12 o'clock
All my family I found well—at ½ past 2 left Boston with Mrs. Mason for Medfield to see my Parents.

Thursday 2nd Nov. 1837
Returned to Boston at 6 o'clock P.M.

Friday Nov. 3 1837
Mr. Thomas and Mr. Harmon passengers in the Oxford called on me, and I spent all the morning with them—going about the City—to Charleston—Cambridge and Mr. Auburn. ~~~~~~~
Called on Mr. Webb and Mr. Eliot but found neither of them.
Evening—Preparatory Lecture Mr. Winslow preached.
The whole exercise was delightful to me.
Mr. John Slade and his brother called after Lecture.

Saturday 4. Nov. 1837
Spent most of forenoon with Mr. Webb. Spent the day in making calls and received from all a kind welcome home.
Evening meeting of the Choirs. On my entering the room the Choir rose and sang a hymn composed by Mr. Benson and set to music by Mr. Woodman—welcoming me home.

Sunday 5th. Nov. 1837
(Absent from Boston 28 Sundays.)
Mr. Winslow preached in the morning on the duty of making a profession of religion.
Afternoon Mr. Bliss—and Communion—
Evening Mr. Winslow on duties etc. of Females. ~~~~~~~

Monday 6 Nov. 1837
Spent most of the morning with Mr. Palmer in my room—Mr. David Sawyer—Quincy (Teacher of Music) called to enquire about a book for
Juvenile School etc.
[END OF DAILY ENTRIES IN JOURNAL THREE]

Abbreviations Used in Appendixes

Works frequently cited in the appendices have been assigned the following abbreviations. Full bibliographic information for these works can be found in Works Cited.

BMB   Brown, James D. and Stephen S. Stratton. *British Musical Biography: A Dictionary of Musical Artists, Authors and Composers, Born in Britain and Its Colonies.*

CAB   *The National Cyclopedia of American Biography.*

DAB   Johnson, Allen, et al. *Dictionary of American Biography.*

DNB   Stephen, Leslie and Sidney Lee, ed. *The Dictionary of National Biography.*

Grove I   Grove, George, ed. *A Dictionary of Music and Musicians.* First edition.

Mason B   Mason, Henry Lowell. "Lowell Mason: His Life and Works."

Mason P   "Lowell Mason Papers, MSS 33."

MGG   Blume, Frederich, ed. *Die Musik in Geschichte und Gegenwart.*

NG   Sadie, Stanley, ed. *The New Grove Dictionary of Music and Musicians.*

NUC   *The National Union Catalogue: Pre-1956 Imprints.*

Report I   *First Annual Report of the Boston Academy of Music.*

Report IX   *Ninth Annual Report of the Boston Academy of Music.*

Appendix 1

Flyleafs

The flyleafs contain considerable notes and jottings. They may be divided into several categories:

Information regarding itinerary and distances.
Lists of names.
Information regarding finances.
Memoranda Mason wrote to himself.
Music and ideas for the church service.
Jottings in the form of notes and reflections on readings.

Itinerary and Distances

Left London for Hamburg Wednesday Morning [June
    28] ½ past 6 and arrived at Hamburg Friday morning
    at 12   500

Left Hamburg at 8 Monday Evening and arrived at Berlin
    [July 5] ½ past 7 Wednesday morning
    4 days at H   170

Left Berlin Saturday morning at 8 and arrived at Dresden
    Sunday morning at 8. 4 [days at] B.   120

Left Dresden Wednesday [July 12] Evening at 8 and
    arrived at Leipsig on Thursday morning [July 13] at 7
    5 days D.   61 ¼

Left Leipsig on Thursday Evening [July 13] 7 o'clock
    and arrived at Frankfurt on Saturday morning [July 15]
    at 11. 1 day L.   215 ½

Left Frankfurt on Wednesday morning July 19 at 6
o'clock morning and arrived Mainz same day at 10
o'clock morning. 4 d a F.   21¾

Left Mainz on Friday morning 21. July at 5 and arrived
at Carlsruhe at ½ past 11 at night—by Steam Boat on
Rhine by water distance greater 2 days at M.   about 60

Left Carlsruhe on Tuesday morning [July 25] at 7
and arrived at Stuttgart (Wurtemberg) at ½ past 4.
3 days at C.   50

Left Stuttgart on Friday morning at 5 o'clock [July 28]
and arrived at St. Gallen—Switzerland on Saturday at
½ past 10. 2½ days at Stuttgart.   120

Left St. Gallen on Tuesday morning (7 o'clock) Aug. 1
and arrived at Zurick same Evening at 5. 3 days
St. Gallen   50

Left Zurich on Thursday morning 3rd. August at 6
o'clock and arrived at Berne at 9 o'clock evening   75

Left Berne at 12 o'clock on Saturday [August 5] and
arrived in Freiburg at 4 o'clock   25
                                                                            _____
                                                                                1468

Left Freyburg at ½ past 5 in the morning August 7 and
arrived at Vevay at 4 and at Mr. Woodbridge's at about
5 "Chateau de Blonay."   35

Left Vevay at ½ past 1 on Thursday 10th August and
arrived at Geneva at ½ past 6—about   75

Left Geneva at 7 o'clock on Tuesday morning 15th
August and arrived in Paris on Friday 18th at ½
past 11.   375

Left Paris at 6 o'clock on Thursday evening 31. August
and arrived at Boulonge on Friday Evening at 6.   65

Left Bologne Saturday morning [September 2] and
crossed the chanel to Dover—11 to 3½ o'clock   30

Left Dover on Monday Morning 4th September at 10 and
arrived in London evening at 8.   95
                                                              ———
                                                              2143

[Daily mileage on the Virginian, New York to Liverpool.]

Apr. 26, 1837	74	m
27	137½	
28	137	
29	136	
30	111	
May 1	148	
2	214½	
3	191	
4	198½	
5	239	
6	191	
7	141½	
8	234	
9	155	
10	217	
11	196	
12	204	
	———	
	2925	

Boston to N.Y.	210
Liverpool to London	205
London to Isle of Wight	110
and /?/	
Isle of Wight to London	110
Dover to London	70
Oxford to Birmingham	116
Birmingham to Liverpool	90
Edinburg to York	188
London to Hamburg—	
Hamburg to Berlin	152
Left H. at 8 Monday Morn—	
at Berlin Wednesday 7	

Berlin to Dresden
Dresden to Leipsig   61¼
Leipsig to Frankfort/m   215½

List of Names

Mrs. Ann Anderson ⎫
Mr. Robert Anderson ⎪
   "   James Anderson ⎬ Scotland
   "   John Anderson ⎪
   "   Weir Anderson ⎭
   "   Lowell Mason   Boston, Ms.
Capt. R. F. Stockton & Servt.   U.S. Navy
Mr. H. Schaeffer—Antwerp
  "   J. G. Chapman   New York
  "   Jno. F. King   Manchester
Walsin Vignaud   New Orleans
F. G. W. Fincke   Port au Prince
Joseph Sturge & Servt.   Birmingham
Dr. Pliny Earle   Philadelphia

The above is list of Cabin Passangers on Board Ship Virginian Apr. 25 to May 15 from N.Y. to Liverpool.

Col. James Hammond S.C.
Rev. Robt. Neill[1]

Finances

Chk. in Baring & Co.		£ 25.00
		25.00
		25.00
	June 23, 1827	25
		100.00
	June 26	25.00
		125.00
Frankfurt July 18, 1827		30.00
Do Do Do		20.00
		175.00
Berne—Aug. 4, 1837		25.00
		200.00

Paris Aug. 23, 1837	25.00
	225.00
London: Sept. 5, 1837	25
	250.00
" " 10	50.
	300.00
" " 12	25.00
	325.00
Liverpool 23rd	25
	350.00
"	60
	410

12 groshens is 54 Kreutzers
60 Kreutzers make 1 florin
11 Florins and 54 Kr. is £
1 Hamburg doll. is 2 florins and 42 K
1 Prussian doll. is 1 fl. and 45 K

1 Prussian dollar is 2/11
7   "   "   £1.0.5

Memoranda

Any letters that come for me previous to 10th July to be sent to Grey &
Co. Leipsic Mssrs. Baring & Co. London June 27.

London—Religous Tract 100. [?]

Cherith
Zarephath

The first Rudiments of Harmony
G.[George] Herbert Rodwell
Goulding and D'Almaine

[Tho]mas anderson

To be sent   One Common packing case
                  containing an earthen Filter

One Leather Portmanteau Trunk
Brass plated on end marked L. Mason
Virginian   One Square Paper Covered Ladies Trunk
One small hair Trunk
One Band Box.

The above were expected in Liverpool on Tuesday next—directed to me—care of Baring Brothers & Co.

Left orders for the Packing cases to be sent to me direct to Boston by first vessel,—and for the other things to be sent to care of Goodhue & Co. N.Y. by Ship Virginian (8th Oct.) for me.

Liverpool 1 Oct. 1837

L. Mason

Mr. Widows is the young man who will attend to it.

Memorandum

Cantata's composed by Zumsteg [Zumsteeg]—published at Leipsig—Partitur almost 15 or 18 in number

Easter Morn by Neukomm

These order from Crantz—Aug: Crantz, Hamburg. from Geneva 11 Aug.1837

Lammibungverschiedener [?] etc.
composed by W.[ilhelm] A.[dolph] Müller
Partitur
10 or 12 numbers
pub. near Leipsig.

Salva Regina by Jos. Hazon [?]
recommended by Mr. Kocker
get it in Paris

[All of the above crossed out]

Mem: for Paris

Solfeg: pub. by Picini
Principles Elementarie, De Musique etc. No. 17 vis-a-vis Fresor Boyce
[above in brackets with notation]: Recommended by Mr. Rider Carlsruhe

Rehearsal at Birmingham St. 16th Sept.
Performance 19th, 20th, 21, and 22nd.
[?]ill Mon Thu Friday

Ar'nt they and not Ai'nt they.
[?] 14½
1/2½ per yd the poplin cost

J. H. & G. von Zengerke
    Bremen
Mr. André's agent

order at Leipsig for letters to be sent to Schott—Mainz—orders with
Mr. Schott to send letters to Mr. Woodbridge, Vevay.
Note to Messrs. Barings Bro. etc. from Carlesruhe July 24. Requesting them
to forward all letters received before 20th August to their agent Hottingen
[?] Paris.

Memorandum for N. York

Holbrook & Nelson—my music from Schott [paragraph emended]

Mr. Palmer to write to me care of Holbrook & Nelson—informing who is
his agent so that I may enquire about things sent from Paris.—Porcelain
etc. [paragraph emended]

Goodhue & Co.—Messrs. Baring & Co. will send my things to them—to
be forwarded to Boston by Steam Boat.

Sword's Bookseller Broadway
Make Mr. Webb's respects—relation

Mrs. Skinner—tell her of Mrs. Bruen [paragraph emended]

Mr. Buck
    who married Miss Wolf of Geneva—give text to her.

Mr. Eastman
    Letter from Mr. Goodhue [paragraph emended]

Mr. Chubb
    Letter from Mr. Banister

Corner of Pine and Broadway—Foster, Publisher for Reviews
Livom [?] & Westminster
Edinburg etc.

---

131 William G. Candy Van ill

Der Erbarmer
    is Romberg's last work—he did not live to finish the score ~ ~ ~ ~ ~ ~ ~

Daniel ⌐┼┼┘ |
Mrs. M ⌐┼┼┘ ⌐┼┼┘ | | | | [2]
Letters received from Mrs. M. ⌐┼┘

            Dinner at Frankfurt
1   Soup
        =
2   Boiled Beef
    Cucumbers
    Potatoes
        =
3   String beans
    Spinnage & eggs
    Fried Cakes
        =
4   Plumb Puddings
    Sallad
    Calves feet—stewed or boiled
    Stewed cherries
        =
5   Lobsters
    Roast Goose & Potatoes
    Fish with Lemon Juice
        =
6   Calves foot Jelly
        =
7   Cherries
    Cherry Tort

Currants
Confectionary
Cheese & butter
=
8   Smoking
=

Music and Ideas

October 5. At Sea Sick in my berth

Sailor's Song

Solo   Cho   Solo   Cho   Solo   Cho

8's and 7! Double   Bis

Duet   Ad Lib

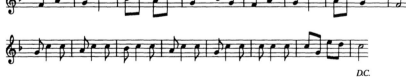

D.C.

Chant

Chant for 23rd Psalm
Ship Oxford 15 Oct. 1837

The Lord is etc.[3]
Chant—either Major or Minor

Voices always to be equivocal or undecided—
Organ to be decided as to major or minor.
Chant in Unison—equivocal

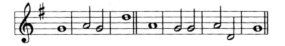

Ship Oxford Sunday Oct. 8, 1837

11th Oct. 1837

Is. 53. 5, 6, 10 and Acts 13.38 for a sentence introductory to public worship "He was wounded etc.—and also "Be it known unto you therefore etc."—

Chant

Mem. For of worship
1. /*Chant or Anthem—Choir
2. Gloria Patri
     Congregation rise
3. Short Prayer
4. Scriptures
5. Chant or Hymn
6. Prayer

7. Hymn
   Notices
8. Sermon
9. Hymn—Congregation
10. Concluding Prayer and Benediction

Hymns all to be given out from the organ Loft and not from Pulpit and never to beread.

(Order of exercises to be printed, pasted on a thin board and 2 or 3 hungup in every pew.[)]

*Or this to be one exercise. Congregation to rise when it commences.

Ship Oxford Oct. 7, 1837

Lord's Prayer[4]

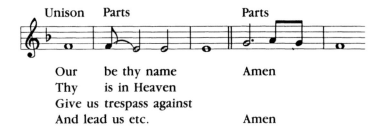

Unison	Parts		Parts
Our	be thy name		Amen
Thy	is in Heaven		
Give us	trespass against		
And lead us etc.			Amen

It seems to me that this chant would be highly devotional. Improved by
making it a regular single chant—chanting note f unison 2nd cadence on
Amen.

Jottings

At Sea

The day is divided into 6 watches of 4 hours each—12 to 4 = 4 to 8 =
8 to 12 etc. The bell of the ship strikes every ½ hour—as follows—at ½
past 12 the bell strikes 1—at 1 o'clock it strikes 2 at ½ past 1 it strikes 3

at 2 it strikes 4—at ½ past 2 it strikes 5
at 3 it strikes 6
at ½ past 3 it strikes 7
at 4 it strikes 8

Different dispositions of men.

Choleric. Example. James and John when filled with indignation at the
inhabitants of a Samaritan village, who refused to receive the
Saviour, exclaimed "Lord wilt thou that we command fire["] etc.

Sanguine. He who came up to Jesus and said "Lord I will follow
thee,["] etc.

Phlegmatic. He who said "Lord suffer me first to go and bury my
Father" = by which he appears to mean, "Allow me to remain in
the house of my parents till my father dies["]; I will then reflect
further on the subject.

Melancholy. Ex. "Let me go bid them farewell that are home at my
house." He thinks of the dark and fearful consequences of following
Christ—he therefore desires to embrace his family once more—

perhaps, as he thinks for the last time. Observe the different answers of the Saviour to these different dispositions.

See Luke 9, 54 to 62.
Elijah the Tishbite—XXI.

Appendix 2

Itinerary

April	25 - Sailed from New York
May	15 - Landed in Liverpool
	16 - Manchester
	18 - London
June	30 - Hamburg
July	5 - Berlin
	9 - Dresden
	13 - Leipzig
	15 - Frankfort am Mein
	19 - Mainz
	21 - Carlsruhe
	25 - Stuttgart
	29 - St. Gallen, Switzerland
August	1 - Zurich
	3 - Berne
	5 - Friburg
	7 - Vevay
	10 - Geneva
	18 - Paris
September	1 - Boulogne
	2 - Dover
	4 - London
	14 - Oxford
	26 - Birmingham
	22 - Liverpool
October	1 - Sailed from Liverpool
	28 - Arrived in New York
November	1 - Arrived in Boston

Appendix 3

Names

ACADÉMIE ROYALE DE MUSIQUE   In 1669 "Abbé" Pierre Perrin received a royal Privilège to found an Académie d'Opera. Lully acquired this Privilège in 1672, at which time the name was changed to the Académie Royal de Musique. Its establishment was part of Louis XIV's efforts to centralize French artistic and intellectual life. Its principal function was the performance of opera, and later it became identical with the Paris Opera (Demuth 1963, 105, 116). A transcription of the original charter is found in Demuth, 282–83.

ADAMS, THOMAS   Thomas Adams (1785–1858), called the "Thalberg of the Organ," was known for his technical skill, improvisation, and ability to imitate orchestral effects upon the organ. He was also considered highly adept in the contrapuntal style. He held two positions in 1837, at St. George's Camberwell (since 1824) and at St. Dunstan-in-the-West, Fleet Street (since 1833). He is not to be confused with another Thomas Adams, who was organist at St. Alban's, Holborn, and who composed a great deal of sacred music. (Young 1967, 456.)

ADAMS, WILLIAM   William Adams (1807–80), Presbyterian clergyman, graduated from Andover Theological Seminary in 1830 and became Pastor of the Congregational Church in Brighton, Massachusetts, in 1831. He moved to New York city as pastor of Central Presbyterian Church in 1835, which was where Mason probably heard him, and in 1836 he became one of the founders of Union Theological Seminary. He was elected president of the Seminary in 1874. (*DAB* 1:101–2.)

ALBERTASSI   Emma Albertassi (*née* Howson, 1814–47), a pupil of Costa, made her first public appearance in 1828, and from 1830 to 1837 sang in Italy, Spain, and France. According to Julian Marshall her "agreeable presence and musical voice" was hindered by her "lifelessness on the stage—a resigned and automatic indifference, which first wearied and then irritated her audiences (Grove I 1:49). Her voice began failing in the 1840s and she died of consumption at age 33. (*The Gentleman's Magazine* 29:320.)

ANDRÉ, CARL   Carl André (1806–87) was the son of Johann Anton André. In 1837 he headed the Frankfurt branch of the André publishing house, which had been founded by his father in 1828.

ANDRÉ, JOHANN ANTON   Upon his father's death in 1799, Johann Anton André (1775–1842) took over the publishing house that the elder André had founded. He purchased all of Mozart's manuscripts from Mozart's widow, Constanze, and not only published many Mozart compositions in carefully edited versions but also began compiling a chronological catalogue of Mozart's works. The latter was never brought to fruition, but André's efforts laid the foundation for much later Mozart scholarship, including Köchel's catalogue. André was also technologically innovative, switching to the lithographic printing process in 1800.

ANGLOIS   Luigi Anglois (1801–1872), the son of the well-known bass player, Giorgi Anglois, was a double bass virtuoso. Highly acclaimed for his technical and interpretive skills in the early nineteenth century, he performed in Paris, London, Lisbon, and the United States, as well as his native Italy. (Fétis 1878.)

ATTWOOD   Thomas Attwood (1765–1838), a pupil of Mozart, became Organist at St. Paul's Cathedral in 1795 and was appointed Composer to the Chapel Royal in 1796. From 1792 to 1801 he composed music for over thirty theatrical productions, many of which were highly successful. After 1801 he concentrated more on glees and various types of anthems. He was a founding member and conductor of the Philharmonic Society as well as one of the first professors of the Royal Academy of Music. (Obituary essay by W. Ayrton in *The Gentleman's Magazine,* May 1838, 549–51.)

AUBER   Daniel-François-Esprit Auber (1782–1871) is considered the preeminent composer of *opéras comiques* in the nineteenth century. His first large success came with *Le maçon* in 1824. His best known opera, *Fra Diavolo,* was composed in 1830 and remains in the repertoire. *La muette de Portici* was composed for the Académie Royale de Musique.

AUGUSTA   Sophie Augusta (1768–1840) was the sixth child of George III. Little is known of her other than an occasional social reference. Reports exist of her playing and singing some of her own musical compositions in private performances. She did not marry. (*DNB* 1:727.)

AYRTON   As the "director" of the Italian opera at the King's Theatre in Haymarket in 1817 and 1821, William Ayrton (1777–1858) is credited with reforming Italian opera in England. He edited *The Harmonicon* from 1823–33 and *The Musical Library* from 1834–37. In 1837 he published *The Sacred Minstrelsy,* with which Mason was apparently not previously familiar (cf. Mason's entry of May 31). He was also one of the founding members of the Philharmonic Society. (Young 1967, 392, 439, 441.)

BACH   In many ways the career of August Wilhelm Bach (1796–1869) parallels that of Mason. He was director of the Institute for Church Music and published a popular collection of church music, *Choralbuch für das Gesangbuch zum gottesdienstlichen Gebrauch für evangelische Gemeinden.* He also composed other vocal music. He was an organist, although, unlike Mason, he was considered a virtuoso, and he included Mendelssohn among his organ students. He was not a descendant of Johann Sebastian Bach. (Young 1970, 288.)

BAIRD   After graduating from Princeton Seminary in 1822, Robert Baird (1798–1863) spent several years promoting public education and Sunday schools in New Jersey. John MacLean, president of Princeton, credited him with doing more than any other man "to direct the public attention to this subject [education] and to induce the Legislature to pass the requisite laws for the establishment and maintenance of a system of common schools." He became active in a temperance movement in Paris after having been sent there in 1834 by the French Association, a group that wished to aid the Protestant church in France. He published a number of works in both English and French on temperance and education. (*DAB* I:512.)

BALFE   Michael William Balfe (1808–70) began his career as a violinist, making his debut at the Oratorio Concerts when he was fifteen. Shortly after that he began to appear as a baritone and, aided by Rossini's patronage, embarked upon a successful operatic career in Italy and France. He returned to England in 1833, where he achieved his greatest fame as an opera composer. His first opera, *The Siege of Rochelle* (1835), was an instant success. This was followed by twenty-five others, of which *The Bohemian Girl* (1843) is best known. (Barrett, *passim*.)

BANISTER   Henry Joshua Banister (1803–47) was active as a cellist in London in the 1830s. More important to Mason, however, Banister edited the complete works of his father, Charles William Banister (1761–1831), who was a composer of sacred vocal music. The edition appeared between 1831 and 1833. (*BMB*, 24.)

BARING   Baring Brothers & Co., Limited, 8, Bishopsgate Street, London, was founded in 1763 as a mercantile banking house. Between 1828 and 1861 it concentrated on the financing of American trade and the marketing of American securities. It was commonly referred to as Barings. Hidy discusses its importance to Atlantic trade and finance in detail (Hidy 1949, *passim*).

BARNETT   John Barnett (1802–90) composed his first and most successful full-scale opera, *The Mountain Sylph,* in 1834, for the newly reopened English Opera House (previously the Lyceum Theatre). He had previously composed music for several popular stage works. In 1837 he became the musical director of the Olympic Theatre. After three attempts at serious opera between 1834 and 1840, which were only mildly successful, he abruptly retired from the stage.

BELCHER, ELIZABETH C. AND JULIA   Elizabeth C. and Julia A. Belcher were the sisters of the publisher Joshua Belcher (d. 1816). They would have been fifty to sixty years old in 1837.

BENEDICT   Julius Benedict (1804–1885), German-born conductor and pianist, settled in London permanently in 1835. He served as either conductor or musical director for several organizations: the Opera Buffa, the Lyceum Theater, Covent Garden, the Monday Popular Concerts, and later the Norwich Festivals and the Liverpool Philharmonic Society. He was particularly active as a conductor at provincial festivals, and he accompanied Jenny Lind on her American tour of 1850–52. Benedict composed much piano music and several operas, only one of which, *The Lily of Killarney* (1862), achieved any success. (Young 1967, 486; Loesser 1954, 489.)

BENNETT William Sterndale Bennett (1816–75) was only twenty-one when Mason heard his compositions. He had already composed three piano concertos, five symphonies, and two overtures by 1835. In early 1837 he had just returned from a highly successful stay in Germany, during which both Mendelssohn and Schumann prophesied greatness for him. Unfortunately, his output dropped precipitously after his appointment to the Royal Academy of Music in the fall of 1837, and he was never able to equal the fecundity of his early years.

BERIOT, DE The Belgian violinist Charles de Beriot (1802–1870) was a touring virtuoso when Mason heard him in 1837, having not yet been appointed to either the Paris or the Brussels Conservatoires. From 1829 to 1836 he had toured, giving joint concerts, with Maria Felicita Malibran. They were married in 1836, only six months before she was killed in a riding accident (see chap. 2, n. 7). In 1837 he was still in a period of despondency over her death, and he did not resume a full concert schedule until 1838.

BIDDULPH Thomas Tregenna Biddulph (1763–1838), a British evangelical priest, was the incumbent at St. James, Bristol, from 1799 to 1838. He published many books, of which *The Inconsistency of Conformity to This World with the Profession of Christianity* (Bristol, 1803) is one of his best known. (Obituary in *The Gentleman's Magazine* 10:1838.)

BIRCH Charlotte Ann Birch (1815–1901), was educated at the Royal Academy of Music and sang with the Sacred Harmonic Society from 1836. She occasionally sang in opera and oratorio productions, including Mendelssohn's *Elijah,* conducted by the composer in 1847. (Obituary in *The Musical Times,* vol. 42, March 1, 1901.)

BISHOP Anna Bishop (*née* Riviere) (1810–1884) made her London debut in 1831, the same year in which she married the composer Henry Bishop. After touring the English provinces for several years she eloped with her accompanist, the harpist Nicholas Boschsa, to the Continent. From 1839 to the end of her life she traveled extensively, first in Europe and then throughout the world, including Australia, the Pacific islands, and the Orient. Following Boscha's death in Australia in 1856 she moved to America and married an American diamond merchant, Martin Schultz. She continued to perform, giving her last concert in New York in April, 1883. (Jones, 14.)

BLACKMAN William Blackman was located at 15, Union Street, Southwark, from ca. 1810–22 and at 5, Bridge Street, Southwark, from ca. 1822–45. Upon William Blackman's death the business was continued by Mrs. Blackman and their son Josiah and later by Josiah alone. (Humphries 1954, 75.)

BOOSEY Boosey and Company was founded by Thomas Boosey in 1816 as a branch of his book-publishing business. They published many standard European works, especially operas, in inexpensive editions. In 1855 they began to manufacture flutes, and in 1930 amalgamated with Hawkes & Son to found Boosey and Hawkes. (Humphries 1954, 82.)

BOSTON ACADEMY OF MUSIC   The Boston Academy of Music was founded in 1833 by a group of private citizens for the avowed purpose of improving vocal music among both adults and children (*Report I*). Lowell Mason was one of the leaders of the founding group, although he is listed only as a "professor." Near the end of the 1830s the Boston Academy began to place greater emphasis upon instrumental music and was crucial in securing the public acceptance of orchestral music (*Report IX*).

BRAHAM   John Braham (1774–1856, real name Abraham) made his debut at Covent Garden as a boy soprano in 1787. After touring in Italy and Germany from 1798 to 1801 he returned to England for a highly successful career as a singer and a composer of ballads. He was originally re-nowned as a tenor with a smooth, musical sound and an exceptional range, which extended from A to e″. His voice became lower in the 1830s, and by 1838 he was appearing in baritone roles.

BRUEN   Mary Ann Bruen (*née* Davenport) was the widow of Matthias Bruen (1793–1829), who was originally licensed to preach in 1816. Because of poor health, Bruen made two trips to Europe, where he preached occasionally. Following his return, he was active as a missionary in New York City and in 1825 was appointed pastor of the Bleecker Street Congregation. (Sprague 1857, 4:543–45; McClintock 1883, 902.)

BURGERSH   John Fane, Lord Burgersh (1784–1859), became the eleventh Earl of Westmorland in 1841. It was through his perseverance as president of the Royal Academy of Music from 1823 that the Academy was sustained through its first difficult years (Cazalett). In 1837 he came under considerable criticism for the authoritarian control he still exercised over it, and on the very day that Mason met with him, *The Musical World* contained a scathing letter from a former student about the pitiful quality of education at the Royal Academy, placing the blame squarely upon Lord Burgersh (vol. 67, June 23, 1837). Subsequent letters confirmed this as well as the degree of coercion that Lord Burgersh exercised (vol. 70, July 14, 1837, pp. 71–74; vol. 71, August 11, 1837, pp. 129–32). It is likely that Mason saw the original letter, but probably not before meeting with Lord Burgersh.

BULL   Ole Bull (1810–80) had alread acquired a reputation in the 1830s as a brilliant but controversial violinst. He was frequently compared to Paganini and considered without peer in the use of multiple stops, an ability related to modifications Bull made on his bow and bridge. Bull was criticized even then, however, for empty showmanship and an undisciplined improvisatory manner of playing. Mason of course heard Bull before he became well known in America; Bull's two American trips occurred in 1843 and 1852.

CABOT   Henry Cabot (1782–1864), was a prominent attorney in Boston. Although he did not hold political office, he was an active member of the Whig Party and a close friend of Daniel Webster, until differing political views forced a rupture. His grandson Henry Cabot Lodge described him in his later years as "over seventy . . . a tall, erect very fine-looking man who gave no impression of age or feebleness." (Lodge 1925, 7–8, 40, 43, 113.)

CASTELLI   A singer engaged at the King's Theatre in 1825, Castelli performed, among other roles, that of Cherubino in Mozart's *Le Nozze di Figaro*. She sang again in 1828 and in 1832–33 after the King's Theatre reopened under new management. Castelli was not, however, listed as one of the principal singers by the management at that time, although she did appear as Clotilde in the London premier of Bellini's *Norma* in 1833. Little is known of her other than her activity at the King's Theatre. (Grove I, 1:319; *The Harmonicon* 1832, p. 122; 1833, p. 159.)

CHAPMAN   In 1837 John Gadsby Chapman (1808–89) receved a highly coveted prize to paint one of eight large paintings in the Capitol Rotunda. Soon thereafter he went to Europe to begin work on his commission, *The Baptism of Pocahontas* (Fairman, quoted in Barker, 463). Chapman had been in Europe before between ca. 1827 and 1831. In 1847 he published *The American Drawing Book,* considered one of the finest books on the subject. In 1848 he returned to Rome, to live there the remainder of his life. Today he is known principally for his landscapes and etchings. (*DAB* 7:18, 19.)

CHERUBINI   Luigi Cherubini (1760–1842) served as director of the Paris Conservatory from 1822 until 1842. He had achieved his greatest fame with his Revolutionary operas, written principally between 1795 and 1805. After 1810 he concentrated more on church music, composing eight masses, including two coronation masses and two requiem masses, as well as many smaller works. As director of the Paris Conservatory he was considered relatively conservative and autocratic, winning esteem from some students, such as Boieldieu and Auber, and drawing the censure of others, such as Berlioz. (Berlioz 1935, 33–39.)

CLAYTON   George Clayton (1783–1862) was one of three sons of John Clayton (1754–1853), all of whom attained distinction as Congregational ministers. He had been at York Chapel, Walworth Surrey, since at least 1820, as indicated by several sermons that he published. (*DNB* 4:470–71; *NUC* 112:5.)

CODMAN   John Codman (1782–1847) served as Pastor of the Second Congregational Church of Dorchester from 1808–47. He was also the first president of the American Peace Society and a delegate to the Congregational Union of England and Wales (1834–35). He published *A Narrative of a Visit to England* (Boston, 1836), which recounted his English travels of 1834–35. (Dunning 1894, 292–95.)

COGSWELL   Joseph Green Cogswell (1786–1871) practiced law in Boston until 1813, when he became Latin tutor at Harvard, his alma mater. He later founded schools at Round Hill, Mass. (with the historian George Bancroft) and Raleigh, N.C. He traveled extensively in Europe, making a number of trips to purchase books for a library that John Jacob Astor wished to endow. (*DAB* 2:273–74.)

COLBY   Daniel Colby is listed as a representative from Green Street Church on a committee that was formed in 1826 for the purpose of improving music in the Boston churches. One of the committee's recommendations was that Lowell Mason relocate from Savannah to Boston. (Mason P, Box 4, Folder 38.)

CONCERT OF ANTIENT MUSIC   The Concert of Antient Music was a society founded in 1776 by the Earl of Sandwich and other noblemen for the purpose of performing older music, which was defined as music at least twenty years old. The society prospered especially after 1785, when George III bestowed royal patronage by becomong a regular subscriber. It moved to the Hanover Square Rooms in 1804, but its repertory remained conservative, centered mostly upon the works of Handel. Compositions by Haydn and Beethoven were introduced only in the 1830s.

COOPER   George Cooper (ca. 1783–1843), father of the more well-known George Cooper (1826–76), served at St. Sepulchre, Holborn, from 1799 until his death in a position that, according to Young, was a sinecure (Young 1967, 453). He was thus able to serve as assistant at St. Paul's Cathedral until 1838 when he was succeeded by his son. (Young 1967, 99.)

COOPER   George Cooper, Jr. (1826–76) began to substitute for his father when he was eleven years old. In 1836 he was appointed organist at St. Ann and St. Agnes. He succeeded his father at St. Sepulchre's upon the elder Cooper's death. In 1867 he became organist at the Chapel Royal. He published several works on the organ and did much to familiarize the British public with the organ music of Johann Sebastian Bach. (Grove I 1:398.)

COSTA   Italian-born Michael Costa (1806–84) came to London in 1829 and became director and conductor of the King's Theatre in London in 1833. He later held conducting positions at the Philharmonic Society and the Royal Italian Opera at Covent Garden. Acclaimed as a conductor, Costa was less successful as a composer. *Malek Adel* was his best received work. Chorley, a not entirely sympathetic critic, referred to it (1862) as a ''thoroughly conscientious work containing an amount of melody with which he has never been credited'' (Grove I 1:406). Mason heard the English premier.

CRAMER   Cramer, Addison & Beale, located at 201, Regent St., was founded in 1824 by J. B. Cramer, Robert Addison, and T. Frederick Beale. They published piano music principally, including works by Clementi, Dussek, Haydn, Mozart, and Beethoven. In 1844 Addison withdrew and William Chappell entered the partnership, creating Cramer, Beale & Chapell. (Humphries 1954, 120–21.)

CROCKETT   Although it is not clear who M. E. Crockett was, the Crockett family was closely associated with music in Bowdoin Street Church. George W. Crockett (1789–1859), president of the Bank of North America, had served earlier as organist at Bowdoin Street. The death of his daughter, Martha Jane Crockett, at age 16 in 1833 was the impetus for Mason's hymn tune ''Mount Vernon.'' (Mason B, 216.)

CROFT   William Croft (1678–1727) was organist of Westminster Abbey and Composer of the Chapel Royal. His anthems, written in the late Baroque idiom, were considered highly progressive in the early eighteenth century, and they remained popular throughout the nineteenth century.

CROTCH   William Crotch (1775–1847) held several organ and academic positions at Cambridge and then at Oxford before coming to London in 1807. In 1822 he was appointed principal of the new Royal Music Academy. He composed three oratorios in addition to a considerable quantity of vocal and keyboard music, and he wrote several theoretical and didactic works that were extremely popular.

CUMMINGS   Joseph Cummings (1790–1846), a merchant in Savannah, worked closely with Mason as Sunday School superintendent of the First Presbyterian Church in Savannah, and Mason became close to the entire Cummings family (Pemberton, 62). Lowell and Abigail Mason were fond enough of Joseph's son William to name their third son after him. (Mason B, 177.)

D'ALMAINE   D'Almaine & Co., musical instrument makers, music printers and publishers, was founded by Thomas D'Almaine, and was at 20 Soho Square from ca. 1834–58. In the 1840s D'Almaine formed a partnership with Thomas Mackinlay, and upon D'Almaine's death in 1866, the business was sold to Joseph Emery, a piano manufacturer. (Humphries 1954, 126.)

DRAGONETTI   The Venetian-born double bass virtuoso Domenico Dragonetti (1763–1846) took up permanent residence in London in 1794 and performed for over half a century in concerts of the Society of Antient Music and the Philharmonic Society. He often appeared in concert with his close friend, the cellist Robert Lindley. During this time he toured extensively throughout Europe, playing a three-string double bass, and won the admiration of many musicians, including Beethoven, Paganini, Liszt and Rossini.

DULCKEN   Madame Louise Dulcken (1811–50) was born in Hamburg and acquired a considerable reputation in Germany during the 1820s as a solo pianist and as a duo-pianist with her brother Ferdinand David. She settled in London after her marriage in 1828 and quickly became one of the most prominent and respected musicians in the city. (Grove I 469.)

DUPREZ   Gilbert-Louis Duprez (1806–96), referred to by some as the first Romantic tenor in France, had his initial successes during a ten-year period in Italy, beginning in 1828. His Italian stay was capped by his creation of Edgardo in Donizetti's *Lucia de Lammermoor* in Naples in 1835. In 1837 he had just established himself upon his return to Paris with his debut in *Guillaume Tell*. Mason was fortunate to hear him when he did because Duprez' vocal powers declined rapidly, probably through strain, and by the 1840s he was considered past his prime.

EARLE   Dr. Pliny Earle (1809–92), a physician and psychiatrist, had just graduated from the University of Pennsylvania in 1837 and was on his way to Europe to study hospitals and insane asylums. He made two other European trips after that and published several articles about his findings. He held various posts in psychiatric hospitals in Pennsylvania, New York, the District of Columbia, and Massachusetts, and was one of the co-founders of the American Medical Association. (*CAB* 11:146.)

EGERTON   Sir Thomas Egerton, was the Second Earl of Wilton (1799–1882). Egerton composed numerous anthems, Anglican chants and other vocal works. (Young 1967, 146.)

ELIOT   Samuel Atkins Eliot (1798–1862) was mayor of Boston from 1836–39, and a member of Congress 1850–51. A graduate of Harvard Divinity School, he was keenly interested in both education and music. He was in charge of music at King's Chapel, Boston, and he served as president of the Boston Academy of Music from 1835. (Mason B 262–65; *CAB* 11:248.)

FELLENBERG   The Swiss educational reformer Phillip Emanuel von Fellenberg (1771–1844) founded a common school with Pestalozzi in 1804. The experiment failed, however, because of differences in philosophy and Pestalozzi's apprehension about Fellenberg's dominating personality. (Silber 1965, 161–63.)

FINK   Charlotte Fink (1819?–43) appeared as a pianist in Leipzig, Dessau, and Dresden before her career was cut short by her early death. (*MGG* 4:col. 224.)

FOUNDLING HOSPITAL   Under the leadership of Thomas Coram, the Foundling Hospital of London was officially established as an orphanage by an Act of Parliament and approval of the Crown in 1740. Children were given some education and then usually apprenticed out. The administrators were careful, however, not to given them enough education to allow them to compete with sons of merchants. In the twentieth century the hospital became the Thomas Coram Foundation for Children and concentrated upon the placement of children in foster homes. (McClure 37–48, 249.)

FOWLE   William Bentley Fowle (1795–1859) founded the Female Monitorial School in 1821, a progressive school that abandoned corporal punishment and made use of then such novel techniques as the blackboard and the drawing of maps. Its most innovative change was the monitorial system, in which advanced pupils helped teach others. Fowle published more than fifty textbooks and later edited *Common School Journal,* a publication founded by Horace Mann. Like Mason, Fowle lectured at many of the teacher's institutes that were organized by Mann. (*CAB* 10:720–21; Ohles 1978, 1:476–77.)

FRANCHOMME   Auguste-Joseph Franchomme (1808–84) spent most of his career in Paris where he was first cellist in various opera orchestras and, from 1846, professor of cello at the Paris Conservatory. Chopin's Grand Duo Concertante and Cello Sonata were both written for Franchomme. Franchomme composed several works for cello, and his various studies are still used. (Fétis 1860, 306.)

GALLLI   Filippo Galli (1783–1853) was a leading bass at La Scala between 1811 and 1825. Noted for a very deep and flexible voice, he premiered in eight of Rossini's operas. He first appeared in London in 1827, and in the 1830s frequently sang in Spain and Mexico. After 1840 he returned to La Scala.

GARDINER   William Gardiner (1770–1853), a clothing manufacturer by profession, was active as a choral singer and conductor, and composer of anthems. He also traveled widely and published several books of musical recollections. He most important influence upon Mason was as a compiler. His *Sacred Melodies* (London, 1812), a collection of hymns and anthems with bowdlerized melodies adapted from Haydn, Mozart and Beethoven, among others, was the principal model for Mason's *Handel and Haydn Society Collection of Church Music.*

GASSNER   Ferdinand Simon Gassner (1798–1851) began his professional career as a violinist. He began writing theoretical works on music while music director at Gissen University in Mainz from 1818–26. His most important treatises, however, were written after 1837. In 1830 he was appointed chorusmaster and musical director of the Court Chapel in Karlsruhe. (van der Straeten 1933, 2:110–11.)

GAUNTLETT   Henry John Gauntlett (1805–76) studied both music and law. In 1827 he accepted his first post as organist at St. Olive's, Southwark, and in 1831 began practice as a solicitor in London. He gave up his law practice in 1842. Today he is remembered mostly for psalm and hymn tunes, the most famous being "Irby" (sung to "Once in Royal David's City"). That phase of his career did not begin until after 1837, however. In 1837 Gauntlett was recognized as a brilliant, if quasi-amateur, organist. (*The Musical Times,* 66:455–56; see also Staples 1941, 184–88.)

GERSBACH, ANTON AND JOSEPH   Both Anton Gersbach (1803–48) and his older brother Joseph Gersbach (1787–1830) published several volumes of vocal music and works relating to singing schools. Shortly after Mason's trip, Anton published *Hundert Choral-Gesänge der Evangelischen Kirche für vier Männerstimmen gesetz* (Karlsruhe, 1838). (*NUC* 197:291.)

GESSNER   Solomon Gessner (1730–1788) was a leading poet and artist of the rococo movement. A prolific writer of pastoral poetry and prose, his two most important works were *Idyllen* and *Der Tod Abels.* (Robertson 1970, 233–34.)

GORDON   George William Gordon was a prosperous importer and was active in Boston politics, having served on the Boston City Council from 1831–36. He was one of the founding members of the Boston Academy of Music and served as its first recording secretary. (*Report I* 9; Mason B 266.)

GRAY   Robert Gray founded his organ company in London in 1774. He was succeeded by William Gray, who in turn was succeeded by John Gray in 1820. From 1839 the company was known as Gray and Davison. They built a number of important organs in the nineteenth century, including the Crystal Palace organ, those at St. Paul's, Wilton Palace, Magdalen College, Oxford, and at the town halls of Leeds Bolton and Glasgow. (Sumner 1962, 233.)

GRAY, FRANCIS CALLEY   Francis Calley Gray (1790–1856) spent the years 1809–13 as a secretary with the U.S. Legation at St. Petersburg. In 1826 he was elected a Fellow at Harvard, a position he held until 1836, and from 1836 to 1843 he served as state senator from Suffolk County. Even after 1836 he dedicated much of his time to providing lay support for his alma mater, Harvard University. (*DAB* 4:514–15.)

GREATOREX   Both of the brothers, Henry John (1812–79) and Thomas Westrop (1816–81) Greatorex, were violinists active in London in the 1830s. Henry John was the better known; he was violinist with the Italian Opera and the Philharmonic Society, conductor of the Choral Harmonist's Society, and member of the Royal Society of Musicians. Thomas composed sacred vocal music and comic songs and later published *Universal Violin Tutor* (1862) and *Complete Organ Tutor* (1863). According to Paige (408), the American psalmodist Henry W. Greatorex (1816–58), who published the *Greatorex Collection* in 1851, was probably another brother. (See also Jones 1886, 68.)

GREEN   The firm of John Green was at 33 Soho Square from ca. 1820–48. Green was the inventor and sole manufacturer of the Royal Seraphine, a small free-reed keyboard instrument. (Humphries 1954, 162; Grove I 2:346.)

GREGORY   Abigail Mason's mother Hannah Buckminster Gregory (1776–1860) married Daniel Gregory in 1795. In 1800 she and her husband acquired and jointly ran an inn in Medfield. They had two daughters, one of whom died as a child. (Pemberton 1971, 67–69.)

GRISI   Giulia Grisi (1811–1869) was already established as a leading singer of bel canto opera in Paris when she made her London debut in 1834. For the next twelve years Grisi sang regularly in London in the summer. In 1854 she toured the United States. Chorley was effusive in his praise of Grisi: "In our day there has been no woman so beautiful, so liberally endowed with voice and with dramatic impulses as herself—Catalani excepted." (Chorley 1862, 75.)

HACH   H. Theodore Hach founded, with T. B. Haywood in 1839, *The Musical Magazine, or Repository of Musical Science, Literature and Intelligence.* Unlike other American musical journals of this time, *The Musical Magazine* had a strong continental European orientation, which probably reflected Hach's own Germanic origins. It drew upon many French and German as well as English sources. (*The Musical Magazine,* vol. 1, no. 1, pp. 2–3.)

HAMMOND   James Henry Hammond (1807–1864) was admitted to the bar in 1828 and was elected to Congress in 1834. He traveled to Europe in 1836 for health reasons, and in 1842 was elected governor of South Carolina. He was elected senator in 1857 and resigned in 1860 to support the secession of southern states from the union, which he had advocated for over twenty years. (*DAB* 4:207.)

HARPER   Thomas Harper (1786–1853) played in various theatre orchestras from 1806 and joined the Royal Academy of Music in 1814. By 1820 he was considered the leading trumpet player in England. He played the slide trumpet and performed regularly at the Concert of Antient Music and the leading musical festivals. He was active through the 1840s, when he was succeeded by his son, Thomas Jr. (Cazalett 1854, 293–95.)

HART   From ca. 1834–58 Joseph Hart was at 109 Hutton Garden. He was previously a partner in Hart & Fellows. Hart published primarily engraved sacred music. (Humphries 1954, 173–74.)

HASTINGS   Like Mason, Thomas Hastings (1784–1872) enjoyed considerable success as an anthologist and composer of hymns, his most famous being "Toplady" ("Rock of Ages"). His *Dissertation on Musical Taste* (Albany, N.Y., 1822) was one of the most influential statements of the psalmodic reformer's point of view. He and Mason collaborated on some collections, most notably *Spiritual Songs for Social Worship* (New York, 1833), and, as Hastings' correspondence reflects, they maintained a spirited although mostly friendly rivalry as church music composers. (Dooley 1963, 51–2; Stevenson 1966, 81.)

HAWES   William Hawes (1785–1846) was appointed Master of the Choristers at St. Paul's Cathedral in 1814 and Master of the Children of the Chapel Royal in 1817.

He was criticized for ignoring his charges for other pursuits, particularly secular vocal and theatrical activities. He edited the madrigal book, *The Triumphs of Oriana,* and composed many songs and glees. He sought to bring foreign works to the English stage and is credited with the 1824 London production of *Der Freischütz.* (Young 1967 453; *DNB* 9:190–91.)

HERSCHEL   The astronomer Sir William Herschel (1738–1822) was probably best known for discovering the planet Uranus. He actually began professional life as an organist rather than astronomer. (Clerke 1895.)

HEWITT   James Lang Hewitt (1807–53), the son of the composer James Hewitt, was associated with the Boston publishing firm of J. A. Dickson until 1827, at which time he moved to New York to manage his father's publishing business.

HILL & SON   The company that was to become Hill & Son was founded in 1755 by John Snetzler. It was later owned by Thomas Elliot, the father-in-law of William Hill. Upon Elliot's death in 1832 Hill became sole owner. Hill's company led British organ builders in the nineteenth century in expanding the tonal spectrum of organs, of which the Christ Church organ was one of his first experiments. In 1827 he and Eliot rebuilt it with pedal pipes one octave below the manuals, giving GGG, as opposed to most church organs of the time that only went down to GG. (Norman 1984, 109, 111.)

HILLER   In 1837 Ferdinand Hiller (1811–85) had just returned from Italy where his opera *Romilda* had been performed in Milan without success. Prior to that he had been in Paris from 1828 to 1835 where he was not only praised for his skills as a pianist and conductor but had earned, for his teaching at Choron's Institute of Church Music, the appellation "le savant Hiller." After 1837 his reputation continued to grow, particularly as a conductor in Germany.

HIME   Humphrey Hime & Son, Music Seller and Publisher, was founded in 1790 and was located at Castle Street and Church Street from 1805–40. (Humphries 1954, 181.)

HOBBS   John William Hobbs (1799–1877) was named Gentleman of the Chapel Royal in 1827 and lay vicar of Westminster Abbey in 1836. According to contemporaries, his singing was characterized by taste, refinement and expression. He also composed over 100 songs, mostly glees. (Obituary notice, *Musical Times* 18:67.)

HODGES   Edward Hodges (1796–1867) received the degree of Doctor of Music from Sidney Sussex College, Cambridge, in 1825 and served as an organist and composer in Bristol until 1838, when he emigrated to America. He held an organ post briefly in Toronto and then moved to New York. There he occupied various appointments until illness forced him to return to England in 1863.

HOGARTH   Shortly after arriving in London in 1830, George Hogarth (1783–1870) began contributing to *The Harmonicon* and then to the *Morning Chronicle.* Writing on both political and musical topics, he became joint editor of the *Chronicle* and as such encouraged some of the first efforts of the young Charles Dickens. When Mason met him he had only recently, in 1835, published his *Musical History,*

Biography and Criticism, which according to George Clement Boase was considered "a standard work of reference on its special subject" in nineteenth-century England. (*DNB* 8:976.)

HOMER FAMILY   When a committee was attempting to secure the services of Lowell Mason for the churches in Boston in 1827, they put together a list of 26 subscribers who pledged $50 or $100 each in order to guarantee an annual salary of $1500 to Mason. These subscribers included a Henry Homer and a George Homer, who were probably related to the Homer family that Mason saw in London. (Mason P Box 4, Folder 38.)

HORSLEY   William Horsley (1774–1858) became organist of the Asylum for Female Orphans in 1802 and was one of the founders of the Philharmonic Society. In 1837 he was also organist at Belgrave Chapel. He composed numerous glees, which were highly regarded, as well as church pieces and piano sonatas and symphonies, which tended to be conservative. (*DNB* 8:1280–81.)

INSTITUTE FOR CHURCH MUSIC   The Institute for Church Music was founded by Carl Friedrich Zelter in 1822 to improve the quality of music in German Protestant churches. In 1822 it was called the *Institut für die Ausbildung von Organisten und Musiklehrern,* and in 1875 it became the *Königliches Akademisches Institut für Kirchenmusik.* Upon Zelter's death in 1832, August Wilhelm Bach succeeded him as director.

IVANOFF   Nicolai Ivanoff (1810–80) emigrated to Italy in 1830 and made his debut at San Carlo in 1832. He first appeared in London in 1834 although he spent most of his career in Italy, with his greatest successes coming after 1840. He had a particularly sweet and gentle tone which was ruined by his attempts at heavier roles in the 1840s. Mason heard him when his voice was still relatively pure.

JAMES   John Angell James (1785–1859) was ordained at Carr's Lane Chapel in 1806 as a dissenting preacher under the Toleration Act. He remained there until his death. He became well known for his sermons and addresses, many of which were published. They were so popular that James was awarded honorary doctorates on both sides of the Atlantic, at Glasgow and at Princeton Universities. Charles Creighton described James as "a Calvinist in creed," whose "rugged features indicated strength of purpose more fully than benevolence of heart." (*DNB* 10:652–53; *see also* James 1861.)

KIRK   Edward N. Kirk (1802–74) was a Presbyterian pastor and a leader of revivals in New York. In 1829 he became pastor of the Fourth Presbyterian Church, Albany, and from 1837–39 he toured Europe. Intensely evangelical, he was a strong advocate of missions, temperance, and abolition. According to Winsor he was almost as well known in England, France, Germany, and Italy as in the United States. In 1842 he became pastor of the Mt. Vernon Congregational Church in Boston. (*DAB* 5:427–28; Winsor 1880, 407.)

KOCHER   Conrad Kocher (1786–1872) wrote several theoretical works, including *Die Tonkunst in der Kirche, oder Ideen zu einem allgemeinen, vierstimmigen Choral— und einem Figural-Gesang für einen kleineren Chor* (Stuttgart, 1823). (*NUC* 301:360.)

KOLLOCK   Henry Kollock was the pastor of the Independent Presbyterian Church of Savannah from 1806 until his death in 1819. (LaFar 1944, 127; Mason B 88–89.)

KRUMMACHER   The Lutheran minister F. W. Krummacher (1796–1868) was an ardent opponent of rationalism and in 1840 initiated the "Bremen Controversy" through the publication of a sermon "Paul Not a Man to Suit the Taste of Our Age." (Jackson 6:385–86.)

LABARRE   Theodore Labarre (1805–70) lived alternately in London and Paris between 1824 and 1847, when he was appointed conductor of the *Opéra-Comique*. In 1852 he became director of the imperial chapel, and after 1867 he was professor of harp at the Paris Conservatory, in which capacity he wrote *Méthode complète pour la harpe*. He composed numerous stage works as well as songs and pieces for harp. (Rensch 1969, 112–15, 125, 136.)

LABLACHE   Luigi or Louis Lablache (1794–1858), an Italian bass of French descent, made his debut at La Scala in Milan in 1817, and for the next thirteen years sang throughout Italy and in Vienna and Paris. He made the first of many regular London appearances in 1830. He was noted not only for an exceptionally powerful voice but also for a keen understanding of musical style that enabled him to sing Palestrina as well as bel canto (Chorley 1862, 13). According to Chorley, "Musical history contains no account of a bass singer so gifted by nature, so accomplished by art, so popular without measure or drawback, as Louis Lablache." (Chorley 1862, 11.)

LAVATER   Johann Casper Lavater (1741–1801) was well known in the eighteenth century as a writer and as the founder of physiognomics, the study of psychological characteristics in relation to facial features or body structure. He was pastor of St. Peter's Church in Zurich from 1787.

LEIFCHILD   John Leifchild (1770–1862), English Independent minister, was raised as a Methodist, but left Methodism when he embraced Calvinism. He held posts in Kensington and Bristol before coming to London in 1830. From 1830 until his retirement in 1854 he was minister of Craven Chapel, Bayswater, London. (*DNB* 11:868.)

LINDLEY   Robert Lindley (1776–1855) became principal cellist of the Opera orchestra in 1794 and held that position for fifty-eight years. He was considered the outstanding cellist in London in the 1830s. Lindley was known particularly for his recitative accompaniment, in which he would ornament the bass line with elaborate arpeggios.

LOEWE   By 1837 Carl Loewe (1796–1869) had composed five operas and six oratorios. The two most successful of these, the oratorio *Die Zerstörung Jerusalems* and the opera *Die drei Wünsche,* were received with enough favor in Berlin to secure his election to the Berlin Academy in 1837. His Lieder were compared favorably to Schubert's, even in Vienna. Loewe also composed a great deal of instrumental music, mostly programmatic.

LORD   Melvin Lord was a Boston publisher who was a partner at various times in several firms that published some of Mason's books. Among them were the *Boston Handel and Haydn Society Collection of Church Music* (Richardson and Lord, 1822),

Select Chants, Doxologies &c. (Richardson and Lord, 1824), *Choral Harmony* (Richardson and Lord, 1828), *The Juvenile Psalmist* (Richardson, Lord and Holbrook, 1829), *Juvenile Lyre* (Richardson, Lord and Holbrook, 1831), *Lyra Sacra* (Richardson, Lord and Holbrook, 1832), and *Occasional Psalm and Hymn Tunes, Selected and Original.* (Melvin Lord, 1836, Nos. 1–3 singly.)

LUCAS   Charles Lucas (1808–69) was appointed conductor of the Royal Academy of Music in 1832, at which time he also played cello in several orchestras. He conducted occasionally at the Antient Concerts and became principal cellist at the Italian Opera upon Lindley's retirement. In 1859 he succeeded Cipriani Potter as Principal of the Royal Academy of Music. (Young 1967, 446.)

MAINZER   Joseph Mainzer (1801–1851) inaugurated music classes for workmen in Paris in 1834, and between 1835–41 published several educational works on music as well as the *Chronique musicale de Paris* (1838). The popularity of the classes, combined with Mainzer's left-wing political sentiments, led the authorities to ban them in 1839. As a result Mainzer emigrated to England in 1841, where he started the periodical *Mainzer's Musical Times,* which eventually became *The Musical Times.* (Scholes 1947, 3–10.)

MALAN   Henri-Abraham-César Malan (1787–1864) was ordained to preach in Switzerland in 1810, but his unorthodox beliefs, regarding hereditary sin, predestination, and divine grace, which were dogmatically held and promulgated with great fervor, led to his expulsion from the Swiss Canton in 1828. By then he had formed his own church, which continued to flourish. Malan wrote many polemical tracts, which were very popular, and over one thousand hymns. (Malan 1869, *passim;* Jackson 7:138.)

MALIBRAN   Maria-Felicia Malibran (*née* Garcia, 1808–36) went to America in 1826 to marry Eugene Malibran, a disastrous marriage provoked by her desire to escape her authoritarian father (and voice teacher). Returning to England in 1829, she appeared in London regularly until 1833. In 1836 she married Charles de Beriot, with whom she had toured since 1829. She died in a riding accident while appearing at the Manchester Festival in 1836. Chorley relates that her rigorous early training and the intensity of her performances made up for her lack of an outstanding natural voice (Chorley 1862, 7). She thoroughly captivated Mendelssohn, who described her as "a young woman, beautiful and splendidly made, her hair *en toupet,* full of fire and power, very coquettish." (Kupferberg 1972, 185.)

MANN   Horace Mann (1796–1829) was admitted to the bar in 1823 and was elected to the Massachusetts state legislature in 1827. In 1837 he was chosen the first secretary of education in the state of Massachusetts. He transformed the entire school system, vastly improving its quality. He did much to encourage Mason's efforts on behalf of music in the public schools, particularly through the establishment of teacher's institutes in which Mason participated. (Pemberton 1971, 274–76; Mann 1897, *passim.*)

MASON, ABIGAIL   Abigail Mason (*née* Gregory, 1797–1889), married Lowell Mason in 1817, and little is known of her life other than as Mason's wife and the mother of their four sons. Her letters and journals reveal a woman of considerable intelligence. (Pemberton 1971, 63–77; Mason P Box 4, Folders 22–28, Box 10, Folder 2.)

MASON, CATHERINE HARTSHORN   Lowell Mason's mother, Catherine Hartshorn Mason (1768–1852), descended from a family that had been in Medfield since 1651. She and Johnson Mason were married in 1791, and they had one daughter and four sons, of whom Lowell was the eldest. (Pemberton 1971, 2–3; Mason B 3–7.)

MASON, DANIEL GREGORY   Lowell Mason's eldest son, Daniel Gregory Mason (1820–69), (not the composer, who was Lowell Mason's grandson through Mason's son Henry), founded the publishing firm Mason Brothers in 1853 with his brothers Lowell Jr. and Henry. Upon Daniel Gregory's death in 1869 the firm was dissolved and most of its plates, including all of those of Lowell Mason, were sold to Oliver Ditson. (Mason B 197.)

MASON, JOHNSON   Lowell Mason's father, Johnson Mason (1767-1856), spent his entire life in Medfield, Massachusetts, where he was part owner in a dry goods store and manufactured straw hats. Active in civic affairs, he served as town clerk, treasurer, and selectman, and later in the state legislature. (Pemberton 1971, 1–2; Mason B 50.)

MASON, TIMOTHY   Timothy Mason (1801–61), Lowell Mason's younger brother, began his career in Boston as a "teacher, organist, composer and arranger of church and secular music" in 1821. He moved to Cincinnati in 1834 at the urging of Lyman Beecher, who had gone there in 1832. Mason quickly rose to a position of musical prominence in Cincinnati, and in 1837 the combined efforts of Mason and Beecher resulted in the installation of the first pipe organ west of the Allegheny Mountains. (Mason B 200-A.)

MASON, WILLIAM   William Mason (1829–1908) was the third son of Lowell and Abigail Mason. From 1849 to 1854 he studied piano in Europe with Hauptman, Dreyschock and Franz Liszt. Upon his return to the United States he established a successful career as a concert pianist. (Mason 1901, *passim.*)

MASSON   Elizabeth Masson (ca. 1806–65), Scottish-born contralto, made her debut at the Antient Concerts in 1831. She sang frequently at the Philharmonic Society Concerts, after which she devoted herself to teaching, editing, and composition. Her *Twelve Songs by Byron* (London, 1843) became quite popular. In 1838 she founded, with Mary Sarah Steele, the Royal Society of Female Musicians.

MATHER   George Mather (d. 1854), blind organist, served at St. Bride's Fleet St. from 1821 until his death. (Dawe 1983, 116.)

MELANCTHON   Philipp Melancthon (1497–1560) was a Protestant evangelical theologian who worked closely with Luther. For most of his adult life he was a professor at the University of Wittenberg, but his reputation was badly tarnished in his later years, partly over several theological controversies, and partly over an indiscreet letter that he wrote criticizing Luther. (Bodensieck 1965, 2:1517–27.)

MESSER, FRANZ   Franz Messer (1811-60) published *Sechs Gesänge für den Männerchor mit und ohne Begleitung des Pianoforte.* (Mainz: B. Schotts Söhne, [1838?].)

MOESER, AUGUST   August Moeser (1825–59) was the son and pupil of Karl Moeser and would have been twelve (not ten) years old at the time Mason heard him. Given Karl's reputation for questionable activities, it would not have been unlikely for him to present his son as being two years younger than he was. (van der Straeten 1933, 375.)

MOESER, KARL   Karl Moeser (1774–1851), violinist, performed throughout Germany before being engaged by Salomon in London in 1796. A scandal, one of several throughout his life involving women, forced him to leave London in 1797. He went to Berlin and then in 1798 to Russia. His whereabouts between 1806 and 1851 is not clear. There is no record of his playing with Beethoven, as Mason mentions. (van der Straeten 1933, 374.)

MOOSER   Aloys Mooser (1770–1859) was a Swiss organ builder. The large organ at the cathedral at Fribourg is considered his masterpiece. It was built between 1824 and 1834. (*MGG* 4:cols. 879–87.)

MORI   Nicholas Mori (1796 [some sources list 1793]–1839) was a leading violinist in the Philharmonic Society orchestra as well as a frequent soloist in London from 1816 until his death. He was also a partner in the music publishing firm Mori & Lavenu, 28 New Bond Street, which brought out English editions of the works of Mendelssohn. (Humphries 1954, 238; Loesser 1954, 349.)

MOSCHELES   Ignaz Moscheles (1794–1870) was well known as a pianist before he moved to London in 1826. He not only concertized there but taught at the Royal Academy of Music and conducted the Philharmonic Society Orchestra. In 1846 Mendelssohn invited him to join the faculty of the Leipzig Conservatory. Loesser, (145, 285) claims that in 1837 Moscheles was the first person in London to play a solo (totally unaccompanied) recital.

MÜLLER   Wilhelm Adolph Müller (1793–1859) published a number of pedagogical volumes for the piano and the organ, most of which included original compositions. He also published other theoretical works of a practical nature. (*NUC* 400, 226.)

MOTT   Robert Mott's establishment, Mott and Co. Pianoforte Makers, was at 92, Pall Mall, London, in 1837. (Humphries 1954, 239.)

MUSARD   Philippe Musard (1793–1859) was celebrated as a conductor at promenade concerts in Paris, and balls at the Paris Opera in the 1830s. He became known in England in 1840, when he conducted promenade concerts at Drury Lane. During the first half of the century, Musard was considered one of the best composers of dance music.

NAUMANN   Johann Gottlieb Naumann (1741–1801) wrote approximately twenty-five stage works and eleven oratorios, as well as large quantities of sacred music in many genres. In the late nineteenth century his best known compositions were the opera *Cora och Alonzo* (Stockholm, 1782) and the setting of Klopstock's *Vater unser* (Leipzig, 1798) (Grove I, v. 2, 449). Influenced by the *Sturm und Drang* movement, his sacred music in particular has an early Romantic quality, noticeable especially in the harmony, the motivic treatment, the instrumentation, and the choice of texts, which frequently deal with nature.

NEATE   The pianist Charles Neate (1784–1877) was one of the founding members of the Philharmonic Society and served as both performer and conductor. He was in Vienna for several months in 1815 and became particularly close to Beethoven. They subsequently had a disagreement, however, over a proposed commission for Beethoven from the Philharmonic Society.

NEUKOMM   Sigismund Ritter von Neukomm (1778–1858), a pupil of Haydn, composed over 1200 works, according to his own catalogue. His choral works were compared favorably to Haydn's, particularly in England, where they were performed frequently at major music festivals. Neukomm made Paris his permanent home but traveled extensively througout Europe as well as in parts of Africa and South America.

NOVELLO   Cecilia Novello (1812–90), daughter of Vincent Novello, prepared for a career as an actress but limited her theatrical activities after she married the poet and playwright Thomas James Searle in 1836. (Hurd 1981, 14.)

NOVELLO   Clara Novello (1818–1908), daughter of Vincent Novello, made her debut in London in 1832, and by 1837 was singing regularly at festivals and at the principal concerts in London. When Mendelssohn heard her at the Birmingham Festival in 1837, he arranged for her to sing in the Gewandhaus, an engagement that formed the cornerstone of a triumphant European tour which established her as a leading English soprano. (Mackenzie-Grieve 1955, 26–69.)

NOVELLO   Edward Petre Novello (1813–36), son of Vincent Novello, displayed exceptional talent as a painter, winning first prizes at the Royal Academy three years in succession. In 1834 he went to Paris to study, but, probably through overwork, contracted tuberculosis. (Hurd 1981, 15.)

NOVELLO   Joseph Alfred Novello (1810–96), the eldest son of Vincent Novello (1791–1861), entered his father's publishing business in 1829. Most of the success and the growth of the company is attributable to the business acumen and the innovations of Alfred. (Hurd 1981, 38–46.)

NOVELLO   Vincent Novello (1781–1861), pianist, organist and composer of sacred music, founded the publishing house Novello and Co. in 1811. (Hurd 1981, 1–11, 23–37.)

OTIS   Harrison Gray Otis (1765–1848) served in the Massachusetts Legislature from 1802–17 and was elected to the Senate in 1817. He resigned in 1822 to run for mayor of Boston and was defeated, but was elected to serve 1829–31. According to Samuel Eliot Morrison, Otis was "the principal connecting link of the Federalist aristocracy with the Boston democracy." (*DAB* 7:98–100.)

PALMER   Julius A. Palmer (1802–72) was a merchant and financier in Boston and a deacon in the Bowdoin Street Church. He was a brother of Ray Palmer, who composed many hymn texts, the most famous being "My Faith Looks up to Thee." (Mason B, 258.)

PARKER, WILLARD   Willard Parker (1800–1884) received his M.D. from Harvard in 1830 and taught at many schools, the last being the College of Physicians and

Surgeons, New York City. In 1856 he was made president of the New York Academy of Medicine. His European trip in 1837 was undertaken to examine European hospitals. (Atkinson 482–3; Talbott 560.)

PASTA   In the 1820s Giuditta Pasta (*née* Negri, 1798–1865) possessed a voice unmatched in range, power and intensity. She made her debut in Milan in 1815, in Paris in 1816, and in London (at the King's Theatre) in 1817. She had leading roles in many premieres of bel canto operas, including the title roles in Bellini's *La Sonnambula* and *Norma,* and Donizetti's *Anna Bolena.* She sang little after 1832, however, and it was a rare opportunity Mason had to hear her. When she did return to London in 1837, her vocal powers, according to Chorley, were "painfully impaired" compared to her previous appearance in 1828. (Chorley 1862, 87.)

PHILHARMONIC SOCIETY   The Philharmonic Society was formed in 1813 to provide more and better orchestral concerts in London than there had been in the early nineteenth century. It quickly established itself as the leading organization for orchestral performance in London. (Foster 1912, 1–7.)

POTTER   After initially studying piano and theory in England, Philip Cipriani Hambly Potter (1792–1871) went to Vienna where he met Beethoven, and he later introduced three of Beethoven's piano concertos to England. He taught piano at the Royal Academy of Music, where he succeeded William Crotch as principal in 1832, and he also conducted in the Philharmonic Concerts. Potter composed a large number of instrumental works, including at least nine symphonies. His lack of success in that field, however, caused him to virtually abandon composition after 1837. (Young 1967, 443–44.)

PURDAY, THOMAS EDWARD   Thomas Edward Purday, brother of rival Zenas Trivett Purday, was a music dealer and publisher, at 50, St. Paul's Church Yard, ca. 1834–62. After 1862 the firm became Thomas Purday & Son and moved to 531 Oxford Street. (Humphries 1954, 265.)

PURDAY, ZENAS TRIVETT   Zenas Trivett Purday, brother of Thomas Edward Purday, had a music store at 45, Holborn Street, from 1831–60. He published many humorous songs. In 1860 the firm was sold to Pottick and Simpson. (Humphries 1954, 265.)

PUZZI   Giovanni Puzzi (1792–1876) settled in London in 1817 and by 1830 had acquired sufficient fortune and acclaim as the outstanding virtuoso on the French horn in Europe to be able to limit his activities to solo work. In addition to appearing frequently as a soloist with the Philharmonic Society, he organized a wind ensemble called the Classical Concerts for Wind Instruments.

RAFFLES   Thomas Raffles (1788–1862), pastor at Great George Street Chapel from 1812 until 1862, was considered one of the leading Nonconformist ministers of his day. He was one of the principal founders of the Blackburn Academy for the education of Nonconformist ministers, and in 1839 he became chairman of the Congregational Union of England and Wales. (*DNB* 16:603.)

RIES   Ferdinand Ries (1784–1838) is known today principally because of his association with Beethoven, which is described in his *Biographische Notizen über L. van
Beethoven*. Ries originally came to London in 1814. He remained there for eleven
years, frequently appearing as both a composer and pianist in the Philharmonic
Concerts. In 1825 he "retired" to his native Rhineland, where he devoted much
of his time to the Lower Rhine Music Festivals.

RINCK   Johann Christian Heinrich Rinck (1770–1846) was associated with the city of
Darmstadt from 1805 as an organist and teacher. He toured extensively as an organ
virtuoso (*MGG*, v. 11, cols. 538–39). When Mason was in Darmstadt in 1852 he
bought Rinck's entire library from Rinck's son, paying approximately $275 for it.
(O'Meara 1971, 124.)

RIVINUS   Edward Florens Rivinus (1801–1873) was a German immigrant who became
an American citizen in 1830. He was appointed consul to Dresden in 1837. He was
active as an editor, library cataloguer, and translator in several fields, but his most
important contributions were in medical science, his profession. (Rivinus 1945,
13–23.)

ROCHLITZ   Johann Friedrich Rochlitz (1769–1842) was chosen by Breitkopf and Härtel
as the first editor of the *Allgemeine musikalische Zeitung* when it was founded in
1798. He resigned as editor in 1818 but continued to write for the publication. Rochlitz
also provided texts for a number of large vocal compositions, most notably a German translation of Mozart's *Don Giovanni*.

ROMBERG   Bernard Romberg (1767–1841) was a cello virtuoso who toured extensively in the early nineteenth century. He was Hofkapellmeister in Berlin from 1816–20
and resigned in protest over Spontini's appointment as general music director. He
lived in Hamburg after 1820. His ten cello concertos are seldom performed, but,
contrary to Kurt Stephenson's assertion (*NG*, v. 16, 145), several of his sonatas,
written mostly in a light, late-galant style, have remained standard repertoire for
students.

ROSENHAIN   Jacob Rosenhain (1813–94) made his London debut in a Philharmonic
Society concert April 17, 1837. He toured for many years before settling in Baden-
Baden in 1870. He was active as a composer as well as a virtuoso. He composed
three operas, which met with only limited success, and three symphonies, the first
of which, in G minor, was performed by Mendelssohn with the Gewandhaus in 1846.
(Loesser 1954, 407–8.)

ROYAL ACADEMY OF ARTS   The Royal Academy of Arts in London was founded in
1768 by George III, opening in 1769. In the early nineteenth century it was housed
in the National Gallery, although not in the present building, which was built later
(Hutchison 1968, 1–10).

ROYAL SOCIETY OF MUSICIANS   The Royal Society of Musicians of Great Britain was
founded in 1738 as the Society of Musicians. Its purpose was to raise funds for
aged and infirm musicians through concerts. In 1790 it received a charter from
George III, and the word "Royal" was added to its name.

RUBINI   Giovanni Battista Rubini (1794–1854) had been a leading tenor at the Paris Opera since 1825. He was renowned for his performances of principal roles in operas by Bellini and Donizetti. According to Chorley, his popularity was unmatched with the English public, with the purity and beauty of his voice making up for a wooden acting quality and a tendency to engage in excessive ornamentation. (Chorley 1862, 21–22.)

SACRED HARMONIC SOCIETY   The Sacred Harmonic Society was an amateur choral society founded in 1832. In 1834 the Society moved to Exeter Hall, but did not appear in the Large Hall until 1836, when it performed *Messiah* with three hundred musicians. The Sacred Harmonic Society pioneered the presentation of entire oratorios, rather than miscellaneous sections, and on March 7, 1837. gave the first London performance of Mendelssohn's *St. Paul.* (Grove I 3:209–11.)

SALAMAN   Charles Kensington Salaman (1814–1901) began sponsoring orchestral concerts in London in 1833. In 1835 he was one of the founders of the Concerti da Camera. In 1837 he was elected a Member of the Royal Society of Musicians and an Associate of the Philharmonic Society. (Obituary in *The Musical Times* 42:530–31.)

SALE   John Bernard Sale (1779–1856), son of composer John Sale, was made Lay-vicar, Westminster Abbey, in 1800 and a Gentleman of the Chapel Royal in 1803, in which posts he performed as organist. In 1826 he was appointed musical instructor to Princess Victoria, and on the death of Attwood in 1838 became organist of the Chapel Royal. In 1837 he published *Psalms and Hymns,* a collection of church music. (*DNB* 17:670.)

SCHNEIDER   Johann Schneider (1789–1864), son of Johann Gottlob Schneider and brother of Johann Christian Friedrich Schneider, held organ positions in Leipzig and Gorlitz before being appointed court organist in Dresden in 1825. Mendelssohn considered him one of the finest organ virtuosi of his time, and he was also renowned as a teacher. (*MGG* 11:col. 1903.)

SCHNYDER VON WARTENSEE   A civil servant by training, Schnyder von Wartensee (1786–1868) decided to take up music as a profession at age 26. He went to Vienna and then returned to Switzerland, where he established a reputation as a composer and writer on music. He taught briefly at Pestalozzi's Institute in Yverdon before moving to Frankfurt am Main. (*MGG* 11:cols. 1922–26.)

SCHOTT   The music publishing firm of Schott was founded by Bernard Schott in Mainz probably in 1780. By 1837 it was being run by Bernard's two sons, Johann Andreas (1781–1840) and Johann Joseph (1782–1855), who changed the name of the company to B. Schott's Söhne. (*MGG* 12:cols. 50–52.)

SCHROEDER-DEVRIENT   Although the vocal powers of Wilhelmine Schroeder-Devrient (1804–1860) were already beginning to decline in 1837, she sustained her career for many years through her powerful dramatic presence. Celebrated particularly for her role as Leonore in Beethoven's *Fidelio,* her singing was an enormous inspiration to the young Wagner. (Chorley 1862, 9, 38–39.)

SCHWENKE   Johann Friedrich (Fritz) Schwenke (1792–1852), grandson of Johann Gottlieb Schwenke, became organist at St. Nicholai in 1729. His principal work was the *Choral-Buches zum Hamburgischen Gesangbuch.* (*MGG* 12:cols. 401–3.)

SHAW   Mary (Mrs. Alfred) Shaw (1814–76) first sang in public in 1834 and through 1837 limited her career to England, singing in Covent Garden and in many festivals. After 1837 she sang in the Gewandhaus in Leipzig, and in 1839 debuted in Italy in Verdi's *Oberto.* According to William H. Husk, in the 1840s her husband's insanity so deranged her system that "the vocal organs became affected and she was unable to sing in tune," thus ending her career. (Grove I 3:285.)

SHERMAN   James Sherman became pastor of Surrey St. Chapel in 1836, after having served for sixteen years at the Independent Church in Reading. (Independent Churches in England were the equivalent of Congrega-tional Churches in the United States.) While at Surrey St., Sherman was considered the most popular preacher in England, with Sunday attendance reportedly averaging three thousand. (Grant 1839, 313–19.)

SINGAKADEMIE   The Singakademie of Berlin was founded in 1791 by C. F. Fasch and is still in existence. In the early nineteenth century it introduced a number of significant works to Berlin, including Bach's *St. Matthew Passion* under Mendelssohn's direction in 1829. C. F. Rungenhangen served as its director from 1833 to 1851. (*MGG* 1:col. 1722.)

SKINNER   In 1827 Thomas Harvey Skinner (1791–1871) became the first pastor of the Berkeley Congregational Church in Boston. He was pastor of the Mercer Street Presbyterian Church from 1835–40. Skinner later became professor of Sacred Rhetoric and Pastoral Theology at the Union Theological Seminary and a leader in the New School Branch of the Presbyterian Church. (Prentiss 1871, *passim.*)

SMART   Although Sir George Smart enjoyed considerable success as an organist, pianist, violinist, and composer, it was as a conductor that he became most well known. He conducted Philharmonic Concerts from 1813 to 1844 and at many festivals throughout England. He conducted Mendelssohn's *St. Paul* in Liverpool in 1836 and the music for the coronations of both William IV and Victoria. (*DNB* 18:389–90; Smart 1907, 282–89 and *passim.*)

SOCIETA ARMONICA   Societa Armonica was founded in 1827 for the purpose of giving subscription concerts which consisted mostly of orchestral and some chamber instrumental music and vocal pieces drawn mainly from Italian opera. The Society flourished until about 1850. (Grove I 3:543.)

SPONTINI   Gasparo Spontini (1774–1851), considered an extremely successful composer of French *opera seria,* was appointed General Music Director in Berlin in 1820 and lived there until 1842. Arriving just as German national sentiment peaked with the success of Weber's *Der Freischütz,* he remained the center of controversy, his position sustained principally because he had the ardent support of King Wilhelm III.

STOCKTON   Robert Field Stockton (1795–1866) entered the navy during the war of 1812 and had risen to the rank of Captain by 1837. He was offered the position of Secretary of Navy under Tyler in 1841 but refused and took an active part in the war with Mexico. He resigned from the Navy in 1850 and was elected to the United States Senate, serving from 1851–53. (*DAB* 9, pt. 2:48–49.)

STURGE   Joseph Sturge (1793–1858) was an outspoken leader in a number of reform causes in England: the Chartist Movement (to establish the rights of unions and better the conditions of the working class), worldwide abolitionism, and universal suffrage. Upon his return from the West Indies in 1837, he published, with Thomas Harvey of Leeds, *The West Indies* (London,1837), which documented the ill-treatment of slaves there. (Cole 1941, 163–86.)

SUTTON   William Walter Sutton (1793–1874), a native of Dover, was a composer, teacher, pianist and organist. His publications consisted mostly of arrangements for the piano. (*BMB* 402.)

TAMBURINI   Antonio Tamburini (1800–1876) sang throughout Italy from the age of eighteen, and in London and Paris from 1832 to 1841, after which he returned to Italy. Famous as an interpreter of Rossini, he was considered second only to Lablache as a baritone in London. (Chorley 1862, 34, 109, 124.)

THALBERG   Sigismund Thalberg (1812–71) was considered the chief rival to Franz Liszt as a pianist in the early nineteenth century. His cool, reserved manner was in marked contrast to that of the more flamboyant Liszt, and each profited handsomely from the publicity attendant to their rivalry. (Loesser 1954, 372–73.)

THAYER   Gideon French Thayer (1793–1864) established the Chauncy-Hall School in Boston in 1828. He was a founder of several educational associations, including the American Institute of Instruction, the American Association for the Advancement of Education, and the Massachusetts State Teachers Association. He stressed the importance of a balanced program that included physical education and music, and he organized his school by departments, with competent teachers in charge of each. This was an innovative concept in the 1830s. (*DAB* 9:404–5.)

TWIGGS   David Emanuel Twiggs (1790–1862) served in the War of 1812, rising to the rank of major in 1814. He fought in the war with Mexico and was made a major general in the Confederate Army. Although too old to take the field, he was for a time the ranking general in the Confederate forces. (*DAB* 10:82.)

VOGT   Jacques Vogt (1810–69) was organist at St. Nicholas Cathedral, from the time that the organ was built to his death, and was then succeeded by his son Eduard (1847–1911). (*MGG* 4:col. 885.)

WARD   Cornelius Ward (b. 1814) was an organist at Speen, Buckinghamshire, his birthplace. He published several collections of church music and composed at least one oratorio and one cantata. Ward's interest in the mechanics of instruments extended to the flute, about which he published *The Flute Explained Being an Examination of the Principles of Its Structure and Action* (London, 1844). (*BMB* 431.)

WATTS   Isaac Watts (1674–1748) became pastor of Mark Lane Independent Church in 1702. After a serious illness in 1712, he relinquished his pastoral duties to a co-pastor and concentrated upon writing. He was well known in the early nineteenth century as his many hymn texts and psalm paraphrases were still in use. (Julian 1907, 2:1236.)

WEBB, GEORGE J. George J. Webb (1803–87) emigrated from England to Boston in 1830, where he assumed the position as organist of Old South Church. He helped Mason found the Boston Academy of Music and was later President of the Handel and Haydn Society. He and Mason enjoyed a particularly close personal and professional relationship, although shortly after Mason returned from Europe he and Webb were temporarily estranged. Mason's son William married Webb's daughter Mary. (See Paige 1967, 434–37, for a brief summary of Webb's career including a list of joint publications with Lowell Mason; Pemberton 1971, *passim,* for a more detailed discussion of their relationship.)

WEBB, JOHN John Webb (1776–1869) was ordained in 1800 and had a sixty-year career as a minister, serving in a number of churches. Facile in both Latin and Norman French as well as in paleography, he was elected a Fellow of the Society of Antiquaries in 1819. He supplied the libretto for a number of sacred works, including Mendelssohn's projected but incomplete "The Hebrew Mother." (*DNB* 20:1011.)

WILHEM Guillaume-Louis Bocquillon Wilhem (1781–1842) pioneered the teaching of singing in Paris. He opened his own school, l'Orphéon, and published a highly influential *Manuel musicale,* which had the same relationship to English musical education that Kübler's *Anleitung* did to American; through a translation by John Hullah it formed the basis of musical education in England beginning in 1840. (Mackerness 1964, 154.)

WINSLOW Hubbard Winslow succeeded Lyman Beecher as pastor at Bowdoin St. Church in 1832. He served there until 1844. According to Winsor, Bowdoin St. Church was full to overflowing during his ministry, no other church in Boston being more popular (Winsor, v. 3, 412). After Winslow retired from the ministry in 1844 he wrote a large number of books, some under the pseudonym Evangelicus Pacificus. (List in *CAB* 1:178.)

WOODMAN, HANNAH CALL Hannah Call Woodman was one of the principal singers in Mason's church choir and in the choir of the Boston Academy of Music. Several members of the Woodman family sang in Mason's choirs, including Mary Olive Woodman, who married George F. Root in 1845. (Mason B, 185.)

WOODMAN, JONATHAN CALL Jonathan Call Woodman, brother of Hannah Call Woodman, was a principal bass and an assistant at the Boston Academy. He also composed some hymn tunes.

ZEUNER Charles Zeuner (1795–1857) emigrated from Germany to Boston in 1830. He assumed the posts of organist at Park Street Church and the Boston Handel and Haydn Society and became the Society's president in 1839. His oratorio *The Feast of the Tabernacle* was one of the first oratorios to be written and performed in America. (Hitchcock 1986, 4:593.)

ZINGARELLI   Nicola Antonio Zingarelli (1752–1837), considered the last major composer of *opera seria*, was highly prolific as a composer of both sacred and secular vocal music, with at least forty-two operas, twenty-three masses, and eight oratorios to his credit, in addition to many other works. His style was extremely conservative and his reputation today suffers from the nineteenth-century verdict that his music is frequently trivial. *Giulietta e Romeo* was first performed at Milan in 1796.

Appendix 4

Annotations to *Messiah* Programs

Messiah, performed by the Royal Society of Musicians,
Wednesday Evening, June 7, 1837,
The King's Concert Rooms, Hanover Square, London.

TEXT FROM PROGRAM	MASON'S COMMENTS
	[Back of title page]:
	Chorus 60
	Double base 4
	Violoncello 4
	Violins 10

PART I.

OVERTURE.

RECIT. acc. Mr. Braham

Comfort ye, comfort ye my people, saith your God; speak ye comfortably to Jerusalem; and cry unto her that her warfare is accomplished, that her iniquity is pardoned.

The voice of him that crieth in the wilderness, Prepare ye the way of the Lord;* make straight in the desert a highway for our God.

L/aord ["a" inserted by Mason]

SONG

Every valley shall be exalted, and
every mountain and hill made low; the
crooked straight, and the rough places
plain.

CHORUS

And the glory of the Lord shall be re-
vealed . . .[1]   Rather slow

RECITATIVE, acc.
Mr. STRETTON (Rehearsal),
Mr. MACHIN (Performance)

Thus saith the Lord of Hosts: yet
once a little while and I will shake the
heavens and the earth . . .

SONG.

But who may abide the day of his
coming? And who shall <u>stand</u>* when he
appear<u>eth</u>?*   *[underlined by Mason]
    For he is like a refiner's fire.

CHORUS

And he shall purify the sons of Levi,
that they may offer unto the Lord an offering in righteousness.

RECITATIVE, Mrs. A. SHAW.

Behold! a virgin shall conceive . . .

SONG and CHORUS
O thou that tellest good tidings to*   [added by Mason:]
Zion . . .   *tidings to

RECITATIVE, acc.
Mr. STRETTON (Reh.), Mr. MACHIN

For, behold! darkness shall cover the earth, . . .

SONG

The people that walked in darkness have seen a great light . . .

CHORUS.

For unto us a Child is born, . . .   rather slow and steady
                                                       audience stood

PASTORAL SYMPHONY.
RECITATIVE, Madame CARADORI ALLAN.

There were shepherds abiding in the
field, . . .   slow

RECITATIVE, acc.

And lo! the angel of the Lord came   Count 4 slowly or 8
upon them, and the glory of the Lord   quick
shone round about them, and they were   [illegible]
sore afraid.*   common march time
                                              *afraid
                                              ◡⟶

RECITATIVE.

And the angel said unto them, Fear
not, for behold I bring you good tidings
of great joy, which shall be to all people;
for unto you is born, this day, in the city
of David, a Saviour, which is Christ the   *cres ff [under words
Lord!*   "Christ the Lord"]

RECITATIVE, acc.

And suddenly there was with the
angel a multitude of the heavenly host,   same time as before—
praising God, and saying,   common march

CHORUS

Glory to God in the highest, and*   *ff [placed under
peace on earth, good-will towards men!   word "and"]
audience rose   Some of the runs—
                                                 echoed very soft

SONG, Madame CARODORI ALLAN.

Rejoice greatly, O daughter of Zion!   quick
shout, O daughter of Jerusalem! behold,
thy King cometh* unto thee!
He is the righteous Saviour, and he
shall speak peace unto the heathen. *Da
Capo*

RECIT. Mrs. A. SHAW

Then shall the eyes of the blind be
opened . . .

SONG, Mrs A. SHAW.

He shall feed his flock like a   Key of F.
shepherd; . . .

Second Part, Miss CLARA NOVELLO.

Come unto him, all ye that labour   B♭
and are heavy laden . . .

CHORUS.

His yoke is easy, and his burthen is   8 in a measure—or 4 and
light.*   Too loud
                                                 *They sing this word as

though it was used in
opposition to darkness as
in Creation

PART II

I should think 15 minutes

CHORUS.

Behold the Lamb of God, that taketh
away the sin of the world.

SONG, Mrs. A. SHAW

He was despised and rejected of men,
a man of sorrows, and acquainted with
grief.

(applauded)
great effect of f and p—
particularly p's
ex. despised—rejected
      f   p

CHORUS.

Surely he hath borne our griefs . . .
And with his stripes we are healed.

*count 4—rather quick—
a common march

CHORUS.

All we, like sheep, have gone astray:*
we have turned every one to his own way.
   And** the Lord hath laid on him the
iniquity of us all.***

Count 4 rather quickly so
that the r's are as quick as
they can easily be sung.
*a-strah-ey
**slow
***Latter part soft—close
soft

RECITATIVE, acc.

All they that see him laugh him to
scorn . . .

CHORUS.

He trusted in God that he would
deliver him, if he delight in him.

delight—delauight

RECIT. acc. Mr. BENNETT

Thy rebuke hath* broken his heart;   *harth
he is full of heaviness; he looked for some
to have pity on him, but there was no
man, neither found he any to comfort
him.

SONG.

Behold and see, if there by any sor-   slow
row like unto his sorrow!

RECITATIVE, acc. Mrs. KNYVETT

He was cut off out of the land of the   slow
living; for the transgression of thy people
was he stricken.

SONG.

But thou didst not leave his soul in   rather quick
hell; nor didst thou suffer thy Holy One
to see corruption.

SEMI-CHORUS.
ALL THE PRINCIPAL SINGERS.

Lift up your heads, O ye gates . . .

SEMI-CHORUS.

Who is the King of Glory?   same time as usual

SEMI-CHORUS

The Lord strong and mighty, the
Lord mighty in battle.

SEMI-CHORUS.

Lift up your heads, O ye gates . . .

SEMI-CHORUS.

Who is the King of Glory?

SEMI-CHORUS.

The Lord of Hosts:

FULL CHORUS

He is the King of Glory.

RECITATIVE.

Let all the angels of God worship him.

SONG, Miss CLARA NOVELLO

How beautiful are the feet of them that preach the gospel of peace . . .

QUARTET, Miss BIRCH,
Mrs. A. SHAW, Mr. BENNETT, and Mr. SALE
and CHORUS

Their sound is gone out into all the lands, and their words unto the end of the world.

break in time

SONG, Mr. PHILLIPS.

Why do the nations so furiously rage together? and why do the people imagine a* vain thing.
The kings of the earth rise up . . .

*a cadenza on this a.

CHORUS.

Let us break their bonds asunder, and cast away their yokes from us.

spirited

SONG.

Thou shalt break them with a rod of iron . . .

GRAND CHORUS.

Hallelujah! for the Lord God Omnipotent reigneth . . .

Hallelujah—altos on A— (King of Kings) harsh— trebles leading off from D to E, F♯ and G—same difficulty as in Boston— want of promptness, energy—unity.

PART III.

(Two or three minutes)

SONG, Mrs. W. KNYVETT.

I know that my Redeemer liveth, and that he shall stand at the latter day upon the earth;* and though worms destroy this body . . .

*9th taken before 8th

SEMI-CHORUS

Since by man came death,

rather—ad lib

FULL CHORUS.

By man came also the resurrection of the dead;

SEMI-CHORUS

For as in Adam all die,

FULL CHORUS.

Even so in Christ shall all be made alive

The organ gave a short staccato chord before the choruses commenced

RECITATIVE, acc. Mr. PHILLIPS.
Trumpet Obligato, Mr. HARPER.

Behold!* I tell you a mystery; we shall not all sleep; but we shall all be changed in a moment, in the twinkling of an eye, at the last trumpet.**

*slow

**very slow

SONG.

The trumpet shall sound, and the dead shall be raised incorruptible, and we shall be changed.

Trumpet beautiful every note

RECITATIVE.

Then shall be brought to pass the saying that is written, Death is swallowed up in victory!

Mrs. Shaw

DUET, Mrs. A. SHAW and Mr. BENNETT.

O Death! where is thy sting? . . .

CHORUS.

But thanks be to God, who giveth us the victory through our Lord Jesus Christ.

SONG, Miss BIRCH

If God be for us, who can be against us? . . .

GRAND CHORUS.

Worthy is the Lamb that was slain . . .
Blessing and honour, glory and power, be unto Him that sitteth upon the throne, and unto the Lamb, for ever and ever! Amen.

Amen slow and firm
I was never so sensible of the dependence of a performance upon the solo singers.

Messiah,
performed at the Birmingham Musical Festival,
September 21, 1837.

TEXT FROM PROGRAM	MASON'S COMMENTS

PART I

OVERTURE

RECIT. ACCOMPANIED—Mr. BENNETT

Comfort ye, comfort ye my people, saith your God; speak ye comfortably to Jerusalem; and cry unto her that her warfare is accomplished,* that her iniquity is pardoned.—*Isa.* xl. 1, 2.
    The voice of him that crieth in the wilderness, . . . —*Isa.* xl. 3.

*hard
appogiatures many

AIR.

Every valley* shall be exalted, and every mountain and hill made low, the crooked** straight, and the rough places plain.***—*Isa.* xl. 4.

*varley
**kard
***moving [?] passage
ah

CHORUS.

And the glory of the* Lord shall be revealed, . . . —*Isa.* xl. 5.

*Glory of the
𝅘𝅥𝅭 𝅗𝅥 𝅘𝅥 𝅘𝅥

RECITATIVE, accompanied.—Mr. MACHIN

Thus saith the Lord of Hosts: yet once a little while and I will shake* the heavens and the earth, . . . —*Haggai* ii. 6, 7.
    The Lord, whom ye seek, shall suddenly come to his temple; . . . —*Mal.* iii. 1.

*moving passage
very distinct

AIR.

But who may abide the day of his coming? And who shall stand when he appeareth?*—*Mal.* iii. 2

                                                              *or
For he is like a refiner's** fire.—*Mal.* iii. 2

*or

**awe
on the last cadence

CHORUS

And he shall purify the sons of Levi, that they may offer unto the Lord an offering of righteousness.—*Mal.* iii. 3.

RECITATIVE—Mr. HAWKINS.

Behold! a virgin shall conceive and bear a son, and shall call his name EMANUEL, God with us.—*Isa.* vii. 14.

[referring to both Recitative and Air]: Too high for his voice—but well done

AIR AND CHORUS.

O thou that tellest good tidings to Zion, get thee up into the high mountain . . .—*Isa.* xl. 9.
Arise, shine, for thy light is come, and the glory of the Lord is risen upon thee.—*Isa.* ix 1.

RECIT. accompanied.—Mr. PHILLIPS.

For, behold! darkness shall cover the earth, and gross darkness the people! but the Lord shall arise upon thee, and his glory shall be seen upon thee, and the Gentiles shall come to thy light,* and kings to the brightness of thy rising.—*Isa.* ix. 2.

*distinct

AIR.

The people that walked in darkness have seen a great light . . . —*Isa.* ix. 2.

[Referring to both Recitative and Air]: admirably done

CHORUS.

For unto us a child is born, unto us   splendid beyond description
a Son is given . . . —*Isa.* ix. 6.

PASTORAL SYMPHONY.
RECIT.—Madame ALBERTAZZI.

There were shepherds abiding in the
field, keeping watch over their flocks by   sub base highly effective
night.—*Luke* ii. 8.   CCC

RECIT. ACCOMPANIED.

And lo! the angel of the Lord came
upon them, and the glory of the Lord
shone round about them, and they were
sore afraid.—*Luke* ii. 9.

RECITATIVE

And the angel said unto them, Fear
not; for, behold! I bring you good tidings
of great joy . . . —*Luke* ii. 10, 11.

RECIT. ACCOMPANIED.

And suddenly there was with the
angel a multitude of the heavenly host,
praising God and saying—*Luke* ii. 13.

CHORUS.

Glory to God in the highest, and
peace on earth, good-will towards men.   [Written on brackets:]
—*Luke* ii. 14.   pure—free from ornament.

AIR.—Madame GRISI.

Rejoice greatly, O daughter of Zion;   splendidly done
shout, O daughter of Jerusalem: behold,
thy King cometh unto thee.—*Zach.* ix. 9.
He is the righteous Saviour, and he

shall speak peace unto the heathen.* —
Zach. ix. 10.

*tr.

RECIT.—Mrs. A. SHAW

Then shall the eyes of the blind be
opened, and the ears of the deaf unstopped
. . . —*Isa.* xxxv. 5, 6.

He   shall   feed   his

AIR.

He shall feed his flock like a shepherd;
and he shall gather the lambs with his arm,
and carry them in his bosum, and gently*
lead those that are with young.— *Isa.* xi.
11.

The F. of Mrs. Shaw—how
rich! beyond all praise
*word gently—differently
adapted Mrs. Shaw's song—
surpassed all description—
Remember her passing
 from medium to di petto in
the lowest passage—chaste
cadenza—feeling—tender-
ness

SECOND PART.—Miss NOVELLO.

Come unto him, all ye that labour, and
are heavy laden, and he will give you
rest.—*Matt.* xi. 28.
Take his yoke upon you, and learn of
him . . . —*Matt.* xi. 29.

B♭

CHORUS.

His yoke is easy, and his burthen is
light.—*Matt.* xi. 30.

commenced too loud and
harsh
Chorus too loud—not
light and easy enough

PART SECOND.

CHORUS.

BEHOLD the Lamb of God, that
taketh away the sins of the world.—*John*
i. 29.

AIR. Mrs. A. SHAW.

He was despised and rejected of men;
a man of sorrow . . . —*Isa.* liii. 4,5.

CHORUS

Surely he hath borne our griefs, and
carried our sorrows . . . *Isa.* liii 4, 5.
And with his stripes we are healed.—   Count 4 moderately or 8
Isa. liii.5.   rather quickly—time steady.

CHORUS

All we, like sheep, have gone astray;   Allegro—rather quick
we have turned every one to his own   Time change—to andante
way.—*Isa.* liii.6.   or largo
And the Lord hath laid* on him the   *pp on this word but not
iniquity of us all.—*Isa.* liii. 6.   the first time it occurred.

RECIT. accompanied.—Mr. VAUGHAN.

All they that see him laugh him to
scorn; they shoot out their lips and shake
their heads, saying—*Ps.* xxii. 7.

CHORUS.

He trusted in God that he would   allegro moderato
deliver him: let him deliver him,if he   tone firm and sure
delight in him.—*Ps.* xxii. 8.

RECIT. accompanied.—Mr. VAUGHAN.

Thy rebuke hath broken his heart; he
is full of of [sic] heaviness . . . —*Ps.* lxix.
21.

AIR.

Behold, and see if there be any sorrow like unto his sorrow.—*Lam. of Jer.* i.
12.

RECIT. accompanied.—Mrs. KNYVETT.

He was cut off out of the land of the living, for the transgression of thy people was he stricken.—*Isa.* liii. 8.

AIR.

But thou didst not leave his soul in hell; nor didst thou suffer thy Holy One to see corruption.—*Acts* ii. 27.

rather quick

SEMI-CHORUS.

ALL THE PRINCIPAL SINGERS.

Lift up your heads, O ye gates, and be ye lift up, ye everlasting doors, and the King of Glory shall come in.—*Ps.* xxiv. 7.

Who is the King of Glory?—*Ps.* xxiv. 8.

The Lord strong and mighty, the Lord mighty in battle.—*Ps.* xxiv. 9.

The Lord of hosts.—*Ps.* xxiv. 10.

FULL CHORUS.

The Lord of hosts, he is the King of Glory.—*Ps.* xxiv. 10.

RECITATIVE—Mr. HOBBS.

Unto which of the Angels said he at any time, Thou art my Son, this day have I begotten thee?—*Heb.* i, 5.

CHORUS.

Let all the angels of God worship h him.—*Heb.* i, 6.

AIR.—Miss C. NOVELLO.

How beautiful are the feet of them that preach the gospel of peace, and bring glad tidings of good things!—*Isa.* lii. 7.

great purity of tone

QUARTET—Mrs. KNYVETT, Messrs. HAWKINS, BENNETT, and NOVELLO; AND CHORUS

Their sound is gone out into all the lands, and their words unto the ends of the world.—*Ps.* xix. 4.

admirable chorus

AIR—Mr. MACHIN.

Why do the nations so furiously rage together; and why do the people imagine a* vaine thing?—*Ps.* ii, i.

The kings of the earth rise up, and the rulers take counsel together against the Lord, and against his anointed.—*Ps.* ii. 2.

*It is certainly absurd to stop upon the particle 'a and make a cadenza, shake, etc.

CHORUS.

Let us break their bonds asunder, and cast away their yokes from us.—*Ps.* ii. 3.

powerful Cho. next to Hails tone;

RECITATIVE.—Mr. HOBBS.

He that dwelleth in heaven shall laugh them to scorn; the Lord shall hve them in derision.—*Ps.* ii. 4.

AIR.

Thou shalt break them with a rod of iron; thou shalt dash them in pieces like a potter's vessel.—*Ps.* ii. 9.

GRAND CHORUS.

Hallelujah! for the Lord God Omnipotent reigneth.—*Rev.* xix. 6.

The kingdom of this world is become the kingdom of our Lord, and of his Christ: and he shall reign for ever and ever.—*Rev.* xi. 15.

King of kings, and Lord of lords. — *Rev.* xi. 16.

Hallelujah.

What shall I say of this Cho.? I shall never hear any thing like it again in this world. The Lord God reigns—so I submit to his reign with all my heart— Oh! what an impression of the majesty and glorious province of God is produced by hearing this Cho. Myrids of Angels will shout Hallelujah throughout all eternity at the thought that God reigns. And the the emotions produced at the change "The Kingdom of this world are becometh. ["] Christ the Lamb of God will reign and to him all creatures shall bow. Does he now reign in my heart—have I submitted to him when whom angels now adore and who always will be worshipped by all that have breath—

How sublime the thought that all shall bow down shall cast the crown at the feet of the Saviour. The pause before the final cadence—produces a wonderful effect and seems like a moments pause in the praises of heaven—and at that moment the glory of God seems to fill the place,

and his glorious presence
to fill every heart with
awe and reverence but the
final long Hallelujah bursts
upon the ear—as written
of those eternal Hallelu-
jahs [praises written below
word Hallelujah] in which
all the repenters will be
permitted to join.

[Inserted between the Se-
cond and Third Parts:]

Tr

PART THIRD.

AIR.—Mrs. KNYVETT.

I know that my Redeemer liveth, and
that he shall stand at the latter day upon
the earth; *and though worms destroy this
body, yet in my flesh shall I see God.—
Job xix. 25, 26.

For now is Christ risen from the
dead,** the first fruits of them that
sleep.***—*I Cor.* xv. 20.

*the passage just before
this was done exeedingly
soft and with great
tenderness of feeling
**when this goes up to
G♮ (dim) and down por-
tamen to [pp under words
"from the dead"]
***closing cadences all pp
and with the greatest
tenderness imaginable.

QUARTET.—Mrs. KNYVETT, Mesrs.
HAWKINS, HOBBS, and MACHIN.

Since by man came death.—*I Cor.*
xv. 21.

CHORUS

By man came also the resurrection of
the dead;—*I Cor.* xv. 22.

Quartet (written in by Mason)

For, as in Adam all die,—*1 Cor.* xv. 22.

CHORUS

Even so in Christ shall all be made alive.—*1 Cor.* xv. 22.

[Written on brackets:]
exquisitely fine
the effect is astonishingly
good, melting, overcoming

RECIT. acompanied.—Mr. PHILLIPS.

Behold! I tell you a mystery; we shall not all sleep . . . —*1 Cor.* xv. 51, 52.

AIR.

TRUMPET OBLIGATO—Mr. HARPER.

The trumpet shall sound, and the dead shall be raised incorruptible, and we shall be changed.— *1 Cor.* xv. 52.

This was done to perfection. His trumpet has not valves but a slide. It seemed too very hard for him. He shut his eyes—face very red—the echoes where the same strain was repeated were fine.

RECITATIVE.—Mr. HAWKINS.

Then shall be brought to pass the saying that is written, Death is swallowed up in victory.—*1 Cor.* xv. 54.

DUET—Messrs. HAWKINS and HOBBS.

O Death! where is thy sting? *1 Cor.* xv. 55.
O Grave! where is thy victory?
The sting of death is sin,—*1 Cor.* xv. 56.
And the strength of sin is the law.

CHORUS.

But thanks be to God who giveth us the victory through our Lord Jesus Christ.—*1 Cor.* xv. 57.

admirable

AIR—Miss C. NOVELLO.

If God be for us, who can be against us? . . . —*Rom.* viii, 31, 33, 34.
It is Christ that died, yea, rather that is risen again . . . —*Rom.* viii. 31, 33, 34.

This song was in as a delicious moral—bringing consolation and peace to the soul and then all heaven and earth unite to ascribe [illegible]—angels and hea[then] seem to vie with each other—there seem to be neither words nor deeds sufficient for them to give vent to the overflowings of grateful hearts to him who hath redeemed—Blessing

GRAND CHORUS

Worthy is the lamb that was slain, and hath redeemed us . . . *Rev.* v. 12.
Blessing and honour, glory and power, be unto him that sitteth upon the throne, and unto the Lamb, for ever and ever! Amen.* *Rev.* vii. 12.

*moderato—careful time

Appendix 5

Letters from Europe

We know from Mason's Diary that he wrote many letters to America while he was in Europe. Unfortunately, only two of those have survived. Although they repeat some information in the journals they do give a different twist to much of it. The two letters are transcribed here in their entirety.

Letter to Melvin Lord

London, June 6, 1837

Mr. Melvin Lord

My dear Sir

I have now been in this great city of the world for three weeks. I have had time to look around a little among the musical people—to become acquainted—hear etc.

I have not as yet devoted any time to the wonders etc. of London but have been wholly devoted to the leading business of my tours in Music. I have been very cordially received by musical people, and have in general only found it necessary to announce my name and residence, an I am on intimate terms at once. Indeed I am quite surprised that I am so well known here among musical men of repute.

I have become acquainted amongst others with Mr. Novello—the father and the son—with Mr. Gardiner,—Sir George Smart—Mr. Atwood—Purday—these are some of the principals. I am daily attending concerts etc. twice have I heard Handels Messiah—once the Mount of Olives, once The Bell etc. besides much secular music. Being known as professional I receive many tickets gratuitously to concerts. This is quite a matter of consequence here, where the lowest price is a ½ a guinea—and often double that price. As to style of perfomance I do not find that the Choruses are on the whole much better done than with us. But the Orchestras here are much more complete—every instrument is well played and the part is sure—and the stringed instruments are far more numerous in all their concerts—about 30 or 40 violins is not uncommen—but the very common orchestra would not have less than 12 to 18 violins.

The solos are far better here—being all done by professional singers. I happened to come to London in a most favorable time for hearing music—it is said that there never was so much talent assembled here before—and this is the very best season. There are Concerts almost every day twice a day—i.e. a morning concert beginning at 12 or 2—and continuing about 3 or 4 hours, and an evening concert beginning at 7 or 8. I yesterday attended the performance of Handels Messiah in the Hanover Square rooms at 12 oclock. The room was crowded at this hour, and for a good part of the time I could not get a seat. Braham sung and others of like character as vocalists. Among the great stars now in London are Grisi—perhaps the best Soprano in the world—Albertassi, Schroeder-Devrient, Rubini, Tamburini, Ivanoff and Lablache. These and also the best English singers I am hearing often.

I have also made some considerable purchases of music—say perhaps 200$ or 300$ worth, and find some things that I think will work up well. There remain many music Shops and publishers for me yet to visit. I stroll about and call into them daily—make selections and then tell them that I must have the music at professional price. "Have you a ticket?" they ask. "No" I reply. "What address?" I write my name, or hand out my card—and it is sufficient. Mr. Novello's is my packing place and whatever I purchase I have sent to him.

Novello will publish a book of Children's music for me [*The Juvenile Songster*] while I am here—and also a number of psalm tunes—probably a selection of a few from Occasionals. This will give us some hold on the people at home. What of the times? I suppose they are severe enough—I fear I shall lose by several failures of which I have already heard, and I fear more. Before this reaches you, you will have heard of the failure of the great American Houses here—Wilson and co—Wiggen and Co—and Wilder and Co—besides others since of less note. I hope our friends W and C will go through.

I know not how soon I may leave London but probably in a few weeks more.

Church music here is miserably low—I have not heard a tolerable Choir although I have been to the Chapel Royal, Westminster Abbey, St. Paul's and other important Churches. My best regards to Mrs. Lord and to all friends.

Very truly yrs.

L. Mason

The original of the above letter is in the Library of the American Antiquarian Society, Worcester, Mass.

Letter of Lowell Mason to the Bowdoin Street Choir

London, June 27, 1837

To the Bowdoin Street Choir, all of whom I love to remember
My dear Friends,

When I wrote to you last (These directed to Deborah) I gave you some little account of what I had been doing from day to day up to the 8th instant;—I find my journal is getting rather behind, and I must be brief. On the 9th, Mr. Benedict, a distinguished German [?] professor gave a concert which I attended. I went half an hour before the time, Viz: one o'clock, but found every seat occupied, and I could only get a little way into the room the crowd was so great. Ladies old and young most superbly dressed—with feathers and diamonds, and laces and silks—and gentlemen were all crowded up together in a complete jam. I was so closely pressed a good part of the time that I could not without inconvenience to others raise my hand to my head—on which I kept my hat for it was the only place—here I stood on a warm summer's day in June from 1:00 to half past 5:00 o'clock—listening to the strains of melody poured forth by Pasta, Grisi, Schroeder-Devrient, Albertazzi, Clara Novello, Rubini, Ivanoff, Tambourini, Lablache, and others—accompanied by full and splendid orchestra. I had just time to get my dinner from 6:00 to 7:00 when I returned to the same room to a concert of the "Societa Armonica"—where was a full orchestra and a full room—home at 12:00 o'clock.

The next day Saturday at 12:00 o'clock I attended a rehearsal of the Philharmonic orchestra. This is the greatest concert orchestra as it relates to instrumental music, after all—but as I have already mentioned it in a former letter I will not enlarge. In the evening I listened to Miss Clara Novello, while her father accompanied her on piano. On Sunday morning a friend called on me to take me to hear a favorite preacher at Surrey Chapel. I went with him—but soon after we got in he informed me that the regular preacher was absent and that they were to have a stranger—it proved to be Reverend Mr. Kirk of Albany with whom I am acquainted. He preached a very faithful sermon from the text "I am the vine, ye are the branches"—after the service I saw him. Here they sing by the whole congregation—it was rather poor and uninteresting.

In the afternoon I went with the same friend to a Baptist church—Text—"For the soul to be without knowledge is not good."—heard—

1. All knowledge is useful
   First. Mechanical knowledge
   Second. Musical knowledge
   Third. Intellectual knowledge
2. Spiritual knowledge is preeminently important
   First—Its excellence

Second—Its accompaniments
Third—Its permanency
Fourth—Its prospects.

I could not help thinking a little logical knowledge would have been an advantage to the preacher. It was, however, a spiritual and good sermon. I could hardly help smiling at his mention of musical knowledge. On Monday 12th attended the concert of philharmonic and heard the celebrated Symphony Pastoral by Beethoven—performed by a band of 60 almost perfect.

Spent Sunday forenoon Chev. Neukomm. He arrived in London from Paris a day or two since and I had been introduced to him at the Philharmonic. On Thursday morning at half past 10:00 I started in the stage coach from South Hampton on my way to the Isle of Wight to visit the parents and sisters of our Mr. Webb. I had a delightful ride and was gone from London three days and got home Saturday evening. It was a pleasant visit—from Mr. and Mrs. W., I received constant attentions—I heard the young ladies (our Mr. W's sisters) play the piano forte and harp on Saturday evening after I got home I attended a very fine concert by Mr. Neate. The next day Sunday I spent mostly with Mr. Sharp—brother of James Sharp of Boston. Attended church with him and heard a very excellent sermon by Reverend W. Clayton to whom I had a letter of introduction from S. Codman. In the evening I heard [Thomas] Adams the great organist—I think his execution is wonderful indeed.

Monday night 19th June

This morning we heard of the death of the king—the shops are presently closed and all the people seem to regret his loss very much. It did not however prevent my attending a concert in the evening. On Wednesday the new queen Victoria (18 years of age) was proclaimed—Queen of these realms. The ceremony commenced at St. James Palace where the queen appeared at the balcony dressed in plain black—a pretty little girl enough—but how strange that she should be the sovereign of the empire. The procession consisted of horse guards, heralds, trumpets, drummers, etc. etc. etc. who at certain places in the city would stop and proclaim Victoria queen and then all the people would shout Huzza—"God save the Queen"—etc.

During the remainder of the week I continued to attend my music as before—and on Friday (day before yesterday) I attended at six different churches—in one of which (Crown Chapel) I heard some congregational singing with which I was quite pleased. It was truly devotional and it seemed to refresh not only my musical ears but my soul. I expect to leave London 28 June for Hamburg and from thence to travel some in Germany from whence I hope to write you in due time. May you all be prospered and especially be blessed with all spiritual blessings and made heirs of the kingdom of eternal life.

Sincerely yrs.

L. Mason

The original of the above letter is in Mason P.

Notes

Introduction

1. According to the publisher's claims, Mason's anthology, *The Carmina Sacrae,* had sold over 400,000 copies by 1855, at a time when sales of 50,000–80,000 were considered outstanding. Although these figures are unsubstantiated, they may be compared with similar claims made by Stephen Foster's publisher, Firth and Pond, to have sold 130,000 copies of "Old Folks at Home," and 90,000 copies of "My Old Kentucky Home" by 1853.

2. Boston (O. Ditson & Co.), 1853.

3. These letters were not written as such on the tour. Both Mason and his wife Abigail kept a detailed diary of their activities, and Mason drew upon both diaries in compiling the "letters." Both diaries are now in the John Herrick Jackson Music Library at Yale University, listed under "Lowell Mason Papers, MSS 33" [Mason P]. Mason's diary is in Series V, Box 9, Folders 4–6; Abigail Mason's, entitled "Mrs. Lowell Mason. Journal," is in Box 10, Folder 2.

4. A principal difference between Mason's 1837 trip and his later one was the very ease of travel itself. By 1852 steam travel across the Atlantic had become common and rail travel in Europe was a reality. Mason's scrapbook contains a rail map and schedule for 1852, which dramatically reflects the changes in transportation that occurred between his two journeys.

5. Vol. 9, pp. 577–81; vol. 10, pp. 16–18; and vol. 10, pp. 62–67.

6. Immediately prior to 1970, the 1837 Journals were in the possession of Mrs. Helen Endicott, great-granddaughter of Lowell Mason. They are now in Mason P, Series II, Box 9, Folders 1–3. The most extensive discussion of the journals occurs in Pemberton 1971.

7. In 1837 the Oxford movement had just gotten under way. See Temperley 1979, 249–52.

8. Mason, for instance, recorded several occurrences of "lining out," a practice whereby the minister, or more often a clerk, intoned the hymn a line or two at a time to guide the congregation in singing it. Lining out was quite common in the seventeenth and early eighteenth centuries but had come under attack during the eighteenth century and was thought to have been mostly eliminated in the larger churches and towns by the nineteenth. While most of the churches in which Mason observed lining out were dissenting, some were among the larger churches in London. For a discussion of this practice and its disappearance see Temperley 1981, 511–44.

9. For a fuller discussion of this point, see Broyles 1985, 316–48.

10. See Temperley 1979, 249–52, for a discussion of the Oxford movement in relation to musical activity.

11. Mason singled out Thomas Adams of London, August Wilhelm Bach of Berlin, and Johann Gottlob Schneider of Dresden as particularly outstanding organ virtuosi.

12. All of the three standard histories of American music that have provided the basic interpretive framework for the past generation of musicologists represent Mason as one of the pivotal figures in American musical history: Gilbert Chase states that "of all musicians active in the United States during the nineteenth century, Lowell Mason has left the strongest, the widest, and the most lasting impress on our musical culture" (Chase 1966, 151), a comment quoted by Wiley Hitchcock (1969, 56). More recently Charles Hamm characterized Mason as "a man who had as much impact on the musical life of nineteenth-century America as any other person" (Hamm 1983, 163).

13. This is certainly true of the many letters by Mason that have been preserved. We know that Mason kept other diaries of this sort, but most have not survived. In his incomplete biography of Lowell Mason, Henry Lowell Mason (Mason's grandson) refers to some that have subsequently disappeared [Mason B. 89].

14. Some of the more important studies are Whitney Cross, *The Burned-Over District* (Ithaca, N.Y., 1950); Paul, Johnson, *A Shopkeeper's Millennium* (New York, 1978); Perry Miller, *The Life of the Mind in America* (New York, 1965); and Robert H. Wiebe, *The Opening of American Society* (New York, 1984).

15. Letter dated April 12, 1855. The letter is reproduced in Mason 1927.

16. For a discussion of the influence of evangelicalism upon national purpose see Nagel 1971; see also Wiebe 1984.

17. In 1831 Mason moved to the Bowdoin Street Church, which at the time was under the leadership of Lyman Beecher.

18. This report was published in the *Boston Musical Gazette* 1, no. 16 (Nov. 28, 1838): 121.

19. These are now in Mason P, Series II, Box 4, Folder 67.

20. One other fragment of a letter to Mason from Neukomm survives in which Neukomm tentatively agrees to Mason's offer, if he is assured of success. The fragment has no date, but almost certainly predates the more detailed acceptance.

21. The original of the second page containing the names of persons to whom the letter was addressed has disappeared, but according to the notes of Lowell Mason's grandson Henry Lowell Mason, it listed the following persons: (Hamburg) Johann Friedrich Schwenke, Bernhard Romberg; (Berlin) Gasparo L. P. Spontini, Madame Milder, Karl Friedrich Rungenhagen, Karl Hennig, August Wilhelm Bach; (Dresden) Johann Gottlob Schneider, August Alexander Klengel; (Leipzig) Johann Friedrich Rochlitz, Gottfried Wilhelm Fink; (Frankfurt) Ferdinand von Hiller, Xaver Schnyder von Wartensee; (Offenbach) Johann Anton André; (Mainz) Andreas Schott; (Bonn) Peter Simrock; (Darmstadt) Karl Ludwig, Amand Mangold, Johann Christian Markwort; (Mannheim) Franz Lachner; (Paris) Luigi Cherubini, P. M. François de Sales Baillot, G. L. Wilhem.

22. Woodbridge's letter was addressed to the following persons: Monsieur Le Dr. Eilen, Coblenz, Monsieur Le Directeur Braun, Neuwied Seminary, Monsieur Le Directeur Baggé, Muster Schule, Frankfort Sur Mayne, Monsieur le Directeur Stern, Seminary de Carlsruhe, and Prof. Gernsbach, Monsieur Le Professeur Leonhard, Univ. de Heidelberg, M. Le Prof. Klumpp, Stuttgard, M. Le Prof. Köcher, M. Le Directeur Densel, Eslinger Wurtemberg, M. Le Prof.

Stendel, Tübingen, M. Le Directeur Vehrli, Kreuzlingen (near Constance), M. Le Directeur Zellwegen, Trogen Appenzel, M. Le Pasteur Fry, M. Le Directeur Krusi, M. Le Prof. Nägeli, Zurich, M. Le. Prof. Pfeiffer, Lenzburg Argovie, M. Le Directeur Keller, M. Fellenberg, Hofwell, M. Le Directeur Rickle, Buchsee Sem., M. le Rev'd Pere Giraud, Freibourg, M. Le Prof. Monnard, Lausanne, M. Le Syndri Vornet Pictete, Casora, M. le Directeur Blumhardt, Basle, M. le Directeur Zeller, Beugger. The list is incomplete; in the letter addressed to Mason that accompanied this one Woodbridge refers to twenty-four names. A second page is probably missing. The letter also contains a number of awkward or incorrect French usages, such as the odd and inconsistent capitalization of "*le*" in the list of names, which has been reproduced here exactly as Woodbridge wrote it.

23. The organists August Wilhelm Bach and Johann Gottlob Schneider, the cellist Bernard Romberg and the composer-theorist Xaver Schnyder von Wartensee.

24. For a discussion of the concept of a gentleman in antebellum America and its historical significance, see Persons 1973, and Wiebe 1984.

25. See Broyles 1985, 316–48.

26. See chap. 2, entry for May 20, for the strongest statement to this effect: "What a wonderful place this is—what New York is to a country village London is to N York."

Chapter 1

1. The term packet comes from the French word *pacquebot* (mail carrying), and means any ship that travels a regular route. For a discussion of conditions on the packets, see Spiller, 3–13.

2. The change in the size and shape of the ships actually began in the revolutionary era, when the necessity of running blockades and escaping pirates put a premium upon speed and maneuverability.

3. Harriet Martineau's *Retrospect of Western Travel* (London, 1838), contains one of the most well-known and informative accounts of the same New York-Liverpool route that Mason took. Martineau made the voyage in August–September, 1834, embarking from Liverpool.

4. Speed was determined by the heaving of the log, in which a triangular piece of wood sufficiently weighted to remain relatively stationary in the water was attached to a rope and thrown overboard. The amount of cord that unwound while an hourglass emptied was then measured.

5. Mother Cary's chickens were storm petrels. The term is derived from the Spanish "Madre cara," (beloved Mother), a term used because sailors believed that the birds would protect them.

6. "Arlington" is a hymn tune written by Charles Hutcheson in 1832.

7. Mason is referring to Thomas Tregenna Biddulph, *The Inconsistency of Conformity to This World with the Profession of Christianity* (Bristol, 1803).

8. Mason lived in Savannah from 1812 to 1827. During that time he worked in a dry goods store and later a bank and was extremely active in the Independent Presbyterian Church. He was also a founder and Superintendent of the Savannah Sabbath School, the first Sunday school in the city. La Far has the most detailed discussion of this phase of Mason's activity.

9. Mason is referring to Bowdoin Street Congregational Church, for which he had been organist and choir director since 1831.

10. Those persons identifiable from Mason's list are: Billy, Lowell, Daniel, and Henry—Mason's sons William (1829–1908), Lowell, Jr. (1823–85), Daniel Gregory (1820–69), and Henry (1831–90); Father and Mother could refer to Lowell Mason, himself, and his wife Abigail, or to Lowell Mason's father, Johnson Mason (1767–1856) and either Mason's mother Catherine Hartshorn Mason (1769–1851) or Abigail Mason's mother, Hannah Buckminster Gregory. Elizabeth and Julia may refer to Elizabeth C. and Julia Belcher, the sisters of the publisher Joshua Belcher (d. 1816). They would have been fifty to sixty years old at the time. Mason later records writing a letter to Elizabeth C. Belcher (see chap. 2, entry for May 15).

11. Mason is probably referring to James David Knowles, *Memoir of Mrs. Ann H. Judson, Late Missionary to Burmah. Including a History of the American Baptist Mission in the Burman Empire*. (Boston, Lincoln and Edmands, 1829). Mrs. Judson's memoirs were originally published as *Memoir of the American Baptist Mission to the Burman Empire in a Series of Letters Addressed to a Gentleman in London* (London, 1827).

Chapter 2

1. In 1835 George Hogarth complained bitterly of the German domination of English music and the effect that this had upon aspiring English musicians (Hogarth 1835, 421–22).

2. It is not clear who Dr. Wainwright or the other persons that Mason refers to in this May 15 entry are. Mason undoubtedly had letters of introduction from persons in Boston.

3. The Liverpool and Manchester Railway, the world's first modern railway, opened in 1829. The train originally traveled at the unheard-of speed of 25–30 miles an hour and made the journey of slightly more than thirty miles in 90 minutes. This included several stops. Roscoe's description of the London–Birmingham Railway, which was completed in 1838, illustrates the dramatic difference that rail travel could make. It cut the time from thirty to five-and-one-half hours (Roscoe, 6–7). The tunnel to which Mason refers is in Liverpool, just outside the railway station.

4. When a committee was attempting to secure the services of Lowell Mason for the churches in Boston in 1827, they put together a list of twenty-six subscribers who pledged $50 or $100 each in order to guarantee an annual salary of $1500 to Mason. These subscribers included a Henry Homer and a George Homer, who were probably related to this Homer family (Mason P, Box 4, Folder 38).

5. Neukomm had indicated in previous correspondence with Mason that he was to be reached through P. F. Willert.

6. The Collegiate Church became Manchester Cathedral in 1848 when the first diocese since the sixteenth century was founded.

7. The 1836 Manchester Festival was the third of four great music festivals held in Manchester. The first occurred in 1777 and the others in 1828, 1836 and 1844. Maria-Felicia Malibran died in a riding accident while appearing at the Manchester Festival in 1836.

8. Neither Salabert, nor anyone similar, is listed on the program that Mason retained.

9. This may be John Slade, Jr. who was a member of the Boston Academy of Music (Mason B, 269).

10. The panic of 1837, which precipitated the worst depression the country had seen, began in New Orleans in March and by April had spread to the rest of the country. Proctor and Palmer was a banking firm in Boston.

11. Mason later refers to Novello in reference to St. George's Chapel. That was probably the church Mason attended.

12. Mark Lane Independent Church.

13. John Rippon, *A Collection of Psalm and Hymn Tunes* (London, [1792] and subsequent editions).

14. An illegible word is crossed out and "distinguished" is added, probably by HLM.

15. Mason's original plan was to have Mr. Hach accompany him on his tour of Germany and Switzerland. See Mason's entry for June 30.

16. Princess Victoria became Queen Victoria less than one month later when her father, William IV, died. See Mason's entries of June 20 and following.

17. It is unclear who Alfred and Jarris Slade are, but they are probably related to John Slade. See entry of May 19.

18. This was the premier performance.

19. As the title page to Mason's program indicates (Scrapbook) this was an annual celebration for which the various charity schools of London banded together.

Chapter 3

1. Emended, probably by HLM.

2. *The Juvenile Songster,* according to HLM (Mason B, 329), was published simultaneously in London and Boston in 1837 or early 1838. See Mason's entry below, June 24.

3. Emended, probably by HLM.

4. Emended, probably by HLM.

5. This was the title of the concert, which consisted of string trios, quartets and quintets by Onslow, Bernard Romberg, Mozart, Corelli and Beethoven, as well as a violin sonata by Beethoven. H. J. Banister was the cellist for this concert.

6. The Thames Tunnel was planned in 1823 by M. I. Brunel. Although it was not actually completed until 1843, it was open to visitors during construction when construction permitted. It was one of the favorite tourist attractions of London in the early nineteenth century, and even the Duke of Wellington led parties to it.

7. Emended, probably by HLM.

8. This could be Mason's own "Missionary Tune," which originally had the words, "From Greenland's Icy Mountains," or it could be "Missionary Chant," by Charles Zeuner, which first appeared in *The American Harp* (Boston, 1832).

9. In 1837 Cornelius Ward patented a cable-tuned kettledrum, which allowed a timpani to be tuned with one screw (Specifications Patent Office, 1837–7505, London). The method ultimately proved unsuccessful as it resulted in uneven tension around the surface of the drum. Ward wrote several letters to *The Musical World* describing and then defending his invention, the last one containing a drawing of the mechanism. (*The Musical World,* 60, vol. 5, May 5, 1837, pp. 118–19; 61, vol. 5., May 12, 1837, pp. 134–35; and 86, vol. 7, Nov. 3, 1837, pp. 118–20.)

Chapter 4

1. See Mason's entry of June 10. Mason had heard a work of Bernard Romberg in London. See entry of May 27.

2. The museum was founded in 1830 but only later became one of the world's great museums.

3. Given Mason's complete ignorance of German, to which he frequently refers, he probably meant Breitkopf and Härtel. There is no other firm that even resembles "Bechtold and Hartje."

4. This gallery was founded in 1722 under August II. Before 1855, when a new building was opened, the paintings were exhibited in the Stable Buildings of the Judenhof.

5. By Musical Gazette, Mason means the *Allgemeine musikalische Zeitung,* of which Gottfried Wilhelm Fink (1783–1846) had been editor since 1828. Fink had written criticism for *AMZ* since 1808 in addition to many other articles on music in various publications.

6. It should not be overlooked that Mason made no attempt to visit St. Thomas Kirche while in Leipzig or even to associate that town with Johann Sebastian Bach.

7. There are no references to any members of the André family in Mason's London entries.

8. I was unable to locate any record of Stricker having founded his own company. He probably continued with the firm of C. A. André, with which he was associated.

9. This oratorio, by Carl Loewe, was first performed at Mainz in 1836.

10. Both of these songs appeared in *The Primary School Song Book* (Mason 1846, 58, 50).

11. Clearly a version of "Wie Schön leuchtet der Morgenstern" by Philipp Nicolai, 1599.

12. Mason was obviously familiar with Kübler's work, as his *Manual of the Boston Academy of Music* is, in Mason's own words, "to a great extent . . . a translation of" G. F. Kübler's *Anleitung zum Gesang-Unterrichte in Schulen* (Stuttgart, 1826) (Mason 1841, 3).

Chapter 5

1. This is the large organ at St. Nicholas Cathedral in Fribourg built by Aloys Mooser (1770–1859) between 1824 and 1834. This particular organ is considered his masterpiece, and the vox humana, with swell mechanism, is its most famous characteristic. The organ was enlarged in 1912, but it has remained essentially Mooser's organ. There is a photograph of it in *MGG* 4:col. 881.

2. Mason later published a description of this organ: "The Organ at Freiburg, Switzerland," *The Musical World* 7 (September 22, 1837): 19–21.

3. Mason is referring to Jacques Vogt's pastoral fantasia, *Gewitter,* which was written specifically for the St. Nicholas Cathedral organ and which helped make the organ famous. The piece remains in the repertory in Fribourg (*MGG* 4:col. 885).

4. Mason first published "Greenville" in *The Hallelujah* (Mason 1854, 154).

5. This is probably Joseph Cummings's son. See entry of June 29.

6. The same Edward N. Kirk that Mason heard in London on June 11.

7. A diorama was a scene painted in linear perspective on a large back cloth that was housed in a cubicle and viewed through an aperture or frame. Objects placed in front of the cloth, translucent curtains and lighting effects heightened the illusion of depth. Diorama exhibi-

tions were opened in both Paris and London in the 1820s by Louis Daguerre, who later invented the daguerreotype, the first commercially successful type of photography (Altick, 163–65).

8. The organ of St. Etienne-du-Mont dates from 1631. A photograph of the richly carved case is found in Wilson, 133.

Chapter 6

1. Mason had heard him on June 25. See entry in chap. 3.

2. Depicting the Roman basilica of St. Paul, which burned in 1823, was one of the "hits" of the Diorama of 1837. An eyewitness describes it as follows: First the scene was portrayed intact, then "as we gaze, the dark cedar roof disappears, and we see nothing but the pure blue Italian sky, whilst below, some of the pillars have fallen—the floor is covered with wrecks; the whole, in short, has almost instantaneously changed to a perfect and mournful picture of the church after the desolation wrought by fire" (Altick 1978, 170).

3. The Surrey Zoological Gardens, one of several outdoor amusement gardens in London, opened in 1831 and continued until 1877. In the early nineteenth century the evening's entertainment usually featured large orchestral concerts intermingled with spectacular effects.

4. A large chamber organ constructed by Flight and Robson between 1812 and 1817. It attempted to reproduce mechanically the sound of the entire orchestra and could be played simultaneously by several performers. For many years it was exhibited in the Flight and Robson showroom on St. Martin's Lane (Sumner 1962, 233).

5. Mott invented the "Sostinente Pianoforte," which sustained tone by means of a revolving roller and a movable bridge that divided the strings in two, producing the first harmonic (Brindsmead 1889, 76).

6. It is not clear what a Filtera, or filter as Mason refers to it later, was. As Mason's entry of September 12 indicates, it was apparently large enough to necessitate being shipped in a separate container.

7. "St. Georges," first found in Thomas Greatorex, *Parochial Psalmody* (London, ca. 1820). An earlier version, that begins 5 | 3 - 8 | 8 is called "Wiltshire," and is by Sir George Smart, in his *Divine Amusement* (London, ca. 1795).

8. See appendix 4 for Mason's annotations in his program of this performance of *Messiah*.

9. See entry of May 15.

10. This tune is similar in the beginning and end to Hackney by E. Lees, found in Thomas Williams *Psalmodia Evangelica* (London, 1789). The middle, however, is quite different.

11. Anthem by James Kent (1700–1776), organist at Winchester Cathedral, 1737–74 (*BMB*, 229), published in Kent 1773.

12. Mason was not alone in his opinion of Ole Bull, who was often charged with indulging in virtuosic feats with music of questionable merit. He used a flat bridge and heavy bowing, which facilitated much multiple stopping. In 1843 he made his first, highly successful tour of America (Smith 1947, 42–45).

Chapter 7

1. See appendix 1.

2. Harriet Martineau describes a similar scene in even more detail. Her reactions are much the same as Mason's, although in order to stay on deck throughout the storm, she had to lash herself to a post (Martineau 1838, 27–30).

3. It is not clear, from either the author or the title, to which book Mason is referring.

4. F. W. Krummacher, *Elijah the Tishbite,* was written in 1826 but came out in English only in 1836.

5. There is no earlier reference in Mason's diary to either Mrs. Bauer or Chateau de Bloney.

Appendix 1

1. The above names are listed separately in journal no. 3.

2. Almost certainly refers to letters written.

3. In Mason 1842, 108.

4. Ibid., 127.

Appendix 4

1. The entire text is included in the program. In sections where Mason made no annotations, only the text incipit is printed here.

Works Cited

Altick, Richard D. *The Shows of London*. Cambridge, Mass.: The Belknap Press of Harvard University Press, 1978.

Aston, Peter. *The Music of York Minster*. London: Stainer & Bell, 1972.

Atkinson, William, ed. *The Physicians and Surgeons of the United States*. Philadelphia: C. Robson, 1878.

Barker, Virgil. *American Painting: History and Interpretation*. New York: Macmillan, 1950.

Barrett, Alexander. *Balfe: His Life and Work*. London: Reeves, n.d.

Berlioz, Hector. *Memoirs of Hector Berlioz from 1803 to 1865*. Translated by Rachel (Scott Russell) Holmes and Eleanor Holmes. Annotated and translation revised by Ernest Newman. New York: Tudor Publishing Co., 1935.

Blume, Frederich, ed. *Die Musik in Geschichte und Gegenwart*. 16 vols. Kassel: Bärenreiter-Verlag, 1949.

Bodensieck, Julius, ed. *The Encyclopedia of the Lutheran Church*. 3 vols. Minneapolis: Augsburg Publishing House, 1965.

Brindsmead, Edgar. *The History of the Pianoforte*. London: Simpkin, Marshal, 1889.

Brown, James D. and Stephen S. Stratton. *British Musical Biography: A Dictionary of Musical Artists, Authors and Composers, Born in Britain and Its Colonies*. New York: Da Capo, 1971; orig. pub. London, 1897.

Broyles, Michael. "Lowell Mason on European Church Music and Transatlantic Cultural Identification: A Reconsideration," *Journal of the American Musicological Society* 38 (Summer 1985): 316–48.

Cazalett, William. *The History of the Royal Academy of Music*. London: T. Bosworth, 1854.

Chase, Gilbert. *America's Music From the Pilgrims to the Present*. New York: McGraw-Hill, 1966.

Chorley, Henry F. *Thirty Years' Musical Recollections*. London: Hurst and Blackett, 1862.

Clerke, Agnes M. *The Herschels and Modern Astronomy*. London: Cassell & Co., 1895.

Clutton, Cecil, and Austin Nilano. *The British Organ*. London: B. T. Batesford, 1963.

Cole, G. D. H. *Chartist Portraits*. London: MacMillan, 1941.

Cross, Whitney. *The Burned-Over District: The Social and Intellectual History of Enthusiastic Religion in Western New York, 1800–1850*. New York: Harper and Row, 1950.

Dawe, Donovan. *Organists of the City of London 1666–1850: A Record of One Thousand Organists with an Annotated Index*. London: Donovan Dawe, 1983.

Demuth, Norman. *French Opera: Its Development to the Revolution*. New York: Da Capo, 1978; orig. pub. Sussex, England, 1963.

Dooley, James Edward. "Thomas Hastings, American Church Musician." Ph.D. diss., Florida State University, 1963.

Dunning, Albert E. *Congregationalists in America*. New York: J. A. Hall, 1894.

Fairman, Charles E. *Art and Artists of the Capitol of the United States.* Washington: U.S. Government Printing Office, 1927.

Fétis, François-Joseph. *Biographie Universelle des Musiciens: Supplément et Complément.* Paris: Libraire de Firmin Didot, 1860–65; 1878–80.

First Annual Report of the Boston Academy of Music. Boston: Issaac R. Butts, 1833.

Forbes, Abner. *The Rich Men of Massachussets.* 2d. ed. Boston: Redding, 1852.

Foster, Myles Birket, comp. *History of the Philharmonic Society of London: 1813–1912.* London: J. Lane, 1912.

Galignani [publisher]. *New Paris Guide, Compiled from the Best Authorities, Carefully Verified by Personal Inspection, and Arranged on an Entirely New Plan.* Paris, 1837.

The Gentleman's Magazine. Ed. Sylvanus Urban, Gentleman. London, 1731–1907.

Grant, James. *The Metropolitan Pulpit; or, Sketches of the Most Popular Preachers in London.* New York: Appleton, 1839.

Grove, George, ed. *A Dictionary of Music and Musicians.* 4 vols. London: Macmillan and Co., 1889.

Hamm, Charles. *Music in the New World.* New York: W. W. Norton, 1983.

The Harmonicon. Ed. William Ayrton. London: W. Pinnock, 1823–33.

Hastings, Thomas, ed. *Musica Sacra.* Utica, N.Y.: Seward and Williams, 1815.

Hidy, Ralph W. *The House of Baring in American Trade and Finance.* Cambridge, Mass.: Harvard University Press, 1949.

Hitchcock, H. Wiley, and Stanley Sadie. *The New Grove Dictionary of American Music.* London: Macmillan Press Limited, 1986.

Hitchcock, Wiley. *Music in the United States: A Historical Introduction.* Englewood Cliffs, N.J.: Prentice-Hall, 1969.

Hogarth, George. *Musical History, Biography and Criticism: Being a Survey of Music from the Earliest Period to the Present Time.* London: J. W. Parker, 1835.

Hopkins, Edward J. *The Organ, Its History and Construction.* London: Robt. Cocks, 1877.

Humphries, Charles, and William C. Smith. *Music Publishing in the British Isles.* London: Cassell, 1954.

Hunziker, Rudolf. *Hans Georg Nägeli.* Zurich: Gebrüder Hug, 1938.

Hurd, Michael. *Vincent Novello—and Company.* Granada: Granada Publishing, 1981.

Hutchison, Sidney C. *The History of the Royal Academy.* London: Chapman and Hall, 1968.

Jackson, Samuel MaCauley, and George William Gilmore, eds. *The New Schaff-Herzog Encyclopedia of Religious Knowledge.* Grand Rapids, Mich.: Baker Book House, 1963.

James, John Angell. *The Life and Letters of John Angell James: Including an Unfinished Autobiography.* Ed. R. W. Dale. New York: R. Carter and Brothers, 1861.

Johnson, Allen, et al. *Dictionary of American Biography.* 11 vols. New York: Charles Scribner's Sons, 1963; orig. pub. 20 vols. New York: American Council of Learned Societies, 1928–37.

Johnson, Paul E. *A Shopkeeper's Millennium: Society and Revivals in Rochester, New York 1815–1837.* New York: Hill and Wang, 1978.

Jones, F. O., ed. *A Handbook of American Music and Musicians.* Canaseraga, N.Y.: F. O. Jones, 1886.

Julian, John, ed. *Dictionary of Hymnology.* 2 vols. Grand Rapids, Mich.: Kregel Publications, 1985; orig. pub. 1907.

Kent, James. *Twelve Anthems, Composed by James Kent.* London, 1773.

Krummacher, F. W. *Elijah the Tishbite.* Trans. from the German. New York, n.d.; London, n.d.

Kupferberg, Herbert. *The Mendelssohns: Three Generations of Genius.* New York: Charles Scribner's Sons, 1972.

LaFar, Margaret Freeman. "Lowell Mason's Varied Activities in Savannah." *The Georgia Historical Quarterly* 28 (Sept. 1944): 113–37.

Lavignac, Albert, fondateur. *Encyclopédie de la musique et dictionnaire du conservatoire, Deuxième partie: Technique—esthétique—Pédagogie*. Directeur, Lionel de la Laurencie. Paris: Librairie Delagrave, 1925.

Lodge, Henry Cabot. *Early Memories*. New York: Charles Scribner's Sons, 1925.

Loesser, Arthur. *Men, Women, and Pianos*. New York: Simon and Schuster, 1954.

"Lowell Mason Papers, MSS 33." In the John Herrick Jackson Music Library at Yale.

McClintock, John, and James Strong. *Cyclopaedia of Biblical, Theological, and Ecclesiastical Literature*. New York: Harper & Bros., 1883.

McClure, Ruth K. *Coram's Children: The London Foundling Hospital in the Eighteenth Century*. New Haven: Yale University Press, 1981.

MacKenzie-Grieve, Averil. *Clara Novello, 1818–1908*. London: Geoffrey Bles, 1955.

Mackerness, Eric. D. *A Social History of English Music*. London: Routledge and Kegan Paul, 1964.

Malan, César. *Chants de Sion; ou Recueil de cantiques de louanges, de prières et d'actions de graces a la gloire de L 'Eternal*. Geneva, 1824.

Malan, César. *The Life, Labours, and Writing of Caesar Malan . . . by One of His Sons*. London: James Nisbet, 1869.

Mann, Mary Tyler (Peabody), ed. *Life and Works of Horace Mann*. 5 vols. Boston: Walker, Fuller, 1897.

Martineau, Harriet. *Retrospect of Western Travel*. 2 vols. London: Saunders and Otley, 1838.

Mason, Daniel Gregory. "A Glimpse of Lowell Mason from an Old Bundle of Letters." *The New Music Review* 26 (January 1927): 49–52.

Mason, Henry Lowell. "Lowell Mason: His Life and Works." Manuscript, in the "Lowell Mason Papers," Yale University. Box 12.

Mason, Lowel [*sic*], ed. *The Juvenile Songster*. 1st ed., n.p., n.d.

_____. *Carmina Sacra: Or Boston Collection of Church Music*. Boston: J. H. Wilkins and R. B. Carter, 1841.

_____. *Manual of the Boston Academy of Music, for Instruction in the Elements of Vocal Music on the System of Pestalozzi*. Boston: Carter, Hendee, 1834.

Mason, Lowell. *Book of Chants*. Boston: Wilkens, Carter, 1842.

_____, ed. *The Boston Academy Collection of Church Music*. Boston: Carter, Hendee, 1835.

_____, ed. *The Hallelujah: A Book for the Service of Song in the House of the Lord*. New York: Mason Brothers, 1854.

Mason, Lowell, and G. J. Webb, eds. *The Primary School Song Book*. Boston: Wilkins, Carter, 1846.

Mason, Lowell, and Thomas Hastings, eds. *Spiritual Songs for Social Worship*. Utica, N. Y.: Hastings & Tracy and W. Williams, 1832.

Mason, William. *Memories of a Musical Life*. New York: The Century Company, 1901.

Miller, Perry. *The Life of the Mind in America*. New York: Harcourt, Brace and World, 1965.

The Musical Magazine; or, Repository of Musical Science, Literture, and Intelligence. Boston: Otis, Broaders and Company, n.d.

The Musical World. London: J. Alfred Novello, 1837–80.

Nagel, Paul C. *This Sacred Trust: American Nationality 1798–1898*. New York: Oxford University Press, 1971.

The National Cyclopedia of American Biography. Ed. by "Distinguished Biographers Selected from Each State." Permanent Series, v. 1–62. Ann Arbor, Michigan; University Microfilms, 1967; orig. pub. New York, 1901, 1909.

The National Union Catalogue: Pre-1956 Imprints. Chicago: American Library Association, 1970.

Neukomm, Sigismund Ritter. *Equisses biographiques de Sigismund Neukomm*. Paris, 1859.

Ninth Annual Report of the Boston Academy of Music. Boston: T. R. Marvin, 1841.

Norman, John. *The Organs of Britain: An Appreciation and Gazetteer*. London: David and Charles, 1984.

Ohles, John F. *Biographical Dictionary of American Educators.* 3 vols. Westport, Conn.: Greenwood Press, 1978.

O'Meara, Eva J. "The Lowell Mason Papers." *The Yale University Library Gazette* 45 (Jan. 1971): 123–26.

Paige, Paul Eric. "Musical Organizations in Boston: 1830–1850." Ph.D. diss., Boston University, 1967.

Pemberton, Carol. "Lowell Mason: His Life and Work." Ph.D. diss.‚ University of Minnessota, 1971.

Persons, Stow. *The Decline of American Gentility.* New York: Columbia University Press, 1973.

Prentiss, G. L. *A Discourse on the Memory of T. H. Skinner.* New York, 1871.

Rensch, Roslyn, *The Harp: Its History, Technique and Repertoire.* New York: Praeger Publishers, 1969.

Rich, Arthur. *Lowell Mason, the Father of Singing Among the Children.* Chapel Hill, N.C.: University of North Carolina Press, 1946.

Ritter, Frédéric Louis. *Music in America.* New York: B. Franklin, 1890.

Rivinus, Emille Marckoe. *Riviniana.* Philadelphia: Author's publication, 1945.

Robertson, J. G. *A History of German Literature.* 3rd. ed. Edinburgh: William Blackwood, 1970.

Rodwell, George Herbert Buonaparte. *The First Rudiments of Harmony.* London: Goulding and D'Almaine, 1830.

Roscoe, Thomas. *The London and Birmingham Railway; with the Home and Country Scenes on Each Side of the Line.* London: Charles Tilt, n.d.

Sadie, Stanley, ed. *The New Grove Dictionary of Music and Musicians.* 20 vols. London: Macmillan and Co., 1880.

Scholes, Percy. "The Mainzer Movement." *The Mirror of Music.* London, 1947, 1:3–10.

"Scrapbook (1829–70) Assembled by Joel Summer Smith? . . . entitled 'Programmes preserved by Dr. Mason.' " Lowell Mason Papers, MSS 33, Box 6. In the John Herrick Jackson Music Library at Yale University.

Silber, Kate. *Pestalozzi, the Man and His Work.* London: Routledge and Kegan Paul, 1965.

Smart, George. *Leaves from the Journals of Sir George Smart.* Ed. H. Bertram Cox and C. L. E. Cox. New York: Da Capo Press, 1971; orig. pub. London, 1907.

Smith, Mortimer. *The Life of Ole Bull.* Princeton: Princeton University Press, 1947.

Spiller, Robert E. *The American in England during the First Half Century of Independence.* New York: Henry Holt, 1926.

Sprague, William Buell. *Annals of the American Pulpit.* New York: R. Carter and Brothers, 1857–69.

Staples, H. J. "The Hymn Tunes of Dr. Gauntlett." *The Choir* 32 (1941): 184–88.

Stephen, Leslie, and Sidney Lee, eds. *The Dictionary of National Biography.* 22 vols. London: Oxford University Press, 1964; orig. pub. London, 1908–9.

Stevenson, Robert M. *Protestant Church Music in America.* New York: W. W. Norton, 1966.

Sumner, William Leslie. *The Organ: Its Evolution, Principles of Construction and Use.* New York: St. Martin's, 1962.

Talbott, John H. *Biographical History of Medicine: Excerpts and Essays on the Men and Their Work.* New York: Grune and Stratton, 1970.

Temperley, Nicholas, ed. *Music in Britain: The Romantic Age, 1800–1914.* London: Anthlone Press, 1981.

_____. *The Music of the English Parish Church.* Cambridge: Cambridge University Press, 1979.

_____. "The Old Way of Singing." *Journal of the American Musicological Society* 34 (Fall 1981): 511–44.

Thayer, Alexander Wheelock. *Thayer's Life of Beethoven.* Rev. and ed. by Elliot Forbes. Princeton, N.J.: Princeton University Press, 1967.

U.S. Census Office, *Compendium of the Enumeration of the Inhabitants and Statistics of the United States as Obtained from the Returns of the Sixth Census.* Washington, D.C.: T. Allen, 1841.

van der Straeten, E. *The History of the Violin, Its Ancestors, and Collateral Instruments.* 2 vols. London: Cassel, 1933.

Wiebe, Robert H. *The Opening of American Society.* New York: Alfred A. Knopf, 1984.

Wilson, Michael I. *Organ Cases of Western Europe.* Montclair, N.J., 1879.

Winsor, Justin, ed. *The Memorial History of Boston, Including Suffolk County, Mass., 1630–1880.* 4 vols. Boston: Ticknor, 1880–81.

Young, Percy M. *The Bachs, 1500–1850.* London: J. M. Dent & Sons, 1970.

Young, Percy. *A History of British Music.* New York: W. W. Norton, 1967.

Index

Mason frequently does not provide sufficient information to allow positive identification of an individual. In such cases the index entry will contain only a last name and the exact prefix, such as Mr. or Miss, or M. Le Directeur, that Mason himself used. Entries such as John Green or Oliver Ditson refer to the name of a business. In cases when Mason used variant spellings of proper or surnames, those variants are indicated in brackets following the main spelling.

Earl of Sandwioh, 173
Earle, Dr. Pliny, 24, 154, 174
Eastman, Mr., 146, 157
Eckerlin, Signor, 42
Edwards and Stoddard, 41, 111
Egerton, Sir Thomas, 52, 174
Eilen, Monsieur Le Dr., 220n.22
Elevator, 123
Elijah the Tishbite, 164
Eliot, Samuel Atkins, 55, 147, 174
Elliot, Thomas, 178
Emery, Joseph, 174
Endicott, Helen, 219n.6
Evangelicalism, in antebellum America, 5
Evangelicus Pacificus. *see* Winslow,
  Hubbard

Fasch, C. F., 188
Faszman, Miss, 64
Fellenberg, Phillip Emanuel von, 98, 101,
  175, 220–21n.22
Fichte, Johann Gottlieb, 57
Field, Miss, 47
Filtera, 225n.6
Fincke, F. G. W., 59, 154
Fink, Charlotte, 70, 175
Fink, Gottfried Wilhelm, 70, 220n.21, 224n.5
Flight and Robson, 225n.4
Forbes, Miss, 41
Foster, Stephen: "My Old Kentucky Home,"
  219n.1; "Old Folks at Home," 219n.1
Foster (publisher), 158
Foundling Hospital, 40
Fowle, William Bentley, 17, 55, 87, 175
Franchomme, Auguste-Joseph, 42, 175
French Association, 169
Fribourg [Freiburg, Friburg, Freyburg],
  99–103, 152; St. Nicholas Cathedral, 100,
  101, 102, 224nn.1,3
Fry, Mr. Le Pasteur, 92, 220–21n.22

Galignani's Guide, 116
Galli, Filippo, 28, 175
Gardiner, William, 32–33, 175, 213; *Sacred
  Melodies,* 33, 175; *Judah,* 33
Gassner, Ferdinand Simon, 83, 176;
  Tabellen, 79
Gauntlett, Henry John [Gauntlet], 53, 176;
  "Irby," 176
Gear, Mr., 42, 52
George III, 168, 173, 186

Gersbach, Anton, 78, 79, 82; *Hundert
  Choral-Gesänge der Evangelischen Kirche
  für vier Männerstimmen gesetz,* 176
Gersbach, Joseph, 176
Gessner, Solomon, 96, 176; *Der Tod Abels,*
  176; *Idyllen,* 176
Giannoni, Madame, 52
Giraud, M. le Rev'd Pere, 220–21n.22
Gluck, Christoph Willibald: *Alceste,* 64
Goethe, Johann Wolfgang von, 57, 71
Goodhue, Mr., 157
Goodhue & Co., 146, 157
Gordon, George William, 29, 176
Gordon & Goddard, 113
Gossler, Mr., 59
Gottschalk, Louis Moreau, 12
Goulding and D'Almaine, 155
Grant, Miss, 109
Gray, Francis Calley, 106, 176
Gray, John, 176
Gray, Robert, 10, 28, 176
Gray, William, 176
Gray and Davison, 176
Greatorex, Mr., 129
Greatorex, Henry John, 53, 176
Greatorex, Henry W., 176
Greatorex, Thomas Westrop, 53, 176;
  Universal Violin Tutor, 176
Greatorex Collection, 176
Gregorian chant, 30, 35
Gregory, Daniel, 177
Gregory, Hannah Buckminster, 177,
  222n.10
Grétry, André Ernst Modeste, 112
Grisi, Giulia, 28, 42, 177, 204, 214, 215
Gutenberg: Festival, 76

Haas, William, 83
Hach, H. Theodore, 31, 46, 58, 60, 61,
  177, 223n.15
Hamburg: St. Nicolai Church, organ,
  description, 60; St. Jacob's Church,
  59–60
Hamilton, Frederick, 50, 51
Hamm, Charles, 220n.12
Hammond, James Henry, 139, 146, 154,
  177
Handel, George Frideric, 38, 40, 52;
  cadenzas in *Messiah,* 33; Fugue in E
  Minor, 70; *Messiah,* 2, 33, 41, 88, 119,
  130, 187, 213, 214

Lightning Source UK Ltd.
Milton Keynes UK
15 March 2010

151445UK00001B/160/P